Villainous Kingpin

KINGPINS OF THE SYNDICATE BOOK ONE

EVA WINNERS

Kingpins of The Syndicate Series Collection

Each book in this series can be read as a standalone.

This series is also connected to the characters in the Belles & Mobsters series and Corrupted Pleasure. Certain events in this book referred to prior books.

Playlist

IF YOU'D LIKE to hear a soundtrack with songs that are featured in this book, as well as songs that inspired me, here's the link:

https://open.spotify.com/playlist/2pS7DbRok206rj1qwrXXI2?si=Rzvog3ggTBmj-gZP8jfqaw

Triggers

This e-book contains disturbing scenes and adult language. It may be offensive to some readers and touches on darker themes.

Please proceed with awareness.

To my daughters—love you always and forever.

To my readers—THANK YOU for reading my creations and all your wonderful messages.

To my Happy Hour Ladies—what happens at the happy hour, stays at the happy hour!

Prologue

BASILIO

Cruelty ran in my veins.

It was part of me. Just like blood, oxygen, and hustling. It was who we DiLustros were. People shit their pants when they see me.

Yet, the girl with the golden curls didn't even bat an eyelash. She literally fell off a balcony and straight into my arms, then turned my life upside down. Well, more like, she tilted my world upright, and for the first time in my life, it wasn't all about blood and money.

It was about a woman. My woman.

I had never felt so goddamn happy. So right, and it was thanks to her. Wynter Star. And just like her name, she had become my star. My guiding light in the darkness of my underworld.

The last few weeks had been hands down the best days of my entire life. And now that she pledged her love and allegiance to me, I knew our future would be happy. Together.

And it was all thanks to her. My angel with golden curls and big eyes that shone like beautiful, precious stones when she looked at me. Only at me.

I'd seen and done enough fucked-up shit and ended more than a few miserable lives to know that when you found *this*, you had to snatch it up and keep it. My one shot at happiness.

She was my once-in-a-lifetime chance at keeping humanity in my soul. Unlike everyone else in my world, she was untainted and gentle, giving love without wanting anything tangible in return. Just me.

She held power over me, without trying. I wouldn't fuck around and chance losing her.

To anyone—cousins, family, rival mafia, or anyone else stupid enough to fuck around and try something.

I'd put a stop to the thieving schemes she had going with her friends. Fuck it. If those four had some kleptomania issues, I'd set up stores they could rob that were mine. I had plenty of money to go around for the next twenty lifetimes.

I pushed my hand into my pocket, the little velvet box burning through my three-piece suit. I patted it for the hundredth time since I'd picked it up.

I couldn't wait to slide a promise onto her finger. As long as she wore my ring, that was all that mattered to me.

My lips curved into a smile thinking of how I left her. Naked. The softest smile I had ever seen on a woman's face. Her skin flushed from what we had just done. Her eyes shining like the most beautiful emeralds. And her hair. Jesus, her golden curls sprawled all over my black satin sheets. She was like an angel captured in the devil's bed.

A willing angel in the devil's bed. *Mine.*

I'd never give her up. I didn't give a fuck who I'd have to ruin or kill. She was my perfection. The best part was that she'd let me because she wanted to be mine.

My enemies called me the Villainous Kingpin. The devil in a three-piece suit. She just called me hers. She loved me, just the way I was. And God knew I loved her just the way she was. My most beautiful perfection.

I turned the corner to my street and my steps picked up.

My father's car was here.

What the fuck was he doing here?

Dread climbed up my spine and my sixth sense set off warning bells. He never came to visit. Fucking ever. Every cell of my being went on alert, I unbuttoned my jacket to ensure I had easy access to my gun.

Then I shoved the front door open. *Blood.*

Bloody handprints decorated the walls of the foyer. Small hands. The taste of fear was new. Something I hadn't felt in so long, I forgot its bitter taste in the back of my throat. Like metal and gunpowder that was sure to take something you loved, more than anything in this world, away from you.

It took hold of my throat and choked the living daylights out of me. My vision blurred and a red haze descended over everything.

Like a fucked-up, bloody film.

I pulled out my gun, and with each step I took, my foot crunched on broken glass, shattering the ominous silence. The kind that brought news that changed you forever.

Just not her, I prayed for the first time in my life. *Take it all, but leave me her.*

I heard men's hushed voices, grunts, and I screwed the silencer onto the muzzle never pausing my steps. Each second counted right now. I rounded the corner to my living room.

Then I saw him.

My father, bleeding like a pig in the middle of my living room. Two bullets in his right leg. A piece of glass jabbed in his neck, and the right side of his face sliced. Angelo, his hacker and right-hand man, tended to him, wrapping up his wounds.

Both of their eyes lifted my way. One wary set and one furious. The latter one belonged to my father.

"Where is she?" I asked, my voice vibrating with rage as I glanced around. Dread was like a chain around my heart, squeezing harder and harder. "Where the fuck is she?" I bellowed, my voice bouncing off the walls and returning my own echo in answer.

I had to keep my cool; otherwise, the rage would blind me and I'd stop thinking rationally. But the adrenaline rushing through my veins refused to heed the warning. It only cared about finding my woman.

The living room was in complete disarray. The hardwood floors were stained with blood and broken glass and overturned furniture was scattered across the room.

"Russians," my father spat out, blood spurting out of the corner of his mouth. "They took her."

"Names," I growled, kneeling to lock gazes with my father.

I had to swallow down the burning rage until I had the facts so I could get my girl. I wanted to kill him for allowing them to take her. For not laying his life down to protect her.

Fury rushed through me, blood drummed in my ears. My control was slipping.

"Didn't recognize them." Something about the tone of his voice warned me he was lying. "She tried to run," my father said. "Fucking girl tried to run and you know how they love the chase."

The red haze in my vision darkened to crimson, picturing how terrified she must have been. The images of how fear would have flooded her big eyes kept playing in my mind. I swear to God, if those fuckers laid a single finger on her, I'd burn down their homes, their cities, and kill their families.

"Where were you two?" I growled. "Did you lead them here? How come they didn't kill you?"

Bratva didn't leave survivors. Just as none of us kingpins left witnesses behind. For a reason.

"We caught them on their way out," my father retorted, spitting blood on my floor. A tooth bounced off the hardwood. "Fuckers," he cussed.

I closed my eyes, took a deep breath, and stood up.

They better not have touched my girl. Not a single goddamn piece of her golden hair. And if someone brought her any harm, I'd rain hell down on them and their motherfucking world.

I stormed out of the living room, the gun still in my hand as I rushed up the stairs to my bedroom. As I climbed the stairs three at a time, my fingers dug into the mahogany rail, the marble stairs echoing loud under my feet, and I couldn't help but recall her teasing me about it. She called it a fancy mobster home.

It was supposed to be the safest goddamn home in this country. I promised her she'd be safe here.

The bedroom door ajar, I pushed through it, but it was as if nothing happened up here. I could still smell her faint flowery scent. The sheets were tousled, just as they were when I left her. Except she wasn't in between them.

Her duffle bag sat on the windowsill where she loved to sit.

They'd taken her.

My star. My light. My life.

Anyone but her, I prayed. *Bring her back.*

And for the first time in my life, I dropped to my knees.

Unless I got her back, I'd be the world's most ruthless villain.

There was no life without her.

Chapter One

Four Months Earlier

"This is a girls' night," Juliette complained, glaring angrily at me. "Stay."

I shook my head. I didn't have the luxury of wasting time. Theoretically, I should be in California right now, vigorously training every damn day with Derek. I was a champion in singles figure skating, but couples skating was new to me. My mother had been an up-and-coming figure skater but having a child and knee injury cut her career very short. She had skated with my father, but I knew very little of him. She never said anything about him except that she trusted him on the ice. I guess that was all that mattered to her.

For me, trust came harder. Trusting someone to catch me after throwing me in the air took some getting used to. My instinct wanted me to land on my feet rather than rely on Derek, my skating partner, to catch me. I was used to relying on my own strength and confidence to fly through the air, jump, and skate on the ice with speed and precision.

Figure skating. I freaking loved it. For me, it was one of those things I enjoyed doing alone. But after I won my Olympic gold in singles figure skating, Mom kept bringing up trying for couples figure skating. I resisted it for a few years and finally caved.

It wasn't in my nature to cave to people, but I hated to see my mother upset. The ghosts that lurked in her eyes, the way she'd watch me on the ice with that wistful look on her face, but with her bad knee she could barely walk with a cane let alone skate.

I wanted to make her happy.

"I know, but I need to take every hour I can to practice," I told her for the millionth time as I pulled on my Chucks.

I wore my black tights, leg warmers, and a large white sweater that came down to my mid-thighs. Winters in New York were brutal. Yes, my name was Wynter, but there was nothing I loved about freezing my ass off.

Ice-skating was different. It was exercise, my blood pumped with adrenaline and kept me warm.

"Well, you heard my dad," Juliette replied, smug with her reasoning. She should know better, we'd done plenty of sneaking around growing up. "We can't roam the house."

I never stopped my movements. I shoved my ice skates into my duffle bag, where I had a change of clothes. My phone followed and I zipped the bag.

Davina, Juliette, Ivy, and I decided at the last minute to spend the weekend at Uncle Liam's city house. We'd been friends for four years, and after this semester, our time at Yale would come to an end. I couldn't quite decide if I was happy about it or not.

My mother was relentless and a hard coach to please. I'd achieved more in figure skating than she had ever dreamed, but for some reason, it didn't seem to be enough for her. I suspected it wouldn't be enough until I got that medal that she was aiming for with my father. Olympic pairs figure skating.

"Which is the reason I'll be going over the balcony," I told her calmly. "Someone just throw me my bag when I'm down."

I threw a glance in the mirror. My hair was pulled up in a ponytail, keeping it out of my face. It was a major pain to skate with hair in your face.

"Is that wise?" Ivy asked concerned, her eyes blinking. "You could break your legs."

I waved my hand. I had good reflexes and strong legs.

Juliette grumbled and complained, calling me the worst cousin ever. She kept forgetting I was her only cousin, so not much competition in that arena. At least that we knew about since much like the nonexistent knowledge of my father, the same was true for Juliette's mother.

Shaking my hands to loosen up my joints, I inhaled and then slowly exhaled.

"Okay, here we go," I murmured, cracking the large French door open. I almost expected Quinn, my uncle's right-hand man, to shout at us from somewhere out there, but nothing happened.

I stepped out onto the balcony, then I eyed the distance to the ground.

"Fuck, I hope I don't break my legs," I muttered. It was ridiculous that I had to resort to this. But I knew my uncle. If he said, stay put and stick to the second floor, nothing would dissuade him.

I flipped my leg over the marble rail, testing the ivy that snaked down the manor. I hoped it would support my weight. My other leg followed and I balanced on the edge as both my hands gripped the ivy.

"I swear, if I fall and break my neck," I grumbled as I searched for the best spot to find my footing, "I'll kill my uncle and his visitor."

Whoever his guest was.

I knew if the visitor hadn't arrived, he'd be coming soon and the balcony was ten feet from the front entrance. I had to get out of here

9

beforehand. I glanced down, eyeing the ground longingly. I had to focus on lowering one foot at a time.

I sought out the thickest ivy branch and reached out my hand to pull on it. It seemed sturdy enough. I moved my leg, searching for footing on another tangled vine. I put my weight into it and the branch snapped.

"Fucking hell," I rasped, hanging off, my hands gripping the branches for dear life.

"That drop's gonna hurt." I stiffened at the man's voice and glanced over my shoulder to find dark eyes staring up at me. It was too dark to see his face.

"Hey," I whispered, trying to act nonchalant. "How are you?"

My arms burned. My body was strong but Derek's upper strength was much better than mine. After all, he lifted my weight up above his head, not the other way around.

"It seems I'm better than you are," he answered.

Smarty pants.

I peeked over my shoulder again. I wished I could see his face.

"Could you help me, please?" I asked. "I'll pay you," I offered hopefully, my muscles shaking already. I'd have to start lifting weights. This was unacceptable.

In my head I ran through my allowance. Uncle and Mom were generous, but I tended to spend a lot of money on my gear. And then, we never cooked, so we spent a lot of money on food, parties, and other junk.

"Five hundred bucks," I added, grunting as I shifted my weight. "Just don't let me break my legs. They are worth a lot."

"Yeah, they look pretty good from down here," he mused, humor coloring his deep voice. "Priceless."

"Thank God I'm wearing pants," I grumbled.

"Shame." Gosh this guy was something. "I bet that'd be an even better sight."

"C'mon," I begged. "I'll give you anything. Just catch me."

A soft chuckle. "Okay, runaway principessa. Let go and I'll catch you." *Principessa?* He said it with an Italian accent.

Unable to dwell on that right now, I closed my eyes for a moment, praying the guy wasn't a dick and wasn't joking about catching me.

"Promise?" I breathed, my muscles aching and shaking by this point.

"On my life. I promise to catch you."

I closed my eyes and let go.

Throughout petite, slim body landed in my arms and a light flowery scent hit my nostrils as her long, blonde curls brushed across my face. Surprisingly, her body was all lean muscles. Strong with the most amazing ass I had ever seen on a woman.

She twisted around, her body brushing against my three-piece suit as if she needed to see who just saved her precious legs. She had nicely shaped legs, but it was her face with those light green eyes that hit me right in the chest. An angel stared at me with long golden curls, glowing like a star. But it was nothing compared to her eyes. They were big, almond shaped, and brilliant. Shining like light emeralds with flecks of gold in their depths.

Chest to chest, when our eyes connected, the world stopped turning for a fraction of a heartbeat. We watched each other, and I was certain from that moment, nothing would ever be the same.

Her luscious red lips curved into a smile as she tilted her head.

"I guess I owe you five hundred bucks," she said, her eyes shining.

No accidental grinding herself against me. No flirtatious look. Just pure curiosity as those light green orbs studied me. She was *different*.

I couldn't decide if I minded it or not. For the first time in my life, I actually wanted a woman to show interest. I had no shortage of women, thrill-seekers, and shallow pampered girls bored with their lives that wanted a taste of danger. They flirted and were always eager, but there was always an underlying look of fear in their eyes.

If they were smart.

Yet, I sensed no fear from this girl, and I didn't think she was dumb. Intelligence shone from her eyes.

"Keep the money," I told her.

She chuckled softly and her eyes glittered like stars in the sky. She gently slid down my body and landed on her feet, taking a small step back. Then she craned her neck, her head tilted up and her eyes continued to study me.

She was much shorter than my six foot four. Almost fragile. Yet, I felt her muscles firsthand when she landed in my arms.

"Normally I'd argue and insist I pay you the promised money," she teased, her full lips in an amused smile. "But I spent too much money on my gear this month and my allowance doesn't kick in for another two weeks." She shrugged her shoulders. "I tried to convince her to increase my allowance." She blew a piece of unruly curl that escaped her ponytail out of her face, then rolled her eyes. "It teaches you to manage money, Star," she spoke nasally, and I gathered she imitated her mother.

I lifted my eyebrow. This girl really had no qualms talking to me. And was her name really Star? It would be the most appropriate.

"Oh shit, my duffle bag," she muttered, then turned around and looked back up at the balcony but nobody was there.

"Throw my bag." Her voice was like a hoarse whisper as she whisper-yelled. I guessed she didn't want to get caught. What was she doing in Liam Brennan's house anyhow? She didn't look Irish and he had no daughters. The thought of her being his woman didn't sit well with me at all.

"What the fuck?" I spat out and stepped to the right, pulling her to me just in time, so she wouldn't get hit by the bag traveling through the air.

"Damn drunks," Star muttered, glaring towards the balcony. "Trying to kill us?"

"Us?" a voice questioned, but I couldn't see anyone on the balcony.

Star groaned softly and put her finger on my lip. I guess to ensure I wouldn't make my presence known.

"Me and my fabulous self. Us," she explained to whoever she was talking to. *I'll be her little secret,* I mused.

"Are you okay, Wyn?"

"Yes, I'm fine," she assured her. She shot me a glance, her finger still on my lips. Then as if she realized, she quickly removed it and stepped away from me, her cheeks lightly flushed. She returned her attention to the balcony. "Let me guess. She's pissed off and threw my precious cargo hoping it would land on my head."

It would seem there were quite a few girls up there.

"Nah. Be careful. And keep your phone on." It would seem Star didn't like being told what to do because she rolled her eyes again.

Her eyes came back to me.

"Anyhow, I have to go," she whispered, keeping her voice low. "Thank you for catching me." She snatched her duffle bag off the ground and threw it onto her shoulder. Just by the way she did it, I could tell she had done it many times.

She tucked a wild blonde curl behind her ear, smiling, those sage eyes captivating. She was breathtakingly beautiful. Stunning in fact.

"See you around."

My eyes focused on her red duffle bag, but the only thing on it were three embroidered letters in white.

W. S. F.

With a last smile, she whirled around, then hurried away. I

watched after her until her blonde head disappeared from my view. Something about her made me want to go after her to ensure she got to her destination safely. There was no way she was part of the underworld. There was no trace of guardedness or fear on her face and she was too free with her smiles. Too happy.

It didn't take long before a car engine roared and loud music blasted through the speakers.

"Youngblood" by 5 Seconds of Summer.

It was loud enough to wake the dead. It certainly alerted the owner of the house. The front door of Brennan's house swung open and Liam stood there in all his fury. The man was my height but was built like an MMA fighter.

"DiLustro," he spat out, but his eyes weren't on me. He must have been searching for Star. When he returned his attention to me, he stepped aside to let me in. "Who did you see?" he inquired, seemingly casual but his shoulders were too tense.

"Nobody," I answered nonchalantly. "Though you might have some gangsters driving around your neighborhood with obnoxiously loud music. And no, I don't mean me or my cousins."

That seemed to appease him.

Who is she? I wondered. Though that question didn't matter right now. Loud music turned up in volume from upstairs, and from the sounds coming down, it was quite a wild party. Liam's lips thinned in annoyance.

"Party?" I asked as the door shut behind me, leaving me alone with the head of the Irish mafia.

"I rented the upstairs," he grumbled and I cocked an eyebrow at the unexpected response. Not that it fucking mattered to me. Instead, I kept my eyes sharp on the man who ran the Brennan mafia.

The Irish and Italians had been at war for as long as I remembered. The same was true for the Irish and Russians. In fact, things were even worse between the Bratva and the Brennans. The hate ran exceptionally deep there. The word among the Bratva was that the Russians blame the Brennans for a long-lost Russian mafia princess. And recently, they believed they'd found her among the Irish. Whoever she was, the Russians wanted her back at all cost.

The DiLustros' relationship with the Brennans wasn't much better. It was about twenty-one years ago or so that things escalated. When Liam Brennan lost his sister. He was left without any family. The word on the street was that members of the Brennan family in Ireland refused to recognize his adopted son and already eyed Liam's position. The Russians kept attacking him. He couldn't afford to fight us, the Russians, and his own members. So I had a suggestion for him, one that would strengthen my position.

Mine, my sister's, and my cousins' positions. Definitely not my father's.

My father was a sadistic bastard and some days I'd considered putting a bullet in his head. End all this shit and rule New York the right way. He left too much unnecessary blood and death in his wake. He had no issues torturing innocent women and children. He fucking loved inflicting pain. It made him hard; I saw it firsthand.

He insisted cruelty and blood were a necessity in our positions. I disagreed. Yes, a firm hand was needed but misplaced cruelty and killings weren't. Unfortunately, my father was one of the men who started the Syndicate. People followed him despite his barbaric methods.

But I'd been strengthening my position in the Syndicate, my wealth already exceeding my father's. My cousins, Priest and Dante, my sister, and I succeeded in growing our empire without a constant bloodbath and fighting amongst each other. If there was a way to operate within this city without a constant battle, I'd take it. Achieving some kind of peace with the Irish in my city was a step in the right direction.

"I have a proposition for you, Brennan," I started, shoving my hands into my pockets. "I believe it will make you happy and hopefully end this bloodshed between us. Keep the Irish to the west side and Italians to the east side of New York.

An hour later the deal was made. I knew Liam Brennan had more common sense than my own father.

As I made my way out of Brennan's home, my eyes roamed the large courtyard covered in darkness.

The golden princess was nowhere in sight.

Chapter Three

WYNTER

Three Months Later

We sat in my Jeep in the parking lot of Whole Foods on the Upper West Side in New York. The top was down, the May breeze blowing, and it was a welcomed reprieve. I was fuming on the inside, like flames licking at my skin. Ironic really given our current situation.

We just meant to go get Davina's stuff while Garrett, her now ex-boyfriend, was still at work. Unfortunately, Juliette went all rogue and Ivy clumsily dropped a match on his alcohol-soaked rug.

I could scream at them, but it wouldn't do me any good. I was just as guilty as they were.

I pressed my head against the steering wheel, regret and hindsight plaguing me. It was so damn stupid. I should have known better. Now Davina's ex-boyfriend's entire goddamn house had burned down. We were lucky the entire neighborhood didn't go up in flames.

Soot marred my cheek and my clothes, but I was too tired to keep rubbing it off. It seemed like I cleaned one spot and another would appear. Like a damn disease. I just needed a shower.

"Oh my God. Oh my God." Davina's panicked voice pierced through and her breathing was labored. "We're going to jail."

God, if Garrett's threat was serious, and I was attached to a crime, my chances at the Olympics would go down the toilet. I'd disappoint my mother. This was her dream as much as my own. Sometimes it felt like my mother's love only came when I skated. Naturally, I always wanted to appease her, so I ensured I skated the best.

And this... This would ruin it all. My mother would be disappointed.

Garrett's text message to Davina played in my mind over and over again, like a broken record.

> Stupid bitches. I know it was the four of you. The cameras were on. Five hundred thousand dollars. Twenty-four hours. Bring me the money by 10 p.m. tomorrow. Or I'm going to the police.

If my name was connected to something like that, I'd be banned from competing. All of it would go down the toilet.

"I'm sorry," Ivy cried. "It was an accident. Maybe we can explain."

She was the clumsiest one out of the four of us. I gently banged my head on the steering wheel, wishing pointlessly that I could turn back time.

"Explain what?" Juliette muttered, her eyes wide with shock. I guess her temporary insanity wore off. "We had matches and alcohol. We had intent."

Suddenly my cousin knew the law. It was a tad bit too late. She should have thought about that before she handed the goddamn matches to anyone.

"*You* had intent." Davina was furious. Rightly so. "I just wanted my stuff and then to get the hell out of there!"

"Davina's right," Juliette muttered, looking slightly defeated.

"I shouldn't have let y'all go," I groaned, then followed up with a few creative cuss words. I heard plenty from my cousin Killian. "I shouldn't have driven you. Made us all stay back at the dorms. We should have called Uncle Liam and asked him to send someone there."

I straightened up, meeting my friends' eyes. We did this together and we'd get out of it together. That's what friends and family were for, we stuck together.

"Maybe we ask Uncle to help us now," I suggested, pushing both hands through my curls. My hands trembled badly. "We're out of our element here."

"No!" Juliette screeched, her eyes bulging out of their sockets.

"No," Davina protested firmly. "You have all done enough. I should go to the police and just tell them I did it. I was mad and lost my temper."

"Fuck no," Juliette, Ivy, and I retorted in unison.

"Besides, that fucker said he has all four of us on tape," I told her, trying to reason with her. "No sense in admitting anything with such evidence."

"That weaselly little fucker," Juliette snapped. "We should just kill him."

"Yeah, let's add murder to the destruction-of-property and arson charges," I snickered. That was sure to get me expelled from the Olympics.

Only if caught, my mind whispered.

One of these days, Juliette would bark at the wrong person and end up getting us killed. She was too rash at times. And seriously, killing him? We weren't killers. Heck, we weren't even criminals.

Uncle Liam and Killian did a good job keeping Juliette and me in the dark about their underworld activities. Despite not being part of the Brennan mafia and geographical distance from Uncle's territory, we've heard rumors about Uncle's war with the Russians and DiLustros. We didn't know the reasons for it. Heck, Uncle and Killian could make people disappear and we didn't even know how to sneak into a house undetected. Of course, setting Garrett's house on fire wasn't in the original plan.

Ugh, I wished Uncle and Killian taught us some criminal activities, rather than treating us like fragile things that needed protection. We might have known how to get out of this clusterfuck.

"But the tape will show that it happened by accident," Ivy reasoned.

Assuming someone gave us that much credit, for being dumb and clumsy, we'd still be guilty of starting a fire. Accident or not.

"Juliette, we should get out of town," I said. Seeking refuge in Uncle's Hampton home would give us time to regroup and maybe even come up with an idea of how to handle the mess we'd found ourselves in. "Let's go to Uncle's beach house in the Hamptons."

"You want to go on vacation *now*?" Ivy asked in shock, her hazel eyes darting between me and the girls.

"You might be onto something," Juliette agreed pensively. The two of us shared a glance, then Juliette explained, "We might be able to find something of value and pay off this prick. Or at the minimum, lie low until we figure out how to get out of this mess."

Cash would be better, I mused silently, though there was nothing amusing about this shitstorm.

"And what about when he doesn't stop at just five hundred thousand?" Davina questioned. At least she was smart. More than likely Garrett would try and blackmail us again. "At this point, I wouldn't be surprised if he blackmails us for the rest of our lives."

"Then we kill him," Juliette concluded, as if that was a normal solution to any blackmailer. If you listened to Killian, it was indeed a solution.

"Let's not become killers quite yet," I retorted dryly, rolling my eyes at my cousin's idiotic suggestion, then started the Jeep so we could head to the beach house.

"God, I need a drink," Juliette muttered from the back seat.

"Me too," Ivy agreed.

Juliette and Ivy continued to throw out ideas as I placed the Jeep in drive and pulled from the Whole Foods parking lot. I tuned those two out, not in the mood to listen to their ideas. Most of them would land us behind bars before we got our diplomas from Yale.

Davina sat next to me, her mood somber and matching mine. I knew she blamed herself, but truthfully, we all fucked up. We all knew right from wrong.

My phone buzzed and I glanced at the caller ID. It was Uncle Liam. I ignored the message. He had been demanding either Juliette or I call him. Neither one of us responded. There was only so much shit I could put up with today. Juliette had been ignoring him for months now, and I wasn't in the mood to play peacemaker.

I sped down the streets as my brain vigorously worked on possibilities. I wasn't a criminal mastermind, but there should be a way to get out of this unscathed. All four of us.

Killing Garrett, Davina's cheating ex, was a no go. It'd put us in more trouble.

Giving him money was an option, but just as Davina said, I wouldn't put it past him to blackmail us again. Assuming we could come up with five hundred grand. Uncle Liam was loaded but it didn't mean he threw money at us. Both Mom and Uncle believed it would build character if Juliette and I earned our own money.

Not that the proceeds from his criminal activities were actually hard-earned money.

My fingers gripped the steering wheel. I hated this feeling of helplessness. Mom always said hard work would get me anywhere I wished. Well, I worked my fucking ass off for as long as I could remember. I was amazing on the ice and the pair figure skating gold medal was what I wished for.

The lights turned red and I came to a stop at a four-way crosswalk. I watched the lights, but in my head, I was far away. The stranger with dark eyes and even darker hair flashed in my mind. It had been three months since I'd seen him, but he'd often crossed my mind.

Something about him piqued my curiosity even before I learned who he was. When I snuck back after my training session, I overheard my uncle mention the visit from *him* to Quinn.

Basilio DiLustro. Kingpin to the New York Syndicate.

I had heard of the DiLustros, but truthfully, I didn't know a lot of specifics about them. So I looked him up. Google was full of information on the DiLustro family. The Kingpins of the Syndicate were whispered to be one of the most dangerous crime families in the world. The speculation was that the Syndicate consisted of top dogs of Yakuza, all the way to the rússkaya máfiya, and everyone in between. They had connections to the most influential families in the States. Reading about Gio DiLustro didn't particularly interest me. Basilio DiLustro, on the other hand, I devoured all I could find.

One day, Basilio would become head of the New York Syndicate. And he was just as deadly, if not more, than his father. Although, he didn't strike me as being as cruel as the infamous Gio DiLustro.

After all, he caught me falling off the balcony. It was kind of romantic, if you really thought about it. Like a *Romeo and Juliette* kind of romance. My brows furrowed. Those two had a tragic love story.

Maybe I should refrain from that comparison.

Either way, my breath was cut short the moment our eyes connected. It felt like the world stopped turning for a single breath and my life was forever changed. It was ridiculous, I knew it. But I hadn't been able to stop thinking about him since.

I looked him up. More than once.

Unlike my best friends, I didn't waste my time on boys. Boys were a distraction I didn't need. But that man. He wasn't a boy. Basilio DiLustro was a man who knew what he wanted and how to get it. I'd stake my whole life on it. My Olympic gold medals. A warm rush ran down my spine when I met his heavy gaze with the darkest brown eyes and longest eyelashes I had ever seen on a man. Even now, thinking about him, something unsettling fluttered in the pit of my belly.

Davina's hand covered my hand gripping the steering wheel forcing my focus back to now.

"I'm sorry, Wynter," Davina rasped.

I looked at her, pushing all the thoughts of Basilio DiLustro aside. My mouth turned down and I shook my head, my damn curls bouncing with each movement.

"It's as much my fault as yours." I smiled tiredly. I didn't like to see her upset. Out of the four of us, Davina worked her ass off. She was at the top of her class and worked in a coffee shop in the mornings and closed the shifts at night. "Everything happened so fast."

A loud horn sounded behind us, startling us all. Juliette and Ivy jumped up in their seats and started cussing the car like native New Yorkers. I shook my head at them, glancing in the rearview mirror, then returned my eyes onto the road.

That was when I saw *him*. He was coming from the opposite direction, driving a sleek black sports car.

My eyes widened and immediately an idea popped into my head. Basilio DiLustro was the answer to all my prayers. Our eyes connected. That same fluttery feeling shot through me, but also hope.

The doors of my red Jeep were all off and I regretted it now. Because I was a mess and in his full view. Soot marks were on my legs and my snug white shorts weren't so white anymore. My soot-stained pink off-the-shoulder blouse was sheer, giving a glimpse of my pink bra.

Though it seemed he liked what he saw. His gaze felt like a warm breeze over my bare skin and heat rushed to my cheeks. The moment barely lasted a second, but it felt like long minutes. My brain furiously worked up an idea.

"What is it, Wynter?" Davina asked, her eyes behind me, following the man who invaded my dreams and thoughts for the past three months.

"I—I have an idea," I mumbled. Though I wasn't sure whether it was a good or bad idea.

"What?"

Without delay, before he got too far away, I spun the wheel. The tires screeched and I made a sharp U-turn in the middle of the city, violating multiple traffic laws. Speeding up, I passed two cars, before we found ourselves behind the black McLaren.

I bet he'd know how to get rid of that surveillance video and any evidence tying us to Garrett's place, I thought to myself. He wasn't clueless like us and he probably had vast resources at his disposal. All we had was each other. Yes, Uncle Liam and Killian would never allow harm to come to us but what good was it when you had to depend on someone else to save you all the time.

I pressed my palm against the horn.

Honk. Honk. Honk.

"What are you doing?" Davina questioned, her eyes wide.

Honk. Honk. Honk.

The car came to a sudden stop and I slammed on my own brakes so I wouldn't run into his expensive car. The traffic around us was already blaring their horns. My heart drummed in anticipation and anxiety, ignoring everything and everyone. This could be our way out.

"What are you doing?" Juliette demanded to know.

"I have an idea," I told them all. "There might be a way to delete the surveillance."

Everyone knew the DiLustros made things happen. So did the Brennans but going to my uncle or Killian wasn't an option. The latter would have been if he wasn't leaving the country, but he was chasing his own ghosts apparently. His text to Juliette and me was literally,

I'll be back. Going to hunt some ghosts.

Whatever the fuck that meant.

I started to feel like Juliette and I were kept in the dark in a lot more matters than just criminal activities.

"How?" Davina demanded to know.

I jumped out of the Jeep, then combed my fingers through my hair, hoping to look somewhat presentable, but probably failing miserably. I was tempted to ask the three of them how I looked, but I knew it would raise suspicion, so I opted not to.

My eyes traveled over the three of them. "Just trust me."

I heard their gasps behind me as I walked towards the sleek black car but ignored them all.

Basilio DiLustro could get us out of this mess. The question was, what would it cost us?

Or me.

My hands grew clammy as I made my way to his car. I performed in front of millions, and yet, I had never been so nervous before. I pushed my fingers through my curls one more time, then smoothed them out. I just hoped in the process I didn't smear soot all over my damn head.

When I reached the car, I noted he wasn't alone. All I could see of his passenger were long legs and a three-piece suit. Basilio was in a three-piece black suit too, and under the sunshine of the warm May day, he looked even more striking.

A frisson of recognition ran down my spine as our gazes met. Something amusing and dangerous danced in Basilio's gaze, tempting me to fall under his dark spell. My heartbeat sped up and I smiled.

Though I wasn't sure why. There was nothing happy about the current situation or talking to a man with the worst reputation in New York.

I liked him. I mean, how could you not with that gorgeous, full smile and dark eyes that could consume your soul.

Tousled, coal-black hair. Sharp cheekbones, strong jaw. Overall gorgeous face. Beautiful mouth with an arrogant smile. Brooding, dark expression as he watched me. His whole persona screamed ruthless power and his sex appeal oozed all around him. I could practically taste it. And for the first time in my life, I wanted to let myself go so this man could catch me.

I mentally slapped myself. This had to be the swoon effect that girls always talked about.

"Hey," I greeted him, my voice slightly breathless.

"Hello again," he said. *He remembers me!* I thought giddily, then immediately mentally reprimanded myself. No time for swooning now.

Though as his eyes raked over me from head to toe, my cheeks instantly flushed.

"Umm." I shifted from foot to foot. My nerves were a tad bit tattered. I never had issues talking to boys, no matter how cute they were. They were either too shallow, too wild, or just too demanding. And I never had time for any of it or those qualities.

Yet, this one... Well, he was hot. Anyone with two eyes could see it. But it was more than that. The way his dark eyes watched me, like I was his already, had my heart fluttering like a butterfly caught in a jar.

"Yes?" A corner of his lips lifted and amusement shone in his eyes. Then as if he revealed too much, he schooled his expression and ran a thumb across his bottom lip, his eyes darkening even further. I hoped that didn't mean he was mad at me. I haven't even done anything yet.

Okay, here we go.

I took a deep breath and exhaled.

"I know who you are," I started.

One heartbeat.

"You're at an advantage, then," he said, smoothing a hand down his tie, in an absentminded move. "All I have is your first name. Star." My brows knitted. I didn't recall giving him my name. "You imitated your mother's voice," he reminded me.

Ahhh. His words were deep and soft, and a strange kind of warmth traveled through every inch of me. But the way he watched me made my cheeks blush.

"It's only fair if you tell me who you are."

Two heartbeats.

"Wynter," I breathed. I loved the way he watched me. Possessive. And he didn't even know who I was. "Wynter Star," I rasped, giving him my first and middle name only.

Chapter Four

BASILIO

Wynter Star.

The name suited her. She gave off ice-princess vibes, except when she smiled and her eyes twinkled, it felt like warm sunshine on my skin.

Look at me going all poetic, I mocked myself silently.

She tucked an unruly piece of hair behind her ear, her hand visibly trembling. I wondered if I scared her. Or something bad happened to her. She had soot smeared on her cheek and some on her clothes. Though she still looked breathtakingly beautiful. Even more so under the bright rays of the sun. Her blonde curls shone like gold under the daylight, and her green eyes reminded me of the colors of Lake Como right before a storm hit it.

A mixture of light green, gray, and blue.

"I—my friends and I need help." Her eyes darted around nervously, as if someone was chasing her. Something protective reared its head in my chest. It was unexpected, startling. "We set a house on fire."

Dante, my cousin, who sat in the passenger seat, coughed, probably stifling a laugh.

"Is that all?" Dante mused.

Wynter's eyes flashed behind me, but unless she ducked down, she couldn't see him. And I had a feeling she didn't want to lean forward and flash me her cleavage. I was glad for it, because I didn't want Dante to see it.

"It was an accident," she added, her tone miserable. "Well, kind of. It was either set his house on fire or cut his dick off. Neither was ideal, but at least this way he's alive." The words flew out of her mouth like she couldn't contain them anymore. "And now he's blackmailing us with surveillance of us setting his house on fire. Though it was truly an accident. The girls got a bit too wild."

Dante's chuckle filled the car. I bet the fucker never had shit like that happen in Chicago. Welcome to New York where anything and everything was possible.

Wynter chewed on her bottom lip nervously. "My mom will kill me if—"

Her voice trailed off. She knew who I was, but instead of being scared of me, she was scared of her mother and getting in trouble. Another car flew by, honking their horn like their life depended on it.

I pulled the door handle and stepped out onto the pavement. Let them try and sit on the car horn with me out here. If they knew me, and most of New York did, they'd know I'd come for them.

Wynter didn't step away and no fear entered her eyes. In fact, relief flashed across her face, and it was a novelty. She looked at me like I was her savior. And fuck, I wanted to be.

Though, if she needed saving, it meant she had nothing going on with Liam Brennan. Otherwise, he'd be doing all the saving. Speaking of the head of the Irish mafia, I had just left his office, settling a truce which would help us eliminate constant fighting over territory. Tomorrow, I'd get the deed to The Eastside Club.

"Tell me what you need help with," I demanded, soaking her in like my personal sunshine.

"Is there a way you could—"

She couldn't finish the statement, so I did it for her. "Kill him?"

A gasp slipped through her parted lips. And fuck, my cock stirred just from that little innocent gesture.

"No, not kill him," she clarified, her eyes watching me like I was a god. "Maybe erase the evidence?"

She nervously licked her lips and my eyes lowered to them. They were tempting, full and pink. I bet they were soft too. I had never felt the instant need for someone. Fucking ever! But something about her did it for me. How many times has she crossed my mind over the last three months? More than I cared to admit.

And here she was now. Needing a favor and free for my taking.

My eyes fleeted to her red Jeep. Her girlfriends' attention was on me. The two in the back seat looked slightly disheveled, their faces smeared with soot. Like they went down the chimney or something. It made sense if they set fire to someone's home.

I returned my attention to the blonde young woman in front of me and a smile tugged at my lips.

"What do I get in return?" I drawled.

I want her. And nothing else would do. I schooled my features, worried I'd scare her off if she read my thoughts.

Her pale cheeks flushed a deeper red. Still no fear. Brave little thing.

"What do you want?" she asked, tilting her chin up. She never hesitated to meet my gaze, though it required her to crane her neck. She only reached up to my chest, her frame petite compared to my six foot four.

I shoved my hands into my pockets as I studied her. That hair of hers was something, like a curly mane with a glow of halo above her head. If there was ever a picture for a golden child, she was it.

"Wyn, get away from him," one of her girlfriends or maybe all three yelled. "He looks like a damn Italian."

An exasperated sigh slipped through Wynter's lips. She gave them an eye roll, then waved her hand, mouthing *shut up* to them. Then her sparkling gaze returned to me.

"Sorry," she muttered, smoothing down her curls. "Jules, my cousin, can be a bit too much. But she means well." She rambled, a slight pitch to her voice. She was even cute when she was rambling. "Her name is Juliette really."

I noted an angry red burn mark on her right forearm and took her hand into mine, running a thumb over her soft skin. A slight wince crossed her expression and I pulled out a handkerchief.

"Put some aloe vera over it when you get home," I told her, wrapping her forearm.

She didn't try to tug on her arm, her eyes on me, watching my every move. "I'll do that. Now tell me what you want in return."

"Your phone number," I drawled. "And a dinner date."

For a moment she watched me, her expression guarded.

"That's all?" she asked suspiciously.

She was right to be suspicious. But I wanted her surrender, because *she* wanted it. Not as repayment to a favor.

"Yes."

I pulled out a pen from inside of my suit, my gun holster exposed. Luckily, she was too focused on my face to have noticed. I handed it to her.

"If that's it, you got it," she replied, stifling a soft chuckle by biting her lower lip. "Though I have a feeling you're letting me get off cheap."

My lips tugged up into a smile. Beautiful and smart. She took my hand, her fingers small compared to mine. She started writing her number on the palm of my hand. Talk about retro moves. Didn't kids used to do that in high school? Thankfully, I was great with numbers, so I immediately memorized the phone number.

"What's the address?" I asked her. She recited it, her eyes never leaving my face. If she kept looking at me like that, I might succumb and kiss her right now. "I'll message you when it's done," I told her.

"Thank you." She squeezed my fingers gently, her eyes lifting to mine again. There was something calming about her gaze on me. My thumb brushed over her soft skin, loving the feel of it. A pink flush rose on her cheeks, though she didn't pull away.

I hoped it wasn't because she worried I wouldn't do this favor for her. Though I didn't think so. Her smile was too sincere, her eyes too sparkling, her expression too soft.

"Well, I better get going," she murmured softly, lowering her eyes to my thumb caressing her skin. She still hadn't pulled her hand away. "We don't want to run into Garrett by accident."

Reluctantly, I let go and the loss was instant. It slammed into me like a runaway train.

I watched her run back to her car and get behind the wheel, and only once her Jeep was out of my sight did I get into my car.

"She really wanted to talk to you, huh?" Dante smirked. "Who is Wynter Star?"

"The girl I'm going to marry."

Chapter Five

BASILIO

The next day, Dante and I strode into The Eastside Club. The guard at the front didn't bother asking us anything as we walked in. Everyone knew by this point the bar was transitioning to the DiLustro family.

I took the fact it was packed as a good sign. It was barely approaching eight at night and the club was pumping. It was one of the most popular establishments in east New York.

Glancing at my phone, I checked for messages. Angelo, my father's right-hand man, was supposed to confirm he had erased all evidence of Wynter and her friends setting the house on fire. He was going over all the surveillances to ensure he covered all the bases and nothing pointed to the young women. And he'd send *me* all the evidence.

"He's expecting us, right?" Dante asked as the song switched to Selena Gomez. Absentmindedly, I made a note to improve the music here. Since it'd be my club, I'd ensure everything was top notch.

"Yes, he's handing over the deed," I told him. "His deadline is midnight."

Hopefully, he wouldn't wait until the last goddamn minute.

My phone buzzed and I glanced at the phone, hoping it was Wynter. I had sent her a message over three hours ago, letting her know the wipeout was almost done. It was Angelo.

Wiped clean. You have the only copy.

I pressed the recording and watched the women frantically run around the house. The one with auburn hair kept trying to make the fire bigger, while the others screamed. Wynter seemed to be the only one who tried to keep a cool head and extinguish it.

Satisfied with it, I put the phone away.

"Where the fuck is he, then?" Dante pondered, his eyes traveling over the crowd. Brennan would be here, I had no doubt.

The beat drummed through the floors. Rowdy men cheering sounded out in the main area, but we hadn't gotten there yet.

"So did you do it?" Dante asked.

The two of us were raised like brothers. We weren't far off as cousins. His father ran the Chicago Syndicate, just as mine ran New York. And just like I surprised my father, so did Dante. Our old men might be the heads of the Syndicate, but we were the kingpins. Dante, Priest, who ruled Philadelphia, and I. My sister ran Las Vegas but only my cousins, father, uncle, and I knew she was really the one pulling the strings.

With each day, we grew more powerful and stronger than our fathers ever were.

"Do what?" I responded distractedly. I had to get my head screwed on right. Ever since I ran into Wynter again, I couldn't get her out of my mind.

"Did you have the surveillance wiped out for the golden princess?" Dante chuckled darkly. The amusement crossed his expression though his eyes were sharp on the crowd around us. Neither one

35

of us trusted the Irish. "I've never seen you look at a woman like that before."

I shrugged. It didn't mean anything. She was a stunning woman, and I was certain she was used to male attention with her looks.

The song switched to "Legends Are Made" by Sam Tinnesz and the whole bar became even more riled up than a few minutes ago. The sound of cheering and yowling rang through the whole establishment while the speakers pumped with the beat and lyrics of the song.

It was way too goddamn loud.

"Does the entertainment come with the club?" Dante mused. "I spy your golden principessa and a couple more troublemakers."

I followed his gaze to find three women dancing on top of the bar, their dresses together making the color of the damn Irish flag. And my principessa with the golden halo dancing on top of it, seducing everyone like a temptress. Wynter Star moved seductively, each sway of her body graceful like she had done this a million times before.

Men's eyes ate her up, greedy for a glimpse of her smooth skin. My eyes traveled over her body in what must have been the shortest white dress on the planet. I had never complained about a woman wearing so little before. So this was a first.

Every single pair of eyes in this bar was on them.

A burning ball of energy shot through me and singed my insides.

"What the fuck?" I growled, glaring at all the men. I wanted to kill them all. Maybe I could break a beer bottle and use it as a weapon. Slash everyone's throat one at a time. Albeit, it'd probably be quicker to just shoot them.

The three girls shared a glance, then their heads turned in the same direction. Dante and I followed their line of sight to see Liam Brennan striding towards them with a seriously pissed-off expression.

"I guess the head of the Irish doesn't approve," Dante sneered, though amusement colored his voice.

The two of us watched Liam growl at the women, trying to get through the wild crowd of men.

"Get the fucking brats off the bar," he shouted but it was a moot point. The crowd was way too wild by now. "Where is the fourth woman?" he growled, his eyes roaming the crowd and searching for who the fuck knew.

Dante and I watched the women up on the bar. It was clear they were up to something. The question was what and why were they giving Liam Brennan a hard time?

Liam turned to his man, Quinn, and barked an order, though his head was turned and I couldn't read his lips.

Quinn's eyes turned to the girls and he nodded, then pushed through the crowd. I watched as the three women on the bar shared a glance, switched the position and one of them unzipped the dress for Wynter as she swayed, kicking off her heels.

The dress slid off her body, leaving her in white boyshorts and a full-coverage white bra.

Jesus Christ!

The men went crazy, but all I could hear was buzzing in my ears. Blood rushed through my body and went straight into my groin. Wynter Star had the sweetest body I had ever seen. It was fucking centerfold-worthy. It called to me, like a song called to a mockingjay.

She was every man's wet dream. More importantly, she was my dream. Perfectly toned body, petite with curves. And her ass.

Fuck!

The two women went to the furthest right end of the bartop while Wynter strode like she was on the catwalk to the left, wearing her undergarments. Truthfully it looked like a bathing suit, but if she attempted to take it off, I'd follow through with the killing spree.

"Are they Irish?" Dante questioned.

Fuck if I knew. I searched the name Wynter Star, but barely any information came up. I had Angelo run a background on her. Nothing. I had Priest run it too. Nothing. It was like the girl barely existed. Born and raised in California. No family. Nothing really worthwhile or remarkable in her background. Yet, the way she carried herself told me there had to be more to her. She carried herself with confidence, like she knew her worth and wouldn't allow anyone to take it from her. She gave out ice-princess vibes, but I'd bet my life underneath it all was a warm, glowing heart.

Either way, I had no intention to stop my digging. I'd find every single piece of information on this woman.

"I don't think so," I muttered as I watched Wynter twerk her ass on top of that bar. The other women shook their ass like they were in a twerking competition too, but I just couldn't peel my eyes from Wynter's form.

Then out of the blue, Wynter picked up her dress, then straightened up, barely five feet away from where I stood. Glancing at Quinn, she winked while he cursed like a motherfucker.

"You three will be banned," he raged. "Need a good arse whooping."

The girl with wild red hair flipped him the bird. She could be Irish; she looked like it. A last shared look by the three women, Wynter nodded and then faced the rowdy crowd with a sweet smile.

"Everybody," she shouted and the room quieted a notch. "Fucking move so I can jump off." The men parted like the Red Sea. Leveling her hands up in the air, Wynter lifted off into the air into a somersault and landed on her feet, right in front of me.

Without looking, she went forward and ran straight into my chest.

"Ouch," she yelped, taking a small step back and her hand on her forehead, rubbing it.

She raised her eyes. A flicker of recognition and surprise flashed in them.

"Hey there," she greeted me in her musical voice, those luscious full lips curved into a smile. Glancing over her shoulder, I followed her gaze. Quinn was too far away and couldn't quite see us. Not yet anyhow.

"You often dance on bartops half-naked?" I inquired, my tone slightly possessive. If she noticed it, she didn't let on. This overwhelming feeling to keep her all to myself was a novelty. There hadn't been a single woman in my entire life that I obsessed over. Fucking ever. But Wynter's curves. Her breasts. I needed to be the only man to ever see them.

"Oh this is nothing," she mused. "I'm used to being half-naked with all my training." A growl rose deep in my throat. From the corner of my eyes, I noted Dante's twisted grin. "Want to have that dinner now?" she asked, pulling her dress over her head and tugging it down her body like it was nothing. "I want to pay off my debt."

Now dressed, my eyes traveled down her body, the white dress hugging her curves. Fuck! That sight would forever be tattooed into my memory. Every square inch of her was perfect. Toned and smooth skin. Her wild, blonde curls. Her sparkling eyes. And her mouth that smiled, like we were alone in the world.

"Your shoes are missing," I told her, trying to get a grip.

She laughed, her eyes glittering like fucking emeralds. This girl lit up when she laughed. She fucking glowed. Grabbing my hand, she tugged on it, pulling me along.

"Buy me a new pair, and I'll repay you with another dinner," she suggested mischievously. "But you've got to pay. I'm broke." She kept glancing over her shoulder, in the general direction of Quinn. She never even noticed Dante. "Come on." She tugged on my hand.

Dante's eyes met mine over her head.

"I got this," Dante mouthed reassuringly, a smirk on his face. I'd have to wipe that smirk off his face the next time I saw him. But then again, he was doing me a big favor, so maybe I'd let him get away with it.

"Let's go." She tugged on me again, tempting me with her smile and I went willingly. Like a dying man being led to water.

I wrapped my arm around her shoulders and tucked her into me, then started using my height and strength to shove men out of the way. Once outside, she searched over the people standing around. I spotted her girlfriends at the same time that she put her fingers into her mouth, then whistled loudly.

I cocked my eyebrow, surprised at her ability. Somehow she seemed too polished to whistle like a sailor.

"Come on, Wyn," the red-haired one yelled. "Before the fucking asshole comes out and catches us."

Wynter waved her head. "You guys go. I'll meet you at the dorms later."

"What?" the woman with dark hair and blue eyes screeched. I guessed that had to be her cousin by the way she scowled my way. "Why?"

Wynter rolled her eyes. "I don't interrogate you when you go out with boys," she protested.

I had to scoff at her calling me a boy. I couldn't even remember the last time I felt like a boy. Probably the day my mother left me.

"What's his name?" her cousin hissed.

"None of your business," Wynter retorted dryly. "Where is Davina?" she asked.

The two women shrugged, and pointed to the cell phone. Wynter reached underneath her dress, and I realized she had a secret pocket in it. She pulled out her phone and read a message.

> All good. Go without me. I'll meet you back in the dorms.

"That's weird," she mumbled.

"Are you and your friends getting into trouble?"

Tilting her head up, her shining eyes met my gaze.

"Never," she deadpanned, but her eyes twinkled with mischief.

Chapter Six

WYNTER

L eaving Juliette and Ivy gaping after me, I followed Bas to
his car.

He opened the passenger door for me and I slid into the
seat of his Lamborghini. As I watched him go around the car, I
combed my fingers through my hair. It wasn't exactly how I envi-
sioned running into him again, but it couldn't be helped. It wasn't
like I'd admit to the Italian Kingpin my friends and I were a distraction while our fourth friend was stealing from my uncle. Oh, who
happened to be head of the Brennan Irish mafia.

Yeah, I'd pass on that explanation.

The driver's door opened and he got behind the wheel.

"No more dancing half-naked on bartops," Bas growled softly as
he started the car and took off down the street.

"Nice to see you too," I drawled and gave him my brightest smile.
"Don't tell me your eyes were offended?"

My cheeks heated at my flirting attempt. I never bothered with it
before, though now I wished I had more practice. I lowered my eyes,
stretching my legs while I stared at my French pedicure.

"Are you even legal to be in the clubs?" he demanded to know.

I peeked at him under my lashes. He was right, I wasn't legal enough to enter that club. But that was never a problem considering its owner. Of course, telling Bas I was related to the well-known mafia owner of the club was out of the question. Uncle Liam kept us in the dark about his activities, but I knew enough to understand fraternizing with any DiLustro would be frowned upon, seriously. Besides, my mother hated anything connected to the underworld.

"I'll be twenty-one in a few weeks," I admitted softly.

"Jesus, you're younger than I thought," he grumbled quietly under his breath. "How did you get into The Eastside?"

"The old-fashioned way," I scoffed. "With a fake ID." He smirked. "How old did you think I was?" I asked him bravely, turning my head to watch his profile.

And what a gorgeous profile it was. My heart thumped to an uneven beat, unlike ever before. The only thing that ever got me excited before was ice-skating. As pathetic as that sounded. But it was my life. I lived and breathed figure skating.

Yet now, I feared I would live and breathe this man.

Fuck, this had to be karma for all my snarky remarks about insta-love.

"Well, I had hoped you were at least twenty-one," he answered.

I shrugged my shoulders. "I will be in a few weeks," I retorted. "Does that help?" His chuckle filled the car and I quite liked the sound. I had a feeling he didn't laugh often. "How old are you?"

"Twenty-seven."

"Hmmm."

"I'll be twenty-eight soon."

"Hmmm."

"And what does hmmm mean?" he challenged.

I looked at him playfully. "I'm trying to decide if you're old."

Another chuckle. "Maybe I'm just old enough."

It was my turn to laugh. "Maybe."

"I see I'm going to have to convince you," he drawled.

I made a *hmm* noise again while my breath was cut short at all the potential ways he could convince me. And let me tell you, the images in my mind were X-rated. For someone who had never had sex, I was a bit shocked at myself.

A strange thrill shot through my veins and heat rushed to my cheeks.

Another chuckle by Bas followed. "Something tells me your thoughts are not so pure right now, *Wynter*."

I rolled my eyes at him. "Oh, and yours are, *Bas*?"

"Touché." Something amused and seductive played in his gaze as his eyes flicked to me. "Bas?" he asked in a smooth voice, his eyes burning.

My heart fluttered so fast, I thought it'd fly out of my chest. I was used to high-intensity interval training on the ice and treadmill to get my heart ready for the 200 beats per minute for my performances. Yet, none of that exercise could ever prepare me for this kind of heart racing.

"Isn't that your name?" I breathed.

A quick flicker my way, his eyes on my lips, he returned his attention to the road.

"Nobody ever calls me Bas. Only Basilio." His voice was deep and soft.

"Oh. Basilio is so stiff, you know." He shrugged. "Do you know your name means 'kingly'?" I blurted out, probably sounding like a fool. The fact that I knew what his name meant probably revealed how detailed my lookup of him was.

"I did," he mused.

"Well, I like your name, but I like Bas better."

He chuckled amused, offering me a fleeting glance.

"I like it, but only you can call me Bas."

My breaths turned shallow and something warm flickered in my chest. Something so simple and innocent, yet I felt like I'd done something right and earned his praise. It was stupid, I knew it. But I couldn't shake the feeling off.

"Okay, *Bas*," I accentuated his name. "Where are we eating? I'm starving."

My skin was burning up. This reaction to the opposite sex was a novelty. I read about it. Heard about it. But I've never *felt* it. Never experienced even a hint of a possibility of attraction to anyone. And here, with this man, the wave of attraction slammed into me and soaked into my every cell.

"I'm assuming you didn't read my message?" he inquired and I remembered. He sent me a text earlier today, but I was in the midst of holding Ivy's head above the toilet.

We spent last night in Uncle's Hampton home. We had to get out of town, and once we devised the plan to rob my uncle's safe in The Eastside, Ivy, Juliette, and Davina started drinking. Admittedly, I joined in, but I didn't get hammered like those three.

"I'm so sorry," I apologized quickly and reached for my phone. "I opened your message but then didn't get to read it. Ivy started puking her guts out."

"Drunken night?" he mused. I nodded my head, smiling. "Forget your phone. I'm here now, so I can deliver the message personally."

"So damn bossy," I retorted, feigning irritation. I was used to people bossing me around. Trainers, tutors, coaches. As long as their advice was sound, I always listened. I had a feeling Bas always gave sound advice.

I reached for the radio to hide my smile, though I suspected nothing would escape this man. The song that came on couldn't be more appropriate, "Eastside" with Halsey & Khalid. How convenient since I ran into him at The Eastside and we were *running* away together from Quinn and Uncle. Poetically speaking.

The silence stretched, the words playing over his speakers at a low volume. Goose bumps rose on my skin and a kindled flame drifted through me. My stomach made somersaults.

Get a grip, Wynter.

I must be losing my damn head. Or heart? I mean, it didn't happen that fast. I've only seen him twice before. I barely knew him.

"The surveillance is wiped out."

My eyes widened. "Seriously?" I gasped. Suddenly the week was looking up.

"Yes," he confirmed.

"What about neighbors and their cameras?"

"Everything is wiped out," he assured me. "Garrett's surveillance. Neighbors'. Even the city's. There is no sign that you ever ventured that way."

I grinned widely, beaming at him. He might be a notorious criminal, but he was my hero right now. "Thank you so much, Bas."

"No problem," he drawled. "After all, you're paying for it."

He came to a stop at the red light, in the heart of Manhattan. The city lights flickered. The wail of an ambulance echoed in the distance. The bus came to a screeching halt next to us. But all of it was just background noise to me. Distant and faint.

All my senses honed in on this man next to me.

"Not much of a hardship," I breathed.

"I'm glad to hear it." Our gazes collided, his burning me. In the best way possible.

His eyes traveled down my body, slowly like he was memorizing every inch of it. His eyes lingered on my bare feet before he took my hand into his and it felt like he branded me as his. The heat of his touch leaked into my bloodstream while his thumb brushed my knuckles.

Just like he had when I asked him to erase the surveillance.

"Let's go get you some shoes," he said. My eyes fell to where he held my hand. His big one against my small one. His grip was firm, possessive. As if he considered me *his* already. And I didn't mind. I knew he killed men with that same hand, and yet fear within me was absent.

His stare traveled back up my body, and I felt every inch of my skin buzz under the scrutiny of it. My pulse fluttered, my chest heaved.

"Bas?" I rasped, my voice barely above a whisper.

"Yes?"

"Why did you just ask for a dinner date?" He could have asked for a lot more and I would have done it.

"Because, Wynter Star," his deep voice rasped. "... you'll *give* me everything else. Of your own free will."

Chapter Seven

BASILIO

The light turned green and I drove down the road until we came to a stop in front of Corso Vittorio, a high-end shoe store that was owned by one of the wives of the men who worked for me.

Wynter remained quiet after my declaration. Speechless more like it. I really dropped it on her.

But fuck it! Why beat around the bush?

I knew what I wanted and *she* was it. Without a single shred of doubt in my mind, I fucking *knew* it. And I'd have her. But I meant what I said. She'd want me too. Until then, this would be purely platonic.

"Corso Vittorio's shoes are expensive," she muttered. "Way too expensive."

I pulled on the car door handle and came around the car, then opened the passenger door.

"Let me worry about the money," I answered her. "We're getting your shoes here."

Her eyes flickered toward the store. "It looks like they are closing," she protested.

"They'll stay open for us," I assured her. I extended my hand, and without hesitation, she placed her fingers into the palm of my hand and met my eyes. God, I loved the way she looked at me. Trust, curiosity, and something else.

Stars flickered above us, lights and passersby of Manhattan buzzed around us. Yet, if you asked me who stood next to me or behind me, I'd never be able to tell you.

There were two rules I always followed. Never go anywhere without my .45, and never care for someone so much that losing them could destroy you. Yet now as I stared at this young woman with stars in her eyes, I knew I had broken the second rule. I wouldn't be able to handle losing her.

I had barely touched her and I was burning up. I wanted to nurture the fire until it consumed both of us.

Dante and Priest would laugh their asses off if they knew. The smallest touch and it had me worked up, hungering for more.

Wynter Star settled me and unsettled me. Such a confusing, contradicting feeling that I was unfamiliar with.

"Let's go get you shoes, Cinderella," I drawled as I shut the car door.

She chuckled warmly, leaving her hand in mine. "Lead the way, Prince Charming."

Prince Charming. Nobody ever called me that. The devil prince maybe. A villain definitely. Certainly never charming.

Without her shoes, she barely reached my chest. She appeared too small and fragile. Though breathtakingly beautiful. And I wasn't the only one who noticed. Pedestrians that rushed left and right couldn't help themselves but to give her a double take. Admiration and hunger on men's faces and envy on women's.

Pulling her closer to me, our fingers intertwined and we walked into the store just as Vittorio's wife, Emilia, was about to lock the door. Emilia was the wife of one of my father's men.

"Basilio," she exclaimed with a big grin. "What are you doing here? Vittorio is not here."

Emilia fluttered her eyes and smiled seductively. She had been trying to crawl into my bed for years. It'd never happen, but it never stopped her from trying.

"I'm not here for Vittorio," I told her, pulling Wynter closer to me. I'd never understand why that man married her, though I suspected my father had a hand in it and Vittorio regretted it immensely. The woman was a snake.

Her eyes darted to Wynter, watching her curiously. Emilia was in her forties, but still carried herself as if she was in her twenties. Dressed like it too. She wore a thin red dress that matched her bright lipstick and knee-high boots.

"We have an emergency," I told her, glancing down at Wynter's feet. "We lost her shoes. Do you mind helping us out?"

"Who is she?" Emilia's eyes narrowed on Wynter. "She looks like those damn Russian women." I felt Wynter stiffen slightly next to me. A threatening growl formed in my throat, overprotectiveness surging through every ounce of me.

"She's important to me," I said, locking the lazy, autocratic stare I was known for on Vittorio's wife. The warning was clear on my face. Besides, who in the fuck was she to judge when she put her own daughter up on the auction block back a few years ago. She didn't hesitate to use her daughter, Thalia, to settle her debt to Benito King. Unfortunately for her, it was my father who jumped to purchase her. Not that there were many upstanding men participating in those auctions she'd have fared better with.

Emilia was a disgrace of a mother. She always feigned sadness, but I didn't buy it for one fucking second. She offered Thalia up instead of using herself to pay her own debt.

49

Displeasure shone in her dark eyes. "I never heard of her," she sneered, her cold expression on Wynter. It pissed me the fuck off. "She looks like a Russian whore."

I leaned over Emilia, scowling. "I'll cut your tongue out if you say another fucking rude word. Or even look at her wrong. And you know it's never a good thing to be on my bad side, Emilia. For you or your husband. So you *will* show my woman respect."

She paled. I wanted to hammer the point home. Wynter was mine and Emilia would never be. And if she upset Wynter, there'd be hell to pay. She knew my threats weren't empty. It was a quality of my father's that had been passed down to me. Except, I could be much more vicious than the old man.

In this case, I didn't mind because Emilia would think twice before she said another word about her.

A forced, fake smile flashed on her face. "Of course. Shoe size?"

Again, she barely glanced at Wynter. I wondered if she ever even thought of Thalia, her own daughter. Emilia was selfish beyond reason.

"Seven," Wynter muttered, her shoulders tense while Emilia disappeared to the back of the store.

Holding her hand, we strode toward the sitting area.

"She seems mad," Wynter whispered with Emilia out of earshot. "Don't make her more upset."

Her gaze met mine, and I could see worry swimming in those big eyes.

"Don't worry about it."

We'd get the shoes, I'd leave Emilia with extra cash, and we'd be on our way. Let that fucking woman ponder on the consequences of her words and actions.

Her teeth tugged at her bottom lip, her gaze fleeting in the direction of Emilia's clacking heels. Then she sighed a resigned breath.

"Why does that make me worry more?" Because Wynter had good instincts. "Bas?"

"Yeah."

"I—I just can't get in trouble." Her gaze came back to me. It was an odd comment but I chalked it up to her knowing who I was. If she had looked me up, she'd know trouble followed where I went. "Okay?"

"Principessa, I'll keep you out of trouble," I assured her softly. "Nobody will hurt you."

At that moment, Emilia was back with several boxes, placing them on the little ottoman and opening the first one. Pink designer heels and Wynter's soft gasp filled the space around me. It seemed Wynter, like many other women, loved shoes.

Emilia handed the shoe to Wynter, but I took it before Wynter could.

"Let me," I told Wynter.

I dropped to my knees, grabbed her foot and slipped the shoe on. "Look at that. A perfect fit."

Wynter's soft chuckle filled the space. "And they don't disappear at midnight," she teased. Her gaze traveled to Emilia who watched us like a hawk. It was almost comical. "Your shoe designs are incredible," Wynter commended her. "I've loved them forever."

"Have you come to this store before?" Emilia questioned her and Wynter shook her head.

"Not to this one," she explained as I watched the exchange. "I've been to the one in San Francisco."

A second of silence.

"You seem familiar." Emilia eyed her, as if she was trying to remember something. There was no chance in hell that anyone who had seen Wynter would forget her.

"I get that all the time," Wynter told her.

"Who are your parents?" Emilia continued grilling her and I was about to cut her off, when Wynter answered her.

"Well, my father is dead and my mother's a sports coach," Wynter told her, the softness of her voice an unmistakable tale that she cared about her mother. "She's one of the best. Of course, I'm biased."

Wynter chuckled but Emilia didn't bother responding to her and Wynter averted the gaze from her back to me.

"Umm, these are fine. Can we just go?"

I never hurt women. Nor intimidated them. Though I was seriously tempted to do so now. Around Wynter my protectiveness surged tenfold. Emilia made Wynter uncomfortable and I wouldn't tolerate it. I suspected the warning glare I just bestowed on Emilia came out murderous.

"We'll take all of them, Emilia. Are there any flats in those boxes?"

"No, no, Bas," Wynter protested quietly. "It's too much. Just one pair."

"Yes, one pair of black and one pair of white flats," Emilia answered, ignoring Wynter's protests.

"Bas—"

I grabbed her chin gently and stopped her protest. "Which do you prefer to wear tonight?" I asked her softly, keeping her eyes on me. Emilia would pay for her disrespect.

"White flats, please."

Wynter slipped on her shoes with my help and I rose to my full height, meeting Emilia's gaze. Taking an advanced step toward her, I gave her a cold smile.

"Keep your mouth shut about our visit," I warned. "If you do anything to jeopardize Wynter or speak of her to anyone, I'll be back." The warning of what would follow hung in the air. Emilia's expression slipped for a moment and her eyes filled with fear, but she quickly masked it with defiance. "Understood?" I growled.

She took a step back, quickly nodded and lowered her eyes. Emilia liked to stir trouble for those she considered less worthy. Wynter was definitely more worthy than her, but Emilia didn't see it like that. Unless she had power and status, she was nobody to her.

My muscles brimmed with tension, the need to make her pay for upsetting my woman clawing at me.

"Bas?" Wynter's soft voice soothed the anger inside me and I inhaled deeply, her honey scent seeping into my lungs. She was so goddamn beautiful and kind, it almost hurt to look at her. She was so much better than I deserved. "Are we ready?"

I nodded, wrapping my arms around her and meeting her gaze. God, those eyes of hers could soothe the beast inside me on the darkest days. There was something remarkably calming and consoling when you drowned in her eyes.

Twenty minutes later, we were back in my car.

"Thanks again," she said softly. "I—I didn't want to say anything at the store, but I can't take all those shoes home."

"Why not?"

"Well, I'm still in the dorm. I'll be moving soon and explaining to the girls about twenty thousand dollars' worth of shoes will be hard."

"What university are you attending?" I asked her. "Here in the city?"

She shook her head, her golden curls bouncing. "Not in the city. I go to Yale."

My lips curved into a smile. "Smart girl, huh?"

She chuckled. "I'm not super smart. Davina, my friend, is brilliant and savvy. I got in on an athletic scholarship."

"What type of athletics?"

She shrugged her shoulders. "The general kind."

Odd. She avoided specifics and it struck me odd that she'd feel uncomfortable to share it.

"What are you studying?" I inquired curiously. Maybe Wynter's family wasn't well off financially and it made her feel uncomfortable to talk about the scholarship. Of course, she'd never have to worry about money again.

"Mathematics and physics."

"And you say you're not smart," I teased. "Math and business were my majors, but not even I could pull off physics."

She let out a bell-like laugh, the sound ringing through the car.

"Somehow I doubt it." She smacked my forearm playfully. The girl really did not fear me. I fucking loved it, and as she beamed with happiness, I couldn't peel my eyes from her.

Noticing my eyes on her, she raised her eyebrows. "What?" she asked, her beautiful lips curved up and her eyes shining.

"I like your laugh," I admitted. And then decided to bring it back to her original question. "I'll keep the shoes for you at my place," I offered. "I want to see you wear them all."

Her face lit up, and I found myself pondering how I could keep all her smiles and attention to myself.

"So does that mean I get to see you again?" She locked her eyes with me, her gaze soft and hopeful. If she only knew the ideas floating through my brain. I wanted to lock her up and throw away the key.

"I'm counting on it, principessa."

Because I'd never let you go.

Chapter Eight

WYNTER

"This is beautiful," I breathed, looking at the New York City skyline. "I've been here for four years and never knew this existed."

I convinced Bas to bypass a dinner sitting in a fancy restaurant. Instead, we got sushi carryout from a small Japanese restaurant. He swore they had the best sushi in town. We walked into the crowded restaurant together, where people stared at Bas with wide eyes. I had never been more glad to convince someone to do carryout.

Once in a while, I'd run into a figure skating fanatic and it'd get awkward. But this time, Bas took all the show. He was probably well-known, considering who he was.

When we picked up our order, Bas drove us to Hamilton Park and now we sat on the hood of his Lamborghini, shoulder to shoulder, with the best view in town stretching for miles in front of us. The lights glittered, yet the city noise didn't reach here. It was so quiet that all I heard was our breathing and the soft sounds of the waves separating us from the Big Apple.

He pulled chopsticks out of the bag and handed them to me. I fumbled a bit, trying to figure out the best way to grip them.

"Don't tell me you never used chopsticks before?"

I shoved my shoulder into his. "I haven't," I admitted. "But not to worry, I'm a fast learner."

"Want me to help you?" he offered, as he pulled food out of the bag. Then opened the first box with tuna rolls.

I was starving. The last few days, with all the shenanigans we found ourselves, I'd burned more calories than consumed.

Gripping the chopsticks, I kept trying to grab a roll without dropping it. After a few tries, I gave up. I was too hungry for this right now.

"Ah, screw it." Getting rid of one chopstick, I held the other one as a fork and stabbed the sushi roll, then picked it up and dipped it into a soy sauce.

He laughed as I shoved the roll into my mouth and instantly the wasabi taste flared on my tongue.

"Holy shit," I breathed, my nose and tongue burning as I searched for the drink.

His continued booming laughter filled the quiet night air as he dug out a bottle of sparkling water and handed it to me. If my tongue wasn't on fire, I'd have laughed that he ensured we had pricey mineral water. Like a drunk, I snatched the bottle from him and brought it to my lips.

I gulped it down like a man dying of thirst, blinking tears away.

"You okay?" he asked.

"What the fuck?" I rasped, putting the bottle down. "How much wasabi was in that soy sauce?"

"I should have warned you," he said, humor still in his voice. "That place knows I like it extra spicy, so they usually prepare it that way." He produced a handkerchief out of somewhere and dabbed at my eyes. "I'm sorry."

I sniffed, letting him wipe the tears rolling down my cheek with his thumb. His touch was gentle, almost reverent and had my chest fluttering. The only thing that ever rattled my heart was ice-skating and to feel it around this man shocked me every goddamn time.

Even more concerning was how much I liked it.

"Not your fault," I murmured, sniffling. "It was just unexpected. Next one will be fine. I won't let my sushi roll soak as long in the soy sauce."

Bas picked up another roll and dipped it in for a mere second. Then brought it up, holding it in front of me. I leaned forward, holding his gaze, and closed my lips around the sticks, then pulled back.

"Hmmm." I savored the taste. "So much better."

Bas's eyes darkened, his gaze glued to me like I was the best sight he had ever seen. Nobody had ever looked at me that way or made my stomach flutter with butterflies. The feeling thrilled me and scared me at the same time.

I swallowed the food, while the words of my mother echoed somewhere in the far corner of my mind. The words she used to say to Juliette and me during our teenage years all the time. She hadn't said them in a while. Yet now they screamed in my brain.

First love shatters your innocence and ends your dreams.

Was that the reason I never bothered with boys? Boys always intrigued Juliette, even more after those words. I didn't heed the warning because ice-skating was everything to me and that seemed to please Mom immensely.

Of course, my mother didn't behave like our friends' moms. They'd chaperone the dates, get their daughters educated on safe sex, and put them on birth control. Mine crammed my schedule with training and Juliette's with ballet.

"What's on your mind?" Bas inquired, his gaze burning me with its intensity.

"I remembered something my mother used to tell me and my cousin."

"What's that?" he asked curiously.

It was a silly thing to say to a twenty-seven-year-old man whose reputation as a skilled killer and sought-after bachelor preceded him. Call me stupid, but I trusted him and wanted to share whatever I could with him.

"When we started showing interest in boys in high school, she'd tell us that first love shatters dreams and innocence," I said, keeping my voice low.

"Rather morbid," he mused.

I nodded. I didn't tell him it had never resonated with me until now. Because something about this man could shatter me. I'd stake my life on it. Worst of all, I'd let him.

He picked up another piece of sushi and I took it eagerly. Food was always easier to handle than deep discussions of love. Since I gave up on my own chopsticks, I let him feed me.

"Don't forget to get some," I reminded him before taking a bite, so he took the next one and we ate in silence. This moment under the stars would forever stay with me. It was simple and complicated. Romantic and dangerous.

None of it stopped me. I liked this man. The dark edge that surrounded him pulled at strings that I never knew existed and whispered to something deep down in my soul.

"Do you eat sushi often?" he asked.

I thought back to the last time I had sushi. It was with my mother right before leaving for Yale. She took Juliette and me to a little hole-in-the-wall, but they had the best sushi in California. At least she believed so.

Of course, all three of us opted for forks rather than chopsticks. I still remembered that tense but comfortable silence as we ate our California rolls. I guess we were all disappointed that day. I hoped that for once she'd accompany me to the East Coast and see me off to college. She hoped I'd pick a college on the West Coast. Juliette was on my side, just for the principle of it.

I sighed. "My last night in California, before Jules and I came to college, Mom took us out for sushi," I told him softly, glancing at the sky. She was a good mother. I knew she loved me. Both Juliette and me. But sometimes she felt more like a coach than a mother. It was like she died right along with my father. "She was disappointed we picked Yale rather than a university on the West Coast, so it wasn't the most pleasant evening."

The starry sky glittered against the darkness, whispering secrets in a language I'd never understand. And I knew without a doubt there were many secrets. It wasn't until recently that I started pondering what my uncle and mom were hiding. Her refusal to ever come to New York or the East Coast, and the whole thing with Juliette finding birth certificates that had names of the Cullens as her and Killian's parents. There was a lot being withheld from us, leaving us blind to who we really were.

I glanced at him to see he'd been watching me and I smiled.

"How did you end up so—" *Dangerous.* But that wasn't the right word. Papers called him dangerous and ruthless. The Villainous King-pin. Those weren't the right words either. Yet, none others fit better than those. So at the loss of how to say it delicately, I just spit it out. "How did you end up being one of the most feared men in New York?"

I was curious about this man. I wanted to know everything, not only what reporters and paparazzi reported.

"Following my father's footsteps," he answered, his voice slightly bitter.

I tilted my head pensively. I doubted there was a person on the entire East Coast who hadn't heard of Gio DiLustro. Monsters were real, and from everything I heard, Gio DiLustro was one of them. All you had to do was google his name and hints to his cruelty and crimes were everywhere. Owner of suspicious businesses, deaths in his strip club and his restaurants.

He was a man to keep your distance from. So was his son. According to the press, Basilio DiLustro wasn't any less ruthless or lethal than his father. Except I had already fallen under his spell the moment he caught me sneaking over the balcony.

Thanks to Bas's looks, reports labeled him as charismatic, intriguing, and one of the most sought-after bachelors. They weren't wrong, but I had a feeling he hid a lot underneath all that.

"I'm not like your Yale boys," Bas growled, his voice low and dark.

But as I watched him, I didn't feel fear. I could sense his darkness, seeping through each word and glance. The slight psychotic possessive need lurked underneath every word and every look. Regardless, I faced it head-on. I loved it and that was the part that scared me. The way it seemed to draw me in like an undercurrent that would swallow me whole.

"You're not," I acknowledged in a whisper. Nobody could mistake Basilio for just any boy. His power and confidence oozed through every fiber of his three-piece suit.

"I'm not a good man, Wynter." I nodded, his eyes dark and possessive. Every look and touch by him exuded dominance, control, and power. "I've killed many."

My heart hammered against my ribs, threatening to break down. God, I wished I could say it was from fear. Maybe even with Uncle Liam shielding Juliette and me from the underworld, it was for naught. We'd been born into it, we'd been unknowingly part of it, and we'd die in it.

"I know," I rasped.

"Do you want to go?" The last chance to get out. His voice was deep, even emotionless, as if he prepared for me to run. I shook my head in answer. "Even knowing I've seen and done some bad things?"

I shook my head, so he continued, "Even knowing I have blood on my hands? I'm not going to pretend that I'm someone good and lie to you."

My heart, soul, and mind were in agreement here. I'd stay. I wanted this. Him. Was it smart? No, probably not. But that wouldn't stop me. Not when it came to all these new feelings swelling inside my chest, and we had barely gotten started.

"I'm not going anywhere," I breathed.

He grabbed the back of my neck and tilted my head so I'd stare in his eyes, our noses were inches apart. "Once you're mine, I won't let go."

His words were deep. Smooth. *Final.* And God help me, I felt like I was *his* already.

My family wouldn't approve. Uncle wouldn't. Mother definitely wouldn't. I wasn't even sure that Juliette would be on my side with this. And all my life she'd always taken my side. None of that stopped me.

The tip of his nose brushed against mine. "Your family will probably know my reputation," he said.

Fuck if I cared at this moment. His hand felt warm on my skin, his fingers firm on the back of my neck, holding me in his control. My heartbeat ricocheted erratically in my chest and excitement swam through my veins. That was all I cared about. This was stronger than my passion for ice-skating.

"I don't think you're all bad," I murmured. "There is good in you, Bas," I whispered softly. Maybe I was stupid, but I was convinced of it. A bad man wouldn't have come to my rescue. A villain would have demanded a higher price to help me. "And my family will see it too."

I was certain of it.

If only I wasn't proven wrong.

We shared sushi, water, and stories for hours. It was hands down the best date I've ever had.

"Juliette, my cousin, is a bit on the wild side," I told him, when he asked me about my family. "It's just her, her brother, and me. Her brother stayed with Uncle," I told him. Uncle Liam and Killian were active members of the underworld, so I withheld their names. "Jules stayed with me and my mom. So we were really raised like sisters."

"I bet she got you into trouble all the time," he mused.

It seemed he read my cousin well without even meeting her. "Here and there," I admitted with a smile. "But she's one of those people who would never betray me. She always stands by me. No matter what."

He nodded. "I have a few cousins like that too. It's important to have people who will stand by you, no matter what."

Something told me he spoke from experience. Though who would dare to betray him or be so stupid was beyond me.

"I'm lucky to have Davina and Ivy, along with Jules," I told him. "Juliette and I only met Davina and Ivy when we started Yale, but we hit it right off. Ivy and Juliette are a tad bit on the wild side. Davina is too serious."

"The girl quad squad, huh?" Amusement lurked in his eyes and I'd bet all my money he had watched the surveillance of the crazy four of us burning down Davina's ex's house.

"You come here often?" I asked him instead, trying to change the subject while glancing back at the view. It'd be better to focus on Bas than think about secrets I couldn't unravel about my uncle and Killian.

"No, not since I was like five."

I tilted my head regarding him. He met my gaze but there was something vulnerable in it that pierced me right through my chest. Without thinking, my hand reached out to his free hand.

"You okay?"

And just like that, his expression was wiped out of all emotions.

"Before my mother left, she brought me here," he said, his voice detached. His explanation shocked me. I expected everything but that kind of admission. "She left me here and took off with my baby sister. She was still an infant. My father didn't tolerate disobedience. Nor betrayal. He found her. She died."

The unspoken words were clearer than the starfall night sky. And a shudder ghosted through me. His father killed his mother. I'd stake my life on it.

"Why did you bring us here?" I asked quietly, squeezing his hand gently. "Do you want to go?"

He was quiet for a moment, his dark eyes meeting mine. My heart ached in my chest for him even though he wiped out any trace of vulnerability in him.

"We can replace it with a better memory," I offered softly, watching him.

A corner of his lips lifted and he regarded me with a hooded expression. It felt like looking into the sun, getting blinded by his darkness, and loving every second of it.

My pulse fluttered. My cheeks heated and warmth pooled in the pit of my stomach.

The girls would argue it was my first crush. I didn't think so. It felt like so much more than that. Like the world tilted off its axis and only this man could keep me standing. I've liked boys before, even fooled around a bit. But I never found it to be that exciting, so it ended before it even started.

Yet now, as I watched this man, I knew it was him I was waiting for. Nothing ever made me feel like a mere glance by him. Warm all over. He tore down invisible walls inside me, unraveled me, then engraved himself into the marrow of my bones.

And he hadn't even kissed me. *Yet.*

I knew it was only a matter of time. It was part of every glance we shared. Every breath. Every heartbeat.

"Want to dance?" It wasn't a question, though he framed it as one. But neither was it a demand.

I slid off the hood of his expensive car. He followed. Pulling out his phone, he opened an app and started his car. Soft music came through his speakers and he took my hand.

For a breath of a moment we stood facing each other, heartbeat to heartbeat and our gazes locked.

I let out a shallow breath and took a step closer to him, bringing us chest to chest. The way he towered above me should scare me. Instead, this man made something hot unravel inside me and I dove into it, needing every ounce of it.

He took my hand into his, interlocked our fingers and we started to move. Our bodies danced, fitting perfectly against each other.

Slow. Sensual. Magical.

Through the buzzing in my ears came lyrics of the song "I Found" by Amber Run.

My breasts brushed against his three-piece suit, my nipples tightened. My heart raced so hard I couldn't inhale enough oxygen into my lungs.

Towering over me like a dark, protective cloud, his eyes fell to my lips. I swallowed hard but I refused to look away. Instead, I drowned in his warm, spicy scent and his dark gaze, getting drunk off it. The butterflies in my stomach took flight and tingles vibrated under my skin.

I had never wanted anything more than *him* at this moment and somehow I knew he could see it in my eyes. Or maybe he could feel it.

He bent his head and brought his lips close to mine.

"I found you," he whispered, his breath brushing against my lips.

Not caring of consequences, or who he was, I wrapped my hands around his neck and closed the small gap between us. Our lips connected and fireworks exploded through every cell of my body.

Kissing Basilio DiLustro felt like committing the most delicious sin.

My mouth parted and he deepened the kiss, his tongue brushing against my lower lip and a moan climbed up my throat. My insides shook with an unfamiliar need.

The touch of his lips on mine set every inch of my skin on fire. I couldn't breathe; it was too much. It wasn't enough. I grew light-headed, lost in the sensation of him. His lips were soft, my veins burned with something hot and an ache pulsed between my thighs that only he could sate. Kissing him was better than anything else I had ever experienced. Better than figure skating or the highest and hardest jumps on ice. Better than experiencing that first perfect quad Axel jump on ice or the triple Lutz.

Kissing Bas was like standing on the edge of a cliff as a warm breeze caressed your face, watching the world spread out before you. It was euphoric.

Nothing and nobody ever came close to this feeling. Not even my quad Lutz or quad flip.

Chapter Nine

BASILIO

The most platonic thing I had ever done with a woman. My body came to life unlike ever before. The scent of her seeped through my skin and into my lungs. The second she parted her lips and my tongue stroked her full bottom lip, she surrendered to me without a second thought. That alone set my desire into a raging fire.

She tasted like honey and snow flurries. The oddest fucking combination, but I loved it. She tasted right. Like my perfection.

My kiss turned more demanding. And fuck it, she didn't seem to mind. Her body pressed harder against mine. I had no fucking clue when my hands traveled down her body but my fingers gripped her ass. Tightly, needing every inch of her.

I wanted to lay my claim on her. Never let her go.

It was that very moment I realized if there was anything in this world that could weaken me, it was *her*. I'd sacrifice everything and everyone for her. To keep her with me.

I'd never let her go.

My kiss turned harder with that self-revelation. I wanted her to feel the same spell I fell under. For her to hold on to me like I was her everything. For her never to leave.

From the moment I laid eyes on her, something in me reset.

Letting go of her ass, I brought up my one hand and pushed it into her golden curls and gripped her mane gently. Another moan.

"Look at me," I demanded.

Her eyes fluttered open. The golden halo of her hair made her appear like an angel. Like she was born just for me. To be mine.

"Now you're mine," I murmured against her mouth, her soft breaths fanning my mouth.

She remained silent, watching me. No confirmation. No denial.

I took her chin between my fingers. Gently but firmly. My heart pounded in my chest, worried she'd deny me. She was young. Not part of the Syndicate or underworld. I refused to lose her before I tied her to me.

"Wynter, I'm not the sharing type," I growled, letting a hint of my darkness seep into my words.

Still no fear entered her eyes. Her lips actually curved into a smile and she lifted on her tiptoes, her lips brushing against mine.

"Good. Neither am I," she said, surprising me. "I'll be yours for as long as you're mine."

Her eyes shone with promises and a future that would be happier with her beside me.

"Yours," I vowed.

"Yours," she repeated my vow in her soft voice and goddamn it if it didn't feel like vows spoken before God.

I crashed my lips into hers and our tongues collided. I wanted to consume her, taste every inch of her mouth and her body. The way she responded to me was addictive. It had me worked up more than I'd ever been. Her body melted into me and her hands fisted my shirt as if she couldn't get me close enough. I moved my mouth down her jaw, over the soft skin below her ear.

Her hips ground against me, her moves jerky and unpracticed. And it was the most erotic sight.

"Bas," she moaned, pink tainting her cheeks.

"You're so fucking beautiful," I rasped, nipping her neck. I hoped it left marks for the world to see. I kept sucking on the soft skin of her neck as my hand slipped between her thighs.

"Ohhh."

I never thought such a soft, needy whimper by a woman could get me so goddamn hard. I pressed my fingers to her core, the only thing separating me from her pussy was the thin material of her panties. And she was soaked.

She rocked her hips, grinding herself against my hand. "Oh my God," she breathed.

"Not God, principessa," I growled, jealous that she'd call out to him and not me. "Say my name when you come," I demanded, tightening my grip on her hair and tilting her face up so she'd watch me. So she'd know who brings her pleasure.

Her emerald eyes darkened, her gaze locked on mine and a sense of satisfaction filled me. Her gaze grew heavy as I increased pressure against her clit, through the damp material. Her pink lips parted. As we stared at each other, her hips ground against my hand harder and faster.

I growled watching her, not willing to miss the flicker of a single emotion across her face.

"Want to come?"

Wynter's eyes dropped to my lips as her tongue swept across her lower lip. She nodded and I kissed her again while my other hand still rested between her thighs. I pushed her panties aside and slid my finger over her clit and she started to tremble, her breathing ragged. I stroked my fingers over her folds and then slid a finger inside.

She was so fucking tight and I couldn't help but imagine how she'd feel as I thrust into her. I thought I'd fucking blow a load in my pants right here and now. Her insides greedily clenched around my fingers as she moaned softly into my mouth.

It was like corrupting an angel, yet I felt no guilt. I guided her gently back, until her legs hit the front of my Lamborghini. Sitting her down on the hood of my car, I half bent over her. And all the while, my fingers rubbed her clit and my tongue teased hers.

I felt her body shiver underneath mine, her hips rose to rub against me. God, she was so responsive. So fucking beautiful.

Her hands gripped my shoulders, her fingernails digging into my muscles as she quivered underneath me.

"Bas," she moaned, needy. "*Bas. Bas. Bas.*"

Her body rocked against my hand and I could taste her orgasm almost as if it were my own. I could smell her arousal, sweet and delicious. Her juices drenched my fingers and I refused to let up. Sliding my finger in and out of her slickness, she writhed under me.

"Look at me," I ordered and she opened her eyes to watch me through heavy lids.

She was close. Her beautiful face was so expressive as I guided her closer and closer to her orgasm. Her first one with me, but definitely not the last one. I'd own all of them from this day forward.

I was so fucking hard, but blue balls would be worth seeing her unravel for me. Shudders rolled down her body and she panted, her moans increasing in volume. Sliding in and out of her folds, while keeping one finger pressed against her clit, I rubbed it faster and thrust my fingers harder.

Her hands tightened around me and I loved how she needed me.

She came hard, her body shivering, her pussy convulsing around my fingers, and my name on her lips. She buried her head in the crook of my neck and peace washed over me.

For the first time in my life, I actually tasted the light.

Chapter Ten

WYNTER

"See me tomorrow."

Warmth filled through every fiber of me. We sat in his car in front of my dorm building. It was almost midnight and I truly felt like Cinderella. My body still hummed with the aftermath of the strongest orgasm I had ever experienced. It was my first orgasm with a man, so maybe that's why. Though I didn't think so.

His touch seared. His lips consumed. And his fingers delivered.

I felt him everywhere, though our clothes stayed on.

"You still want to see me?" I breathed the question, my tongue sweeping over my lower lip nervously. I could still taste him on my lips. It was an aphrodisiac.

I expected him to take it all the way after I came all over his fingers. Instead, I watched him lick his fingers clean. And oh my God, it was so damn erotic that a delightful shudder ghosted down my spine in anticipation. I wanted to feel him inside me. Give him my virginity.

He was the one I'd been waiting for.

Yet, rather than taking me, he helped me off the hood and settled me into the car.

"You're mine now," he repeated his earlier statement. I didn't mind his possessiveness, but it confused me.

"But you didn't—" My voice faltered and my cheeks heated. I was pretty sure my body clearly showed him that I wanted him. I didn't hold back. Did I?

He took my chin and held it between his fingers. My eyes met his, drowning in his darkness.

"I didn't what?" he demanded to know.

I rolled my eyes. "You didn't try to sleep with me," I rasped, slightly agitated he'd make me say it out loud.

He chuckled softly, his Adam's apple moving in his throat, and I found it so damn sexy. I had to fight the urge to lean forward and lick his neck. Everything about this man was attractive.

He took my hand and placed it over his groin and I gasped, my cheeks heating. He was hard. And so damn big I didn't think he'd fit inside me.

"Tell me now I don't want to fuck you," he gritted.

My cheeks flushed crimson and my insides were burning up.

"Then why didn't you?" I breathed the question bravely.

"Wynter Star." He leaned forward and brushed his tongue at the corner of my lip. "When I fuck you, it won't be a quick fuck in the back seat. It will be in a bed, so I can spread you wide and take my time worshiping every inch of you." A shiver rolled down my body at his words. "I'll eat your pussy. Then I'll fuck it. And you're going to ride me all fucking night." My mouth parted and my eyes widened. "I want your lips, your pussy, and your body because you want to give it, Wynter. Not because you want to repay a debt."

Something hot burned deep inside me, causing a dull ache between my thighs.

"Holy shit," I murmured, my whole body lit on fire. I was almost tempted to beg him to take me to his place tonight. "I'd invite you to start that tonight," I said, trying to come off seductive but my voice

71

was too throaty. It was coated in thick, deep lust that I felt in the pit of my stomach. "But I have roommates."

"See me tomorrow," he asked again, his own voice deeper than usual and his eyes burning with dark flames I felt inside me.

There was nothing and nobody that would stop me from seeing him.

"Okay," I breathed. "I have ballet class with Madame Sylvie tomorrow afternoon. After that?"

He nodded without delay.

"Text me the address and time."

He exited the car and came around to open the door for me. For a mobster, he was such a gentleman. The romantic part of me, that lay dormant until I met this guy, was giddy.

Taking his extended hand, I stood up and he pulled me against his tall, hard body. Before I could relish his strong arms around me, he grabbed the nape of my neck and pressed his lips into an all-consuming kiss.

The toe-curling kind.

It was the kiss that songs were written about. The kind that changed you forever.

I walked through my home entrance a little after two a.m. After dropping Wynter off at Yale, I sped down the dark road back to New York City.

Her scent still lingered in the car. It was like a drug to me. Intoxicating and, at the same time, soothing. I never thought there'd be light in my life. All I had ever known was the piercing darkness that was my life. Cruelty that surrounded the Syndicate world. Each Kingpin was known for it, and I was no different.

From a young age I fought against becoming *him*. My father. His blood was my blood. His monsters were my monsters. Our cruelty was like poison. It ran through our veins until it infected your heart.

More monster than man. It was what people whispered behind my back. Behind every DiLustro's back.

Yet, in Wynter's presence all I felt was the warmth of sunshine. Even under the night sky, I swore her golden halo projected sun.

"What are you still doing up?" I asked when I spotted Dante with his feet on the coffee table, watching baseball.

He glanced over his shoulder. "Watching the Yankees lose to the Cubs."

I scoffed. "You wish."

He reached over to the side table, picked up a piece of paper and threw it at me.

"Deed to The Eastside," he retorted, his eyes back on screen. "Your fucking father showed up."

My shoulders tensed. He was supposed to stay out of that club. Fuck! I hated that fucking nosey bastard. He was so paranoid about everyone, including his own family, overthrowing him and ending his pathetic life that he had to insert himself into everything. Of course, he wasn't wrong when it came to his family. We hated his guts, me most of all.

"Don't worry; Liam actually let him believe you already picked up the deed."

"Why?"

"I guess he hates us less than him," he muttered. I grabbed a bottle of water and sat next to him, stretching my legs. "Were you out there getting your dick wet?"

I didn't bother answering him. I wouldn't talk about Wynter. She wasn't like other women. Anything that would pass between her and I was only for the two of us to know. She was mine alone.

"So the blonde is it for you, huh?" Dante asked when I remained quiet.

"Yes."

Wynter was not up for discussion, regardless that there hadn't been anything I kept away from Dante, his brother, Priest, or my sister. The four of us were the only family I ever counted on, despite the distance. Emory stuck to Las Vegas, as far away from our father and uncle, Priest ruled Philly and Dante ruled Chicago.

We all hated our fathers. Their sadistic ways. And most of all, we hated knowing we'd become them. Though Gio, my own father, won the first spot in cruelty. At least my uncle's cruelty didn't extend to his family. My father's did.

For a while now, I feared I'd already become him. Until the day Wynter fell into my arms. Literally. The way she looked at me breathed hope and light into my soul. Corny, yes. But fuck it, the way she made me feel was intense. Possessive. She was the first woman who made me *feel*.

I took a swig of water, the scent of Wynter's arousal still on my fingers. I almost didn't want to take a shower, so I could keep her scent on me.

Tomorrow, I calmed myself. I'd see her again tomorrow.

"Did you pick up on Liam's comment yesterday?" I asked Dante, setting the topic of Wynter aside.

Before Liam handed over the deed to The Eastside Club, we met with Liam in his office building. He'd gotten part of the property I owned on the west side in exchange for the club. Unfortunately, my father came along and made things more tense than they usually were. Liam hated his guts and his comment to my father alluded to the past.

It was you who started this clusterfuck between our families. Those were his exact words. DiLustros and Brennans never got along, but I never heard of my father starting it.

"Which one?" Dante snickered. "Your father and Liam behaved as if they were ready for a battle. We're lucky they didn't draw guns."

He was right. Those two hated each other's guts for as long as I could remember. They didn't even bother hiding their animosity.

"Liam calling out Father for starting this war." It had lingered in the back of my mind ever since. Liam Brennan was our enemy but he was a fair man. Unlike my own father.

Dante's dry gaze flickered my way. "They're probably keeping some secrets. Worried to show us their true colors." Sardonic breath left me. It was too late for that. I'd seen my father's true colors when I was five and he killed my mother in front of me. "If I had to guess, I'd say Liam's comment probably has something to do with the fact that Gio shot Brennan's sister."

I frowned. "What?"

"Gio shot Liam's sister," Dante explained.

"No, I didn't know that." There was barely any information on Liam's sister. No pictures. Killian was his adopted son but even his information was hard to come by. "How do you know?"

Dante shrugged. "Priest. You know he likes to dig shit up. Plus he overheard Father's conversation with Uncle Gio. Gio didn't want to support your deal with Brennan and debated dragging it in front of the Syndicate." Fuck, that would have been risky. Especially with the older members, since they were stuck in their ways. "Your father's hate for the Brennans goes beyond normal rivalry. But Father convinced him to take it and put to rest the entire business of shooting Liam's sister."

Jesus Christ!

"Did Priest happen to overhear why he would shoot a woman?" I questioned. Regardless that she was a Brennan, she was a woman. Killing women and children was frowned upon. Not unless they've done something to compromise us. Dante shook his head. "Of course not. It wouldn't be that easy."

"If I had to guess, it had to be about the power," Dante speculated. "It's the only thing that he cares about."

Our fathers still run the Syndicate in name only. Over the last eight years, Dante, Priest, and I had worked at increasing our influence, power, and wealth. Even Emory. For the past three years, she ruled Las Vegas, building the Syndicate's power there. In my father's world, it was either sink or swim. And he applied that to my sister too. I protected her as much as I could but it wasn't enough. She had to become strong and ruthless. So I helped her become that, with Dante's and Priest's assistance, and she exceeded our expectations.

She made me so goddamn proud. Despite what our father did to her, she came out on top. He'd pay one day for what he'd done to her. I vowed it to her and had been working at slowly clawing away at the things he cared the most about.

Power. Money. Connections.

Our power and wealth now superseded our fathers' by tenfold. Unfortunately, there was a certain hierarchy and patriarchy in our circles that was followed. And killing your own father was frowned upon. Very frowned upon. So I kept looking for other options. I wasn't beyond hiring a killer, the problem was finding someone you could trust not to turn on you.

"How did Liam's sister die?" I asked him.

"I was curious and looked it up," Dante muttered, and by the tone of his voice, I knew I wouldn't like what was to follow. "She died after getting shot. Her unborn child didn't make it either."

"Fuck," I muttered.

"It's odd though," Dante continued, his voice low as if he tried to give respect to the woman we've never met. "There was no mention of her getting shot or anything. According to the official paperwork, her death was an accident. Not a single picture of her anywhere. You'd think Liam would have gone full force to lock Gio up. If Priest wouldn't have told me about the conversation between your father and mine, we wouldn't have known. There are no traces of her anywhere on the web."

"Brennan should have killed him," I grumbled.

It would have saved us all so many years of brutality and pain. To my mother. My younger sister. It was the reason my mother left. She couldn't handle it. Even more because she didn't want to see her son grow up into a monster like his father. So she took Emory and ran.

Like a thief in the night she left, except it wasn't night. It was the middle of the day when she dropped me at the park and left me there. A head start that didn't save her. Father found her and killed her, then brought my infant sister back. She should have known a head start wouldn't have mattered. There was no hiding from him. Nowhere to run that he wouldn't find her.

Albeit, she was right to worry about me because I'd become just like my father. I killed my first man at twelve. And I still remembered that first kill. The way hot, sticky blood stained my hands, the scent of copper and piss mixed with the sound of the man's screams in the damp basement. I was shaped into a monster by my father's fists, blades, and harsh words.

Power is offering no mercy, only brutality. That had been my bedtime story since my mother's death.

Staring at the rerun of the baseball game, both Dante and I lost in our thoughts, ghosts came chasing, lurking in the darkness of our minds. Except I saw the light in the form of a young woman.

Wynter's light shone in my darkness brighter than the moon in the night sky. And I'd keep it that way. I'd never let anyone extinguish that light. If they'd try, they'd earn my wrath, and I wouldn't hesitate to use the brutality I was taught.

And most importantly, I'd keep Wynter away from my father at all costs. He destroyed everything he touched, young women in particular. He thought them only good for fucking and breaking. If he ever dared to touch her, I'd kill him. My hands curled into tight fists itching to cut him piece by fucking piece, to kill him, consequences be damned.

"You know one of these days we'll have to kill him." It was the first time I uttered those words out loud.

Dante met my gaze.

"Don't bring your woman around him," he warned, reflecting my exact thoughts. "Why do you think I'm avoiding the whole idea of commitment?"

I knew it. Until Wynter, it was exactly how I felt about commitments and marriage. When she fell into my arms three months ago, something clicked in my chest. I still let her walk away from me. But then life threw her right back into my arms.

It had to mean something. That she was mine to keep.

I got up and headed out of the room with ghosts at my tail.

"I'm taking a shower and then hitting the sheets. You should try and get some rest."

Neither of us slept much. I supposed it was a result of years of *training*.

As I readied for my shower, those old ghosts came calling and my mind wandered to the past that I never visited willingly.

I watched my mother rush, scurrying away with little Emory in her arms, wailing. She was still a baby and cried a lot. She needed a lot of attention, but I was okay with it. As long as my mother kept me with her. Sometimes she'd send me with Papà to his club. I didn't like it.

Standing still in the park full of happiness and laughter, all I felt was my racing heart. I kept waiting for her to turn around. She never did. Not fucking once.

Minutes turned into hours. Strangers threw curious glances my way. So did the other children, but I never left my spot, staring in the direction my mother left.

"She'll be back," I whispered under my breath. "She'll be back for me. She loves me."

My eyes stung, my head throbbed, my mouth dried.

The humid August air made it hard to breathe. It was hot, my forehead sticky. My stomach rumbled with hunger. But I didn't move. I refused. I needed to be here when she came back. One moment and I could miss her.

It took me years to understand she couldn't bear to look at me. She saw my father every time her eyes landed on me, and taking me with her, I would have been her reminder of what she endured with him every single fucking day.

A dark shadow cast over me, and I slowly looked up to find my father's furious face glaring down at me.

"Where is your mother?" he hissed.

I blinked up at my father, not having the answer for him. He seemed kind of blurry, so I blinked again.

He gripped me by the collar and carried me away from there. Like I was a piece of garbage. Once we got to his car, he shook me and threw me into the car.

"Stop crying or I'll give you something to cry about!"

For some stupid reason, the five-year-old in me noted he didn't put me in the car seat. Mamma always put me in the car seat.

My father got behind the wheel and hit the gas so hard, I flew out of my seat and my forehead hit the back of the front seat. I struggled getting up, then climbed up back on the seat, then reached for the seat belt and pulled it over my chest to click it.

I had no idea how long we drove. My father barked a few times for me to stop, but I wasn't sure what to stop. My eyes followed the passing cars and buildings, then the highway. The drive took too long and not long enough. My stomach lurched, threatening to empty the contents out, but deep down, I knew that'd earn me a beating.

Mamma wasn't here to stop him.

The car came to a sudden stop. Before I could blink, the car door opened and Papà hit me hard across the face.

"Stop crying!"

He gripped me by my shirt, glaring at me, but I must have still been crying because he hit me even harder.

"Let's go," he ordered, yanking me by my arm. The neighborhood was rough, glances thrown our way quickly averted.

"That whore thinks she can run away from me," he hissed, his face twisted with rage. "Take my daughter." He gripped my arm tighter,

wrenching me along. My shoulder hurt, his fingers dug into my arm, but I didn't dare to make a sound.

We came to a ragged-looking door, the familiar cry of a baby sounding through it. Father didn't bother knocking. He kicked the door open and familiar dark brown eyes full of fear met Father and me.

Screaming filled the small, dirty space. My father's body collided into my mother's, then the pitch of her screams rose a few notches. So did my baby sister's. I ran to her, took her off the floor and set her down on my lap. Just the way my mother taught me. It was the only way she'd ever let me hold my baby sister, and while her screams pitched, I tried hard to soothe her.

I watched with tight lungs as Father hit Mamma again. "Stop," I yelled at him, my voice wobbly. "Stop, Papà. Please."

His face twisted into an ugly and scary mask as his anger shifted to me. I braced myself because I knew another blow was coming. I shifted my body and sheltered my baby sister on my lap, right as my father backhanded me. His palm connected with my right cheek, the burning sensation instant and tears stung my eyes.

Then his attention returned to my mother, as he pulled out a knife and gripped it tightly. I watched in horror as he took two strides, then sliced her throat before she even had a chance to open her mouth and beg for her life.

I froze, watching my mamma gurgle, choking on her own blood and her eyes wide with terror. She gasped, despair in her eyes as she watched me. No, not me... my baby sister. Father pushed her onto the floor and blood quickly pooled around her, each second taking her further and further away from me. From us.

The scent of copper mixed with Mamma's perfume and fragranced the air. I watched the light slowly extinguish her dark brown eyes, leaving frozen horror on her face. Sad and lonely, scared, staring at me.

Except she didn't see me.

It was the first dead body I had seen and by no means the last one.

Eventually, I learned Father had a chip installed in my mother that allowed him to track her. She was doomed from the start.

———

Later that day, after only a few hours of sleep, I got a message from my father. He wanted to see Dante and me.

What crappy timing, I grumbled silently.

I hoped after the whole ordeal with The Eastside, there'd be no need to see him. At least for another few weeks.

Dante gave me a questioning look. "Why in the fuck does he want to see *me*?"

I grimaced. "Would you like me to relay that message?"

He scoffed, though he looked like he swallowed a bitter pill. "No. We all know how much he likes to be questioned." His voice held sarcasm as he made his remark. "I should have left last night, now I have to talk to him before going to the airport."

"I'm sure your plane won't leave without you," I retorted dryly. "Let's go so you can head back to Chicago."

When we arrived in front of the mansion on Fifth Avenue, I had to fight the urge to torch the whole goddamn building to ashes. I hated this fucking place. I hated my fucking father. And most of all, I hated the darkness that thrived in the memories that this place evoked.

Parking my car at the bottom of the stairs leading to the double doors, just the way my father hated, Dante and I exited the car, then headed up the stairs. This place was secured better than the White House. There were high-tech cameras everywhere and guards.

We ran into Thalia, Emilia's daughter and the woman my father purchased through the Belles and Mobsters auction from Benito King about five years back.

She lingered in the entrance hall, eyeing the exit longingly. Fuck, I

82

wanted to take her out of this hell. Her face was smeared with tears and a black bruise marked the whole right side of her face.

She whimpered at seeing us, taking a step back. Both Dante and I stilled.

"Fuck," he muttered.

She didn't look good. Probably the reason she had stuck to the inside of the house. Waiting for her bruises to fade before she'd show her face in public.

Rage filled me at my own father's brutality. It was one thing to beat men and torture traitors. It was something entirely different abusing the innocents that couldn't fight back. My father was ten times stronger than Thalia, even at his age.

And Thalia was only twenty-five. She hadn't done anything to deserve this.

He'd end up killing her one of these days, just as he killed Brennan's sister. No wonder Liam hated our guts.

"Thalia, you should let us help you," I whispered so low only she and Dante could hear.

She shook her head. "He'd kill my mother."

I clenched my jaw. Thalia worried about her mother and that fucking bitch only thought about herself.

My phone buzzed and I slid the message open without checking who it's from.

Wynter: **I'm so sorry. I have to go out of town. Can we meet when I get back?**

Me: **Don't be too long.**

It had only been less than a half a day and I missed her already. I wanted her with me at all times. Albeit part of me knew that wouldn't be possible. Not with my father around.

With the sound of footsteps that were unmistakably my father's, I shoved the phone back into my pocket while Thalia quickly scurried away. She probably wanted to be anywhere but where my father was. Not that I could blame her.

"Ah, here you are." His voice boomed over the large foyer. I really wasn't in the mood to talk to him. This hate I had for him ran deep and it'll never ease. Not until his dying breath.

He approached us, dressed in his three-piece suit, no gun. He seemed so sure of himself that he believed he didn't need it. It would be so damn easy to pull my gun and shoot him. Except, I knew his surveillance feed went directly to the Syndicate. Fucking sick bastard.

While he roamed around his house weapon-free, I always had my gun on me. When I slept, it was either on my nightstand or under my pillow. You never knew when the attack was coming.

"You wanted to see us," I told him coldly.

"Yes, let's go into my office." He turned around and headed down the hallways, which led to the back of the house where his office was. He expected us to follow him like dogs and I fucking hated it.

Dante and I shared the briefest of glances but said nothing. We knew better than to say anything in front of him.

Once in his office, I shut the door behind me and shoved both of my hands into the pockets of my pantsuit. It was easier to hide the urge to punch my father that way. I leaned against the marble ledge of the fireplace, keeping my composure relaxed and expression bored.

Dante did the same, except he sat down and rested his ankle on his knee as he leaned back in his chair with an equally bored expression.

My father sat behind his desk, his eyes darting between the two of us. He liked to show his power, as well as exercise it. Though he was too blind to see that it was slowly slipping through his fingers. He was too arrogant, too sure that he was invincible.

Neither Dante nor I broke the silence. He wanted to see us squirm, but we weren't little boys anymore. We had done and seen our share of brutality and silence didn't bother us in the slightest. Except let me contemplate a few more creative ways to kill him.

I held his expression, hiding all my plans and turmoil deep down where he'd never see it. After all, I had two decades to perfect it. My old man liked to taunt and I wouldn't give him the satisfaction.

"The Russians attacked Brennan," Father finally broke the silence, a benevolent smile on his lips. "They believe he has something of theirs."

"What's that?" I asked, hiding my curiosity behind a bored tone.

"A woman," he muttered with a dark expression.

A woman would be my father's downfall. Too bad she couldn't get here already.

"I'm sure Brennan has many women at his disposal," I said, shrugging my shoulders. "Do we have specifics?"

"She's the great-granddaughter of a powerful Pakhan," he grumbled, bitterness in his voice. "Both her mother and her daughter are supposed to be dead." Dante and I shared a glance, but neither one of us uttered a word. It was best not to let Father know we knew anything. "The rumor is that both mother and daughter are alive and well, hiding from the underworld. The Pakhan wants to get them back."

"Why does it sound like you want to find them before the Pakhan?" I asked dryly.

"It would give us an upper hand," he said, the cruel and dark expression I have come to know well lurking in his eyes. "Not only over the Russians, but also the Irish."

God, he made me sick. My fingers twitched, the need to pull out my gun and put a bullet between his eyes so strong that my muscles brimmed with tension. If we did find the lost Russian mafia princesses, I'd ensure they disappeared before he'd ever put his hands on them. I wouldn't repeat the same mistake as with Thalia. If that one would let me help her, I'd have her gone too.

"What's the kid's name?" I asked. "How old is the girl?"

"She'd be about twenty," Father drawled. "Her mother was a fine piece of ass. I'm sure her daughter is too. It's in their fucking genes."

My hands curled into fists, the guilt from long ago curling in the pit of my stomach. I didn't save my own mother, maybe I could save this woman and her child. At least from my old man.

"Brennan nor the Russians are our concern," I told him. "If we find or hear anything, we'll follow the lead."

But only to secure her away from the fucker. It made my stomach churn to think what my father would do to the women. What he did to Thalia. That dreaded fear that my mother's words would turn into truth always lurked deep in my mind. Yes, cruelty ran in my veins. It was beaten into me, but it was where I drew the line. I wouldn't harm an *innocent* woman. Cross me and I'd make you pay.

"This is Brennan's weak moment," my father protested. He always wanted to go into attack mode with the Brennans. "We could wipe him and his wretched family off the face of the planet."

I was surprised Brennan allowed the Russians back into the city if in fact his sister and niece were alive. Over the last twenty years, the Russians would attack here and there, but it was always sporadic. They didn't have a presence in New York. Not for some years now. Until about three months ago. From all the intel I had, they bickered with the Russians worse than with DiLustros and he hated our guts.

"It's not a good time." Not to mention I shook his hand and gave him my word we'd have peace. I refused to break it.

"We should take advantage of the opportunity and attack Brennan," Father continued stubbornly. Alert shot up my spine, but I kept my expression unmoving. "He can't fight us both. We should strike him at his weakest."

He let his rage or jealousy, or whatever the fucking personal vendetta he had going with the Brennans, dictate his behavior. It made him stupid and reckless. But I'd be damned if I'd go against my word. My promise to Liam Brennan was I'd keep to the east side, as long as he kept to the west side of New York City.

I didn't intend to break my agreement.

"Brennan has alliances," I told him calmly. "With Cassio King and his gang. Picking a fight with him means going against all of them."

Father waved his hand like it was nothing. "We have Chicago, Philadelphia, and Vegas to support us."

I clenched my jaw tightly. There was nothing I wanted to do more than stride over to him and wrap my hand around his throat, then watch that cruel light as it extinguished in his eyes. Just like he extinguished it in my mother's eyes when he sliced her throat.

But the Syndicate would never accept patricide. If they allow one man to kill his father, then others would follow.

"And Brennan has Cassio King and his gang," I repeated. "That gang is a lot larger."

"We have the Syndicate," he snapped back, slamming his fist on the table and ignoring reason. The bastard never liked to listen to reason. "What do you say, Dante?" he asked my cousin, grinning with a self-satisfied smirk.

"We're strong," Dante answered diplomatically, giving him a tight smile. "Albeit we're currently fighting The Unione Corse in Philadelphia and Canadians in Chicago. Alessio Russo, who's also tight with Cassio King, has had his sights on us too. It'd be hard to support another fight."

The Unione Corse was a Corsican mafia. Their home and main operation was in Corsica and Marseille, but they also had a presence in the States. They'd been trying to expand for years, and it was only thanks to Priest and our efforts that they were unsuccessful.

Bottom line, Dante and Priest had their hands full without adding another clusterfuck that could be avoided.

"We need the Brennans gone," he said in a strange voice, and every single fiber of me stood in alert. "They've been a thorn in our side for far too long."

He narrowed his eyes on me and my muscles tensed. Truthfully, I rarely thought of the Brennans. They didn't bother me. There were plenty of deals to be made to divide it twenty ways. Liam mainly stuck to his shit and we did our own. Except when fucking Father tried to poke the bear.

I forced myself to relax. I started to think it would be inevitable that one day I'd kill my own father but it couldn't be today. Not in his own home. I'd have to kill his entire crew and that'd be hard to hide.

"If the Russians are already attacking him, why not let it ride out?" I asked instead, my smile cold. "Let them finish him."

I stared into his eyes, hammering the point home. My hands itched to draw my gun, but I forced myself to remain immobile.

He narrowed his eyes on me, then on Dante. Could he tell that we all hated his guts? I didn't think so. Dante was just as good at hiding his emotions as I was. Cruelty ran in DiLustro veins and straight into our hearts.

Then as if he figured us out, Father cackled. "Right you are, sSon. We'll let the Russians finish him off." Then he gave me that smile I knew so well. The kind that spoke of hell. "Now tell me about this girl Emilia tells me about."

Anger surged through me. I forced my body to remain motionless or risk flying over his desk and killing him. Emilia had to have told him. She'd pay for that one

"Just a chick I ran into at a club. She's nobody." *She's everything.* But that sentiment would remain buried deep down so he'd never see it.

He shuffled some papers on his desk, seemingly uninterested but I knew him better than that. He waited for me to slip and give him more information because Emilia had none. It was the only explanation for him knowing about Wynter. That bitch probably hoped to gain some points with the fucker.

"Just remember, Basilio," he said, raising his eyes and narrowing them on me. "Women are only good for fucking. Don't forget what happened to your mother."

Anger simmered under my skin and red mist marred my vision. I was ready to pounce on him and strangle him with my bare hands, when Dante's voice came through.

"We know that, Uncle. You taught us well."

Too fucking well.

F rustration clawed at my chest.

It had been several days and my father hadn't eased up.

Fucking Emilia! She had to open her mouth and blab about Wynter to my father. So now on top of riding my ass about the fucking Brennans and wiping them out of existence, he also rode my ass about Wynter. He wanted to know who she was.

I'd rather cut my dick off than tell him about her.

I'd never been so fucking happy that cartel came to visit, interrupting Father's questioning.

Goddamn Emilia.

Apparently, she needed a reminder of who the fuck I was. Right after this, I'd go and teach the jealous wench a lesson. She was a greedy, power-hungry bitch. If there was one thing my father hammered into me, it was forgiveness made you look weak.

So after this meeting, I'd be sure to pay her a visit. And if something happened to Wynter because of her big mouth to my father, I'd fucking slice her to pieces.

The atmosphere around the room was tense. We met the cartel in one of our warehouses that also had a conference room for meetings with higher-ranking members. I preferred not to take them to my establishments and Father pretty much left me free rein when it came to meetings.

I sat back in my chair and cracked my knuckles. I should be focused on the situation in this room, yet all I could think about was Wynter. Her last message to me said she was on her way back. And I knew where she had been. Of course, I knew that because of Dante.

He flew back early this morning after the fiasco at his casino. My woman was directly involved with it. Her girl quad squad was more trouble than I initially thought. What the fuck ever. She accepted me for who I was, so I'd accept her for who she was. If she liked to cheat and steal, fuck it, I'd let her. Maybe I'd contain it to safe environments where I could protect her.

I'd finally see her tomorrow. I couldn't fucking wait.

The burning need and worry concerning Wynter surged through my veins. I worried about what she and her girlfriends were up to and that she'd get herself killed. I worried about my father sniffing around her.

I fucking worried about her, period. I knew I couldn't fucking handle something happening to her.

Dante's shifting gaze flickered to me, warning me to keep my shit together. I would have my shit together when I shoot all these goddamn idiots, including my own father. I had no time for this shit and this supposed negotiation was a fucking waste of my time.

Sebastian fucking Tijuana could have called, instead of insisting on a face-to-face meeting. He should know by now that it'd be my way or the fucking highway.

"Ten million dollars for two truckloads and—"

"Seven million," I cut the head of the Tijuana cartel off, my voice remaining impassive. I heard the fucker's brother gave Raphael Santos a hard time. Hence the reason for his untimely death. "One week. One truckload here and the other in Philadelphia. Take it or get the fuck out."

I didn't have time for this shit. There were plenty of distributors in the market and this fucker knew it. Sebastian Tijuana wasn't dumb and certainly not ignorant to not realize he was overcharging me for the drug shipment.

A tense air crept through the room. I could see even from my spot my father's complexion turning red, but thankfully he said nothing. After all, this was my deal and my warehouse. He hadn't been successful lately in running his businesses. I might have had a thing or two to do with it, chipping away at him.

Payback's a bitch and his payback is way overdue.

Maybe if he'd get his head out of his ass and stop obsessing over the Brennans, he'd notice it. Maybe even succeed in growing some of his own shitty relationships. His loss; my gain.

"Seven million," Sebastian agreed, standing up. We shook on it and he was out the door.

Thank fucking God!

Now if only my father would follow, the day would be looking up.

"Well," my father said from the seat behind me, "if this is how you conduct business, son, I don't know how we're still in business."

I gritted my teeth. He barely hustled with his ancient and outdated ideas. The Italian Syndicate thrived under business dealings that Dante, Priest, Emory, and I made. Though at this very moment, business was the least of my concerns.

"It's not good business to piss off suppliers, Basilio," Father continued, leaning back in his chair, his eyes on me. "Or does this have something to do with the blonde hussy Emilia told me about?"

I decided I'd kill her. Skin her alive. I should have killed her when she sold off Thalia to settle her debt.

"It worked out just fine," I said, glancing down the table to where my father sat with Angelo, his right-hand man. "I wouldn't let him screw us over."

"And the hussy?" He just couldn't let go, although something about the smugness in his eyes rubbed me the wrong way.

"Like I said, she's nobody." A dark edge crept into my voice.

I refused to talk to him about Wynter. My father had a tendency to destroy good things. I'd be damned if I'd let him even attempt to taint the golden-haired woman who smiled innocently and happily.

Wynter and her friends might have some suspicious activities going on, but fuck if I'd judge them. Maybe they were short on money and this was the only way they could get it. I'd ensure Wynter never lacked. I had plenty of money to support anything she had going on.

Though Dante's revelation still made no sense to me. A rigged poker game and some property damage at his casino, Royally Lucky, in Chicago. That's where Wynter and her girlfriends went, why she canceled on me, costing Dante a couple of hundred thousand dollars in lost revenue. Dante recognized the woman he'd seen with Liam and the rest of the girls that danced on the bar at The Eastside.

Apparently, there was a girl squad *Mission Impossible* going on with the four women. Though I had to admit, I was impressed by Wynter's gaming skills. It was clear she counted cards and I never would have guessed she'd be capable of it. Luckily, Dante was my cousin, but if they'd walked into one of the businesses my father owned or someone like him, they'd be dead.

I already started looking into buying clubs that she could rob with her girlfriends. Either that or I'd put a stop to it. For Wynter's own good.

I'd come to the realization that I'd been pining after Wynter since she first landed in my arms three months ago. I thought about her way too often since that night, but I came to terms she'd forever stay a mystery. It was better that way—for her and for me.

But then we crossed paths and I'd made her mine, whether she liked it or not. And she did, just as I did. She had a body I wanted to bury myself in. Her smiles were my own personal version of heaven. It didn't take a genius to realize my control was slipping around her and we had barely gotten started.

I was hung up on her, falling fast, furious, and deep. I knew I'd better marry her fast.

Seeing he'd get nowhere with me, my father stood up and gave both Dante and me a nod before leaving the room. He earned his ten percent just by sitting here and annoying me. *Fucker!*

Once the door clicked, Dante finally broke the silence.

"You have to hide it better, Basilio," he warned. "I swear, I see smoke steaming off your body. It's about to start a wildfire and consume everything."

I flipped him the bird. He had no idea how good it felt to feel Wynter's small body pressed against me. The moment her lips connected with mine was the most vanilla thing I had experienced in over a decade. Yet it unsettled me more than any other sexual act I'd ever done. It replayed on a loop in my mind.

The way she moaned into my mouth. The smell of her arousal. I needed her and I hadn't needed anything in such a long time.

Fuck me.

Dante was right. I should hide it better.

"What's your plan with Brennan's woman?" I asked him. I had Angelo send me information on Davina Hayes. Just like Wynter, she had no connection to the underworld. Well, except for Liam Brennan. It made you wonder how in the hell those two got together, considering their stark age difference.

He shrugged. "I'll collect the poker losses and damages from him."

I still couldn't wrap my mind around the footage of Wynter playing poker. Even more, how good she was at it. If I had known she'd be in Chicago in Dante's casino, I would have ensured I was there. Then I'd have scooped her up and spent days buried inside her.

She looked like a million bucks striding through the casino like she owned the joint. And the way she kept her cool while playing her hand was a fucking turn-on.

The woman was surprising me.

"Let's call the Irish bastard," Dante announced. "It's the only reason I flew back to New York."

So I dialed Liam up from the conference room speakerphone. It took no time for him to answer.

"What?" he barked.

"Is that how you greet all your associates?" I drawled, annoyed I'd even have to talk to him again.

"Only the annoying ones," he grumped. "And you're far from being my associate."

"We all need goals," I deadpanned, though truthfully, I didn't give a shit about ever being Liam's associate.

"Why are you annoying me, DiLustro?"

I nodded at Dante. He might as well explain it. All I cared about was that Wynter's name stayed out of that conversation.

"The woman from The Eastside was in my casino," Dante started.

"She ruined his first floor and cost Dante days' worth of business dealings," I added so he'd understand there'd be a bill to pay.

"She what?" Liam barked with a growl. "Are you fucking with me?"

My lips curved into a smile. I'd rarely seen the man riled up, but whoever that woman was, she managed to get to the Irish fucker. I liked her already.

"You're not my type," I told him dryly.

"Nor mine. Though your girl on the other hand—" Dante left the sentence unfinished, and I could already picture the fucker on the line fuming with anger.

"Your arses approach Davina and I'll slice off both of your dicks," he growled, confirming my suspicions. I didn't give a shit about his woman. Or any other for that matter.

"I'd like to see you try," I said, bored with the conversation.

"I have a few years on you two. You two were still shitting in your diapers while I dealt with the Colombians, Russians, and you fucking Italians."

Yeah, so he was an old prick! If I was in his shoes, I wouldn't have reminded anyone of my age.

"Gosh, I'm feeling loved," I drawled. "How about you, Dante?"

"So damn loved," Dante sneered. "Did you send your woman to my casino?"

"Tell me exactly what happened," he demanded, avoiding the question. It confirmed my suspicion that he had no clue what his woman was doing.

"Well, she pulled the emergency handle, ruined the night's earnings, and then to top it off, she dumped lavender oil all over my marble floors. The fucking building smells like a spa," Dante deadpanned, annoyed. "Not exactly the atmosphere I was going for."

"Was she alone?" Brennan demanded to know.

"The casino was crowded but she stood alone," Dante answered, his tone even. "Not to worry, old man, she didn't have another daddy there with her."

"I want to see proof," he demanded. We expected it.

"Thought you might ask," Dante drawled. "The footage is coming your way now."

We heard Liam's phone dinging over the speakerphone.

"I need other angles too," he added. "If she's at the casino, she has to have played slots or at least a game. Why would she show up there just to pull the fire alarm and dump lavender oil on your precious marble floors?"

"Hold on a second," I jumped in, then muted the line.

"My woman is already on my father's radar thanks to Emilia. I don't want Liam asking questions about her as well," I told Dante. "First time I saw her, she jumped out of his window. So it is likely he'd recognize her."

Fuck! I slipped and he knew it by the knowing smug smile he gave me. "Your woman, huh?" When I didn't answer, he continued, "Does she know?"

"She will." Very soon.

"Fine, Basilio. I'll send him other angles, except for the one where we see your woman."

I unmuted the speakerphone.

"Dante is sending you footage from the south and west cameras. The other cameras have confidential information, so you won't be getting that." There was nothing more that he needed to know.

A minute of silence and I could only picture how he fumed as he watched the tape. No fucking idea what his woman was thinking throwing lavender oil on the marble. I've looked at the footage a few times. It didn't escape me the way Dante looked at the girl who kicked him in the nuts. I knew my cousin well and he wanted her. The fact that he didn't even mention her confirmed the fact.

"What's the goddamn damage?" Liam's voice came through. No other comment, not that I expected it. The evidence was rather convincing.

And another deal was struck.

It was late in the day when I found myself in front of Vittorio's red brick duplex in the city. He lived on one side while his mother lived on the other side. His mother couldn't stand Emilia, and the old woman barely spoke to her son since he married her. She knew, just as others did, how Emilia sacrificed her daughter for her own gain. While her daughter was left at my father's mercy, Emilia went off to marry Vittorio and live a much better life than her daughter.

Naturally, every decent mother despised her.

I banged on the door. Once. Twice.

Then waited. The sounds of footsteps, too heavy to belong to a woman.

The door opened and I came face-to-face with Vittorio.

Surprise flashed on his face. "Basilio, what are you doing here?"

I ran a thumb across my jaw, giving him a hard look. "I came to deal with Emilia."

He clenched his teeth. "What did she do?"

Stepping aside, he motioned for me to enter. I walked through the door as I unbuttoned my jacket to ensure I had quick access to my holster.

Once the door shut behind me, I said, "I warned her to keep her mouth shut about something important to me. And she went behind my back and fucking yapped to my father."

Displeasure crossed his face and the fucker looked tired. Almost defeated. He still wore his suit, but his tie was slightly crooked and his silver hair a wild mess, like he pushed his hand through it one too many times.

"She has to be dealt with, Vittorio," I growled. "Thalia is paying her mother's price every single day. Emilia put someone I care deeply about on my father's radar. She's not worth it."

"Thalia loves her mother," he grumbled. "It will destroy her."

My expression darkened. "She stays with my father just to protect Emilia. She is dying every single day and refuses my help to run away. Because of her mother. To protect her." He knew it, his expression said it all. "He'll kill her one of these days," I hissed. "Thalia is lucky she has survived this long."

Soft footsteps approached us, shuffling over the hardwood floor. The moment Emilia spotted us, her steps halted and she watched us with those dark eyes. The sound of the city buzzed outside, but it didn't compare to the volatile atmosphere inside this home.

"What are you doing here?" she whispered, her eyes wide. She wore a red, satin robe and her dark hair loose down her shoulders. It made me sick to my stomach that she lived her life basking in luxury and content, while her daughter was being tortured thirty minutes down the road.

"What did I say when I came to your shop?" I drawled, seemingly casual.

She held my gaze, the lies and deceit swimming in her gaze. "*Niente.* I said nothing."

"You're a piece of work," I said. "You don't hesitate to destroy anyone in your path, including your own daughter."

"I love my daughter," she whimpered.

Pathetic, selfish liar. "When was the last time you visited Thalia?" I asked, narrowing my eyes. When she didn't answer, I offered her one. "It has been a whole fucking year."

She didn't deserve her daughter.

She glanced at Vittorio hoping for help. She ruined his life too, running around on him and making a fool of his good heart. Why would he back her up?

Realizing no help would come from her husband, Emilia straightened her shoulders and tilted her chin up. "My relationship with my daughter is none of your concern," she spat out. "And Gio is the boss, not you."

Fucking bitch. "How do you want to pay for your betrayal?" I deadpanned. "Quick and relatively painless? Or long and very painful?"

It was more than she deserved, although she'd gotten off easier than her daughter.

Her expression fell for a moment, but then she got herself together. "Y-you must be joking. Your father won't allow it."

"I warned you to keep your mouth shut, didn't I?" I said coldly, fixing her with a hard look.

"I—I didn't say anything," she lied again.

Vittorio's mouth thinned. The guilt was plain as day on Emilia's face. The two of us shared a look. No words were needed. Either he'd do it, or I would.

He tilted his head, allowing me to finish her. Not that his permission meant much. It was either him pulling a trigger. Or me.

I pulled out my gun and then the silencer, my gaze icing over her. She opened her mouth to scream, but not a single tone left her throat.

A muffled *pop* sounded in the room, blood splattered across the hardwood and she slumped down onto the ground.

The bitch was dead.

Chapter Thirteen

WYNTER

I couldn't wait to see him again.

The girls and I drove to Chicago. We had a brilliant, or not, plan to play at Royally Lucky Casino. I played poker and won three hundred thousand. I counted cards, of course. Not that anyone but the girls would ever know. The exit strategy wasn't as graceful as the entrance but we got out of there intact.

I watched the light turn red and groaned silently. Davina's driving was too slow. Realistically, she was obeying the speed limit and traffic laws. It was the reason I let her always drive my Jeep. Unlike Juliette, Davina was responsible. But today, I wished she'd speed down the highway and get me to my destination sooner versus later.

I told Bas I had a ballet class with Madame Sylvie and I could see him afterwards. He was fine with it and asked if I'd be willing to go to Philly with him. Our little weekend getaway. Of course, I said yes and immediately packed my duffle bag with cute clothes, running gear, and the sexiest undergarments I could find.

I wished ditching ballet class was an option. I had skipped the last two days. Missing another day was a hard pass. She'd alert my mom, so it was best I stuck to my schedule.

The moment we drove into the parking lot of Madame Sylvie's building, I spotted him dressed in his three-piece suit, leaning against his sleek black McLaren. The man had way too many cars.

My heart fluttered, his eyes already on me. I didn't expect him to be there. He said he'd pick me up after my class.

I glanced down at myself and thanked all the saints I got dressed up, and blow-dried my hair. I did it so Madame Sylvie didn't find it odd I came in one outfit and left in another. I wore cropped jeans, a shimmering pink blouse and matching pink flats while my hair was pulled up in a high ponytail.

"Call me if you need me," Davina whispered once she parked. I wouldn't need her; I'd have Bas. I leaned over and pressed a kiss on her cheek, unable to stop myself from grinning happily.

Then I grabbed my bag from the back seat, and left her, rushing towards Bas. I missed him over the last few days. We exchanged a few texts, but it wasn't the same as being with him. He waited for me, his hands in his pockets but his eyes on me, and my heart beat a mile a minute.

His dark, burning gaze met mine and warmth rushed to the pit of my stomach, then spread through me like wildfire. It was the exact look he gave me before he kissed me. Like I was everything, and the only thing he wanted and needed.

He consumed me without even trying. My breathing slowed and my heart danced as his eyes trailed over my body. I stopped short barely an inch in front of him. My skin buzzed with excitement and craving the feel of his hands on me again.

"Hello, Bas," I breathed, my heart hammering against my ribs. "I didn't think you'd be here yet."

"I couldn't wait to see you," he admitted softly and I lifted my face to his. His presence was large and could be intimidating, especially if you believed all the rumors about the DiLustros. Yet, I felt none of it around Bas.

The breeze around us grew hot and my breasts tingled in anticipation of feeling his hard body pressing against mine. All these emotions for him flooded my bloodstream, sinking deep into my bones.

He leaned in, his breath hot against my earlobe. "I missed you so fucking much."

The rough edge of his voice ran the length of my neck and a shudder ghosted down my spine. So I lifted on my toes and pressed my mouth against his neck, his heat burning my lips. He tasted so good.

Like sin, whiskey, and bad decisions. Like a man who wanted me for me. Not the figure skater. Not the athlete. Not the woman who broke records. Just *me*.

I had never wanted to ditch my regimented schedule as badly as I did right now.

"I missed you too," I murmured against his neck, his strong pulse vibrating straight to my core. His hand wrapped around my waist and pulled me against him.

"Good," he rasped, his voice deep. "I want you to miss me so much, you'll never leave."

Chapter Fourteen

BASILIO

Fuck me. She was gorgeous when she danced.

I couldn't peel my eyes away from her form. Despite her petite frame, she was fucking strong. I witnessed it firsthand as I watched her jumps and landings.

For the past hour, I watched her dance with a determined look on her face. She and her dance partner kept repeating the same stunt over and over again. It didn't strike me as a ballet type of move but what the fuck did I know. I didn't watch ballet. All I knew was that she looked stunning. Absolutely beautiful.

I caught her rolling her shoulders a few times as her French instructor kept barking shit at her. I had to fight the urge to go and shut the woman up. Whatever she was saying to Wynter, it wasn't good because I could practically taste Wynter's tension.

"Again," Madame Sylvie barked in her thick accent. Wynter's skin glistened with a layer of sweat. She had to be exhausted, but she refused to ask for a reprieve.

Wynter's eyes glanced at the clock, Madame Sylvie caught it, and the latter frowned at her, then a string of French words left her mouth. Wynter shrugged her shoulders and muttered something back that I couldn't hear.

Whatever it was, Madame Sylvie didn't like it.

"Encore," she demanded. *Again.*

Wynter turned to face her partner and said something, then both nodded. More steps, movements so in sync, it was mesmerizing to watch. Then her partner threw her so high up in the air, my heart fucking stopped. I wanted to burst into the studio and beat the living crap out of him.

Wynter twirled in the air, then landed on her feet and balanced herself.

"Bien," Madame Sylvie exclaimed. "Bien."

"Fucking finally," I heard Wynter say, earning herself a glare from her instruction while my lips curved into a smile.

My phone buzzed and I checked the messages. It was from Priest.

> Presidential suite is all yours. Better show up, fucker.

Then I shot a message to Dante.

> Do you have everything in place to get Thalia out?

Now that her mother was dead, we'd get her out. We have set her up with a place and enough money so she never had to work.

Dante's reply came instantly.

> While you're getting laid in Philly, I'll have her out and hidden. The old man will never find her.

Before I had a chance to reply, the door to the suite opened, and Madame Sylvie's eyes narrowed on me.

"Ah! This is why she's distracted," she complained in her thick French accent. "No boys. No boys."

Wynter came right behind her and rolled her eyes, then grabbed my hand and dragged me away.

"She likes to torture people," Wynter complained, still in her bodysuit. "I need to shower. I know this took longer than forty-five minutes. Do we have time?"

"Yes, take your time."

"See, I knew you'd get us here in one piece," I drawled, seated back in the passenger seat of my McLaren as Wynter parked the car in front of my cousin's club and hotel building in Philly.

She shot me a sideways glance, then rolled her eyes. "Bas, either you're crazy or blind. I almost drove into another car at least three times. And don't cry to me when you find a scratch on your expensive, fancy car," she warned.

I grinned widely.

It was the best way I could come up with to distract her from her ballet class. It was either start making out with her or have her drive us to Philly. I'd have preferred the former but making out with Wynter in the parking lot of Madame Sylvie's building was neither the time nor place.

"And don't send me a bill either," she added, narrowing her eyes, but her threat was ruined by a mischievous twinkle in her eyes. "I could have totaled your car. Or even worse, got you hurt. I've never driven a stick shift car."

"It's just a car," I soothed her. "And I paid attention the entire time. I'd never let anything happen to you."

I pulled on the handle and exited the car, then came around to help her out, while grabbing her duffle bag and my own bag from the back seat.

Looping my hand around her, we walked together into the club and hotel my cousin Priest owned.

"Now, I want you to relax and enjoy our little vacation," I demanded.

"Are we sharing a room?" she asked curiously.

"We have the presidential suite. There is plenty of room to sleep ten people." I stopped and she did too, her face turning curiously to me. "Wynter, I don't want you to worry about anything."

Her eyebrows shot up, a puzzled look in her mesmerizing eyes. "What do you mean?"

"I mean that I'll never touch you without your consent." When she didn't say anything, I continued, "If you are more comfortable, I can get another room and you keep the suite."

She shook her head.

"Don't you dare leave me alone," she warned, but her voice was too soft to be effective. "If I was worried you'd force me to do anything, Bas, I wouldn't have come along." She rose to her tiptoes and pressed a kiss on my cheek. "I trust you, Bas. So you better stay in the same room with me."

She was mine. Mine to protect. And mine to love.

Chapter Fifteen

WYNTER

I was used to luxury.

Mom and Liam insisted we earn our own money for certain things, but it wasn't as if Juliette and I ever lacked anything. Yet, it was different with Bas. He went out of his way to ensure I had everything and anything I could possibly want. Like an extra pair of AirPods. To ensure I could go for my jog if mine died, because I forgot to bring a charger. Or packages and packages of clothes and jewelry laid out for me. *Just because*, he said.

But right now, as I sauntered through the entire top floor of the hotel reserved for us, I realized *this* was luxury. We had the entire top floor of the hotel with a magnificent view of the city. I felt like a princess trapped in a tower with a prince by my side, showing me his empire. The glittering city with a river running through it.

Standing on the large balcony of the suite, I admired the city skyline. I never thought of Philadelphia as a romantic city, but it would forever be one for me. The dark sky glittered with stars while the city lights shimmered beneath it.

"You like it?" Bas's voice came from behind me and I turned around to look at him.

He leaned against the glass door with an unlit cigarette in his mouth. He looked like the most handsome bad boy I have ever met or associated with. There was a thrill to it, but it was so much more than just that.

The way he looked at me. The way he smiled at me.

"It's my first time in Philly," I admitted smiling, as the breeze swept through my hair. Tucking my curls behind my ear, I took a step closer to him. "I like it." I like *you*.

I had never been a coward before. But I didn't want to come out like some silly, clingy girl with an infatuation for this man in front of me. It was so much more than that.

"I didn't know you smoked," I remarked, because the way he regarded me unnerved me. It made every fiber of me come alive for him.

Admittedly, I didn't know a lot about him, but for some reason, I had never felt so comfortable around another human being. It was like coming home.

"I quit." His gaze was heavy on me, and with the star-lit sky, the atmosphere gave off romantic vibes.

In my whole life, I had never been accused of being a romantic. More of a realist. But around Bas, it was like a new me was born. I melted with every sweet word or action. His mere presence made something hot unravel inside me, and I suspected it would only react to him that way. My dormant body waited to be awakened just by my own charming prince.

I shook my head and scoffed silently at that notion.

"What are you thinking about?" he asked me, his deep voice made my pulse flutter.

I took another step, leaving two feet of space between us. He must have noticed me eyeing his cigarette because he pulled it from his lips and handed it to me.

"I don't want you to die from lung cancer," I murmured, because admitting my other thoughts wasn't an option. At least not yet.

Dark amusement ghosted through his expression. "You'd miss me?"

Something squeezed in my chest at the thought of losing him. It wasn't anything I had ever felt before.

"I would," I admitted, taking his unlit cigarette. "Very much so."

I watched his beautiful mouth curve into that half-arrogant smile and a languid rush filled my bloodstream. My body reacted to him so strongly, I feared he'd destroy me without even trying. And I'd let him.

My mother's words came back. *First love shatters your innocence and ends your dreams.*

Then why did it feel like my dreams around this man took me higher and higher? He'd never shatter me.

"So why did you bring me to Philly?" I asked in an attempt to change subjects.

"My cousin runs this city." My eyebrows rose. "And I have some business to take care of."

"You have a lot of cousins?" I asked.

He shrugged. "I do. But only Dante and Priest count. And of course, my sister."

"Priest, huh?" I inquired curiously about his cousin. "Nickname?"

Bas nodded. "He recites the last rites to men before he finishes them off."

I felt my eyes widened and a gulp sounded between us. Unsure how to respond to it, I decided it was probably better that I said nothing. Priest must be one scary dude, and now I wasn't quite sure whether it was smart to meet someone like that.

So I reverted to a safer subject. Bas's sister.

"You mentioned your sister before. What's her name?" It was true that I didn't know much about the families of the Syndicate, but I didn't recall seeing anything about a sister when I looked him up. He mentioned his baby sister on our first date too.

"Emory. She's twenty-three." I tilted my head studying him. "And you?"

"Just the two cousins I mentioned," I said. "It's mainly Jules, Mom, and me."

"Jules, the crazy one," he mused. "That should be her title." When I cocked my eyebrow, he explained. "I saw the footage. It was her that gathered the supplies to set the house on fire."

I sighed. "She's going through some rough times."

Jules found a birth certificate naming her birth parents. At first we thought they were fake, but it turned out they were real. It was a shock to all of us, most of all Juliette.

"You're protective of her and your friends."

I nodded.

"Are you close to your mom?" he asked and my eyes shifted back to the city.

It was a complicated answer to a simple question. I sighed, because I had nobody to compare my relationship to Mom with. Davina grew up under her grandfather's care. Juliette and Killian didn't have a mother. And Ivy's mother died when she was very young.

"I think so," I finally answered. When Bas cocked his eyebrow, I tried to explain, "She's my coach too. Some days it feels like she's more my coach than anything else. My breakfast was determined by my coach, not my mother. My class schedule. My holiday. Everything." I returned my attention to the fascinating man in front of me. "It was probably why I picked Yale. It was on the opposite coast from Mom."

"I'm glad you did," he drawled, the deep timbre of his words setting off flames inside me. "What does she coach?"

"A little bit of everything," I told him. "She's versed in choreography, skating, ballet. You name it, she has a knack for it."

"Capable woman."

"She is," I agreed. "Her career was cut short due to her knee injury but she's really good at everything and quite a sought-after coach. I'm lucky to have her."

"I bet she's lucky to have you too." His voice was soft and warm, weaving its web through my heart. Like a moth moving toward the flame but his heat ignited something raw and deep inside me, changing me forever.

"When I looked you up," I whispered, "I didn't see anything about your cousins or sister." I instantly flushed with my admission, every inch of my skin growing hot.

"You looked me up, huh?" he mused. Another nod. "What did you find?"

I glanced up at the starry sky, scared I'd drown in the warmth of his gaze if I kept watching him.

"That you're a very dangerous man," I answered softly.

"Come here, Wynter." His voice was velvet soft with a demand weaving through his deep voice. My body moved of its own accord another two steps and we stood chest to chest.

"Are you scared of me?" My heart stilled before it leaped, my pulse fluttering in my neck.

I wasn't scared of him. At least not in the way he thought. I was scared of the way my body and heart reacted to him. I was scared of what falling for him so deeply could do to me. My mother had been a shell of a woman my entire life. I overheard my grandpa and uncle arguing once that it was because of her relationship. Whatever that meant. I always assumed losing my dad destroyed her.

"No," I whispered. "Should I be?"

He cupped my face between his big palms and this time I let myself drown in his darkness.

"Never be afraid of me, principessa."

Kingpins of the Syndicate.

I observed the sign on the wall with a large skull. It was in contrast to the entire room, as if Priest and Bas wanted the whole world to think they were untouchable. More than likely they were.

The dance floor had a few bodies swaying on it, the reddish lights throwing a glow over them. Music filled the room and the beat vibrated through every inch of me. It was why I loved to skate and dance. I felt the music; it made me sad, happy, mellow.

My fingers tangled in Bas's coal-black hair, his muscled body flush with mine. I felt the happiest I'd ever been. Carefree, despite what was coming.

Six months of intense and vigorous exercise. No social life. Barely time to sleep and eat. My mother was a demanding coach, and the fact that I was her daughter made her even more demanding. Sometimes even to the point where she could have me on the verge of tears. But she hated those, so I've gotten good at hiding my emotions. I knew she meant well and wanted the best for me. She wanted *me* to be the best.

Bas's eyes traveled the length of my body, ignoring everyone around us. It was just the two of us in this club. I'd store this moment forever in my heart.

"What are you thinking about?" Bas asked, and I took a second to collect my thoughts. I didn't want to sound like a complainer.

I smiled. "I have another few weeks at Yale, at most," I told him. "Then I have to fly back to California."

His fingers on my waist tightened and I held my breath. "Stay. Forget California."

My chest brushed his three-piece suit. My pulse beat wildly in my throat, and everywhere he touched me, I felt his heat searing my skin.

He smelled so good that I couldn't help but inhale his scent deep into my lungs.

The club was full. We swayed to the music, everyone around us fading in the background. It was just the two of us. Just like on our first date.

A man as tall and strong as Bas shouldn't move as gracefully on the dance floor. His eyes locked on me and his hands possessive on my waist, he made me feel safe.

Bas's lips crashed down on mine, demanding and hard. "Stay for me," he growled.

Was this normal? We'd seen each other three times now, if you counted that small interaction when he caught me jumping off the balcony. Yet, I felt like I'd known him my entire life. Like my soul had been lost until I ran into him.

I still wanted the Olympic gold. But I wanted him more.

"I want to stay," I rasped. "But I have to work out some things with my mom first."

His eyes never left mine as we danced. The tunes of "Hypnotic" by Zella Day played through the club speakers and our bodies swayed together. It was obvious by the way he moved that he was a good dancer.

Bas's hot breath brushed my ear as he held me against his body. "We can talk to your mom together."

God, that he'd even offer made him a true Prince Charming in my book. This attraction should scare me. It should have me running in the opposite direction. My instincts warned that it was the all-consuming feelings like this that could make you happy but also destroy you.

I tilted my head to stare into his blazing dark gaze and a shiver rolled down my spine. He made me feel protected. Invincible.

Neither one of us noticed a tall, blond man who appeared to our right. "You two having a good time?" he asked, sparkling blue eyes, darting between Bas and me.

I couldn't fight my curiosity nor my manners. "Hello."

"Fuck off, cuz," Bas retorted dryly, without glancing his way.

My eyebrows shot up. They didn't look like cousins, except for the darkness that shone in his light eyes. His dirty-blond hair and blue eyes set him apart from Bas's striking dark hair and eyes. His every movement screamed intrigue, and that full mouth of his probably had ladies falling at his feet.

I couldn't shake off the feeling that there was something familiar about him. I couldn't pinpoint it. Maybe it was the darkness that resembled Basilio's or maybe the way he wore his three-piece suit.

"Hello," I greeted him again. "I'm Wynter."

"I'm Priest," he introduced himself. I stiffened for a second, remembering Bas's explanation for his nickname. This man administered a man's last rites before he killed him. Yet, he looked too handsome to be a psycho. *Jesus!*

"Don't scare my girlfriend," Bas growled and instantly my worry evaporated. He'd never let Priest recite any last rites to me. He'd kick his ass.

So I smiled and extended my right hand. He took it in a firm grip. "Nice to meet you, Wynter."

"You too." I studied him curiously. He was extremely good looking. Kind of mysterious and charismatic. Of course, nothing like Basilio. Though there was one thing the two cousins shared. The ruthless aura about them.

"Let me guess, you were born in winter," Priest teased.

I shook my head. "Actually not even close."

His eyebrow shot up. "I'm intrigued. Why Wynter, then?"

"It was my grandmother's name," I explained. "Mine is just spelled differently. My grandpa insisted on having a grandchild named after his true love."

"Romantic family, huh?" he deadpanned.

I shrugged my shoulders, returning my attention to Bas who listened intently. "Basilio is a romantic name," I said, smiling.

Priest's laugh vibrated through the air, mixing with the beat of music. "Man, I got to share that with Dante. He will piss his pants."

I rolled my eyes. "Okay, that's so mature," I muttered sarcastically and Priest laughed even harder.

"I can see why Basilio likes you."

Heat rushed to my cheeks and I glanced at the man who swept me off my feet. I never blushed, until I met this man.

Bas's gaze was full of promises, his darkness unapologetic. He didn't bother denying it and I loved him even more for it. The way his burning gaze caressed my face promised pleasure and sins.

"I like him too," I murmured, uncaring who heard me while Bas's scorching gaze set fire through my bloodstream.

"Basilio, we are meeting with the distributors in five minutes and I wanted to talk about the other stuff," Priest reminded his cousin. "You two can *play* after that."

I rolled my eyes, smiling at Priest's insinuation. Bas had been nothing but a gentleman all along. Much to my dismay. I might have to take advantage of him if he didn't make a move soon.

Regret washed over his face, and I thought I heard him grumble "fucking business" under his breath.

"It's okay," I said. "Come back when you're done. I'll be here," I assured him.

Bas glanced to the bar and then to the two bouncers on the side, giving them a tense nod. "Those men will keep an eye on you. I'll be back as fast as I can."

I nodded. "It's okay, Bas."

He took my chin between his fingers, and brushed his thumb over my lower lip. "Save me another dance."

I grinned. "You got it." I didn't want to dance with anyone else, just Bas.

Then he and Priest strode through the crowd that parted for them, sensing the danger. I turned around and strode to the bar area, sitting myself on an empty barstool.

In my periphery, I noticed a man sitting next to me, but I didn't bother acknowledging him. Through the years, I learned some people take a simple greeting as a sign to advance. I didn't want anyone's advances. There was only one man for me and he was seated with Priest behind a large glass window.

He had only left me a few minutes ago and promised he wouldn't be long.

I shifted on my barstool and met the bartender's eyes. He wore a white shirt and black vest. It was a different kind of uniform but it kind of worked. It gave it a mobster-bar vibe. I had to chuckle at my description.

"What's so funny, love?" a voice next to me purred, and I shifted away slightly. I could literally feel his hot breath on my neck and I fucking hated it. His light brown hair was ruffled and messy, and his lips curved into a sneering smile.

Choosing to ignore him, I ordered a mineral water. The bartender raised a brow at my choice of drink but said nothing. He saw who seated me here and warned him to give me whatever I wanted. He wouldn't dare to question Basilio DiLustro's drink choice.

"Playing hard to get, huh?" The guy next to me continued.

I shot him an icy glare. He was too close for my taste. "I'm not alone."

Bas might not be here but his bouncers were. Weren't they?

I threw a quick look over my shoulder, but before I could even spot them, the creep's hand came to my thigh. I shoved it away, disgusted at his touch.

"Excuse me," I gritted, suddenly feeling on edge. "Keep your hands to yourself."

He chuckled like I said the funniest thing and I released a breath, sensing agitation simmering underneath my skin. Uncomfortable with the way he was leering at me, I glanced away from him. The man was giving me the creeps.

He reached past me for a toothpick, his arm brushing against me and I shifted even further away. He was giving me serious creep vibes. I readied to stand up and just walk away when his hand grabbed my ass and his stale breath was in my ear.

"You put on that sparkling little dress because you want to get fucked."

I glared at him and slapped his hand away. "Don't touch me," I hissed.

I turned away to get away from him when he gripped my arm and pulled me to him. A woman's yelp sounded somewhere behind me, but I kept my eyes on the danger in front of me.

"Don't play hard to get, cunt." His mouth reeked of stale-cigarette breath. "I'm going to fuck you raw and—"

He never got to finish his sentence because the next sound filling the room was his yelp, followed by an agonizing cry. He released me and stumbled onto the floor. I would have stumbled backwards but a set of strong arms caught me. Bas's scent immediately registered and I exhaled a breath of relief.

My eyes lifted to his face to find his gaze narrowed on the man. His face was devoid of emotion, and if this was the first face I'd seen when I met him, I would have been scared of this man. He wore an unemotional mask but his eyes burned with so much anger, I feared he'd kill someone.

I followed his eyes to the man and I realized Bas had punched him. I had no idea how I missed it but the man was scrambling back to his feet, the area around his right eye already turning blue.

"You touched my woman," Bas snarled at him and the other man looked like he was about to shit himself. "She tells you she doesn't want you and then you threaten to fuck her?"

Bas's voice sent a shiver down my back. I finally saw firsthand the kingpin I read about. This was the version of him that was scary as fuck.

The man shook his head frantically, raising his hands. "I didn't know she was yours."

Bas looked at me, then at the man who stood behind me.

"Priest, watch her," he ordered, then before I even had a chance to blink, Bas wrapped his hand around the other man's throat and lifted him off the ground. My eyes widened, the whole scene playing in slow motion. The man's face turned blood red and his whole body shook as he desperately tried to get footing.

Bas used his free hand to drive his fist into his face. Another punch followed, a crack of a broken nose. And another punch.

Everyone's attention was on us. They didn't even bother to hide their stares. Oh my God, if there was a single reporter here, I'd be ruined. No Olympics. Disappointment to Mom. Impact to my skating partner, Derek.

"Bas, he's not worth it," I rasped, then took a step to grab his hand, but Priest's grip tightened on me, trying to drag me away.

My head whirled around to glare at him, only to find Priest's cold stare aimed at the guy Bas was beating. It was as if he wanted to join his cousin, an excited gleam in his eyes. It was almost terrifying.

Who in the hell gets excited to hurt someone?

My eyes darted around the club. The music no longer played. A few people were recording the whole incident. The two bouncers who were assigned to watch me were keeping the crowd at bay.

"He's going to get in trouble," I muttered quietly, glancing back at Bas who was choking the life out of the man.

"You touched her," Bas roared.

"I—I didn't—" The guy never got to finish his statement because Bas tossed him across the room and the man's body hit the wall with a loud thud, then crumpled to the floor.

"I was just having a bit of fun," the guy whimpered, then began to cry. "I wasn't going to hurt her."

His eyes flitted toward me as if he hoped for my help but that seemed to piss off Bas even more. In five strides, Bas was in front of him again and hunched down, getting into his face.

"Don't fucking look at her," he roared. "Now give me your hand that dared to touch her." The man started bawling. I didn't feel sorry for him but I didn't want to see Bas get arrested. "Your hand, or I'll cut your cock off."

I frantically glanced at Priest. "Do something," I hissed on a whisper. "There are people recording this."

He didn't seem worried at all. Instead he lifted his left wrist and spoke something into it.

My eyes bulged as I watched bouncers make a round through the room, taking guests' devices.

I returned my attention to Bas whose face was twisted with rage. It was as if the glimpse of the man I got to know was gone.

This was the ruthless man who the world knew and feared. Basilio DiLustro. The villain in a three-piece suit.

Chapter Sixteen

BASILIO

He fucking groped her.

Burning rage spread through my veins like fucking acid. I brought Wynter here for a romantic getaway and because I knew she'd be safe in Priest's club. Instead, she had to endure this fucker groping her.

Anger crept beneath my skin, searing and demanding I make him pay.

I shouldn't have been surprised that another man wanted her. I expected hungry gazes thrown her way. She looked fucking gorgeous in her light pink skater dress and white flats that I bought her. She didn't aim for glamorous but she came out looking like a million bucks regardless.

"Which hand did you use?" I asked one last time, my voice cold. Red rage rushed through me, drumming in my ears.

"Please, please," he whimpered.

No amount of begging would work with me. I brought my face close to his, smiling harshly.

"Cock cutting it is," I deadpanned, the corner of my lips lifting into a cruel smile.

I withdrew my knife and the fucker finally got the message. He shot out his right hand, shaking like a leaf. I brought my knife down on his right hand fingers, pressing the blade against his skin and already breaking the skin. Blood trickled down and he screamed like the fucking coward that he was.

"Bas." Wynter's small hand came to my shoulder and some of my rage slithered away. "Bas, look at me."

Lifting my eyes, I met her face etched with worry and apprehension lingered in her emeralds. Priest attempted to pull her back but Wynter refused, pushing him away.

Her hands took my face between her palms. "He's not worth it," she murmured softly, her light green gaze sending calm through me. "Just give him a black eye and call it a day."

I met her gaze that was begging me to stay calm. But the mere thought of this piece of shit touching her drove burning rage into my chest, making me see red.

"Very well," I muttered, then sliced his index and middle finger of his right hand clean off.

His high-pitched scream filled the room, but I ignored it as I nodded at Priest. He'd know what to do. I looked around the group of people that gaped at the scene. I stood up to my full height and focused on Wynter who looked pale.

"That's not exactly a black eye," she said weakly, her gaze focused on me.

"He touched you," I rasped, resting my forehead against hers.

The thought of any other man laying a hand on her sent fury down my spine and marred my vision with a red mist. The anger was so strong that I had to choke it down. For her. Yes, she accepted me for who I was but killing a man in front of her would be taking it too far.

It wasn't rational. Or maybe it was. Fuck if I knew. My moral compass was fucked up. In my entire life, I had never regretted a single thing I'd done. There was no room for regrets in our life. Those got you killed.

"Yes, but cutting his fingers off was a bit too much," she whispered, never breaking our eye contact.

I'd involuntarily given her a glimpse of who I truly was—for better or for worse. Either way, she had seen firsthand who I was, who I was always meant to be. And I was damn good at it. I was born on the wrong side of the law and I thrived on it.

I have never been tempted to follow the law. Today, even less so. Now I knew I'd never be able to handle seeing another man have her. Rage when this fucker touched her burned cold through my veins and I had to fight the urge to beat him some more.

My chest twisted with something unfamiliar.

She'd be mine. For the rest of my life.

Chapter Seventeen

WYNTER

I sat next to Bas, whose knuckles had red marks from beating the man who dared to grab my ass. He and Priest were discussing business. The only reason I was here was because Bas refused to let me out of his sight.

Tonight didn't go exactly as I expected it. I should have just told Bas I'd wait for him in the suite. I chewed the inside of my cheek as thoughts swirled in my mind. Seeing this side of Bas should have scared the living daylights out of me and had me running. Yet, the fierce protectiveness warmed me from the inside out.

Maybe something was wrong with me. Or maybe despite living with Mom in California away from Uncle, Killian, and their underworld, I was just as tainted as them. I'd kill just as they surely did. Just as Bas did.

A heavy sigh left me.

"You good?" Bas's question had me lifting my eyes to find six pairs of eyes on me.

The lighting was low and the air carried a hint of cigarette smoke. It was actually a very stylish office with dark blue accents, several flat-screen TVs and the largest minibar that I'd ever seen. Not that I've seen many. The men seated around the table were tense, discussing some business deal. They alternated between Italian and English, and since the only foreign languages I could speak were Gaelic and Russian, I couldn't follow what they were saying, not that I cared to.

The beat of the music pulsed through the walls and the glass that separated us from the dance floor and bar area where I was groped.

A thick atmosphere hung in the air among the men seated around this round mahogany table.

"Yeah, all good," I said, offering a reassuring smile.

Bas's shoulders tensed as he let out an unamused breath. He didn't say anything else, but I knew he didn't believe me. Except, I didn't know how to reassure him that his slightly disturbing behavior wasn't the cause of my distress.

It was the revelation that it didn't bother me as much as it should. It didn't have me running away from him and all my reason said that it should.

"You look familiar," one of the men at the table commented. "I swear I've seen you somewhere."

I reached for my phone in my pocket and saw I had a bunch of missed messages.

"I get that all the time," I answered, never raising my head and swiping the first message open.

Juliette, Ivy, and Davina threw around a bunch of ideas for the school we planned on founding one day. A missed message from my mom.

"It will come to me," the guy insisted. "You don't forget a pretty girl with your face."

Bas growled and I recognized Priest's voice. "That's Basilio's girl, so rethink your next words."

A smile pulled at my lips. It was dumb that being labeled as

Basilio's girl made me all giddy. I tried to hide it, keeping my gaze downcasted.

Instead I read the text from my mom.

> Three weeks and you need to come home. Derek worked out his routine. Madame Sylvie confirmed yours is set too. She mentioned a boy distraction. What is she talking about?

Another heavy sigh slipped through. It didn't take her long to get an update.

I typed back the reply.

> Not sure what she's talking about.

I groaned in my mind. I should tell her I wanted to stay longer. Instead, I didn't comment on her request to come home. It was the plan all along, except now I had a compelling reason to stay.

Bas stood up from his spot and my eyes darted to him. His focus was on me as he walked over. His mood was dark and I watched him as he unbuttoned his suit jacket. He slipped his hands into his pockets, his gaze intense, then dropped to his haunches before me.

He brought his hands to my thighs and I held his gaze as my heart thundered behind my chest. His spicy scent invaded my lungs, and I reached out to run my hand through his thick hair

"No running, principessa." His voice was a raspy whisper nobody else could hear. "I gave you fair warning."

He was all rough edges around other people, but he offered me glimpses of his vulnerability. I never wanted to be the cause of it.

"No running," I vowed.

He stilled as if I surprised him with my promise, but then his fingers tightened on my thighs and warmth spread through me. God,

I was falling fast and hard for this man. My breathing shallowed at his vicinity, his gaze warm on me. Like he was my gravity, I inched closer to him, inhaling deeply.

"What upset you?" he demanded to know.

"Ah, my mom sent a message," I murmured.

My phone rang at that very moment and the screen flashed with the caller. *Mom.* I frowned, eyeing it with uncertainty. Avoidance was sometimes so much easier.

"You can answer it in the room over there," Bas said, tilting to the room I hadn't spotted before. "Priest's men use that room. That way you can have some privacy."

It wasn't privacy I was worried about. It was getting reprimanded.

"Thank you," I whispered, then pecked him on the cheek. I might as well bite the bullet and talk to her.

Jumping up, I strode towards the room while answering the phone. "Hi, Mom."

"Wynter, who is this man Madame Sylvie mentioned?"

I blew a frustrated breath. No "hello." No "how are you." Nothing. Just straight to inquisition.

"Davina borrowed my Jeep," I told her in an exasperated tone. "So I needed a ride."

I entered the room, just as a man was leaving. "I'm going to the restroom," he mouthed and I nodded. I suspected he just wanted to give me some privacy.

Mom's voice came through the phone. "No distractions," she warned.

"I'm not distracted," I argued softly. "I finished the session and kept to my schedule."

"That's not what Madame Sylvie tells me," she argued and I could hear disapproval in her voice. I could almost picture her knitted brows and critical gaze on me.

"Mom, give me some credit," I protested. "It's not my first rodeo and I know what it takes to win."

"How can I when you're keeping secrets?" she said, her voice full of disapproval. "Both you and Juliette."

"We're not," I groaned. "We've been busy packing up the dorm room." And dealing with the outcome of burning down Garrett's house, as well as planning heists, but those words I'd keep to myself. "I just want—" I paused for a moment, then continued, "I need to be able to take a break, too."

"Wynter, I told you it's important to keep focused." Her measured voice came through the line, but instead of calming me, it fed my frustration. "The Olympics won't happen for another four years. This is it. You are already at a disadvantage since Derek and you are not practicing together. The recordings only go so far."

God, she didn't hear a word I said.

I closed my eyes in disbelief. "Would it kill you to be my mother for just a minute?" The bitter words escaped with a shuddering breath. "Do you have to be my coach all the goddamn time?" I asked tersely.

The tense silence stretched and I realized my mistake. My mother hated theatrics. She lived and breathed discipline. She used it like her own cage and pulled me into it too. I didn't think I'd ever heard her laugh. Her smiles were rare and her praise was reserved only for my skating achievements.

"We could train here," I muttered, words leaving my lips with a hope in my heart.

"Who's the man?" she asked, without answering my question and I knew no amount of begging would make her come.

"Nobody," I answered with resignation.

She made a comment about the dangers of the East Coast, but in my mind, I already stopped listening. My eyes lowered to the document laid out on the table. It was a schedule of dates and routes. I picked it up and turned it over in my hand and the front side read "Cash pickup."

Glancing over my shoulder, I noted the door was shut and I quickly snapped a picture of it, all the while my mother still went on about my discipline and need for a regimented schedule.

This could be our next project.

Chapter Eighteen

BASILIO

Wynter's blonde curls glowed under the lights of the club. Men threw glances her way but none of them dared to get too close to her. Not after what I'd done to the last man who dared to touch her without her permission. Truthfully, I'd have done it even if she gave him permission. Just for daring to touch her.

Nobody touches what's mine and she was mine.

She moved sensually to the rhythm. After seeing her dance at Madame Sylvie's, I wasn't surprised to see her move so gracefully.

I bent down to her ear and whispered, "Are you okay?" Her light green eyes met mine and her eyebrow rose in question. "I overheard a fraction of your conversation with your mom."

A soft sigh slipped through her lips and her shoulders slumped just slightly.

"She's worried about distractions," she explained, shrugging one shoulder. "Boys are a distraction."

I chuckled. "That's easily rectified."

"It is?" she asked curiously.

"Yes, we'll have her come to New York, and she'll see I'm not a boy."

She threw her head back and her melodious laugh rang between us.

"Loophole, huh?" she mused and I grinned. "She hates New York, and says there are too many criminals here."

"Hmmm, odds are stacked against me," I said, but I didn't care. I'd impress her mother if it was the last thing I did. Wynter would be mine.

I pulled her closer to me and she smiled softly. Fuck, she'd bring me to my knees with that smile. This wave of possessiveness was overwhelming and reminded me of my father. I hated the comparison, but I couldn't avoid it. Except, Wynter wanted me. She saw my brutality and still wanted me. She knew I'd never hurt her.

I gripped her hips tighter and we moved together. This moment when nobody and nothing mattered, just the two of us.

I caught her stifling a yawn and I grinned. "Am I boring you, principessa?"

She chuckled softly, her eyes shining with amusement. "Bas, you could never be boring." She lifted on her toes and brushed her lips against mine. "I've been up since dawn. I rarely stay up late. Though the last few weeks have been crazy with the girls."

Considering she and her friends burned down a house, then went to Chicago for a game of poker, while Wynter trained as well, I bet she was tired.

I cupped her cheek, brushing our noses together. If Priest was watching us, he'd know I was whipped. I didn't give a fuck. I'd found my perfection and my light in the darkness of the underworld.

Everything about her fascinated me. Every single word. Every single look. Every-fucking-thing.

She was my perfection. My perfect opposite. My sweetest obsession.

"Want to go back to our room?" I asked as I skimmed a thumb across her full bottom lip.

"Thought you'd never ask," she answered mischievously, her lips curved in a soft smile.

I came out of the shower to find Wynter fast asleep and the *Good Girls* show we were watching still playing. It wouldn't have been my pick. A total chick flick, but I wanted to make her happy. She seemed excited for it and I'd give her anything she wanted just to see her eyes shining.

Although I suspected the show might be a bad influence on her and her friends.

Dropping to my haunches next to her, I watched her sleep for a moment. She was curled up in a fetal position sleeping, facing the bathroom door, as if she was waiting for me. Her hands were folded under her cheek and one of her smooth feet half hanging off the bed. She wore a little tank top and hot-pink boyshorts.

Fuck, her ass was perfection. When she started trailing her fingers over my muscles, her touch feather light, I had to fight the urge not to roll her over and rip her clothes off. Just her scent was enough to get me rock hard.

But I was too worked up from earlier that night, the need to kill burning inside my chest. Wynter didn't deserve an angry fuck. I wouldn't do that to her. Never to her. She deserved romance, wining, and dining.

I rubbed my face. Fuck, I had lost my goddamn mind, pining after a woman so desperately.

Every monster has a weakness and she's mine. My obsession. My addiction. My only salvation.

She looked like an angel with her long, blonde eyelashes fanning her cheeks. She took a deep breath, then sighed softly. How peaceful she looked. I wanted her to keep that peaceful and innocent look she held.

Leaving her to sleep in peace, I headed out of the room and down to the secured basement Priest kept for men like our newest guest. Priest was all about the ironies in life. Three stories up, there were the most luxurious bedrooms of Philly. Down here, it was hell for anyone who dared to double-cross us.

I found our guest tied to a chair and Priest already entertaining himself, reciting his version of the man's last rites.

"May the Holy Spirit free you from this miserable life and your sins swallow you whole with the grace of the Holy Spirit. Amen, motherfucker."

Priest was a sick fucker. Good thing he was my cousin and I loved him.

I stalked toward our guest, fury burning in my veins. The best thing would be to smash his skull into the wall and have his brain spill all over the ground. That would be too quick of an end for this creepy weasel.

"So you think you can grope my woman, huh?" I asked, my voice hoarse with the rage I tried to contain.

"I didn't know she was yours," he cried, his beady eyes full of terror. His hand was covered in blood, the fingers I cut off dangling from a necklace Priest must have made while waiting for me.

Like I said... a sick motherfucker.

"Doesn't matter, buddy," Priest drawled. "No groping of any woman in my club. You just fucked up by touching Basilio's woman." My cousin's eyes met mine. "Time to get dirty."

"And I just took a shower," I feigned disappointment, though anger burned my throat. The only reason I took a shower was to get some space from Wynter before I caved in to the sweetest temptation. I wanted to touch her and fuck her until she felt this same obsession that burned in my chest.

I took a knife from Priest and jabbed it into our guest's thigh. He roared in agony, but I was just getting started. I twisted the knife, turning it sharply and his eyes rolled back.

He wouldn't last long.

"See, fucker," I started with my psychotic smile, "there is one thing I hate more than anything else in the world." He whimpered like the baby that he was. "Ask me what it is," I drawled.

"W-what is it?"

"People who hurt the weaker ones. The innocent ones. Do you know what I do to them?" He whimpered in response, shaking his head. "Kill them."

I watched him pale, his pupils dilated realizing he'd never get out of this one. He was a dead man. But first he'd suffer and beg me to kill him. My eyes settled on him, trying to decide the best way to cause him pain. Or the worst way, depending how you looked at it.

The fucker's chin wobbled and he started crying, his eyes twitching with terror. He started pleading, but I tuned him out. There was no amount of begging that would spare his life.

His face was a bloody mess. I gripped his throat and jerked him up, along with his chair, and choked him. Slicing the rope that bound him, the chair fell with a loud thud, then I threw him through the air. He smashed against the wall, then dropped to the ground. The room was filled with his agonizing screams.

His eyes darted to Priest who leaned against the wall, his hands in his pockets. He looked bored as fuck. I took five steps towards him and knelt in front of him. Priest joined, that crazy and unhinged look in his eyes focused on the fucker who whimpered in front of us.

"You're dead already," Priest announced, his voice bored. "You were the moment I read you your rites."

"You're fucking crazy," the fucker screamed. "Both of you. I barely even touched the girl's ass."

That was when I lost my shit. I jerked down his pants and brought my knife down to his cock. My lip curled with disgust scenting his piss and cheap cologne.

I brought my face close to his, smiling harshly. "You have no idea how fucking crazy I am."

I pushed my knife deeper into his groin, then I brought it to his cock and sliced through the soft flesh. His screams were high-pitched, the fucker gurgling in his own spit and blood pooling around him.

I stood up, his cock discarded in the pool of blood and the fucker twitching in his own vomit and sea of blood around him.

"Now I have to shower again," I growled, my darkness and brutality simmering under my skin.

"And you call *me* a sick motherfucker." Priest grinned stupidly.

Chapter Nineteen

BASILIO

I leaned back in the seat and stretched my legs, enjoying the view of my driver.

Wynter was behind the wheel of Priest's Jeep. Unlike her own, this one was all fancied up. She didn't care for the fancy, but I convinced her to drive. The top was down and so were the doors, and wind whipped her curls around her face that she was unable to tuck into her pink baseball hat.

She glanced over, the big grin on her face. "I'm starting to think you brought me along to be your chauffeur."

She didn't know that I rarely sat in the car with anyone if it wasn't me driving. It ensured I was in control and most people were shit drivers.

"That and some other things," I drawled.

She instantly blushed and I chuckled. I honestly never thought a blush could get me so hard. After another shower last night, I crawled into bed with Wynter, and for the first time in my life, I slept in the same bed as a woman. I never trusted anyone beyond my cousins and my sister. When your own mother betrayed you, it was hard to trust people. But last night, listening to her even, calm, and soft breathing, it was the lullaby I hadn't had the luxury of listening to when I was a kid.

Wynter Star was changing my world. For the better.

I watched her driving, her tiny green shorts having most of her long legs open for viewing, and her pink blouse giving total girly vibes. Girl was seriously obsessed with pink. I didn't think I'd be able to see the color again without thinking about her.

I watched her through my aviator glasses. She didn't bother hiding her eyes, and I was glad for it. She flicked a gaze to me, and her eyes roamed down my body.

She tugged her bottom lip between her teeth and her eyes roamed over me. "I like you in something other than a three-piece suit." I raised a brow, amusement filling me. "It makes you look... younger."

I chuckled. "I aim to please, principessa."

She continued nibbling on her lip. "You're gonna wear a bathing suit too, right?"

A deep laugh left me. "Are you trying to take advantage of me?"

She returned the attention to the road but not before I saw her full lips curve into a smile. "Can you blame me?"

Her honesty was refreshing. Never in my wildest dreams did I think I'd be pining after a girl. Certainly not one who had no connections to the underworld. The way she looked at me with her curious and soft expression burned through my skin and sent blood rushing straight to my dick.

"I'm guessing you'll be wearing a swimsuit too, principessa."

She grinned. "I am. I got one in the hotel shop. I put it on the room tab." Her brows knitted as if she was displeased about it. I insisted she put everything on the room tab and buy herself multiple things. "You know that shop could be charged with extortion for how crazy their prices are."

There were worse crimes than extortion. "I can afford it."

She rolled her eyes. "The richest and youngest gazillionaire."

I chuckled. "Gazillionaire, huh?"

She shrugged. "That's what the papers said."

"You believe everything you read and hear in the media?"

For a moment she stiffened and a shadow passed her expression. "No, not everything."

Rays of sun caught strands of her hair, making them shine like gold. She was a mystery and an open book. She didn't play coy. I sensed her honesty when answering, but there were parts of her she was hiding. I couldn't shake the feeling and usually my sixth sense never failed me.

I overheard part of her conversation with her mother last night. I got the sense she cared about her very much, but there were clearly some issues in their relationship.

The squeal of tires sounded behind me, and I flicked a look into the rearview mirror. I saw the corner of a black Land Rover three cars back. It was a habit to check surroundings and I was glad for it now because I swore the same black Land Rover followed us since we left the hotel.

"Wynter?"

"Hmmmm."

"You think you could lose that black Land Rover three cars behind us?"

She glanced in her rearview mirror and her brows furrowed, worry crossing her face. Then her eyes darted my way. "I don't want to get a ticket," she murmured. I couldn't help smiling. She worried about getting a ticket while I've done much worse.

"You won't," I assured her. "If we get pulled over, I'll handle the cops."

A spark flickered in her eyes. "Promise?"

I nodded. It was all the encouragement she needed. She stepped on the gas and the car accelerated so fast, my back pressed against the seat. *This girl has some recklessness in her*, I mused as I pulled up my phone and shot a message to Priest.

I watched her speedometer hit 80... 90. She was a confident driver. I had yet to find something that I didn't like about this girl.

"You better tell Priest it's your fault if I crash his fancy Jeep," she teased. "And don't ever let him recite my last rites."

I threw my head back and laughed. "I'd crush his throat before he'd be able to say the first word."

She grinned happily, then reached and turned up the music. It was the first thing she did when she sat in the Jeep. Connected her music to the Bluetooth. She had a lot of chick and classical songs, though as long as she was happy, I didn't care.

Glancing behind me, I noted the Land Rover was still there. My phone buzzed. It was a message from Priest. He had a pin on my location and sent men. I didn't expect anyone to be tailing us in Pennsylvania, so I only had a handgun on me, tucked in the back of my pants. I refused to risk Wynter's life if there were men after me.

I pointed to the exit we had to take and Wynter slowed for it, then glanced over her shoulder and cut through three lanes at the right moment to take it, ditching our Land Rover friends.

"Good job," I commended her.

She beamed. "Thank you. My first high-speed chase."

"I might be corrupting you," I mused.

She shrugged, her eyes twinkling. "I like it."

Fuck me. She might be corrupting me too, in the best way possible.

Because this feeling around her was addictive. Her smile. I'd do anything to see her smile.

I stepped up to the two men hanging from the ceiling. Two days in a row in Priest's basement. What was it about Wynter that brought out the crazies? Or maybe she was bringing out the crazy even more in me?

Glancing around, fresh blood covered the concrete floor. It looked like Priest already took a liking to one because he was in rough shape.

The other guy's eyes twitched with fucking terror. It worked well when they got to witness the torture of their fellow accomplice.

"Anything on the reason why they were following me?" I asked Priest.

Priest gripped the throat of the man he had beaten close to death and jerked him up, choking him.

"Tell him what you told me," he ordered.

"Looking for the lost princess," he muttered in his thick accent.

I cocked my eyebrow. "I hate to tell you. I'm not a princess. I'm your worst fucking nightmare."

Rolling up my sleeves, I approached him and stared down at one, then the other. The guy who Priest tortured fainted, or maybe died, I had no fucking idea but the other shook with fear wide in his eyes.

"Tell me, comrade." I smiled darkly as I brought my face close to his. "Why is Bratva following me?"

He attempted to spit on me, despite the clear fear coloring his expression. "Do your worst. I'll never betray our Pakhan."

I straightened and reached for the knife on the little table. "Before you die, you'll tell me everything."

My fingers on the knife tightened, then brought it down to his pinky, cutting through bone and flesh. His screams were music to my ears. I didn't stop there. I moved on to the next finger, then the next. His pussy screams echoed through the basement's concrete walls.

"I didn't know you were an opera singer," Priest remarked. "Lousy as shit but still."

All his fingers cut off, I asked again, "Why were you following me?"

"Fuck you." Idiot.

Grinning wide, I flipped the knife through the air. "I was hoping you'd say that." Before he could blink, I shoved the knife into his gut and turned it sharply. His face turned ashen and his eyes rolled in the back of his head, while he roared in agony.

"No, no," he cried. "Please."

Fucker finally came around. "Now you're coming around."

"I don't know anything," he claimed, whimpering like a coward.

It took two hours and twenty-five minutes and a whole lot of spilled blood to break the whimpering Russian asshole. At this point, I was covered in blood from head to toe. I was taking Wynter out to dinner and I didn't have much time left for this fucker.

I leaned closer to him and growled, his stench invading my senses.

"Tell me again why you're following me."

The blade of my knife pressed against his eye socket and I didn't hold back.

He whimpered. "We're looking for the lost mafia princess."

"What's her name?" I demanded to know.

"I don't know," he cried. "They'll kill me."

"What do you think I'll do to you?" I questioned with a smile as I pressed the tip of the knife harder into his temple.

"We were given this location and told to follow you and the woman with you," he croaked. "That's all I know."

I rammed my blade into his eye and watched the light leave his eyes and end his miserable existence.

Chapter Twenty

WYNTER

For the past two days, I was just Basilio's girl.

I didn't complain.

He told me stories about his cousins and sister. I told him stories about Juliette, Davina, and Ivy. But we both stuck to general comments. Maybe it was a lucky coincidence or maybe it was self-preservation. I had no idea.

I even flipped on the TV, then played a marathon of *Good Girls*. He laughed because I fast-forwarded through a lot of parts. *I just need the bottom line,* I told him grinning. I was the happiest girl in the world at that very moment.

I regularly never had time to watch TV or keep up with the shows, and I knew if I didn't finish it, I wouldn't for the foreseeable future. So he humored me and went along, though it wasn't exactly his kind of show. Admittedly, we got distracted through some of it. We kissed. We touched, but he didn't take it further than that.

Trust me, I tried. When he sat against the headboard, his white shirt unbuttoned and his tie loosely hanging around his collar, I drooled. His abs were mouthwatering. And I couldn't resist his tattoo playing peekaboo with me. It was a peculiar tattoo and it resembled the skull that was above Priest's club, right below the Kingpins of the Syndicate sign. I explored it, trailing my fingers over every hard inch of him.

Until it got so hot, I thought I'd combust. He was hard too; I could see the outline of his hard length pushing against his pants. My heart fluttered with expectation and uncertainty as I slid my hand down and cupped his erection through his pants. He let out a rough groan, while his eyes darkened and encouraged me, I reached for his belt. My pussy throbbed with the need to feel him inside me and his hands gripped my curls, pushing them out of the way.

He pressed himself further into my palm, his hard length big and hot through the fabric. He was thick and big and so damn perfect.

I pressed my lips to his neck. His hot skin burning my lips and his taste imbedding itself into my bloodstream. I went lower, skimming my mouth over his stomach and kissing his hard abs. Then I licked his skin, right above his undone belt that I couldn't even remember unbuckling.

A rumble escaped his chest.

"Wynter," he groaned as I attempted to slip my fingers into his boxers. He grabbed my wrist, then jumped off the bed.

Then he cupped my face and kissed me. "It's late and you're tired."

"I'm not that tired," I protested, shaking my head.

His thumb brushed my cheek. "If you're awake when I'm out of the shower—"

The meaning lingered in the air as he headed for the bathroom while I admired his backside. A man shouldn't be allowed to have such a fine ass.

I shifted over, determined to stay awake while I watched *Good Girls* and the women get into even more trouble than my friends and

I. My eyelids grew heavy but I rubbed my eyes, the sound of the shower still running.

"He'll be out any moment," I whispered to myself, closing my eyes for just a second and sleep took me under. It was the downfall of waking up at the crack of dawn or even earlier.

I woke up with my cheek pressed against his warm chest and his arm wrapped around me. There might have been some drooling involved on my part, but I quickly wiped it away. I remained in his arms, relishing in his body heat and his steady heartbeat thumping under my ear. So strong and confident.

Waking up this way, I wanted to ditch my jogging session and stay in bed longer. To enjoy this moment. But it was hard breaking the habit and guilt of skipping the vigorous exercise. I had miles to burn. A medal to win. Records to break... and shit like that.

I shifted to get out and Bas stirred, his eyes finding mine and my lips curved into a smile. God, nobody had ever made me smile like him. I could get used to waking up next to him. I could get used to this.

"Where are you going?" he demanded to know.

I sighed. "I have ten miles to burn."

He cocked his eyebrow, then checked the time. "At five a.m.?"

I shrugged, then jumped out of bed before temptation got the better of me. As I changed out of my pjs and into jogging shorts and a sports bra, his eyes never wavered from me. His intense gaze burned through me, setting sparks to my insides, and for the first time in my life, I was grateful for a toned body.

Maybe I should push my butt out, twerk it or something, I mused silently and pondered how I could pull it off gracefully.

"I'm coming with you," he announced as he jumped out of bed and startled me out of my twerking plan.

"Stay in bed," I protested.

"Fuck no," he growled. "I'm not staying in bed while my girl is jogging at the crack of dawn."

It was impossible to resist him, so we ran ten miles together and managed to impress each other. After our jog, we showered and went to the beach.

It had been one of the best days ever.

When we got back to the hotel, he met with his cousin and I took a shower. Afterwards, we had a dinner date at one of the fancy restaurants.

And now we waited for the elevator to take us to our hotel suite. It was our last night before we'd get back to New York City.

The elevator door dinged, then opened. We stepped in together, his palm on the small of my back. A tight sensation wrapped around my lungs. I didn't want to leave Philadelphia without having Bas. I needed him to know I wanted him.

"Bas?" I met his gaze bravely, my heart drumming and pulse throbbing between my legs.

"Hmmm?" His shoulders were relaxed. His eyes were hungry on me. But he refused to make a move. Then his words from our first date came back to me.

I want your lips, your pussy, and your body because you want to give it, Wynter. Not because you want to repay a debt.

Maybe I hadn't explicitly told him I wanted him and he was waiting for that. I stepped into his space and took his tie between my fingers. He always seemed to wear a three-piece suit. I remembered hearing Killian joke about the Italians and their three-piece suits.

Rising to my tiptoes, I pressed my lips to his jawline, the stubble rough against my lips. My insides shuddered with delight. I loved feeling his hard chest against my body. His spicy scent. I inhaled a deep breath of his scent. He smelled so good. Nobody would ever smell as good as him.

I kissed a line down his throat, growing dizzy from his smell.

"I want you," I breathed out my admission. "So much that I ache for you."

He stilled, his gaze heavy and dark. It burned, as if I stood in front of a fireplace, the flames licking my skin, threatening to burn me alive. And still, I was unable to move, letting the fire consume me.

Then in one swift move, he grabbed the back of my neck and his mouth pressed on mine. He kissed me deep and slow, setting my body aflame. Hot desire burned through my body as I pressed myself against his. His kiss was all-consuming and my hands wrapped around him.

He pulled away and I whimpered my protest.

"Bas, please," I moaned, leaning forward.

"Not here," he rasped, his eyes burning coals. The elevator door dinged, his arm around my waist, as we rushed into our suite.

The second we entered, a soft gasp tore through me as I glanced around the room mesmerized.

The whole suite was decorated with red and white roses, and candles flickering, giving the entire room a romantic feel.

"Who... what—" I couldn't form a question.

"Our first time together will be special, Wynter Star." His words sent warmth through my body, they burned in my chest and made my heart race. I loved this guy. Whether it was a crush or true love, he made me happy. He made me feel alive.

We stood eye to eye; his lips so close to mine, I could feel his hot breath fanning my lips. I had fallen under Bas's spell and nothing could pull me away.

My fingers roamed over the fabric of his three-piece suit, feeling his muscles beneath. I took a step backwards, my fingers gripping his jacket and he followed. Another step back. He followed again.

"No matter where you go, Wynter," he rasped. "I'll always follow."

My chest swelled. I learned not to let my emotions show over the years. My mother always said it was unbecoming. It showed weakness to the world. Yet, at this very moment, my emotions were so strong, tears stung the back of my eyes.

I had never wanted anyone or anything as much as I did this man. Figure skating included. Nothing *ever* matched the intensity of these feelings.

It scared me and thrilled me at the same time. We had barely gotten started and I felt so much for him.

"Bas?"

His mouth touched mine and my eyes fluttered closed, inhaling his scent deep into my lungs. When his mouth tugged on my lower lip gently, I moaned my approval. Then we kissed, hungry and desperate. Our hot, needy breaths mingling.

The kiss stopped too quickly. "Yes."

My fingers tangled into his hair, tugging him closer to me. I needed him like the desert needed water.

"I'm falling for you," I admitted softly against his lips.

His body stilled for a split second. A heartbeat passed. "I have already fallen for you."

Later, much later, I'd realize I had already given this man my heart long before I realized.

I drowned in his dark gaze, finding safety in them I never thought possible. His tongue swept over my bottom lip, and before I even realized what was happening, my body pressed against his, greedy for him.

"Don't ever leave, Wynter," he murmured, brushing his nose against mine.

I couldn't promise him that. Not yet. My heart wanted to stay with him forever, but I knew there were things I had to resolve. But I couldn't think about that now.

So I gave him everything but words. Pushing my hands up his back, I roamed my palms over his muscles, feeling them contract under his suit. He was kissing me with the sweetest pull as he captured my top lip gently between his. My mouth parted and a moan climbed up my throat. My heartbeat danced happily and I lost myself in the sensation.

My tongue brushed against his lower lip and a groan came from deep in his chest. His hands tightened around me and he deepened the kiss. His tongue slid between my lips and explored my mouth. Every single inch of it.

He cupped the back of my head, angling my head as he kissed me harder and deeper. My pulse thundered in my ears and my chest. He was consuming me and I happily let him. He was the air in my lungs.

"I love you." The words slipped. His dark gaze sought out mine and I held it. A shiver rolled through me, worried I'd ruined the moment. But I wouldn't take the words back.

I didn't know if it was an infatuation kind of love or the kind that stayed with you forever. All I knew was that I wanted to give him everything I had and take his all. Protect him. Love him. Make him laugh. I wanted to share it all with him.

"Are you sure?" I locked eyes with him and nodded. I never did anything halfway, and I wouldn't start now.

"Yes." If he didn't want my love, now was the time for him to say it.

"I love you too." His nose touched mine, brushing against it back and forth. Then he pressed his forehead to mine, his eyes boring into me. "It's like you're a part of me and I have been looking for you all along."

My soul trembled at such a beautiful admission.

Then his lips took mine again as he lifted me up and walked me over to the bed filled with roses.

Chapter Twenty-One

BASILIO

She loves me.

Trust shone in Wynter's beautiful eyes and my chest fucking squeezed. I had never wanted anything as I did this woman. I barely knew her but she spoke to my essence. It was like a part that was missing came back to me and put me back together.

As I lowered her onto the bed, my cock strained against my pants. I got rid of my jacket and discarded it soundlessly on the floor. Then I took off my holster and put it on the nightstand. Her eyes darted to it for a fraction of a second, but she wasn't scared.

Instead, her hungry eyes returned to me. Her hands reached out and her fingers fumbled with the buttons on my vest, so I helped her. My shirt followed.

"You're so beautiful," she whispered, her fingers trailing over my abs. I climbed on top of her, claiming her lips. She tasted perfect, like an addictive brand of honey. I needed to own her completely. I helped her out of her dress.

I knew she was stunning. I saw it that night at The Eastside. But she still took my breath away. I let my eyes trail over her, memorizing every single inch of her.

"You're mine," I growled, watching her hungrily. She looked like an angel, her golden hair spread around her and her eyes shining like diamonds.

"You're mine too," she claimed and nothing was more true. I was only hers. For the rest of my days.

I hooked my fingers in her panties and pushed them down her slim legs.

"Bas, take your clothes off too," Wynter begged, her lust-filled eyes on me. I loved how she didn't pretend to be shy. She gave and she took. So I stood up and got out of my clothes.

Her legs parted and her eyes on me, she looked like a virgin sacrifice, hungry for pleasure. She was so petite; I worried I'd break her. Yet, I saw firsthand how strong her body was. The glow from the city below us shone onto her naked body, and I had never seen anything so achingly beautiful.

I shifted down her body and hovered my mouth over her breasts. Wynter arched her back and it made her slick pussy rub against my abs.

"Bas," she moaned. I tugged her nipple between my teeth, holding her gaze and I relished in her shudders and small noises as she panted. She was magnificent. Perfection, made just for me. I trailed my hands down her ribs and slim waist. All the while she writhed underneath me, whimpering with need. I trailed my mouth lower down her body, worshiping her.

I parted her thighs, opening her pink pussy for my full view. And fuck, my mouth watered. She was glistening wet, the scent of her honeyed arousal seeping into my lungs.

"You're so beautiful," I hummed, pressing a soft kiss on her inner thigh.

She let out a small moan and I lightly bit her inner thigh. "Bas," she gasped, arching up.

"What do you need?" I asked, my gaze lazy on her.

She twisted underneath me, grinding herself against me. "P-please."

"Want me to kiss your pussy?" I asked, watching her body shudder in response.

"Yes," she panted.

"What else?" I looked up to find her emerald gaze on me. She looked beautiful with her eyes hazed and her mouth parted, watching me with so much trust, it fucking hurt my chest.

"Everything," she breathed. "I want it all."

Keeping my eyes locked with her lust-filled emeralds, I wedged my palms under her ass and lifted her pussy to my mouth. I kissed her soaked folds and her lips parted on a soft moan.

"You like that?" I murmured against her soft inner folds. Her scent was intoxicating. I parted her open with my thumb and lapped her juices as she shook underneath me. "Tell me," I demanded, then sucked her lips lightly.

"Yes," she whimpered, grinding herself against my mouth. "Yes, please."

I circled her opening, then thrust my tongue inside her. Her thighs clenched around me, and she lifted her hips.

"Please, Bas," she begged. She was so goddamn responsive to me. She grew wetter, writhing and moaning. I brushed her clit with my tongue and she shuddered violently.

"Want me to suck your clit?" I growled the question.

"Yes, yes, please."

I closed my lips around her clit and began to suck as I slid my finger in and out of Wynter. She was so fucking tight and the thought of her gripping my cock with her walls had my dick throbbing with need.

She quivered underneath me and her face flushed with pleasure, her eyes on me, riding the wave of her orgasm.

"Bas, I need more of you," she pleaded, her face flushed, and I'd never seen anything more beautiful.

I circled her clit with my tongue one last time and moved up, gently pushing her legs further apart.

Lining my cock up with her hot entrance, I could feel her greedy pussy clenching. I kissed the corner of her mouth, then her lower and upper lip as I shifted my hips so my tip nudged into her hot entrance.

Pain flashed across her face and I froze. She was plenty wet, there should be no discomfort.

"Wynter." Her eyes sought me out and my chest squeezed at the trust in her eyes. "Have you—"

Fuck, this should have been something we talked about before.

"I'm on birth control," she murmured, kissing my face. Jesus Christ. That was how much she rattled me. I didn't even think about birth control. I never fucked anyone bareback, yet I wanted nothing separating the two of us.

"I was going to ask if you're a virgin." I didn't need her to confirm to know she was. Her face was expressive and admission was written all over it.

She gave me a small smile. "I should have said something earlier," she murmured, her hands wrapping around me, like she was scared I'd leave.

"Are you sure you want me as your first?" My last shred of honor, just for her.

She cocked her eyebrow. "Why?"

"Because I'm gonna want all your firsts," I rasped. She was it for me.

Her grip around me tightened. "Please don't stop."

Kissing her temple, I shifted my hips so the tip nudged barely an inch into her entrance and she felt like heaven.

"Nothing would make me stop," I rasped. "Except for you. You tell me if it becomes too much. Okay?"

She nodded, and she gripped my biceps.

"It won't be too much," she murmured, her legs wrapping around me. I slid deeper into her, my mouth skimming over her forehead. I'd be the only one to ever feel her clench around me. I'd be the only man to ever have her.

Taking her mouth for a kiss, I thrust forward and swallowed her gasp, her breathing turned ragged. I shuddered out a breath, feeling her walls clench around my cock and milking it. She was heaven on this earth.

I drowned in her big eyes, the light specks of gold, green, and gray in them captivating me. Then in one swift thrust, I slid into her further, breaking her barrier. God, she felt good. The grip of her walls, milking my cock, brought me pleasure unlike any other I had ever experienced.

"You're mine," I whispered into her ear. "Nobody else's."

"Yours." The way she watched me, with those eyes that shone with love, I was falling under her spell. I knew nobody else would ever do it for me. Just her.

"Bas," she whimpered, raising her hips. "Please."

I began to move, small shallow thrusts. Her insides clenched me greedily and I kept my eyes on her face, watching for any signs of pain and fear. There were none. The need to have her was consuming me. I worried my control would snap and I'd fuck her into oblivion.

"Fuck, you feel good," I growled. I pulled out slightly and then eased into her deeper, grinding my pelvis against her clit. Wynter's lips parted and flickers of pleasure crossed her face.

"More, Bas," she begged, her back arching off the bed. My thrusts grew harder, I could feel her fingernails scraping my back.

My muscles quivered as I slid in and out of her, filling her to the hilt. My pleasure coiled tighter and tighter, her moans grew louder and needy. I pressed our mouths together, swallowing all her sounds like a greedy bastard. I pushed into her harder, hitting deeper. Nothing on this earth felt better.

"Don't stop," she begged as if I could even if I wanted to. I was way beyond control. Pleasure tingled at the bottom of my spine and my balls tightened. I reached between our bodies and rubbed her clit furiously as I pounded into her.

"Fuck," I groaned, my thrusts becoming jerky.

Her back arched and I watched mesmerized through heavy lids as pleasure crossed her face. Her pussy milked my cock, clenching it with the tight grip and I shot my cum into her. My dick twitched, filling her with my seed.

A strong emotion burned through me right along with my orgasm. I buried my face into her golden curls, both of us breathing raggedly. Her warm breath fanned over my skin and her palms stroked my back, her touch soft and tender.

Inhaling her scent, I relished in the feel of her soft body under mine and our scents mixing together.

I slid out very slowly and rolled off her, then tugged her into my arms. I wanted her closeness and she obviously needed mine, too, because she nuzzled into my side. She tilted her face, looking up at me with those gorgeous eyes, and I couldn't resist pressing a kiss to her nose.

I brushed my fingers against her cheek. She was breathtakingly beautiful. Her blonde curls crowned her head and her naked body stretched against mine.

"Did I hurt you?" I asked her, but she shook her head.

"No, you could never hurt me."

If only that was the truth.

Chapter Twenty-Two

WYNTER

I missed Bas and it had only been a few days.

The girls and I managed to pull off our plan, though I was hesitant to say our heist in Philadelphia was a success. We followed the armored money truck from Priest's club to the gas station. Ivy seduced the men and drugged them, then we stole it and drove it to Trenton, to the perfect spot at the Delaware River.

Slight hiccup happened.

Alexei and Sasha Nikolaev caught us red-handed, pushing the armored vehicle into the river. We almost shit our pants being cornered by Alexei and Sasha Nikolaev. Yeah, that was unexpected.

In retrospect, it was better that we were caught by the two of them and Davina's sister rather than Priest. After all, he didn't strike me as a forgiving man, especially considering we robbed him of forty million. Priest would have definitely read us our last rites.

A shudder rolled down my spine.

Honestly, I wasn't sure who was scarier. Priest. Alexei Nikolaev. Or a slightly unhinged-looking Sasha Nikolaev. Jesus, we dug ourselves deeper and deeper into the underworld. Uncle and Mom kept us out of it for twenty-one years and we managed to jump right in. Into the deep end.

But we handled it admirably. I think. *Maybe?*

Well, considering we never dealt with mobsters, I'd say we deserved a fucking medal. Though not sure if I'd earn a medal for dating the hottest kingpin. Yeah, I wouldn't share that quite yet.

Uncle Liam was furious enough without divulging that little extra detail. But at least he came clean with Jules. She deserved to know the truth about her real parents. The fact that we weren't blood related didn't diminish the fact she was my cousin. Nothing could take that away. Though it made me wonder—how much did they actually withhold from us?

Maybe it was all the stress from the last night that made my skating lousy. I'd been on the ice for the past two and a half hours and I only became worse at my jumps by the minute.

Usually when I hit the ice, I'd stop thinking. For me, it was all about instinct and feelings as I jumped and glided around the ice. It was such an exhilarating feeling of freedom that it was addictive.

Until recently. But today was especially bad.

With each heartbeat, my heart tugged at me, pushing me towards Bas and away from my mother and the ice.

I didn't want to leave New York. All I could feel was anguish because my days at Yale were approaching the end. I knew the only way to stay with Bas was to hurt Mom.

I wanted to stay with him. I felt alive and happy around him. I knew after my conversation with her while I was in Philly, she'd never consider moving here. And I still sent her a text last night asking if we could continue our practices here in New York. I couldn't stop hoping. I didn't want to disappoint her, and I didn't want to leave Bas.

Her answer was immediate. My hope crushed.

So I'd poured all my frustration into skating. I worked on my technical elements—jumps, triple Salchows, spins, more jumps. I pumped my heart, hoping I'd burn this brimming feeling inside me that I hated.

Helplessness.

I turned my body around to skate backwards as fast as possible so I could go into a triple Lutz. That particular jump always made me feel better. Yet, as I flew through the air, I knew I fucked it up. Yet again. My weight was off; my speed was off; my fucking mind was off.

I landed. Barely. My leg gave out the moment my skates hit the ice. My body tried to compensate and bear the weight. It felt like falling on fucking concrete. In all my years of skating, I had never fallen as many times as I had today.

Blaming exhaustion was pointless. I'd skated with less sleep before. It was my mind that was fucking me all up. Well, my mind and heart.

Sprawled over the ice, I rolled over and stared at the ceiling. It was pointless to keep going. My head was elsewhere. So was my heart. But how do I explain that to my mother? Basilio DiLustro was known to be part of the Syndicate and my mother hated anything to do with that kind of life.

She wouldn't cave in for her brother; she certainly wouldn't for a mere stranger. Yet, I couldn't help but wonder what happened to have her run away from the underworld. Now that Uncle Liam confirmed Jules and Killian weren't his biological children, I couldn't help but wonder what other secrets lurked in our pasts. Somehow, I didn't think the story ended there. My gut feeling warned there were big things Uncle Liam and Mom had kept us in the dark about.

Davina showed up next to me and lowered to her knees. Sometimes I'd use her to record me so I could spot my mistakes when I went through the videos. I wouldn't have to watch this one because every single move I've done for the past two hours was a major fuckup.

"Wynter, how about you take a break?" she suggested. "No sense in bruising your entire body. We had a long night yesterday. You just need a good day of rest."

I stared up at the ceiling. It was so much more than a good day of rest that I needed, but I didn't want to divulge that to Davina. She kept enough secrets on our behalf from her husband. *Davina and Uncle Liam.* Who would have thought it? I was thrilled for them but I was still coming to terms with it.

"Yeah," I agreed. There was no solution to my predicament. At least not one that wouldn't upset someone. Either I break my mother's heart, or I break my own and Bas's.

Davina took my face between her palms, her gray eyes locking on me. "What's the matter?" she asked softly. "Is it the money we stole?"

A heavy sigh slipped through my lips and a cloud of hot breath dusted through the cold air. You'd think our heists would be my problem and dealing with the mobsters. The Nikolaev mobsters.

But no, something as simple as continuing my career on the East Coast versus the West Coast was my problem.

"Is it about your guy?" Davina whispered, glancing around as if to ensure nobody could hear us. When I didn't answer, she continued, "School? About what happened yesterday?"

I just nodded. "I'm glad it all worked out yesterday. And we met your sister."

It was better if I left her thinking it was about that. We got caught. Uncle Liam just about lost his shit.

Shifting my head, I focused on the ceiling again, worry swarming my mind. Why couldn't I stay on the East Coast? Derek, my skating partner, could relocate here for a bit and I could have skating, Bas, and my friends. After all, the property we want to buy for the school would be on this coast.

"Tell me, Wyn," Davina interrupted my scattered thoughts. "I'm worried about you."

A heavy sigh slipped through my lips. I dug my skates, picking at the ice as I folded my legs. "I don't want to go back to California," I admitted. "My mom won't come—"

Finding another coach wasn't an option. Not that I could afford it. My inheritance wouldn't kick in until I was twenty-five or married. But even more importantly, I couldn't do that to my mother. The Olympic gold was for her as much as for me. It was her dream to skate but a freak accident while she was pregnant with me had fucked up her knee and she could never recover.

She never talked about it, but it damaged her more than physically. It killed my father. The details were vague and I never asked her again about what happened, seeing the pain on my mother's face. Though, I always pondered on it. She said her accident happened in New York but refusing to visit your hometown for twenty years seemed a bit extreme. Unless, there was more to it.

There had to be more to it. What had really happened? Was it connected to the death of Juliette's parents and Uncle's best friends?

"I see." Davina's gaze met mine, and somehow, I sensed she saw more than I wanted her to.

Slapping my hands on the ice, I grunted softly as I got onto my feet, balancing on my blades. It was then that I spotted Bas at the exit of the rink. He looked almost out of place, dressed in his dark three-piece suit and his coal-dark hair that glistened like he just took a shower.

Our eyes connected and butterflies fluttered in my belly as warmth spread through my chest. I just couldn't give him up. I loved him. So fucking much that I didn't feel whole without him.

"Your Bas is here," Davina announced unnecessarily. I acknowledged her, keeping my eyes on Bas and my lips curved into a smile for the first time since I woke up today. He made me happy.

"Well, at least he can get you off the ice," she teased. "Your triple Salchows can wait."

I didn't bother correcting her that my last jump was a 3L. Instead, we headed towards the short wall surrounding the rink.

"Ouch," I mumbled under my breath. Now that adrenaline wasn't pumping through my veins, I could feel the ache in my muscles and bones. Falling on the ice was a bitch.

"You're taking my Jeep, right?" I asked, rubbing my left hip as we approached the gate, and where my skate guards were.

"Yes." She'd go back to Uncle Liam and then they'd go see Davina's grandfather to announce the news of their marriage. I was happy for them, though a tad bit envious. "He's hot," she added quietly.

"He's great." So much more than just hot. So thoughtful and kind. Even his crazy psychotic ways made me swoon over him.

Once we reached him, Davina greeted him. "Hello."

"Hello," he greeted her back in a deep voice, but his eyes never left me. I loved the way he watched me. Intense. Consuming. Possessive.

"I'll talk to you later, Wyn." Davina pressed a kiss on my cheek and my eyes looked her way.

"Sounds good," I said. Davina headed out and I returned my eyes back to Bas. "You're early," I murmured softly.

He grabbed my nape, threading his fingers into my hair, and then buried his face in my neck inhaling deeply.

"I missed you," he rasped.

A masculine noise of satisfaction vibrated through his chest and I could feel it deep down between my thighs.

"I missed you too," I admitted. *God, I can't leave him.* Just the thought of it made my heart ache and made me want to scream in agony.

He glanced behind me. "What made you want to ice-skate?"

I shrugged my shoulders. I should tell him it was for competitions, what I'd always done, but for some reason I didn't feel like it. I liked that he didn't know who I was and he still loved me.

"I used to skate in college," he added and my eyes widened. "Hockey," he clarified.

"The fearless kingpin played hockey," I mused incredulously. "When did you have time to play? And why aren't the reporters all over that one?" I teased.

He nipped my bottom lip. "In the morning, I'd practice. Then at night, I was the kingpin. Unless there was a game."

A soft chuckle vibrated in my chest. "That sounds like a busy schedule." I glanced around. The rink was still empty and I had an idea. "Want to skate?" I asked. "I know where they hide the skates."

"Principessa, are you suggesting I steal the skates?" he retorted, pretending to be shocked.

"We'll just borrow them," I justified. "I won't let you fall and we'll keep your impeccable suit intact."

He chuckled. "I'm not worried."

Ten minutes later, we were both on ice. His black skates against my white ones. My leggings and loose shirt compared to his three-piece suit. We probably looked ridiculous; I didn't care. My heart sang as he held my hand, as if he was worried I'd fall and I couldn't help grinning at his thoughtfulness.

"You're surprisingly stable on your skates," he complimented, the deep timbre of his voice seeping into my soul.

I grinned. Maybe I could impress him and fly through the air. Or maybe not, since I've landed more on my ass than on my feet today. Still, this was too much fun.

"So are you, Mr. Kingpin." It was slightly silly because he was still wearing his three-piece suit. He pulled it off with panache though. This man could do no wrong. At least not in my eyes.

He was graceful, dangerous, and fascinating all in one. My own romantic villainous kingpin.

I raised my eyes and watched him, while my chest filled with warmth. He cocked an eyebrow, as if asking if everything was okay and my heart fluttered like a butterfly captured in a jar. Except I was his willing victim.

His arms wrapped around my waist and he lifted me up like I weighed nothing. My hands came around his neck and our lips met, as my body pressed against his. I wasn't experienced with relationships but these feelings... I wanted to see where they took us.

There was something comfortable and easy about being with him. Even better than the exhilarating feeling I had from the moment I stepped on the ice. Reporters and newscasters called me an ice princess. A natural on the ice, like I was born on it. But not even that compared to these feelings I had for Bas.

Our tongues slid against each other, his mouth consuming me and kissing me deeper. I moaned and he swallowed it, then nipped my bottom lip.

"Ready to go home?" he murmured against my lips. *Home.* Yes, I was ready to go home. With him. And see this through. Regardless if it ended in a fairy tale or a broken heart because there was one thing I knew would be even worse. To wonder for the rest of my life whether I lost my chance at love.

I nodded my response.

He skated backwards and I followed. I remembered his words from before. *I'll always follow.* I'd always follow him too, because he was mine as much as I was his.

It was at the very moment I decided I'd stay with him.

Basilio DiLustro engraved himself on my flesh, into my marrow, and I couldn't let go.

Chapter Twenty-Three

BASILIO

I knew something was wrong the moment we left the skating rink to get to my bike. I had parked it a few parking spots away from her Jeep when I arrived.

Wynter stiffened, her eyes frantically darting around and she almost dropped her duffle bag.

"What is it?" I demanded, shuffling her to my left so I could easily retrieve my gun with my right hand.

"My car is still here," she said, looking shaken. "Davina was supposed to take it."

She rushed to her Jeep and I took her hand into mine, squeezing it in comfort. All the while, I kept alert to ensure nobody blindsided us. There was only one car here, and it was Wynter's Jeep.

This side was too secluded, and it left you vulnerable if something was to happen. But the exit out of the rink was on this side. Once by her Jeep, Wynter gasped. I followed her gaze to see a sports bra on the ground, on the driver's side.

"Somebody must have dropped it," I told her but Wynter shook her head.

"It wasn't here when I pulled up." She went to open the door but I stopped her.

"Let me." I put her behind me and then I opened the door to find a bag on the driver's seat, wide open and in plain sight. Wynter came around me and grabbed it.

"Oh my God," she whimpered. "That's Davina's bag." Her face turned my way, and I could see her eyes shimmering with tears she tried to hold back. "Someone took her, Bas."

I reached for my phone to dial up my connections, while Wynter dug her own out. "I have to call my uncle."

While she was calling her uncle, I dialed up Angelo and had him hack into surveillance around here.

Her uncle must have answered on the first ring because words poured out of Wynter's mouth.

"Uncle, Davina is gone. Someone must have taken her. Oh my God. This is bad. Right? This is so bad."

I couldn't hear what her uncle said but he must have told her to calm down because Wynter took a deep breath in and then exhaled. "Davina was supposed to take my Jeep. But it's still here. And her purse is here. That was an hour ago!"

Silence followed, and then Wynter answered. "Northwell Health Ice Center."

Another stretch of silence. "But—"

"Okay," she sighed. "I have a friend here with me. So I won't be alone." I shook my head at her "friend" label for me. She had to have read my thoughts because she gave me an apologetic look. "Don't send anyone to fetch me. I'm fine."

My phone dinged and it was Angelo's response. He was on it. If Davina means so much to Wynter, then she mattered to me too. I never wanted to see Wynter upset. "No, no," she protested, shaking her head like her uncle could see her. "I won't leave my friend's side. I promise."

Damn straight, she wouldn't. Maybe they robbed the wrong person and now their lives are in danger. It wasn't out of the realm of possibility.

"I'm safe," she assured him. "My friend won't leave my side."

This time I heard a muffled question through her headset. "What friend?"

Wynter blushed crimson and my dick instantly responded. Fucked up, I know. "Ummm, you don't know him. From college." Another apologetic look. "You guys go look for Davina. I—I think…"

More muffled questions and silence. Then Wynter continued, "Ummm, no. I don't think so. Nothing other than what you already know."

One thing was for certain. Wynter wasn't a very good liar. I tuned out the rest of their conversation and walked away to send my own message out. I wouldn't tolerate any direct or indirect threat to Wynter.

I wondered if Liam Brennan knew his woman was in trouble. From my spot, I watched Wynter nod while on the phone with her uncle and all the while typing a message to Angelo to check the surveillance around the ice rink. She wore a long white off-the-shoulder t-shirt and black leggings. She seemed to wear those a lot, like it was her signature wardrobe.

Then ending her call, she wiped her nose with the back of her trembling hand. That right there told me how scared she was. It was such a childish gesture. Seeing her upset and tears shine in her eyes was like a stab to my heart. I didn't fucking like it.

This kind of thing didn't get my heart racing. I've seen much scarier shit in my world, and for a fraction of a second, my conscience pointed out how much worse my world would be for her.

Yet, I refused to even consider giving her up. I needed her in my darkness, to keep me sane. To keep me from becoming a monster. Every monster had a weakness and she was mine.

And like a selfish bastard, I shoved any possibility of life without her out of my mind and pulled her into a hug.

"I messaged my guy and he's checking the surveillance," I murmured into her hair. "We won't let anything happen to your friend."

She sniffed into my chest, and fuck, if that didn't make my own chest ache. "I should have let Jules kill him," she mumbled into my chest.

A choked laugh escaped me. "She wanted to kill him?"

She nodded. "Cut his dick off, burn down his house, kill him. She's a bit unhinged."

"I'd say." I rubbed her back, feeling her tense muscles slowly relax. "What will your uncle do?"

She tensed slightly. "He'll call the police," she murmured. "He has some people he knows." Her eyes darted away from me. "I'm worried they won't do anything until twenty-four hours have gone by. Aren't those the rules?"

I shook my head. "Not necessarily." She chewed on her bottom lip nervously. "If his connections in the police can't help, I have my own connections already working it."

Wynter's face lit up hopefully. "Really?"

I nodded. "Don't worry about anything."

She swallowed, her emotions glittering in her eyes. "Thank you so much, Bas," she breathed out. "I can't thank you enough."

"No need for thanks," I told her. "Let's get to my place."

Her eyes flickered to my bike. "We're riding that?"

I grinned. "Don't tell me you're scared?" I teased, trying to get her mind off things.

"Of course not," she replied undignified. "I just don't want to get hurt. I need my legs working perfectly for another ten months or so." My eyes roamed down her leggings, giving me a perfect view of her curves and shape of her legs.

"Your legs are indeed gorgeous," I murmured. "I'll keep them safe, principessa."

She rolled her eyes. "But is a three-piece suit the right apparel for a motorcycle?" she questioned. "We could take the Jeep," she suggested.

I shook my head. "Don't worry about my suit, principessa," I purred. "Get on the bike. I want to feel those gorgeous legs against mine."

The truth was that I fucking hated riding my bike in anything but jeans, but I had to leave my car at the warehouse and take the bike in order to get here on time.

Blush colored her cheeks and I had never seen anything so fucking beautiful.

"Fine," she caved on a sigh.

I swung my leg over the bike seat, then helped her get behind me and handed her a helmet. She fumbled with it and I helped her put it on, her blonde curls peeking underneath it. Once I was satisfied it was secured, I put my own gear on and started the bike. Her hands instantly came around my waist, holding on tight. It felt good having her body pressed hard against mine.

I took the long way to my city home, and with each street behind us, I felt her body relaxing into me. Her slim fingers slid into the loop of my pants and my heart did this weird boom-thump against my ribs. It only did it around her.

It was at that very moment I realized... That the day she landed in my arms was the day I actually started living. She restarted my heart and I'd never let her go.

I watched Wynter drift through my living room, her slim fingers trailing the surface of the furniture. Every so often she'd stop and study a picture. I didn't have many and whatever few I had were there because Emory made them and hung them up.

"Priest looks nothing like you," she observed, throwing me a glance over her shoulder. "Though he seems slightly... ummm... brutal, like you. But the other one looks like you."

"Dante. He's Priest's brother."

"Yes, Dante." She moved to the next one. The only one with Dante, Emory, Priest, and I together. "Does your sister live in New York?"

I knew she was just trying to keep her mind off things, but I tensed nonetheless. She didn't notice it because her attention was on the photograph. We kept a tight lid on Emory's location and that she ran Las Vegas, fearing if people knew it was a woman, they'd find Vegas an easy target.

"No, not in New York," I ended up answering.

If Wynter noticed I avoided answering her, she didn't lead on. "I guess she kind of looks like you. With her dark hair and dark eyes."

That was pretty much where our resemblance ended. I looked like our father. She looked like our mother.

"Who do you resemble?" I asked.

She shrugged her slim shoulders, her curls bouncing down her back. "My mom and my grandmother."

A heavy sigh left her and I stood up, coming behind her.

"Everything will be fine."

She turned around and pressed her face against my chest. "Everything has gotten out of hand," she murmured against my heart.

I took her chin and lifted her face to mine. My gaze found hers and I pressed my forehead against hers. I opened my mouth to tell her I'd fix it all, but my phone rang.

I kissed the tip of her nose and went back to the couch where I left my phone.

It was Dante. "Yeah," I answered.

"You won't fucking believe this shit," he hissed and I instantly tensed.

"Speak."

"Gio put a hit on Liam's woman." My eyes instinctively shot to Wynter. If she heard this, she'd be sure to fucking leave. "It was capture or kill. As long as Brennan no longer had her."

The anger was so strong, I had to choke it down or risk scaring the living daylights out of Wynter. She threw me a hesitant look, probably sensing the fury. It burned my throat, my chest, my fucking lungs.

"How do you know?" I asked, reining in the anger in my voice.

"Priest hacked into Garrett's computer. Apparently, the guy likes to keep notes on his illegal dealings and had all his plans and instructions from Gio recorded. Fucking moron."

"Have you sent our men after her?"

"I have, but Liam's men beat us to it." Fuck, if he learned Father's connection to her kidnapping, we'd have a fucking war. "We have to do something," he growled.

I had to overthrow my father. Or have him killed. Anything before he threw us into fucking chaos. Even more terrifying was that Wynter was with Davina. If I hadn't made plans, the fucker could have taken Wynter too.

"Otherwise, we'll all be dead. Brennan has good connections and we don't need their attention," Dante continued. Fuck, didn't I know it. We didn't need to fuck with Cassio King and his gang. The old fuckers were married and settled. I'd like to keep them focused on their families rather than looking our way. It was our turn to rule and our reach through the Syndicate covered the entire world.

Wynter's phone started vibrating and she jumped, then rushed to it, answering on the first ring. I watched her face and saw relief wash over her expression.

"Yes, we'll have to deal with it," I acknowledged Dante's insinuation.

"Come to Chicago," he grumbled. "Let's make a plan and execute it."

"I have Wynter with me."

"Bring her along," he reasoned. "He already knows you have a woman and he's curious. She won't be safe from him either. Assuming he hasn't already dug up every piece of information on her."

He was right. Albeit, Wynter's background wouldn't divulge anything to him. Her life was simple compared to ours.

"We'll come together." But first I'd marry her. "I'll call you later."

Chapter Twenty-Four

WYNTER

A rush of relief filled me and tears stung my eyes. If something would have happened to Davina, I'd have never forgiven myself. We should have walked her to the Jeep and ensured she left safely.

For a moment, I thought our misdeeds caught up with us. First, we burned down Garrett's house, then counting cards in Chicago, and finally stealing the armored truck. Thank God, Davina was alright.

I settled on the sofa next to Bas and he wrapped his one hand around me. "She's good?"

I nodded. "Yes. For a moment—" I couldn't get the words out. Just thinking about anyone who I loved being hurt caused such anguish. "The girls and I, we did a few stupid things over the last few weeks. I thought it caught up to us."

He stilled, but didn't interrupt me. I chewed on my bottom lip, while Bas watched me intently.

"I—we... the girls and I stole some money," I muttered, peering at him from underneath my lashes. "We shouldn't have and it was stupid. Initially, we did it to pay Garrett's ransom, in case you didn't come through. Then when you did, we kept it. We did a few other stupid things."

Bas's dark eyes assessed me, though he didn't seem surprised. "I thought it caught up to us," I muttered slightly embarrassed.

His hand cupped my chin, tilting my head so I was forced to lock eyes with him.

"No judgment, principessa," he claimed, brushing his lips against mine. "But no more stealing. I have enough money."

A choked laugh escaped me. "I'm not exactly broke either."

I really wasn't. Grandpa had a trust fund established for me. So did Uncle Liam. Mom insisted neither Juliette nor I be given too much so we'd learn the value of money. Uncle agreed, though he never let us go without.

"I have something for you," Bas announced, interrupting my thoughts.

"Really?" I asked excitedly, straightening up. I loved surprises. "What is it?"

He grinned. "It's a birthday present."

I blinked. "But my birthday is not for another few days."

"Do you want to wait?" he teased. "Or you could get it now and tell me if you don't like it so I can buy you something you like."

A giddy smile I couldn't contain curved my lips. He leaned over and opened the drawer of his little coffee table. A handgun lay in it and a small box he pulled out and handed to me. Uncle never kept a gun in the living room.

"Happy birthday, principessa." I twisted it in my hands, wondering what it was. "Open it," he demanded, his palm resting on my hip.

I lifted the lid and my breath stilled as I stared at the beautiful necklace holding a pendant. It was a skull that matched his tattoo. I traced the delicate gold with my finger.

"It's the kingpin pendant," he murmured. "So no matter where you are, if someone hurts you, they'll know whose wrath they'll earn. Priest, Dante, Emory, and I carry the tattoo."

I remembered the tattoo. I traced over it back in Philly. It'd be impossible to forget something that fascinated me and everything about this man interested me.

I took it out of the box carefully. "I love it," I whispered softly. "It's part of you."

Bas lifted me, setting me on his lap, then helped me put on the necklace. Once clasped, his mouth brushed over the back of my neck and goose bumps rose on my skin.

"Bas," I whispered as I tilted my head to allow him better access.

"Hmmm?"

"I'll stay with you," I said and he stilled, his breath ghosting over my skin. Someone might have accused me of making a decision on the fly but it felt so damn right. "Here in New York. I won't go back to California."

I held my breath with anticipation while my heart thumped wildly under my rib cage.

"Yeah?"

"Yeah," I confirmed.

He grabbed my nape, threaded his fingers into my hair and then buried his face in my neck. The masculine noise of satisfaction he made vibrated deep in my stomach and the tightness in my chest loosened.

"Fuck," he groaned. "That makes me so fucking happy." His arm wrapped around my waist and he shifted me around on his lap so I'd face him. "Come to Chicago with me," he rasped against my throat. "Tomorrow."

I nodded, every cell in my body humming with love and such intense longing, it made my heart flutter.

"I'll always follow," I promised in a breathless whisper, repeating his own words back.

I placed my palms against his chest, his heat seeping into me. God, to love someone so much could be thrilling and terrifying at the same time.

I trailed my hands over his vest and my fingers trembled as I unbuttoned one button, then the next. With each button loose, my heart thundered harder and my pulse raced faster.

I closed the distance between us, lingering a breath away, his form unmoving. As if he waited for something. Then I closed the distance. He kissed me with such passion that I couldn't keep my eyes open and every thought left me.

Our kissing quickly turned frantic. A dam broke, leaving in its wake an unhinged desire. I ran my fingers through his hair, tugging him closer. I needed his skin on mine.

"Bas, please," I begged.

His hands grabbed my ass and lifted me up, my legs wrapping around his waist.

He bit my bottom lip, gently but enough to sting and I moaned into his mouth. I could feel his desire blazing and clashing with mine. I had no idea how we found ourselves in the bathroom, my back pressed against the cool tile, cooling my scorched skin.

I opened my eyes to find his gaze on me, drinking me in. His dark gaze blazed with fire, an inferno in its depths.

I slid down his body and he pulled the t-shirt over my head, then undid my bra and tossed it to the side. His fingers trailed down my body, causing goose bumps over every single inch of my body. His rough palm against my soft skin sent shivers down my spine. Then he hooked his fingers in my pants and panties. Then he lowered himself onto his knees, sliding them down my legs.

A hiss of appreciation left his lips. My legs quivered and would have failed me if his strong arms weren't holding me up. He spread my legs, his dark gaze burning holes in my skin and causing a pulsing ache between my thighs. My sex throbbed, the evidence of my arousal trickling down my inner thigh. The moment his mouth connected with my pussy, a loud moan echoed through the bathroom, vibrating against the tile.

He lifted my one leg and draped it over his shoulder, his mouth never leaving the most intimate part of me.

"Mmmmm." The noise of him vibrated through my core and my fingers tangled into his dark hair.

"Bas. Oh my God, Bas." He kissed me with an open mouth, shoving his tongue inside my entrance. "Fuck."

I buckled, my back arching off the tiled wall. The sensation was too much. Not enough. His finger thrust inside me. His tongue swiped through my wet folds, sending a series of shudders through me.

I'm dying. The best kind of death. Sweet, exhilarating, volcanic.

He sucked and licked on my most private part relentlessly. Every single fiber of me shook with pleasure. It was right there, within my grasp.

"Watch me, Wynter," he commanded, his voice hoarse.

I peeled my eyelids open, meeting his dark gaze as the muscles in his jaw contracted as he ate my pussy. He bit my clit and I bucked off the wall, arching into his mouth. His hand moved to my stomach, holding me still, and my hands gripped his head.

"Oh, oh, oh," I panted, his laps never easing. His laps steady, he slid one finger inside me. Pleasure ignited, sending languid heat through my bloodstream. A tremor went through me, as he moved his fingers in and out, again and again. Hard and fast.

God, the deep noises of satisfaction that vibrated through him would be my death. His dark gaze locked on me, he nipped my clit again. The orgasm tore through me like an opened dam. Pleasure swam through my veins, spreading tingles throughout.

His tongue didn't stop, he sucked and lapped, taking every last drop of the orgasm. My legs quivered and my ears buzzed as I lay slack against the wall. His mouth trailed kisses down my inner thigh.

Letting out a shaky breath, Bas's face came back into focus and my fingers still tangled in his dark hair. His eyes burned with hunger but he made no move to undress. He still wore his three-piece suit, my feeble attempt with several buttons loosened.

He stood up, his one hand still on my hip, while with the back of his other hand he wiped his mouth.

Our eyes locked, our breathing synchronized, neither one of us looked away. I wanted to give him the same kind of pleasure. He owned all mine, I wanted to own all his.

When he didn't move, I reached out and shoved his suit coat off his shoulders, then loosened the rest of the buttons on his vest. When he didn't stop me, it fueled my courage, shooting adrenaline through my veins.

Nerves fluttered in my belly but I ignored them. Instead I met his eyes.

"Tell me if I'm not doing it right," I rasped.

"Everything with you is right." His voice was deep and guttural, his control close to unraveling.

I shoved his shirt off his bulky shoulders and threw it onto the floor. His broad shoulders took away my breath. The sight of his muscles and beautiful, golden-tanned skin made my mouth water. I reached for his zipper and unfastened it, the sound of the zipper echoing through the bathroom. And all the while he kept his dark stare on me. I pushed his pants down to his ankles. He wore nothing underneath it.

This man was perfect.

His stomach was rock hard, six-pack abs making my inner thighs pulse with ache. His large cock hung heavy and thick between his legs.

I absorbed it all, drinking him in. Thick veins ran down his hard length.

He kicked his pants and shoes off, leaving him gloriously naked. He stood still, his one hand in my hair, his other by his side as my eyes soaked him in.

I pressed my palm against his chest, his heart thundering under my touch.

"You are so beautiful," I whispered, my eyes dropping lower.

Pre-cum dripped from the end of his cock and my hand wrapped around his thick shaft, rubbing his pre-cum with my thumb. A sharp inhale left his lips and my eyes rose to his dark gaze.

My chest rose and fell, struggling for air. This desperate need for him, the taste of him would be my addiction. I just knew it.

He was my own brand of drug.

My heart drummed inside my chest. My hands trembled as I wrapped my fingers around his erection. He felt so warm and smooth, pre-cum tempting me to taste it. So I did, I licked it and a low groan vibrated against the tiles.

My body hummed in response.

This felt like a dangerous kind of power and I fucking loved it. I ran my tongue around his head before sucking it into my mouth. His dark gaze turned coal black and his head fell back.

"Fuck, that's it, principessa."

Encouraged by his praise, I sucked him again, taking him deeper into my mouth. I bobbed my head, up and down, taking as much of him as I could.

The grip of his hand in my hair tightened and he moved my head, controlling the rhythm. And the way he dominated me made me hot and throbbing for him again.

He moved my head. Up and down, thrusting deeper in my mouth every time.

"Look at me when I fuck your mouth," he demanded, his voice hoarse.

My eyes flicked to him and found his gaze burning. For me.

His hips thrust forward, pushing himself deeper into my mouth and hitting the back of my throat, my eyes watered. But I refused to give up. His breaths came out heavy, the tension in him building to a pinnacle.

His free hand cupped the side of my cheek, his thumb caressing it like I was his everything.

"Can I come in your mouth, principessa?" he asked with a groan.

A light nod and he continued fucking my mouth. Deeper and harder. Both my hands held on to his thighs, my nails digging into his muscles. I moaned, something thrilling about watching him unravel.

His groan rumbled from low in his throat, the sound loud against the tile and I could feel it vibrate between my legs. When he finished, I swallowed all of his cum, wanting every single drop of him. All the while his dark gaze lit me on fire and melted my soul.

The two of us watched each other, the silence between us full of hopes for the future. I remained kneeling, my heart thundering in my chest and a throbbing ache between my legs.

A small squeal escaped me when he stooped down, suddenly lifting me by grabbing my thighs and I wrapped my legs around him. His mouth pressed to mine, our tongues slid against each other.

"I love you, Wynter Star," he murmured against my lips and my heart skidded to a stop, before it went into overdrive. I'd never tire of hearing those words come from him.

"I love you too, Bas. Always." It was my vow to him.

He walked us both into the shower and started it. I squealed, feeling cold droplets on my heated skin. I pressed myself harder against him, stealing his heat.

"Basilio!" I protested.

He chuckled and turned us around so he'd take all the cold. I've taken ice-cold showers before after skating practices, but it didn't mean I cared for it.

"I'll keep you warm," he drawled. "Always. With my body and my c—"

"Bas," I exclaimed, suddenly feeling very hot all over.

He grinned, suddenly looking younger than his twenty-seven years. His fingers gripped my thighs and I rubbed myself against him.

Another groan slipped from his lips and our mouths collided. My heart swelled and emotions burned through me. I was so in love with him, and for the first time in my life, I feared being without someone.

But then he slid inside me and the whole world was forgotten. It was just me and him.

An hour later, we lay between Basilio's tousled black satin sheets. I laid my head on his chest and listened to his heartbeat, lulling me to sleep. There would be nothing that could compare to this. Not even ice-skating, and I freaking love figure skating.

His hand rubbed my back, his touch soothing. Up and down, up and down. I knew something was on his mind, but I didn't want to pry. I figured he'd tell me when he was ready.

"Principessa." His voice was a hot whisper against my earlobe.

"Hmmm," I murmured, my body slack against him and my mind slowly drifting off.

"Marry me." My whole body jolted up, searching his face.

"What?" I didn't hear him right.

He took my shoulders between his hands, his touch firm but gentle and our gazes locked. He brought our faces inches apart.

"Marry me, Wynter Star."

My pulse raced and my ears buzzed. I couldn't have heard him right. The intense orgasm he had just given me must have messed up my brain.

"You've been mine from the moment you fell into my arms," he continued and conviction in his voice sent adrenaline rushing through my blood and straight into my heart. "You said you love me."

"I do," I confirmed in a quiet voice, while blood pulsed in my ears. I *loved* him so much it fucking hurt.

He slid off the bed, wearing only his boxers and a big grin on his face. He lowered himself on one knee, his dark eyes never leaving me.

"Wynter Star, would you do me the honor of becoming my wife?"

A choked laugh escaped me, while I debated whether this was romantic or not. My heart sang as he looked at me with so much intensity, it melted my heart. I'd kill for this man because living without him wouldn't be living.

"Yes," I rasped, shifting on the bed so I'd be closer to him. Then I threw myself on him, knocking him onto the floor. "Yes, yes, yes. I'll marry you."

Chapter Twenty-Five

Dressed in one of Bas's white t-shirts that came to my mid-thighs and my boyshort panties, I roamed his home.

Unlike most bachelors that I'd heard stories about, Basilio's place was spotless. I could go mess around in the kitchen, but it was probably safer that I didn't. While I was good on the ice, I was terrible in the kitchen. I didn't want to risk burning his place down.

I roamed from room to room. Admittedly, I was a tiny bit nosey. Earlier today, I was too worried about Davina and then got wrapped up in Bas to absorb this place, but now, I had time.

His kitchen was grand and fancy for a bachelor. Not that you'd catch me in it. But the rest of his house was the epitome of comfort with a feel of home. An office with a large mahogany desk and matching furniture, a guest bathroom painted all black and white, and a guest room in dark earth-tone colors looked cozy though it didn't compare to Bas's own bedroom.

His bedroom walls were crisp white with a large bed draped with black satin sheets. It fit him perfectly, giving his room the appearance of a devil's lair tempting women with the promises of sin, pleasure, and happiness.

I was floating on a cloud while scouting his place, the words of his proposal playing on repeat. Over and over again, making me gush. I'd marry him. And I couldn't freaking wait.

Since I'd met Basilio, life had been different. I enjoyed it more. I appreciated free moments and relished in spending them off the ice. Besides, I promised Basilio I'd stay here. My hand reached for the necklace around my neck and my fingers twirled the skull pendant.

Tucking it under my shirt, I glanced around, my bare feet cool against the hardwood.

He touched something deep inside me, engraved himself on my flesh, into my marrow and there was no letting go.

I promised him I'd never leave and I intended to keep that promise. Despite the darkness around him, he also had light in him. Or maybe it was exactly his darkness that appealed to me.

I was so deep in my daydreams that I never heard the steps.

"Now I understand what has been keeping my son busy," an unfamiliar voice drifted through the air. I whirled around and came face-to-face with a much older version of Basilio. A much darker, much crueler version.

It was peculiar because physically the son and father looked very much alike. His jet-black hair had silver strands all throughout. Basilio was an inch or two taller than his father, and though both were strong, his father looked stockier because he was shorter. I had no doubt that Basilio would look like his father in his old age.

Yet, something about the cruelty in this man's eyes differentiated him from Bas. Basilio could never become this man.

The ruthless head of the New York Syndicate stood barely five feet away from me.

Uncle and Killian may have kept Juliette and me blind to the underworld, but I'd heard enough stories about Gio DiLustro to know it wasn't smart to be alone with him. Or to be on his radar.

My heart tripped but I kept my face expressionless. After all, I have had years of practice.

Bas's father leaned against the living room doorway, looking like he was in his own home. His own territory. Well, he was in his territory. This side of town belonged to the DiLustros. How many times had Uncle Liam warned us not to cross to this side of the city?

I could taste fear on my tongue as I stood there watching one of the most feared men in New York City. Unlike Bas, this man was all cruelty and corruption. Evil. It was in the wickedness of his gaze. In the darkness of the air that seemed to pulse around him with each slight movement he made.

"Basilio is not home," I said firmly, though my heart thundered so hard it might have cracked my ribs.

"Home, huh?" He chuckled, though there was something menacing about his laugh. Predatory. "You already made yourself at home, I see."

I didn't like his tone. Being caught alone in Basilio's home with this man was bound to end badly.

He hadn't moved, but the way he eyed me, like a predator, I felt like he was too close. The room was closing in on me. His gaze lowered, eyeing my sparkly painted toes, then traveled up over my bare legs. I felt too exposed, too naked.

He took a step towards me, and instinctively, I took a step back. I didn't want him any closer to me, though by the way he smiled, it looked like I made his day. This man liked a chase and right now he looked like a cat who was about to catch the canary.

My eyes darted around for my phone. It was on the coffee table. *Coffee table!*

I saw it when Basilio gave me the necklace. He stored his handgun in it. His father didn't bother looking away from me. He didn't consider me a threat.

I shifted to my right, towards the table. He followed.

"How much?" My heart skidded to a stop and I blinked in confusion. He chuckled darkly. "How much to let me fuck you?" My heart pounded in my chest but I refused to show it. Bas would be home soon. He'd keep me safe. "Name your price. I'm willing to negotiate."

The gun and coffee table temporarily forgotten, I stared at him in shock.

"I don't have a price," I choked out, swallowing a lump in my throat. "This has nothing to do with you."

He leered at me with a cruel smirk on his face. The way he looked at me sent a shiver of fear down my spine. His mouth pulled into a big menacing smile that raised the little hairs on my skin. Terror unlike any before clogged my throat.

I wasn't prepared for this. To fight. To defend myself.

My heart thundered against my rib cage. For the first time in my life, I was scared because the way this man looked at me promised nightmares and retribution. The man didn't like to be denied.

"Everyone has a price."

And this was where my infamous Irish temper kicked in. I squared my shoulders and glared at him.

"Well, I don't," I spat back at him. "I don't want nor need your filthy money."

In two big strides, the man was in my face. I pissed him off. This was the scary, ruthless, and crazy mobster. He literally towered over me, working his intimidation.

But what had taken me aback was the hate in his eyes. What could I have possibly done for this man to hate me so much? Hate was usually personal and this man had only just met me.

Using all my strength from years of training, I kicked him between his legs and sprinted for the coffee table. I wasn't fast enough or I didn't hit him hard enough. His hand grabbed my arm and yanked me back. Losing my balance, I fell to the floor. My head cracked against the hardwood floor. Stars danced in front of my vision.

It was peculiar the thoughts that ran through one's head when in panic. I didn't think about my mom. I didn't think about Basilio. I didn't think about surviving. My only damn thought was not to break anything or get a concussion so I could continue my training.

My priorities were screwed up. Or maybe the ice-skating and training had been ingrained into me for so long, I didn't know how to think about anything else.

My fingers locked around the table leg and I gripped it hard as I scrambled onto my knees. I was desperate to get away from him. I wasn't quick enough. His hands grabbed my hips and jerked me backwards.

Losing my balance, my knees gave out and my head hit the corner of the coffee table. Stars swirled in my vision again.

Fuck!

His harsh laughter filled the room. It pierced my eardrums. It sent fear down to every cell of me. I felt sticky liquid trickling down my temple, red dripped in front of my vision.

I couldn't give up. I had to fight.

His hand wrapped around my throat from the back, his body pressed against my ass and with horror I realized the man was fucking hard. The bulge in his pants couldn't be mistaken for anything else.

The next second, I was flipped onto my back. My head hit the floor again. I jerked against him, fighting him off, but it didn't seem to faze him at all. His fingers ripped the shirt straight down the middle.

My head snapped to the side. He backhanded me; my cheek burned, my vision blurred, and my ears buzzed from the force of it. My mouth filled with blood, the metallic taste overwhelming. It was on my tongue, in my throat. I could smell it.

Tears blurred my eyes, whether from the pain of the slap or the icy terror, I didn't know. I had never been hit in my entire life.

"Don't worry," he hissed against my ear, his other hand fisting my hair and yanking it backwards. "I'll break you in. I knew your mother was alive. That lying, filthy Irish whore."

I blinked, confused at his reference to my mother.

But I couldn't ponder on it. His breathing was hard, his breath vile against my skin as he pried my thighs apart. *Fight*, my mind demanded. *Fight.*

The sound of the zipper was ominous. His penis flopped out and I jerked back, twisting around. Bile rose in my throat and threatened to empty my stomach.

I had to get away from him. I crawled on my hands and knees. "I can fuck your ass too. I'll break you in, girl."

I struggled against him. I elbowed him hard enough to hear his grunts and his disgusting breath on my neck. Glass shattered, a vase from the coffee table. His hands gripped my hair and yanked my head back so hard, sharp pain shot through my neck and down my back.

Nausea curled in my stomach. His laugh sounded in my ears. He reached for my panties, peeling them down my legs. His fingers were between my legs and I tasted vomit in my throat, the acid of it burning it raw.

I jerked my head back and headbutted him. I never saw his fist coming, nor his hand that choked the life out of me. Ignoring the pain on every inch of me, I headbutted him again. His grip loosened just enough for me to jab my elbow into his gut.

I took advantage of his recovery and started crawling, the glass cutting into my palms.

It only took a second for him to react and tighten his grip in my hair. A yelp escaped me and my scalp burned with pain.

His mouth latched on to the back of my neck and bit in hard. I screamed. I screamed so hard and long, my lungs burned. Tears pricked my eyes. This man would rape me. I had to think of a way to escape this monster.

I had to get my hands on that gun. Using all my muscles, I kicked him with the heel of my foot. His grip on me loosened just enough to allow me to move.

Ignoring pain in my palm and my shoulder, I grabbed the handle of the drawer. I pulled hard on it, the whole drawer came out of the sliders and went flying onto the floor.

"Firecracker, aren't we?" he mocked. The next second I felt his hand slap me across my head so hard my ears buzzed.

I won't die like this, I whispered in my mind. *I can't die like this.*

He chuckled, almost as if he heard my thoughts. "Should have taken the offer," he taunted. "I would have given you a few million and fucked you. Now, I'm going to fuck you and kill you."

My face throbbed. My whole body pulsed. Blood stained my hands. My legs. I could see the gun from the corner of my eyes. I scrambled for it, but his hand yanked on my shirt and another sound of cotton ripping filled the air.

The gun was my endgame. I needed that gun.

His hands came to my waist and flipped me over, my back hitting the floor. The ripped shirt couldn't protect my bare back from the shards of glass that were cutting into my skin. A scream tore from my throat. Tears started flowing. His fist hit my jaw and spots danced in front of my vision, shades of black and red. Maybe blue. I couldn't tell.

"Your mother thought she was too good too," he hissed, his breath hitting my nostrils. He smelled like whiskey and cigarettes.

His words made no sense. Maybe he was crazy.

His knee nudged my legs further apart and another scream tore through my lips. Full of anguish. Full of pain. Full of terror.

I kicked. I scratched and slashed his face. His palm connected with my cheek and instantly my cheek exploded in pain.

Think, my mind kept whispering. *Think.*

I relaxed my body and instantly I could see victory flash across his face. The evil in his eyes was black and tarnished.

"I knew you'd see it my way," he hissed, his breathing hard.

I kept my body relaxed and waited. His one hand cupped my breast. His touch disgusted me. It had bile rising in my throat. *Stay focused*, my mind whispered.

"I can see why he likes you," he drawled, his breath hitting my nostrils. I had no idea what the fuck he was talking about but I kept still. I kept watching him through half-closed eyelids, waiting for my opportunity. "Your fire probably turns him on. Just like it turns me on."

God, I wanted to spit into his face. Then smash it against all the glass on the ground.

"But he's just a boy," he purred. "I'll show you how a real man fucks."

He was so excited, he let go of my wrists to bring his dick to my entrance, and that was when I saw my opportunity. With all my strength, I kneed him into his balls and then my fist flew across the air and connected with his face. I pushed him off of me and scrambled for the gun lying two feet away.

Grabbing it, I shuffled to my feet and aimed it at him, sliding the hammer back to ensure there was one in the chamber, ready to fire.

He laughed. "You are not going to shoot me."

"I wouldn't bet on that."

He watched me and he must have seen something on my face that convinced him I'd pull the trigger. I kept my finger readily on it, ensuring he kept away from me while I pulled my boyshorts back on.

"Did you know I knew your mother?" My eyes widened. It was a mistake. He latched on to my surprise and kept on pushing on that weakness. "She was supposed to be mine."

"You're lying," I choked out.

"No, I'm not," he protested. "Ask her. She didn't love your father."

This made no sense. My mother didn't talk about my father, but she said she loved him. Didn't she? My mind worked vigorously, remembering what little she told me.

"I fell in love. It wasn't accepted."

"I had to choose. Love or my career. I ended up losing both."

Gio studied my expression. "You look like her," he drawled. "But she chose wrong."

A gasp tore through the room. My mother loved Gio DiLustro? How did my father come into play? No, no, no. This man was cruel. Evil. It was evident in his eyes and in his expression. There was no chance of missing it.

"The bullet in her knee..." I watched his dark eyes harden. "I put it there." My chest froze and then turned into an angry inferno. It consumed me from the inside and had my hands shaking.

Gio laughed, like it was the funniest thing when that would have ruined her life. It only fueled my anger further. Ice-skating was like breathing for Mom. For me. "Do you think she'll like my son as her son-in-law?"

She wouldn't. It finally made sense why my mother refused to come to the East Coast. The chance for the future with Bas slowly drifted away like a feather on a breeze.

The pain in my chest overwhelmed all my other senses and dulled out the physical pain. It was the kind of pain that made it hard to breathe. The kind of pain that made you weak in the knees in the worst kind of way.

"My mom breathed ice-skating," I croaked, my chest tightening with each breath. "She lived it, and thrived on it."

Not a single muscle moved on Gio's face. No regret. No sorrow. Nothing. "Why would you be so cruel?" I whispered, knowing just how much it broke my mom to have lost her chance to skate. Her passion.

I saw it every day in her limp. Or when her knee bothered her. The way sorrow filled her eyes sometimes when she watched me skate. She had that and she lost it. All because of this man.

"I loved her," he said, his voice cold. "Her Russian heritage was a bonus." My brows knitted. "Yes, her mother was the beloved daughter of the Pakhan. Why do you think the Russians can't stand your family? The Brennans kidnapped your grandmother." Surprise washed over me at that revelation and all I could do was stare. "But your damn mother, all she wanted was my brother. When she left him, instead of coming to me, she married some frilly skater." He scoffed and almost looked like he wanted to spit. "Your father was a fucking joke. So fucking weak."

My hand lowered to my side, the gun suddenly feeling too heavy to hold. My lungs lacked oxygen, each shuddering breath making it harder to breathe. There was too much information. Too much history I didn't understand.

"Of course, the moment Basilio saw you, he knew who you were," he continued and my heart shattered. "We planned this. You are our ticket to the Pakhan and the Russians that keep refusing to join the Syndicate."

I swallowed hard, my heartbeats shattering me with each beat against my chest. It was ironic that the very thing that ensured I lived was so painful.

"You will marry Basilio, and the DiLustro family will make an allegiance with the Pakhan," he boasted. "We'll get rid of the Irish, once and for all."

Over. My. Dead. Body.

"You're crazy," I hissed.

He threw his head back and laughed as if I'd told a joke or this whole situation was funny. "You didn't really think Basilio was chasing a silly girl without an endgame in mind. All along, it was to secure an alliance and end your uncle. He knew this would happen. He knew, that's why he left."

He took a step forward, and instantly I raised my gun.

"You were played," Gio cackled. "After all, I'm the one who taught my son how to play the game."

I'm not a good man. Basilio's words from our first date came back with a vengeance. He told me he was a bad guy, and yet, like a fool, I refused to see it.

"Give me that gun," he drawled. Another step. "You're not a killer, so save us both the time."

He moved towards me and I aimed at his right knee, then pulled the trigger.

Bang.

"You're right," I told him as he fell to the ground. "I'm not a killer. But I'm not beyond making you lose a leg."

I cocked the gun and pulled the trigger again.

Chapter Twenty-Six

WYNTER

My legs quivered, my body ached, and blood covered my hands and face. I held the shreds of my clothes with one hand while I supported myself against the walls in the hallway with my other.

I had to get out of there. Clenching my teeth and ignoring the pain that each step shot through me, I kept moving forward and stumbled out of Bas's red brick home.

Warm air hit me. The noise of the city matched my hectic state. My steps halted.

A car sat parked in front of Basilio's home and a man stood in front of it. Big, bulky. Our eyes connected, and for a moment, I thought he'd kill me or send me back inside, to face my death.

"Go," he mouthed and relief washed over me. I tilted my head, and tears burned my eyes.

I took off running. I was barefoot, blood stained my ripped shirt, leaving my back exposed. I only wore boyshort panties, now stained with blood. My phone was left behind. Everything.

Bas played me. Bas played me.

The words screamed in my ears as I ran down the street, glances thrown my way, but I ignored them all as my chest burned.

Oh my God! Bas's father shot my mother.

How many secrets did our family have? I didn't even know my mother was shot. She had a past with the DiLustros? DiLustro had to be lying.

"Do you need help?" a passerby asked but I ignored him, rushing aimlessly down the street. I couldn't call Uncle Liam. He'd kill Bas.

Idiot, I shouldn't worry about Bas. He betrayed me. Left me for his father to—

A shudder rolled down my spine and fear iced through my veins. *Bas left me.*

The sound of screeching tires. Shouting. I ignored it.

I was such an idiot. I fell right into their trap. Like a lamb to the slaughter.

"Wynter."

My heart sped up. *He* was coming after me. DiLustro was coming to finish me. I sped up, my ears buzzing with adrenaline and terror.

A hand wrapped around my wrist and I screamed, jerking against it.

"Wynter, it's me." Two hands wrapped around me and turned me around. Pale blue eyes met mine and I blinked. "Remember me?"

I frantically looked around. There was nobody else, just him.

"Sasha," I croaked, with despair. My eyes burned and pain scratched at my chest and stole my breath. The sobs I desperately tried to contain choked me, making each inhale and exhale physically painful.

He nodded and I burst into tears. There was no stopping the floodgate of tears. Sasha's big arms wrapped around me and my body shook with sobs.

"Who did this to you?" he growled.

My sobs wrecked me and words refused to come out. How could I tell him? The fucking idiot in me still cared about what would happen to Bas. I shouldn't care. I wouldn't care. One day, but right now, I just couldn't utter those words. Besides, if Bas and his father were so ruthless, it would put Uncle and Mom in danger. Juliette and Killian, my friends. I couldn't let anything happen to them, and I knew the moment I uttered Gio DiLustro, Uncle would go on a warpath against all of them.

"Tell me," he demanded, his chest vibrating under my cheek. I shook my head against it. I'd never say the name.

"We're getting an audience," he grumbled, taking off his suit jacket. I raised a blank stare to his pale blue one. The moment he rested his jacket on my shoulders, I flinched and a muscle in his jaw tightened.

"Let me take you home." Something bitter passed through his eyes, like ghosts haunting him. The thought made no sense, but I couldn't shake it off. "I'll call Brennan from the car."

I jerked my whole body out of his hold and shook my head frantically. "No. Not Uncle," I begged, my voice hoarse. "Not his house. Not yet."

He glanced around us, growling at the audience that immediately dispersed. "Come in the car with me. My brother is there. We'll take you somewhere safe."

"Not home," I repeated, my demand clear. If Uncle saw me, it would be bad. I couldn't let that happen. It was my burden to bear. Even knowing who Bas was, I willingly went to him. Despite the warnings I'd heard, I trusted Basilio DiLustro.

"No, not home," he promised, then his arm came around my waist, urging me forward.

His one, bulky arm around me, he nudged me to the car and I followed while staring at the ink on his fingers. They looked like symbols, but I couldn't distinguish what they were. My sight was blurry from the tears, my focus even more so.

Once by the black Mercedes G-Benz, he opened the back door and helped me into it, then slid next to me. His brother was behind the wheel. I clutched Sasha's jacket as I met Alexei's pale blue eyes in the rearview mirror.

Something dark and unhinged flashed in his eyes that had me shrinking into the seat.

"What in the fuck happened to her? Who?" He spat out in Russian, his voice colder than the Arctic temperatures. Sasha responded in Russian too and my eyes ping-ponged between the two.

"N-nothing," I breathed, my voice sounding slightly distorted from my lip that started to swell. I swept my tongue across it and the cut stung badly.

"You understand Russian?" Sasha and Alexei asked at the same time, surprise on their faces.

I nodded. "It was an elective, and for some reason, it worked for me," I muttered, each muscle on my face hurting as I talked.

"Give me a name," Alexei said, the demand clear in his cold voice.

I shook my head.

"You know we can't let whoever did this to you get away with it," was Sasha's response.

"No," I replied stubbornly.

Sasha ran his tongue across his teeth with agitation. I took Sasha's big hand with both mine and squeezed desperately. "Please. Please, just let it go. I—I won't go around B—" I cut myself off just in time. "I won't go around that area. Please."

Alexei shook his head and reached for something in his pants. I watched with wide eyes, holding my breath. It was his cell, he flipped through and dialed a number.

"Nico, need surveillance on the east side of New York," he said, his voice monotone and raspy. Then he recited the block of the city he found me in.

"Please," I pleaded in a hoarse whisper. "Please, no. I—I'll give you anything."

Alexei ignored me and I turned to Sasha. "Whoever it is, Wynter, don't worry. We'll protect you. They'll never get to you again."

I shook my head with desperation and my vision blurred, with tears and pain. The physical pain didn't compare to the ache in my heart. It was supposed to be an organ that breathed life into a body but each pump and beat of it hurt worse than anything else I had ever experienced before.

"That's impossible," Alexei grumbled into a phone and my eyes left Sasha to stare at Alexei, trying to read his impossibly passive expression.

"Jesus, you're bleeding all over," Sasha hissed, then brought a handkerchief to my face, the movement reminding me of Bas.

My ears started to ring, my lungs closed up and my breaths came out ragged. I couldn't breathe. I gripped the hem of his jacket and my body started to tremble. Tears stung my cuts, streaming down my cheeks.

"Fuck," Alexei muttered from the front seat. "I'll talk to you later, Nico. Keep trying. Sasha and I want that name."

Sasha pulled me into a bear hug and I shook against him. The knowledge I'd never have Bas cut through my chest, splitting my heart wide open. My throat tightened and I squeezed my eyes shut.

I never had him, my heart whispered. It was all a lie.

"What did Nico say?" I could hear fury in Sasha's voice and it burned further fear through my veins. If DiLustro's name came out, they'd go hunting for Bas, his father... every DiLustro. If they didn't, Uncle Liam would for sure. No wonder Mom didn't want to come to New York.

"City surveillance was already erased," Alexei remarked, putting the car into drive. A tiny relief washed over me. "He'll check the private ones."

196

I had no idea what it meant. My body shook uncontrollably, and now that adrenaline wore off, the pain grew with each second.

"We have to take her to the hospital," Alexei grumbled. "Brennan will find out and burn down this fucking city. You know that, Sasha. We have to call him."

My teeth clattered as I desperately shook my head. "N-no. P-ple-ase."

"Wynter, the hospital will call him and you need medical care. Especially if you were r—" *Raped.*

He cut himself off. But I wasn't raped. It came pretty close but I got away.

"N-no h-hospital," I said coarsely, my whole body shaking uncontrollably "P-paper. They'll recognize me."

Sasha gave me a blank look, then turned to meet Alexei's eyes. "She's an Olympic figure skater," Alexei explained. If I wasn't in such a horrible state, I'd be surprised someone of his caliber even knew that.

Sasha must have thought the same because he muttered, "I didn't take you for a figure skating fanatic."

"Fuck off, Sasha," Alexei told him. "Aurora likes it."

He scrolled through his phone and dialed someone else as my whole body shook and a haze swelled in my brain.

"Cassio, we need to bring someone to your penthouse." Alexei's monotone voice filled the fog in my head. An invisible hand wrapped around my throat, cutting off my oxygen.

I tried to hold on to my consciousness, but the ringing in my ears grew and grew. I moved my head, at least I tried. "Sasha, I think—"

And the world went black.

Chapter Twenty-Seven

BASILIO

I should have known villains didn't get a happy ending.

Too much blood on my hands. Too many wrongs. But I realized over the last few hours that I'd tear this world apart. Piece by fucking piece, until I found her or some godforsaken place where I could put my pain.

This ache inside my chest clawed at my heart and soul. The pressure had been a constant companion, from the moment I walked into my home to find blood all over my hallway and living room. Finding my father there. But no Wynter.

I wished they could have traded places. I wished the Russians would have taken my father, not my woman. Though there was a feeling I couldn't shake off. My father *never* came to visit me. Fucking never. He preferred to summon me to his place. When I checked my surveillance, I found it to be wiped clean. Technically, the Russians could have done that too.

I had Angelo run the surrounding street surveillance in my presence, but we found most of it wiped out too. With one little exception. A glimpse of the golden curly hair stained with blood being put into a black Mercedes G-Benz three streets over. It was unmistakably Wynter, the exact shade of her golden-blonde curly hair. Barely two seconds captured, but it was enough to see how battered she was. And all we could get of the man who nudged her into the car was his large back and a glimpse of a tattoo on his finger.

The tag number led us fucking nowhere. Trying to find a different angle was fruitless too.

I'd never felt this helpless. I couldn't even allow myself to consider what happened to Wynter, wondering if she was still alive. Fear and fury simmered under my skin. I couldn't think with a clear head.

The moment I entered my house to find her gone, a gaping hole tore through my chest and grew by the second. My mind rattled, ready to unleash a fucking war and wreak havoc on everyone. Russians, Irish. Every. Fucking. One. They called me a villainous kingpin, but they'd get a taste of a psychotic kingpin.

Unless I got my girl back, I'd lose my goddamn shit.

All I could think was that I failed her. I didn't protect her. Just as I didn't protect my own mother.

My world was worthless without her in it. This hole in my chest hurt worse now than after I lost my mother.

I had Priest digging through Yale records. Surveillance. So far, we found nothing. Not a single fucking clue. Like she disappeared into thin air.

I reached the corner of a building that belonged to the Bratva. This was my second one in a matter of hours. I was desperate to locate her. I kept one captor alive from the last attack and questioned him. No answers. No clues. Fucking nothing.

The Bratva didn't own any buildings in the city, but right outside of it, they had a few warehouses. Crouching down, I peered around and found two men guarding the entrance.

My phone vibrated faintly. I entered the code into my phone to open it and found that the message was from Dante.

Dante: **Where are you?**

Me: **Busy.**

Priest: **Stop hunting blindly.**

Unless either one of them was able to give me information on Wynter, or surveillance on my house so I could see what happened to Wynter or who invaded my home, I had nothing to say. I had the best surveillance control system and for fucking what. There wasn't a second captured of the attack. Angelo must be getting sloppy in his old age, and I wanted to fucking kill him for it. Neither Angelo nor Priest were able to get information on Wynter's friends either.

Dante: **You're going to get yourself killed going after the Bratva alone.**

I wasn't alone. I brought along three of my best men. I locked eyes with them. "Keep one alive," I ordered.

A terse nod. And we raised our guns and fired. One down. Two down.

Bullets started flying. I followed the path and spotted the window where the bullets were coming from. I aimed and pulled the trigger. Another down. We ran towards the entrance, keeping a sharp eye. No bullets came.

I glanced at my man who scanned the building for body heat with our military-grade device. He raised five fingers. Excellent, this should be easy, then.

Bursting through the door, two attackers came after me. I shot one and ran towards the next one. The other three my men could handle. Out of bullets, I pulled my knife. The fucker jabbed at my stomach, but I dodged it and rammed my blade into his shoulder. He cried out and my next move was ramming my blade into his thigh.

Before he could attack me again, I grabbed him from behind and one arm locked around his throat. He kept struggling against me like a fucking madman. He hadn't seen crazy yet. With the butt of my gun, I hit his temple and his body went slack.

Half an hour later, my clothes were drenched in blood and I still had no answers.

His last words before he died were, "Pakhan wants the woman."

Was he talking about my woman?

Chapter Twenty-Eight

WYNTER

Voices in the distance were distorted. They made my head hurt. I could feel the tension so cold in the air. It licked over my flesh, sending a shiver through my body.

"Don't be fucking stupid, Sasha," a clear voice growled. "Brennan will tolerate a lot of things. Keeping something like this from him, he won't. He'll burn the city, the world, and go to war for this."

"She doesn't want to go to him," Sasha argued back. "Let her heal here. Or I can take her to my place but let the doctor finish cleaning out her wounds."

I tried hard to peel my eyelids open or at least move, but my body refused to obey.

"She might have a concussion." Another voice, a woman's. "If she does, this will come up. She's an Olympic skater, she'll have to undergo medical testing to check her physical condition. It will come up. She needs top physicians for this."

"Fuck you all," Sasha's voice grumbled. "As soon as the doctor's done, I'll take her to my place. If Brennan finds out, it will be on me."

"Don't be stupid, Sasha," the same woman's voice retorted dryly.

It sounded vaguely familiar. "Like Alexei or Vasili would let you fight him alone. You're pulling us all into it and forcing us to fight against him."

"You have to call Brennan," a man's voice argued. "At least tell him she's with you and she's okay. He just got his wife back and is preoccupied ensuring she's okay, but he'll be after Wynter. It is only a matter of hours."

"Was she raped?" an unfamiliar female's voice asked. My body shuddered and I opened my mouth to deny it. Except I couldn't hear my voice. Did I tell them that I wasn't?

"Jesus Christ. Brennan will lose his shit. He'll fucking burn us all and take us to war, regardless if he can win it or not." I wished I knew that voice. "Remember how bad it was when his sister was shot by DiLustro?" A sharp pain pierced through my chest. "He fucking burned their side of town. He hunted them and—"

My mind drifted away and a welcomed blackness filled my brain. And all the while voices stayed nearby.

Chapter Twenty-Nine

SASHA

I didn't give a shit what Cassio, Alexei, or anyone said.

I wouldn't break my promise to Wynter. Even after all these years, I remembered failing another woman. It resulted in her death. I'd stay with Wynter through it all, and if war with Brennan was needed to keep my promise, fuck it, I'd do it.

I had nothing better to do anyhow. I refused to fail this woman too.

The doctor examined her body and the sickness sat in the pit of my stomach with bruises and cuts all over her. She fought back whoever attacked her, there was no doubt of that. Her fists and knuckles proved it.

I refused to leave the room when the doctor went over her wounds and the nurse cleaned the blood from her body. There was so much of it. On her face, her hands, her thighs, her legs. She had been out for hours. Way too long. He couldn't speculate concussion, at least not until she woke up.

I just wished she would wake up now.

I'd take her to my place afterwards and she could stay there until she was ready to go. Whenever and wherever that might be. The lights of the city glowed through the windows and reflected against her hair.

Even in her battered state, the girl looked vulnerable and angelic.

I reached out and touched her forehead. No fever.

"I think she's just resting," the nurse said, trying to comfort me. Fuck, I should have continued tailing her. She and her friends were a recipe for disaster, especially among ruthless men like us.

What was Brennan thinking when he sheltered the girls so much that they couldn't distinguish reckless and dangerous from an adventure?

Tatiana, my sister, and Isabella, Vasili's wife, did some adventurous and crazy stuff but never reckless. Never dangerous.

"Should we do a brain scan?" I asked the nurse. Wynter hadn't woken up once.

The door opened behind me and I didn't need to turn around to know who it was. Alexei was just as disturbed with this as I was. For a different reason. He lived through it.

"Anything?" I shook my head in answer. I wasn't much for emotions, but fuck if they weren't choking me right now. Certain ghosts were hard to forget.

Alexei's hand came to my shoulder and rested there. He never fucking touched anyone except his wife, so I knew it shook him up to see Wynter like this.

"She's strong," he said in his monotone way.

I disagreed. She was weak. Too happy. Too careless. Too innocent.

I pulled up different footage of her, and fuck, the girl indeed was a figure skater. A fucking good one. But she was too goddamn soft. She even hugged girls that got disqualified in her competitions to comfort them.

Who fucking did that? You crushed your opponents, not hugged them.

"If you want to keep her," Alexei continued in his way, "I'll help you."

God, he sounded like I wanted to kidnap her and keep her as my pet.

"You two sound like idiots," Aurora's voice scolded us softly. She glanced at the nurse who got up and left the room. I guess the nurse wanted to ensure the girl was never alone with a man. "You can't keep her. She's a human being. I mean, what in the hell runs in the Niko-laev veins."

She shifted the baby on her hip. "She belongs with her family, Sasha. And you know that."

"Aurora," I gritted. I liked my sister-in-law, but God, I'd kill myself if she was my wife. So fucking opinionated. "Wynter will be with her family when she is ready to be with her family. Not a moment sooner."

"Have you met her before?" she asked curiously. When I shook my head, she continued curiously, "What is your obsession with her? She's a bit too young for you."

I clenched my hands. Why did everyone assume I wanted to fuck her, for Pete's sake.

"Aren't you a bit young for Alexei?" I retorted back dryly.

"The girl's not even twenty-one," she objected. "That doesn't compare to Alexei and me."

My jaw tightened and I gritted my teeth or risked snapping at my sister-in-law and then Alexei would go on one of his growl sessions or, even worse, try to fight while Wynter lay there immobile.

"Why isn't she waking up?" I asked again.

"I don't know," she answered as she walked over to Wynter's sleeping form. Little Kostya's eyes studied Wynter, and for the first time since he was born, he stayed focused for longer than a second. It had to be those golden curls. "The doctor said he's not certain whether she was assaulted. He'll have to do a rape kit, but he needs her consent."

She won't give it, I thought immediately. I'd bet my life on it.

Áine, Cassio's wife, offered to help if Wynter wanted someone to talk to when she woke up. It was bad timing to bring her here. Cassio and Alexei planned on having a double date. Of course, that went out the fucking window and everybody hovered in the penthouse.

Another set of footsteps. Fuck, this was like a whole fucking gathering in the sick room.

"Brennan called Nico," Cassio hissed under his voice. "He's been trying to call Wynter and getting no answer. She told him earlier today that she was staying with a friend."

"I thought the four girls were inseparable," Aurora said thoughtfully.

"Brennan said they always stuck together," Alexei confirmed.

"Davina is with Brennan. Juliette and Ivy are at the house, trying to figure out how to plan another heist without getting caught." She rolled her eyes to emphasize how reckless they were. "That means Wynter was probably with a boy."

"And you came up with that before or after she was assaulted?" They were all getting on my nerves. "Considering the state she's in, we can all come to the conclusion she wasn't with a girlfriend."

"Sasha—" Alexei growled.

Wynter's body stirred and all our heads snapped to her. Light green eyes cracked open and met mine. I jerked forward, leaning over her.

"Wyn?"

Dark bruises around her eyes and on the side of her face were stark against her pale skin.

Someone must have called the nurse and doctor back in because suddenly the two pushed us all away from her bed.

"Hello, dear," the doctor cooed to her like she was an infant. I fucking wanted to punch him. "Do you remember your name?" Wynter blinked slowly, then nodded. "Do you know how you got here?"

She stared at him for a moment as if she was trying to remember and then she slowly nodded.

"We cleaned up your cuts and bruises. We need to check for your concussion and do a rape kit." She instantly stiffened and I could have just smacked the stupid doctor upside his head. Cassio should really find a brighter doctor than this moron.

Her tongue swept over her dry lips. "I wasn't raped."

The doctor took her hand and gently patted it. "Let us just do a test and—"

Wynter jerked her hand back. "I just told you," she croaked. "I wasn't raped. I got away."

I watched her for any signs that she might be lying or in denial. I didn't think so. Her eyes came to me, ignoring everyone else.

"How long until the bruises and cuts go away?" she muttered, turning her head to look out the window.

"A few weeks." The doctor didn't look pleased to be shut down. He obviously didn't believe her. Not that it fucking mattered.

"Wynter, we have to call your uncle." Fucking Cassio, always wanted to do the right thing. Goddamn him!

Wynter's head turned back to us, her bruised eyes looking somehow defeated. "No. It'd bring war."

"Did the DiLustros do this to you?" Cassio asked sharply.

"It's none of your business," Wynter rasped, narrowing her eyes, though by the expression on her face, that little movement pained her.

"Wynter, I'm Áine. We can help you. Whatever you need. Someone to talk to, anything."

Wynter slid her legs from under the sheet off the bed and slowly sat up, all the while the nurse and the doctor protested. Ignoring them, her head tilted back and she stared at all of us unblinking.

"If you say anything to my uncle, I'll deny it." She let the words sink in. "I'll blame you if I have to. I'm not going back to Uncle and Mom until I'm healed."

Cassio growled at her and I took a step closer to Wynter, in case the idiot tried something.

"Try something, Cassio, and you're a dead man," I warned.

Silence and tension was thick in the room. Nothing new. It followed me everywhere.

"Please, I don't want anyone dying on my account," Wynter begged, realizing her words were taken as a threat. "I just want to stay away from my family for now."

Cassio let out a soft groan, clearly disagreeing with that request.

"You'll stay at my place until you're ready to go back," I told her firmly, glaring at my friends and daring them to say anything.

Wynter's bruised and swollen lips curved into a smile and I saw the resemblance of that girl who hugged fellow skaters offering comfort. This woman would never be tough.

"Thank you, Sasha."

She had the kind of smile that'd break hearts. Just like someone broke hers.

Chapter Thirty

WYNTER

I watched Sasha remove his holster, then pull his shirt over his head, revealing his muscled and tattooed torso. My heart didn't even skip a beat.

"Wyn, you really have no qualms staring at a man's body," Sasha remarked sarcastically.

"Don't tell me you're shy," I teased softly.

I'd been with Sasha at his place for the past two weeks and grew accustomed to his unique brand of humor. I was almost completely healed. Physically, at least. Nightmares plagued me and emotional scars refused to heal. I wasn't helping myself by not dealing with it. Except, each time I even thought about what happened, panic would tear through my chest, cold and dark, and my breathing would shallow.

So when Sasha had offered to teach me how to fight, I eagerly accepted the offer. I saw it as a way to heal. I'd get stronger and I'd never be caught vulnerable again. Not like that.

Uncle Brennan had gone ballistic. The only thing that kept him from attacking Sasha was Davina. Thank God for her. It had been the longest I'd gone without seeing my best friends. I missed them terribly, but I kept delaying the reunion with them. It would have been hard to explain the marks on my face.

"I'm far from shy," Sasha responded dryly. "Though most women avert their eyes in respect."

I rolled my eyes. "Sure they do," I muttered. "They are probably gawking with their mouths wide open." Sasha shook his head, disbelief crossing his expression. "Anyhow, I've seen plenty of athletes changing in my lifetime. You're nothing special."

Okay, a tiny lie. I had never seen an athlete built like him. Maybe if I dealt with MMA fighters, but certainly not figure skaters.

Sasha grinned that shark smile that I grew used to and hinted that the next thing out of the fearless mobster's mouth would be something inappropriate or just reckless.

"Trust me, Wyn. Everything about me is special."

I huffed but couldn't stop from smiling. He really was the most reckless man I'd ever met, but he had a heart of gold underneath that big chest. Any woman would be lucky to have him.

I turned my back to him as he continued changing. There was a limit to how much I should gawk.

"Do your tattoos mean anything, Sasha?" I asked, staring at the sparring mats he had all over his gym. He had punching bags in the far corner, even fencing equipment, and then one whole wall full of knives. Kind of disturbing but there was no way I'd complain.

I wanted to learn how to fight and how to defend myself successfully. I'd never be vulnerable again.

"Some of them I got when I was in the military," Sasha answered.

"I didn't know mobsters joined the military."

His chuckle filled the space behind me. "You'd be surprised to know how far our reach is."

Something had been on my mind ever since Sasha brought me to his place. It was stupid, but I almost expected Bas to find me. After all, he was able to wipe out surveillance and all related evidence of us burning down Garrett's house. So theoretically, he should be able to find me.

"Okay, I'm decent," Sasha announced, his voice directly behind me.

I slowly turned around and met those remarkable eyes. I truly hoped he knew how grateful I was for his help. For everything.

"Sasha," I started hesitantly and he waited, as if he knew something big would come out of my mouth. "Has anyone... has anyone been looking for me?"

He stilled, his eyes sharp on me. "Like who?"

I still hadn't given him a name. I'd never give him a name, though deep down I knew he guessed.

"Anyone," I whispered.

"No."

The longing in my heart ached. It actually hurt worse than all my bruises. And while my cuts and bruises healed, the ache in my heart didn't. It became part of my heartbeat. And my mind whispered things I didn't want to admit. Bas had used me. He didn't give a shit about me, otherwise he'd have searched for me.

Even more worrisome was that I shot his father. So far, no retaliation had happened. Uncle had placed extra security on everyone. Whether it was a result of Davina's kidnapping, I was unsure.

"Uncle and my friends are safe?" I asked. I debated for weeks whether I should warn them, because there was a chance what I had done could cause my family to be dragged into a war. Except, I didn't know how to say it without risking Basilio's life.

Disgusted at myself for even caring whether he lived or died, I felt like I betrayed my own family each day I kept this secret.

"They are safe, Wyn," Sasha said, his eyes watching me and seeing too much. The man was too insightful. It was probably what kept him safe, but in my case, it was scary.

I forced a smile and gave a terse nod. "Let's get started."

I ran my miles in this gym. I worked my ballet and Pilates here. Even my choreography. The only thing I couldn't do here was ice-skate, but I didn't dare go back to the ice rink. It was too risky.

Sasha handed me the knife he'd made especially for me.

I took a breath and tried to forget everything, gripping it tightly. I focused on Sasha's instructions.

"Keep eye contact. Don't look in the direction you're aiming for. Put all your muscle into it. Aim for the kill."

"You give too many instructions," I muttered my complaint and then advanced on him. Just as he made a grab for me, I aimed for a kick between his legs.

He chuckled. "That's right. Don't play fair," he praised, though unfortunately he caught my foot before I could make contact.

I landed on my back with a heavy thud while my breath swished out of me. I thanked all the saints that Sasha's mats were cushioned so well, otherwise it would have hurt.

I stared at the skylight ceiling, the clear blue sky of his penthouse gym room giving me a glimpse of a gorgeous day outside. So in contrast with how I felt on the inside.

Two weeks. It felt like a lifetime of changes were crammed into two weeks.

"You know, your girl squad is blowing up my phone," Sasha said as he sat down next to me. "Driving me nuts, in fact."

I closed my eyes. "I miss them," I whispered. "I just don't want to upset them. And Juliette would go on a rampage if she knew—"

Sasha chuckled. "I'll help her and ensure she comes out of it alive."

I turned my head to the side to find an unapologetic look on his face. This man would gladly go on a killing spree.

"If we knew you when we were growing up," I told him, "maybe we'd all know how to handle ourselves and take care of our own problems."

But then I probably wouldn't have asked Bas for help. I missed him so much. On one hand, I hoped he'd find me. On the other hand, I had to keep reminding myself that it was all a lie. He didn't love me. Except, I couldn't help but ache for him. I promised him I'd stay, but all along he lied to me. Played me for a fool. There was no future for us.

Did he know what his father had done to mine? Did he know his father destroyed my mother?

"Do you have a sister?" I asked him curiously. I didn't know much about the Nikolaev family other than there were three brothers.

"I do. Tatiana is the youngest of the siblings. She and her friend, who is now married to my oldest brother, were fucking nuts during their college years." His sister and sister-in-law were lucky to have him. The way he talked about them, I knew he cared about them a lot. "Though those two can't quite compete with you and your friends' crime spree."

I scoffed. "We're the worst criminals on this planet."

It didn't escape me that he didn't contradict me. We robbed my uncle and failed. We barely escaped Chicago unscathed. We got caught stealing from Priest, though thankfully not by him. He'd probably recite us our last rites and then kill us all. Obviously, Bas lied when he said he'd protect me.

Goddamn it! I couldn't forget about Bas. I kept going over every single minute of our encounter from the moment I met him, trying to spot the signs I might have missed. I couldn't find any. Maybe he was just exceptionally good at deceit.

"You'll have to talk to someone eventually," Sasha interrupted my thinking. "Àine, Cassio's wife, has seen some shit. Maybe it would help to talk to her?"

I returned my gaze to stare at the skylight and clear blue skies. What could I possibly say to make sense of it all? It was quite simple. I fell in love with the enemy. I could have overlooked that. His father shooting my mother and Bas using me to gain more power for himself, I could not.

Gio DiLustro's words still rang in my ears. How could my mother ever accept Bas when he resembled his father so much? And then there was the matter of Bas using me to strengthen their position with the Russians.

"You promise not to go after them?" I asked quietly.

Ba-boom. Ba-boom. Ba-boom.

"I promise."

I closed my eyes for a moment, then exhaled and opened my eyelids.

"I ran into Basilio as I was sneaking out of my uncle's house several months ago," I started softly, keeping my gaze on the clear blue skies. "I jumped off the balcony and he caught me." I snickered softly, "Romantic, I thought."

"More like *Romeo and Juliet*," he snorted. "Tragic."

"Anyhow, I didn't know who he was until I overheard Uncle and Quinn, his go-to guy, talking. Yes, I knew the DiLustros and Brennans weren't on good terms. I still liked him." I sighed heavily. "And when we burned down Garrett's house, we were out of sorts. A lucky coincidence, I ran into Bas again." Now, I wondered if it was by design. I questioned everything. "I asked for his help."

Sasha listened intently. I kept waiting for him to interrupt but he didn't.

"He asked for a dinner date with me as his payment for helping us out," I rasped, thick emotions choking me. "You can laugh all you want, Sasha, but it was the most amazing date ever." My stupid lip quivered and tears welled in my eyes, while all the feelings I kept hidden squeezed my throat, making it hard to breathe.

"I'm not laughing, Wyn."

My lungs burned and I bit into my lip to get myself together. *Emotions make us weak,* my mother would say. *And love shatters us.* It

215

turned out she was right. Partially anyhow. Losing Bas shattered me. Loving him made me whole.

"I told him I'd stay with him," I continued, my voice barely above a whisper. "I was going to tell Mom I'd practice for the Olympics here or not at all." Maybe what happened was karma, because I was being so damn selfish. "Bas said he forgot something in his club, two blocks away. He left. And his father—" My fingers curled into a fist, my fingernails dug into my palms. It was good though. The pain helped me stay focused. "His father showed up and tried to—"

God, I couldn't even say the words. *He tried to rape me*, my mind screamed. Even knowing what Bas's father said, I couldn't tell Sasha that it was all a setup. I just couldn't. Maybe saying them out loud would make them too real.

So I said nothing. Too scared to face the truth. Too scared it would cost Bas his life.

Sasha stood up, while I still lay immobile. "Want to train some more?"

I nodded.

Holding out his hand, I put my fingers into his palm and he pulled me to my feet.

"Wyn?"

Standing chest to chest, I tilted my head so I'd meet his gaze. "I'll never betray your trust." I swallowed the lump in my throat. "But if either one of them hurt you again, I'll kill them. Promise or no promise."

It was all a girl could ask for.

"Again?" he asked and I nodded.

I'd go as many times as necessary.

Until I could beat men like Gio DiLustro. Because I swore to myself that I'd make that man pay one day.

I'd break him, just the way he broke my mother.

Just the way he attempted to break me.

Chapter Thirty-One

WYNTER

T hree weeks since I felt Bas's lips on mine. Three weeks since I inhaled him deep into my lungs. Three weeks since I felt alive.

I stepped into the shower and turned it on. Cold water washed over my skin, raining droplets, but before shivers started, the water turned hot, painful against my skin. Yet, the pain didn't compare to this all-consuming ache in my chest. I leaned back against the wall and slowly sank down.

The kingpin necklace Basilio gave me no longer hung around my neck. Instead, I wrapped it around my wrist and used it as a bracelet. I kept the kingpin skull hidden under the chain, worried someone would recognize it.

Pulling my legs up against my chest, I started crying. I missed him. No matter what I did, I'd never be able to forget him. Each breath I took was for him. Maybe he just wanted my cursed connection to the Russians, but all of it couldn't have been a lie.

Could it?

I've asked Sasha to look into my grandmother. Winter Volkov. I needed to know more about my family. They've kept me in the dark long enough.

The history wasn't a good one. It began with a kidnapping by my grandfather. Like a thief in the night, Grandpa snuck into Russia and stole a young woman. My grandmother. In order to ensure the Pakhan wouldn't join the Syndicate. He fell in love. But my grandmother died giving birth to my mother and the war between the Brennans and the Volkov Pakhan escalated.

Jesus Christ. Grandfather never stopped mourning her. Even now, after all these years, he never spoke of anyone but the woman he lost. The woman he stole from her home, but he failed to mention that part.

Was it his punishment? To lose something which wasn't meant to be his and then have a reminder in his daughter and granddaughter. How many times has he told me I looked like his true love and the reminder was always bittersweet.

Just like everything reminded me of Bas.

A scent. A word. A song.

The image of Bas kneeling in front of me, with my dirty foot in his hands and looking up at me like he owned me. His father's words were killing me slowly from the inside. Poisonous and shattering words that altered my world forever.

Yet, what if they were lies? Uncle lied too. Yes, his intentions were good, but he had lied to me for so long. Maybe Gio lied too.

Or maybe I was a fool.

God, this was torture. I was falling apart on the inside.

When I was around Sasha, I was able to maintain my composure. It was required of me since I started competing. No outbursts or reactions in public were ever tolerated. But when I was alone, my heart shattered over and over again.

I dragged myself out of the shower and put on my clothes. White jeans and a green t-shirt. Throwing a fleeting glance in the mirror, I made sure the reflection that stared back at me didn't look like my inner state. Thankfully, I looked fine on the outside. Probably thanks to Sasha. He bought me some new clothes and got some of my stuff from the girls so I'd feel more comfortable.

With a heavy sigh, I put my "I'm fine" face on and padded to the living room where a large floor-to-ceiling window offered magnificent views of the city. It was only nine in the morning and Sasha had actual work to do today, so I'd spend it alone.

He probably has to kill someone, I thought wryly to myself. Did it bother me? No, not really. He swore to me he only killed bad people. So I guess that was okay. Fuck, maybe my moral compass has been skewed all along.

My sigh sounded loud in the spacious, empty penthouse decorated in white and black.

Three weeks since I walked away from the DiLustros. I'd stayed with Sasha in his penthouse on the Jersey side overlooking New York City. It was almost torture because it reminded me of my first date with Bas.

And just like a fool that liked to open the wound and let it bleed all over again, I'd stare at the city every morning and night, and remember our first dance. His hot breath against my skin and his words in my ear.

The sound of the doorbell filled the penthouse and I jumped, startled. Glancing around, I stood unsure whether I should answer it or not.

Then banging on the door. Whoever it was, he or she wasn't happy. They banged like maniacs.

"We know you're in there." Juliette's voice was muffled, and I couldn't help but roll my eyes. Well, the maniacal banging on the door made sense now. "Open the goddamn door or I'm going to kick it in."

"Always so dramatic," I muttered under my breath, but I headed for the door and unlocked it, then came face-to-face with my three best girlfriends.

Three sets of blue, gray, and hazel eyes stared back at me. My three best friends regarded me with pity and sorrow. It gutted me and somewhere deep down a scream bubbled in my throat. I didn't want pity. I wanted to scream at them that I had survived and I was stronger now. But instead, I just smiled and opened the door wider.

"Want to come in?" I asked, my voice raspy.

One moment they stared, the next all three threw themselves at me and wrapped their arms around me. It was like getting suffocated with love.

"I missed you, Wyn." Juliette's voice was slightly high-pitched with emotions.

I swallowed the lump in my throat. "I missed y'all, too."

"Killian wanted to attack this building," Ivy announced. A choked laugh escaped me. That sounded like my cousin. "It was so fucking tense without you," she added. "Brennan screams into the phone at everyone and anyone, demanding you be brought home or he'll wipe the Nikolaev men off the face of this planet."

"Davina had to distract him by any means necessary," Jules added, rolling her eyes. "Sex every day, all day long. In the bed, on the desk, in the bathroom... fucking everywhere. I'm trying hard to unhear those noises."

Davina smacked her against her shoulder. "It worked, didn't it?" Davina grumbled. "You wanted to plan the attack with Killian."

Jules smiled guilty. "Well, we have to learn strategy of attack someday."

And just like that, things were back to normal. Like nothing had happened, but a lot did.

"Come in," I urged them in.

Once inside, Juliette whistled. "Wow, so this is how fucking Russians live, huh?"

I winced at the sound of her tone. Uncle Liam's dislike for Russians was always evident, but now that I learned some of my heritage, I didn't know how to take it. Ignoring her usual comments, I led them into the living room, and instead of sitting on the couch, the four of us sat on the floor and crisscrossed our legs.

Just like we did in our small dorm room. It seemed ages ago, yet it was only last month.

"What the hell happened, Wyn?" Juliette wasted no time. "Why did you refuse to see us?"

I sighed.

"Damn it, Jules," Davina scolded her. "We said we'd give her time."

My cousin ignored her. "I was worried sick. Wondering if you are okay or what you're hiding." I swallowed hard. "I know you're hiding something. Something happened and you don't want us to know."

I shook my head and tried to smile but I failed miserably.

"Damn it, Jules," Ivy groaned. "Stop it. You're upsetting her and she'll kick us out. Let her tell us when she's ready."

Since when has Ivy come to her senses.

"I'm fine." I waved my hand.

"You're not fine," my cousin protested. "We grew up together. I know when you're hurting and one look at you and I know you're hurt."

The lump in my throat grew bigger and bigger, and tears burned in the back of my eyes, while my heart and my soul shuddered. Juliette stilled and our eyes connected. She had never seen me like this. After all, it wasn't every day you fell for your enemy.

My villain.

I still thought of him as mine.

A lone tear rolled down my cheek and my lip trembled. Before I saw her take a step, Jules wrapped me into her arms. I wouldn't cry. I couldn't cry. If I started, I wouldn't stop.

"It's okay," she murmured. "I'm sorry, I didn't mean to upset you."

"It's okay," I croaked, barely finding my voice.

"No, it's not."

The next moment, Davina and Ivy joined in, attempting to smother me with love, I guess.

"You know we're here for you," Davina whispered. "Whenever. Wherever. You don't have to hide here. I can keep Liam at bay and warn him to give you space." I nodded. "Just come home with us. We miss you."

I bit into my lip, tasting copper on my tongue. She was right, maybe it was time I stopped hiding. I was running out of training time with Derek too.

"Tell me what I've missed," I asked instead.

"Ah, no, no, no," Ivy protested. "You tell us what we've missed."

"Are you and Sasha a thing?" Juliette reverted to her mouth-without-filter mode. "Is that the reason you want to stay here? Because Brennan hates the Russians?"

I sighed. In the group chat we've had she kept complaining about me staying here. With Russians of all people. I almost regretted that Sasha got me a new phone. Juliette needed a filter.

"I already told you, Jules," I muttered. "We're not a thing. He's just helping me through some stuff."

"We help each other through stuff," she protested. "He's an outsider."

Ivy rolled her eyes. "So are Davina and I."

Juliette shook her head. "No, we are a quad squad and no new applicants are accepted. Sasha has to go."

Davina rolled her eyes. "And what do you want me to do with my husband?" she asked Jules dryly. "Want me to get rid of him too?"

"Well, since you asked—" Juliette started and the three of us groaned.

"We should find *you* a fucking guy, so we can make you get rid of him," Ivy mumbled annoyed.

My cousin just shrugged. "And I would. Men are an unnecessary distraction." Jesus, maybe my mother's words actually rubbed off on Juliette. "Besides, we have bigger problems."

You never knew what'd come out of Juliette's mouth.

"Like what?" I asked, when it became apparent neither Davina nor Ivy wanted to ask her. They probably worried what kind of crazy trouble she'd get us into. Rightly so.

"Well, we're all out of money we stole," Juliette announced and all our eyes snapped to her.

"That was almost fifty million, Jules," I said, appalled that she'd spend so much in just a matter of weeks.

"Well, we bought that extra piece of land and paid all cash," she muttered. "Then there were taxes, architects for the buildings and design, how to lay it out, permits, material. It's all gone. Boom." She waved her hands in the air, as if mimicking an explosion.

"How much are we short to finish?" I asked in an exasperated tone.

She shrugged. "We still need three buildings and one extra dormitory. Then I think we'll be done."

"Did we get features we didn't need?" Davina asked, annoyance on her face. "I really hoped to do this without actually using anyone's money but our own."

"Theoretically, stolen money," Ivy reminded us.

Juliette rolled her eyes. "We don't need a reminder anymore. We need to finish this so we can move on obtaining a license from the board of education, creating a staff, curriculum, and who knows what else."

"Wow," I murmured, slightly impressed. Juliette might have finally found her thing.

"How do you feel about playing a round of poker?" she asked.

"Juliette, we said no more," Davina groaned. "Liam will lose his shit. There is only so much calming, distracting sex I can have."

Juliette raised her palm and faced it at Davina. "Listen, step-mother, I don't need reminders of your hanky-panky with my father, who's not really my father, but I think of him as a father."

"Well, confuse us more, why don't you?" Ivy chimed in. "If we get in trouble and my father finds out, I'll be shipped to Ireland."

"Like a bag of potatoes," Davina added.

"We won't let that happen." Juliette swished her hand. "If we get at least one of the school buildings built, we won't need Dad's place. We can just stay there. The school will need all our attention anyhow."

"Yeah, let's stay there while workers are banging and building shit," Ivy said sarcastically. "It's my dream come true."

I raised my eyebrow, surprised at Ivy's reluctance to get into trouble. Usually it was Jules and Ivy who dove headfirst into mayhem.

"Okay, this is what we need to do," I announced. "Juliette *will not* be paying bills. We need to be smarter about our spending. I know we want everything to be perfect, but we can always upgrade later, once the school brings in profit."

"I'll handle all business arrangements and contracts," Davina agreed. "Wynter, you take care of the funds."

I grinned, feeling lighter for the first time in over two weeks. "I'll be the banker."

"Sounds good to me," Juliette commented. "I want to be the enforcer and kill people."

The three of us shared a glance and rolled our eyes.

"You've handled everything amazingly so far," I commended Jules. "You keep arranging the next steps, but let Davina do negotiations. I know you want everything perfect and it will be, but not at the point where we have to keep playing poker."

Juliette nodded her agreement.

"I can help with decor and furniture," Ivy offered. "When we are at the interior-decorating stage, we should also start making offers to individuals we want working for the school."

The four of us nodded, excited about our long-term goals.

"But until then, we need to find someone to rob." Juliette had to ruin the moment. Ignoring our protests, she continued, "I think we should rob Nico Morrelli."

"Are you crazy?" Ivy hissed. "Didn't I tell you he's known as the Wolf?"

She shrugged. "So what? There are four of us and one of him."

"Jules, stop it. We're going to get in trouble," I told her. "We haven't been successful with any of it. But I can go there and play poker."

That wasn't stealing.

"Exactly," she agreed. "You're counting cards. It's not stealing exactly."

I sighed. "It's not strictly legal either."

"Actually, I agree with Juliette," Davina chimed in, surprising me. She usually sided on the sane side, with me. "Let's go into one of Nico's casinos in Baltimore and play poker."

"You know there is no way to get millions off counting cards," I murmured. "At least not the normal way and not bringing attention to ourselves."

"We're so fucked," Ivy groaned, pushing her hand through her red hair. "So fucking fucked."

"Let's do it for old time's sake," Davina said, locking her eyes with me. "But then if we fail, then we look at *normal* ways to get money. Investors. Liam wants to invest and he doesn't want any stake in the school."

Ah, so that was the reason she agreed with Jules. "If we do this, no more stealing," Davina told her firmly. "And I want your word, Juliette. Promise, blood vow, the whole fucking nine yards."

It would be comical if it was anyone else.

"Fine, you have my blood vow and all that shit," Juliette agreed. "I'll be a better enforcer anyhow."

"I'm sure," Ivy grumbled. "But first you have to catch a bad guy and kill him without shitting your pants."

And just like that, the four of us rolled over Sasha's Persian rug laughing like four idiots.

"Taking Sasha's car was a good call." Davina beamed, glancing around with wide eyes. "This freaking car is nice."

I shrugged. Sasha offered if I had to go anywhere to take his Mercedes G-Benz. He had one in every color. Davina drove the girls over in my Jeep, but I thought it was too risky driving around in it. DiLustro would notice it, I was certain.

"The back seats are perfectly leveled and wide," Davina continued. "I wouldn't have to bend over to put the baby into a child seat."

Wait? What?

"What?" Juliette screeched, her eyes wide. "What baby? Your sister's?"

Davina kept looking around the car, evaluating it and I glanced in the mirror. The moment our eyes met, I knew it wasn't for her sister's baby.

"I'm pregnant," she announced, chewing on her bottom lip. "Surprise!"

God, the look on Ivy's and Juliette's faces was comical. Maybe I would have had the same reaction if I wasn't driving. I returned my eyes to the road. I was happy for my best friend and my uncle. I really was.

Then why did I feel this slither of envy spreading through my veins. It was ugly and made me feel like shit. It wasn't like I'd have a baby anytime soon. Skating was my priority right now.

"You're quiet, Wyn," Davina noted.

I shook my head and smiled. "Just thinking how wonderful it will be to have a niece or a nephew," I told her. "I'm really happy for you. Both of you."

"Man, I thought you were going to wait to have kids," Juliette groaned.

She shrugged. "It happened sooner than I anticipated. I'm not sorry about it."

"Of course not," Ivy said quickly. "And we're all happy for you."

Ivy's eyes flickered my way, the worry in her hazel gaze unmistakable. I just nodded and returned my attention to the road. We still had another hour to go before we reached Baltimore.

The silence for the next five minutes felt louder than all the screaming Jules could muster. The big elephant in the room, or the car in our case, would eventually be brought up. I didn't think for a moment they'd pretend it never happened. Especially not Juliette.

"Who hurt you, Wyn?" Ivy finally asked. It surprised me that she beat Juliette to the punch.

I stared ahead of me and my vision blurred as tears stung, threatening to spill. I blinked, trying to hold them back. But I lost the fight. Tears burned a hot trail down my cheeks and I wiped them angrily with the back of my hand.

Juliette's hand wrapped around me from behind, the reach awkward because she had to do it over the seat.

"I'm fine," I said with a strained smile.

"No, you're not," Juliette protested softly. "And it's okay to admit it. The fucking Italian broke your heart."

I shook my head. I didn't want Juliette getting any ideas.

"No, it's not that," I muttered. I was sick and tired of the tears and wallowing in self-pity. People went through worse things than a heartbreak and a crazy almost father-in-law who tried to rape and kill you.

"Then what is it?" she spat bitterly. "You've never disappeared on us. You never ignore your mom or uncle. And then you go and stay with that Russian. It had to be something bad."

Anguish flooded my veins and cut through each breath I took.

"Things with Bas didn't work out," I murmured softly. The three of them held their breath, waiting for me to continue. I'd rather they hadn't. I'd rather Juliette started to spit out threats. But none of them said a thing. "I—I found out something Uncle and Mom kept from me."

Juliette stiffened. "Are you adopted too?" she whispered, disbelief on her face.

I shook my head. "No, I found out that Mom was shot in her knee. It was what ended her career. Gio DiLustro." And my boyfriend's father did it.

"What the fuck?" the three of them whispered. "Are you sure?" Jules asked.

I nodded, my eyes on the road. "Yes, I'm sure." My eyes focused on the road, though my mind was somewhere far away. "Brennans and DiLustros are enemies because Gio DiLustro tried to use Mom for her connections."

"What connections?" the three of them asked.

"Oh, just a tiny insignificant detail," I retorted bitterly. "Mom's connection to the Russians. I learned that Grandpa kidnapped my grandmother. She was the daughter of the Pakhan, the head of the Russian mafia."

"Russian mafia?" Juliette repeated, blinking confused.

"But I thought Brennans hated Russians," Ivy muttered.

I shrugged. "I think there is a lot we don't know. Uncle kept us in the dark about a lot of it. Mom, too."

Although, I couldn't blame Mom. I could imagine losing the ability to ice-skate was like losing a limb for her. I've seen her figure skating tapes. She was magnificent on the ice.

"We should talk to them about it," Davina recommended. "Don't let it fester."

"They need to be confronted," Jules agreed.

It was too late for that. They kept us in the dark and I fell into the trap. If I had known what Gio had done to Mom, I'd have never gone around Bas. Would I? The familiar pain swelled in my chest. Love had turned bitter. Betrayal stung. But I pushed it all down into a deep, dark corner for now. I'd deal with it some other time.

"Let's focus on going into Morrelli's casino and me counting cards so we can get some cash," I told her. "Please do that for me," I pleaded softly, my gaze finding her eyes in the rearview mirror. "Please."

Jules's blue eyes held mine, searching my face. For what, I didn't know. But whatever it was, she finally caved in.

"Fine," she agreed and Davina's hand came to my shoulder and squeezed in comfort.

It made no sense that I told so much more to Sasha, not my girl-friends. Maybe it was easier because Sasha was a stranger until three weeks ago.

An hour later, the four of us strode into the Morrelli & Associates casino, downtown Baltimore. We changed into our dresses in the parking garage, then entered the casino. It took exactly twenty-two minutes for Nico Morrelli to show up at the table I sat down at merely five minutes ago.

"Ladies," he greeted us, his wolflike gray eyes traveling over the four of us. The three-piece suit he wore was dark blue with thin gray stripes. He just needed an old-fashioned hat and he'd give Al Capone vibes. Except this guy was a lot hotter than Al Capone and a lot taller. "You'll come with me."

Well, that didn't take long at all. I sighed and put my cards down.

"We want our money back," I said coolly, meeting his steel gaze.

The man was deadly; it was written all over him. But I felt no fear. Maybe after what happened with Gio, my tolerance for threats grew.

His mouth curved into a smile and he pushed his hands into his suit pockets. "Of course, Miss. Flemming." Then he turned to Davina, Juliette, and Ivy. "After you, ladies."

Juliette came up to me and the reckless cousin that she was, she whispered, "You know there are four of us. We could take him down."

I shook my head, suddenly feeling tired of all the bullshit. As if we could take anyone down.

"He's probably calling Uncle," I muttered. "We haven't done anything wrong. So let's not kill the old man and get out of this intact."

"But—" Juliette started and I cut her off.

"Remember the deal with Davina," I reminded her. "No more heists."

She blew out a frustrated breath. "Such bullshit," she huffed. "You are not even trying to be a good criminal."

I rolled my shoulders. "Sorry, I'm preoccupied with other shit."

Her eyes glanced my way and she finally dropped it. Five minutes later, we were in front of the luxury casino with a limo waiting for us. Nico Morrelli shuffled us into it and sat in the back with us, unbuttoning his jacket and revealing his holster.

"I better not get shipped back to Ireland for this shit," Ivy spat. "I told you we're the worst."

Nico glanced at her, amusement in his expression.

"We didn't do anything wrong," Davina assured her. "It's probably because we left town and Liam didn't know."

I huddled in my seat and pressed my cheek to the window, watching the city buildings pass us. I felt Nico's occasional looks my way. I wondered what he knew or didn't know. Over the last two weeks, Sasha gave me previews of who's who in the underworld. According to him, Nico Morrelli was one of the few men who could get information on everyone. Sometimes he knew stuff that people themselves didn't know about themselves.

Did he know who I was? Some fucking Russian mafia princess. Did he know I'd fallen for the enemy?

No, my heart screamed. Basilio couldn't be the enemy. I had to be the stupidest person on this planet, because my heart still wanted him. Only him.

My throat clogged and I dug my fingernails into my palms, focusing on the physical pain. This love for Bas splintered me apart, piece by fucking piece. I closed my eyes, fighting the tears stinging my eyes and threatening to spill.

The drive to Nico's place passed in utter silence. It was only when the car stopped that I finally opened my eyes. We were stopped at the gate, and from the looks of it, the entire property was surrounded by tall fences and trees.

The gate slid to the right and the driver drove through the entry and followed the winding road through the woods until we reached a clearing.

At the end of the clearing a large manor estate stood. It'd look immaculate and pristine, if not for kids running around.

"It's like a fucking daycare here," Juliette muttered and Davina elbowed her to shut up. The car came to a stop in front of the marble grand staircase, cascading in front of the house.

Jesus, talk about elaborate!

The moment Nico exited the vehicle, two identical girls who looked to be roughly seven came running his way.

"Dad, Dad."

And I watched mesmerized as the ruthless mobster lowered down and grinned at his girls. Juliette and I didn't have that. Not because Uncle wasn't a caring man, but because he was on the East Coast, while the two of us were mostly in California.

The pair of identical blue eyes peeked at the open door and we slowly made our way out of the limo too.

"Hello, girls," Davina greeted them. "I'm Davina."

"Wynter," I introduced myself, then Juliette and Ivy followed suit.

"Sasha and the old man are here already, Daddy," one of them announced and Juliette snickered.

"She called your husband the old man," Juliette snorted.

"That's your dad, woman," Davina retorted back dryly. "And I could go for evil stepmother if you don't quit it, Jules."

"Now there is an idea for a Halloween costume," Ivy said, trying to stifle her laugh.

"If you three are finished, let's go find them before Uncle tries to kill Sasha," I snapped at all three. "Which way is it, Mr. Morrelli?"

"Go run and tell Mommy we have four more guests," he told the twins and the two ran off before he even finished the statement. He climbed the stairs and the four of us followed.

We took in his home. The wealth and luxury were evident everywhere. I could hear the echoes of laughter and music. A baby crying.

"Is this how happy homes sound?" I muttered under my breath.

Juliette and I shared a glance. We didn't exactly have an unhappy childhood, but it was a quiet one. Neither one of us understood Mom's need to have a regimented schedule for us. I understood it now, but not before.

Sometimes Jules and I would fantasize about a big family and lots of music and laughter when we were little. But then we grew out of it. We thought it was just a fairy tale.

Then realizing I'd stopped and stared in the direction of the laughter, I resumed walking past the grand foyer with a large crystal chandelier and caught up to Nico.

"We're heading to my office," Nico explained, directing us all to the left wing of his house. As we approached it, I could hear Uncle's and Sasha's voices. They both sounded angry, though I couldn't distinguish the words that were being spoken.

The moment we stepped inside Nico's office, the smell of cigars and viable tension slammed into me.

Two sets of blue eyes, one pale as the clearest sky and one dark as the deepest ocean, and neither looked happy.

"Sorry, Sasha," I muttered, going for the easy first. "We were going to bring back the car."

He shrugged. "Just a car."

I turned to face my uncle for the first time after the night the Nikolaev men dragged us back from our Philly heist mission. His gaze raked over me, as if ensuring I wasn't hurt. There were only a few faint bruises left on my body and my clothes covered those.

"Hello, Uncle Liam," I whispered softly, my emotions choking me. I had never gone this long without talking to him. While I sometimes went months without seeing him, we always talked—messages, calls, emojis.

"Wyn." He took two big strides and was in front of me. "Jesus Christ, I was worried sick."

"I'm fine," I murmured. He glanced at Davina and then Juliette, as if asking for their confirmation. It was the reason I couldn't tell them everything that happened. If they knew, they wouldn't be able to assure him, as they now did, with a straight face.

"Why won't you come home?" he asked, cupping my cheek. "Your mother is worried sick, going out of her mind."

Holding his gaze, I steeled myself for what I knew was coming. "You have to come home. I can have a plane ready to take us to California."

I took a step back and shook my head. "No, not yet."

The tension in the room grew another notch. Uncle's eyes were full of disbelief, evaluating me. "Why not?"

Because the moment I put on a costume, my back would be bare, giving everyone a full view of scars and bruises.

"I need another week or so," I pleaded.

Uncle shoved his hand through his hair. It almost seemed he aged ten years over the last month. We haven't been kind to him with all our bullshit we stirred since we burned down Garrett's house.

"Just give her another week, Liam," Davina jumped in. "She deserves that much before her full-blown training starts."

"Why?" he demanded to know. "You can get a whole goddamn year if you want it, Wyn. I want to know why. Something happened, and I want to know what."

I shook my head. "Nothing happened, Uncle. I—I promise," I lied.

"If nothing happened, then come home." He set that trap beautifully and I fell right into it. He knew it too.

Sasha knew it too and immediately came to my defenses. "Brennan, give her another week. It can't hurt and then I'll personally take her to California."

And Uncle lost his shit. "I don't want you around her, Sasha," he growled. "I asked for tailing, not for my niece to move in with you. You and her... it will never be."

An exasperated breath left me. "There is no me and him, Uncle," I huffed. "Truly. He's just giving me a place to stay."

"Wyn, I'm trying to protect you," Uncle growled. "You have to trust me."

And it was then that I lost my shit. I was so sick and tired of being kept like a fragile, breakable doll and, worst of all, being kept in the dark. I was oblivious to any and all dangers lurking in the shadows. I knew *nothing*.

Nico's wife walked in right at that time with cookies in her hands, but my hands shook and my ears buzzed to even attempt being polite.

"Protect me?" I screeched. "You want to protect me by keeping me oblivious to EVERYTHING." Uncle gave me a confused look. "I could look the enemy in the face and smile, and not even know they are the enemy. You know why? Because you keep me in the dark," I screamed.

My chest rose up and down, my breathing heaved and I knew everyone was staring at me like I had lost my mind. Outbursts were nonexistent in my childhood. It was all about discipline and control. Well, I fucking lost my control. I lost everything.

"Wynter, I—"

"Don't fucking tell me any more lies," I snapped, my voice high-pitched. "If your protection means me being left in the dark and finding out who the fucking enemies are as I'm being—"

I stopped, unable to finish the statement. My ears rang, my lungs closed up, my throat tightened. It was like someone gripped it tight. Like Gio DiLustro himself choked the life out of me.

I couldn't breathe. Every single second that ticked, the panic in my chest grew. Desperate, I fought for air, just an ounce of oxygen. *Fuck, is a panic attack going to kill me*, my mind whispered. I was never prone to those, but I've seen it on my mother once or twice.

My hand clawed at my chest, as if ripping it open would give me air to breathe. They trembled so bad, I couldn't even do that right. The buzzing in my ears grew, this terror twisted something inside me and it wouldn't let go.

Uncle's face inched closer, but my vision was too hazy. I could barely focus on it. Juliette's, Ivy's, and Davina's voices sounded like echoes in my brain, taking them further and further away.

Chapter Thirty-Two

SASHA

Both Brennan and I caught Wynter's body at the same time, before she hit the floor.

"What's wrong with her?" Brennan demanded to know.

He was alarmed, his eyes darting between the women and me, demanding to know.

I knew Wyn didn't tell them anything, not wanting to upset them, but they knew something happened. They weren't dumb, reckless but not dumb.

Yet, the three of them shook their heads and said nothing, and fuck, I was proud of Wyn's crazy, slightly idiotic friends because they refused to betray her.

So his eyes came back to me. "I know you know, Nikolaev," he growled.

"God, so much fucking testosterone. How about you worry about my cousin and not this pissing contest you two seem to be in." Of course it would be Juliette to say something like that.

"Juliette." Her father shot her a warning glare.

"My cousin is lying limp in your arms. How about we focus on helping her and you can growl at people later," she reasoned with him.

"So this is what you were talking about when you advised me to look for a highly guarded school," Nico mused.

And as if the twins knew their father was talking about them, they strolled in at the same time, as I lifted Wynter up into my arms.

"I'm taking her back to my place," I told Brennan.

"The fuck you are," he growled. "She's my niece. My family."

"And she'll come back to you when she's ready," I told him in a cold voice. "Not a moment sooner."

"How about if we lay her in one of the guest rooms," Nico's wife, Bianca, suggested. She reminded me so much of Isabella, it wasn't even funny. The woman had no business being among men like us. Much like Wynter.

Juliette, on the other hand, that one might turn into a goddamn killer.

"Give her to me, Nikolaev," Brennan ordered. I guess the fucker hadn't heard, I fucking sucked at following orders. Did enough of that shit in the military to last me two lifetimes. "Or I'll fucking end you, to hell with your brothers."

My expression darkened. "You can try," I said coldly. "But it won't end well for you. Thank the saints, Brennan, that I have your niece in my arms, or I'd crush your throat."

"Whoa, whoa. Everyone calm down." Brennan's wife jumped in and the girl actually put herself between her husband and me. "Let's leave Wynter with Sasha. She wants it that way and he's kept her safe so far."

"Why don't we let them fight it out?" Nico's twin girls leaned on each side of the doorway. "Let's take bets. I want to see who's better."

"Hannah," Bianca scolded her, giving her the most threatening look she could pull off. It resembled a mean kitten. I was sure her twins were shitting their pants. *Not.*

The little blonde just shrugged her shoulders and folded her arms in front of her chest. "What? I have to earn money somehow."

"Holy fuck, we should get this one to give us some pointers," Ivy mumbled. "They should totally attend our school."

"I was thinking the same thing," Juliette added, then turned to face Nico. "Would you consider sending your kids to our school? It might be ready by the time they are old enough. We just have to find some other mobsters to rob," Juliette muttered. "You were a bad choice."

"You think?" Nico mused, entertained.

"No, no more stealing," Davina hissed, glaring at her friend who batted her eyelashes.

"Can you lay her down and then fight him?" the other twin asked.

"Nobody is fighting," Bianca said firmly. "But you two might earn yourselves a timeout. Separately," she warned, giving them a pointed look.

That seemed to have the desired impact because the two of them made themselves scarce right away.

"Let me show you to the guest room," Bianca offered and I nodded, but before I left the room, Brennan called out.

"When she's awake, I want to talk to her," he said, his voice dark. My shoulders tensed, knowing that it was inevitable that Wynter and Brennan talk. Honestly, I was surprised to have succeeded in keeping him at bay for this long.

I followed Bianca through their estate home. She kept chatting softly, probably her way of releasing her tension. Unlike Cassio's wife or Luciano's wife, Bianca and Bella had never gotten completely comfortable around men like us. Their husbands were the exception, of course.

Once we were in the guest bedroom, I laid Wynter's body on the bed. She lost some weight in the last two weeks. From what I heard, she usually had a healthy appetite but not since her run-in with the old DiLustro.

"Is she going to be okay?" Bianca whispered.

I nodded. I didn't give Wynter enough credit. She *was* strong. I'd seen it over the last three weeks—in her persistence and determination. She just had a very big heart and I feared a romantic one that she hid underneath her ice-princess persona.

"I can't believe I have an Olympic gold medalist in my home," Bianca murmured. "Maybe the twins will take note and try to aim for something more than just being little devious troublemakers."

My lip quirked. "Then you might want to keep them away from Wynter and her friends. They are quite accomplished troublemakers. Reckless too."

She chuckled softly. "I gathered. What were they thinking trying to make money in Nico's casino by counting cards?"

I suspected it was their way to get attention. Davina shot me a message, telling me of their plan. Of course, she waited until they were elbows deep into it.

"How's married life treating you?" I asked her curiously. "I still remember that Hallmark drama wedding. I think the only thing that beat that event was catching these four reckless criminals"—I tilted my head towards Wynter's sleeping form—"pushing an armored vehicle into a river after they stole millions."

"Jesus!" Bianca sounded slightly appalled. She watched Wynter sleep for a few seconds, then added, "You know, I can't help but think she had a point."

I raised an eyebrow. "About?"

"Being kept in the dark," she clarified. "It is in y'all's genes to protect women. It's like it has been beaten into you since you were born." She wasn't far off. "My family did it. Nico still does it, with me and the girls. And while I don't mind it at all, in fact love it, I worry how it will impact our children. Especially the girls. Like Wynter said, she's so protected, she wouldn't know if she was staring into the face of an enemy."

I didn't disagree. Wynter was so oblivious to the cause of the wedge in her and DiLustro's family that she went and fell in love with one. Yeah, she refused to say she loved him. But it was plain as fucking day.

Wynter stirred on the bed and Bianca was forgotten. I took two strides to the side of the bed and lowered to my haunches.

Her eyes fluttered open and those green eyes that had the world falling at her feet met mine.

"Hey, rebel."

For a moment she just stared quietly, probably trying to figure out how she got here.

"Panic attacks aren't good," she finally whispered.

"No, they aren't," I agreed. "But they're manageable."

"Always so positive," she muttered, her lips curving a tiny bit. It was only then that she noticed Bianca was in the room as well.

"How about I bring you some lemonade and cookies?" Bianca offered, always eager to feed everyone.

Wynter shook her head. "No, thank you. But could I talk to my uncle, please?"

"Sure, I'll go get him."

Once Bianca left us, I locked eyes with Wyn. "You can stay at my place for as long as you need to."

She shifted on the bed, then sat up, pulling her knees to her chest. "Thank you. I just need a week for the rest of the bruises to fade."

"You need to think about taking time to recover mentally too, Wyn. Your mother will understand if you explain." She shook her head vigorously. "There is always the next Olympics."

"No, no, no," she protested softly. "I can't keep hiding. You know it's exactly what I've been doing."

I didn't give a fuck. She should hide for as long as she wanted to. It didn't make her a coward, not after everything that happened.

"Jesus, you gave me a scare." Brennan's voice came from behind me and he came around to the other side of the bed to sit. The dude was so large, Wynter almost rolled into him.

"Come home with me," Brennan demanded softly, but Wynter shook her head. "I'll talk to your mom and you can stay in New York if you wish. In another two months, we'll visit your granddad. You can beat him at poker or chess. Davina's grandpa will come. It will be good."

Red blotches of agitation traveled up Wynter's delicate throat. "No, I'll go to California. I'll finish what I started. I can't go back to New York. Not for a while. I'll meet you in Ireland. But please let Ivy and Juliette come with me." Brennan nodded his agreement. "And you come visit with Davina too."

Fuck, if it didn't sound like she was saying goodbye. At least to the East Coast.

"I'm sorry, Wyn." Brennan cupped her chin. "I've always just wanted to protect you. Both you and your mother. It seemed I failed with both of you."

He tucked her curls behind her ear, the move almost father-like. He probably was her father since she never had one.

Wynter took his big hand into her small one and squeezed. "You didn't. It's not your job to protect us."

"Yes, it is," he disagreed with a grumble.

Wynter shook her head. "I know what happened with the DiLustros," she whispered her admission so softly, you could barely hear it.

"How?" Honestly, I couldn't believe he was able to keep such a big secret from her for so long.

"It doesn't matter. The bottom line is that *you* should have told me. I shouldn't be blindsided by someone else about things that concern me. Whose granddaughter I am, my connections to the Russians, about the DiLustros and what they did to my mother."

A growl vibrated deep in Liam. The history and feedback I got was that Liam lost his shit when Aisling was shot. He was known to be a fair man, but during that time, he killed anyone connected to Gio DiLustro.

"That bastard destroyed her," Liam hissed. "If they knew about you and Jules, you'd have been a target. I wanted both of you to have a normal childhood, away from the underworld. It was what my sister wanted. I had to protect you and Jules to keep history from repeating."

"Maybe when we were kids. Not anymore. Make us stronger, not blind and dependent on someone else to save us."

Wynter might have Irish in her, but I could honestly say she didn't inherit a single feature from them. Maybe recklessness. But then, even that could be the Russian side of her.

"Some habits are hard to break," he said darkly.

She met his eyes with the stubbornness I have come to know well. "Well, break them. Otherwise, you'll lose us all."

Chapter Thirty-Three

BASILIO

Four fucking weeks.

I've looked for her everywhere. I even had men watching Brennan's house. Her Jeep was there. Her friends were there. Wynter wasn't.

I went to Yale, and I heard from the building attendant that all her stuff was boxed up and sent to Davina Hayes-Brennan. When I asked why, he just said the girl disappeared and one of her roommates was handling her affairs.

If only I could get my hands on Davina. I seriously contemplated kidnapping her so I could question her. Priest hacked into Wynter's phone to find it was wiped clean. He attempted to hack into Brennan's network, but that was blocked.

"You can't keep this up," Dante muttered. "We're chasing ghosts."

We sat in the back of the graffitied entrance to one of the Bratva's warehouses in Long Island, which served as their lab. There was one thing I learned over the last four weeks. The Russians had been expanding all around New York. That had to end.

"No, we're not," I hissed. The three of us came along with our ten best men. "She is somewhere. People don't disappear into thin air."

There was something that had been bothering me about Wynter's abduction. It lacked logic and reasoning behind it. They left my father alive, much to my regret. I'd rather they have killed him or taken him, and left Wynter behind. But it would seem my father schmoozed the Russians too and somehow talked himself out of getting killed.

"Jesus, Basilio. You have to get yourself together," Priest added, his eyes focused on the blade of his knife as he kept turning it over. "Maybe she escaped the Russians and just changed her mind about marrying you."

Dante punched his younger brother in his shoulder so I wouldn't. I gritted my teeth that he would even say something like that.

"My father shouldn't have been at my place," I said, that fucking day replaying in my mind over and over again. Nothing my father said sat well with me. None of it made sense. Too many inconsistencies.

"Do you suspect he set it up?" Dante inquired. The fact that we had to even wonder about it was fucked up. But that was who my father was. He'd stab anyone in the back, including me.

"Too many coincidences," I said, frustrated that I couldn't solve this puzzle. "It was almost as if the kidnapping of her friend was a distraction." Their expression told me they agreed with it. "My father shows up, surveillance in my home fails, most of the city block around my home was corrupted. The Russians leave him alive. Nobody gets that lucky."

"Except for your father," Priest commented. "Though I have to agree. The Bratva is not known to leave survivors."

The moment he said it, he realized his mistake and a string of curses left him.

"Let's go," I told them all.

There was no time to waste.

The attack was brutal and bloody. We almost lost a man. The Bratva had more men than we anticipated, but we powered through it.

After hours of fighting and killing, and then torturing Russian assholes for information, we were down to the last two bastards.

"Nyet, nyet," one of them started. Then a string of Russian words left his mouth.

Nothing would save them. But first I'd get some information. "Switch to English or Italian," I said as I cocked my gun. The ugly fucker covered in tattoos attempted to spit at us.

Then as if in slow motion, my restraint snapped. Over the last four weeks, I had been hanging by a thread. My rage took over and I lunged at him. The Glock in my hand turned into a weapon. But not to land a bullet in him, but to strike. Again and again.

"Who are you?" I roared. "Why are you in my city?"

He smiled, stupid and gruesome, showing me his bloodstained mouth and teeth.

"Kill this one," Dante said with a twisted smile, eyeing the other captive. "And we'll work on this one. I'd bet my money that this one speaks English."

The other guy's head shook vigorously, then uttered words in Russian. *Suka.* Yeah, I understood that one.

The shot rang out loud and ended the first Russian. Then we all turned our attention to the next one. We'd call him *suka guy* for the duration of his short miserable life.

"He's sensitive to being called a bitch," Priest remarked casually to the other one who just about pissed his pants.

"Can I?" Priest asked when I readied to start working on the fucker. It had been the only way to release my fucking frustration lately. Killing people.

Fuck, I wanted to deny him. I needed to release this rage festering inside me, but I also knew I had been walking the thin line between rage and sanity. And the monster that relished inflicting pain wasn't satisfied. Not yet, but I nodded my head just the same.

Priest produced a piece of glass from somewhere and he stepped forward to drive it into the back of the fucker's hand. Then I watched him pry his mouth open as he drove it into his tongue.

"How in the fuck is he supposed to talk with a hole in his mouth?" Dante complained.

Priest shrugged. "It's not clean off. He can still talk." Dante rolled his eyes. "Fine, since you're so sensitive," Priest caved, then let out an exaggerated sigh. "I'll stop playing with his tongue."

So he sunk the sharpest point of the glass into his ribs. "I'll just play with his ribs."

"You're one sick motherfucker," I told my cousin Priest.

His answer was a slightly unhinged grin.

Dante shot us both a look, then just shrugged. "You're both sick fuckers."

"Thank you," Priest and I answered at the same time.

My demons danced through my veins, eager to play with the fucker. Eager to make him suffer. It had been weeks and I kept waiting for the break. For any piece of information that would bring me a step closer to *her*.

So I caved in to the monster and took a step towards the Russian, while Priest muttered his last rites. While he was twisting the glass in his ribs, my hand wrapped around his throat and I squeezed.

"Why is the Bratva here?" I growled. "Who's your fucking Pakhan?"

Blood spilled from the corner of his mouth as he choked. I released the grip just enough to let him speak.

"You'll never see our Pakhan coming," he garbled out, wheezing. "Death is coming for all of you."

I slammed my forehead against his. Bone against bone. The

buzzing in my head was welcomed. It was exactly the kind of pain I needed. But he didn't. His scream traveled over the empty room like a shockwave.

"Fucking crazy Italians," he hissed, gurgling on his own blood, eyeing us warily.

"You ain't seen crazy yet," Priest laughed, then continued reciting the last rites. Again. "May the Holy Spirit free you from this miserable life and sins swallow you whole with the grace of the Holy Spirit."

Priest really *liked* this one.

I pulled out my knife and stabbed his thigh with it. As Priest twisted the glass into his ribs, I worked on tearing his thigh up.

"Let's start again." Dante leaned against the wall, watching the scene unfold. "See, my cousin and brother quite enjoy torturing. They can last days, playing with their prey. So you might want to speed up and tell us what you know."

Then to prove his point, I struck the Glock into his skull. And again. The crunch of breaking bones mixed with his pained screams.

"Who are the Russians looking for?" I demanded. There was no mistake, they were looking for someone. The fuckers were all over New York, attacking different organizations. Brennans. Me. Russians in New Orleans. Colombians. Even Yakuza. "Who's your fucking Pakhan? Last warning."

Then to show him I meant business, I pushed the knife deeper into his thigh.

"Winter Volkov," he screamed out a name and I froze. So did Priest. Shock washed over me and I stilled.

"Who?" I asked, my voice cold and detached.

"Winter Volkov," he panted, his accent heavy. "Pakhan's daughter. She's dead, but they are looking for Winter Volkov's descendants."

"Who's they?" I asked harshly.

"Akim Kazimir," he whimpered. "He has a lead and works directly with the Pakhan. That's all I know, I swear."

He cried like a baby, repeating it was all he knew. Over and over again.

"I believe you," I told him finally and raised my gun.

"Amen, motherfucker," Priest finally ended his last rite, just as I pulled the trigger.

Turning to Priest, I found him already scouring the web, digging for information.

"You know I'm getting blood all over my fucking electronics," he grumbled as his fingers flew over the screen.

"I'll buy you another one," I vowed.

"You complain about blood on your electronics, while you're soaked in it." Dante shook his head. "You're both fucking idiots. You won't get into my car like that. I have white leather seats."

We flipped him off without raising our gazes off the screen of Priest's fancy device.

All the while my heart thundered and the darkness in my vision slowly lifted. This has to be a sign. The name couldn't be a coincidence. It wasn't exactly a common name and everyone knew of the Volkov Russian family. Practically Russian mafia royalty.

"Fuck. Me." Priest's voice interrupted my thinking and my eyes snapped to his. He flipped over the screen and a picture filled my vision.

I froze, staring at the image of the woman I had been searching for. It was almost identical—same eyes, same curls, same face. The only thing that was different were the freckles on my Wynter's face.

"Winter Volkov," Priest rasped. "Winter with an i, rather than y."

Fuck. Me.

My Wynter was a Russian mafia princess.

Chapter Thirty-Four

BASILIO

"This can't be a coincidence," Dante grumbled, echoing my thoughts exactly. The three of us stayed in my place in the Hamptons. It was easier than going back to the city. After we got cleaned up, we sat on the back patio facing the ocean, pondering on today's findings.

"Agreed."

Once upon a time, my father wanted the Volkov Pakhan at the Syndicate table. It didn't happen. Instead he got a different Russian alliance at the table. A weaker one.

But knowing Father, he held a grudge. There wasn't an ounce of doubt in my mind that either he worked with the Russians to get their dirty paws on my woman or he made up a different story. The one where he'd end up on top.

"What's his angle?" Priest asked.

"Maybe he recognized Wynter," I rasped, ice flowing through my veins. "If he knew the Pakhan and his family decades ago, there's no way he'd miss the resemblance." My eyes flickered to the screen again.

I had never seen two human beings look so alike. "It would explain his hatred for the Brennans."

"None of this shit makes any sense," Dante said. "So the old-fucker Brennan kidnapped Winter Volkov to keep the Pakhan out of the Syndicate. When the woman died, what would have kept the Pakhan from joining?"

"The grandchild. Aisling Brennan," I said. Wynter was part of the underworld all along. Yet, there seemed to be so many disconnects. My sixth sense told me she didn't grow up in the underworld. She couldn't have. Nothing about her behavior indicated that.

"But all the records point that Aisling Brennan and her unborn child died," Dante reasoned.

"We know data can be manipulated," Priest hissed, staring at the pictures. "There's no way in hell this kind of resemblance was coincidental."

Russian princess. "They don't have her," I concluded. "The fucker said they're looking for the descendants. That means they didn't find her."

"Maybe it's time we join forces with other organizations," Dante suggested. "It's clear the Syndicate is making moves without anyone's knowledge."

"Or maybe it's just my father making those moves."

I certainly wouldn't put it past him. He thought himself invincible. The Syndicate was supposed to spread power among different members but my father seemed to conveniently forget that. Or simply ignore it. He used the Syndicate to get what he wanted, at any cost necessary.

"Could this be enough to remove him from the Syndicate?" Priest pondered. "If he made a move without their knowledge, this was a clear attempt to seize power."

I shook my head. "If the Pakhan was a member of the Syndicate, it would have been against the rules. But it's a free-for-all for anyone outside the Syndicate. It's the loophole that allowed Father to continue his attacks on the Brennans."

The three of us sat in silence and the waves crashed against the shoreline. I had wanted to bring Wynter here too. There were so many fucking plans I had for us and now—

She had to be alive. If the Russians had her, she was alive. The Pakhan would never harm his great-grandchild. Marry her off, yes. Benefit off her, yes. But the bastard would never kill her.

My father, on the other hand, he'd break her. Bitterness was like fucking acid, eating away at my insides. It was a fucking joke that I hoped that the Russians had her rather than my own fucking father.

Fuck!

If he touched a single hair on Wynter's head, I'd fucking kill him. Rules be damned, I'd end him.

"Maybe we reach out to Brennan," Dante suggested. "It's his family, after all."

"Then why isn't he tearing apart the city, looking for her?" I hissed. "We can't trust anyone outside the three of us, and Emory." I wouldn't risk it. If Father indeed made a deal with the Russians, Brennan would lose his shit. Attack us, and it would distract us from looking for Wynter. "We keep looking for Wynter, keep our focus on her and the elimination of Gio from the Syndicate."

Priest and Dante nodded their agreement. "If we're to remove Gio from the Syndicate, it's the best plan," Dante muttered. "It makes me fucking sick that we have to play this cat-and-mouse game with him. I wish Liam would have just shot Gio decades ago and ended it all."

I agreed with the sentiment. He might be my father, but it was in name only. In my entire life, he hadn't shown a single fatherly emotion. To me nor Emory. He destroyed her life before it even began.

Screams rang throughout the house, startling me out of my nightmare.

It was always the same one.

The first death I witnessed. The way she gurgled and choked on her own blood as my father stood over her with a harsh smile on his face.

It had been seven years since that day. I was no longer a five-year-old boy. Mother was a faded memory on the floor of a dirty motel room. Emory didn't even know what she looked like, because Father had removed all evidence of our mother's existence.

But when he wasn't around, I'd whisper to her about Mother. What little I remembered. And when she'd ask me how pretty our mother was, I'd tell her to just glance in the mirror. Because Emory was as beautiful as our mother was.

My door swung open and seven-year-old Emory ran to my bed, her eyes wide with fear and her hair disheveled. She padded across the room barefoot, the light of the moon guiding her way.

"What's the matter?" I asked her in a hushed tone. "A nightmare?"

She had them too. Courtesy of our fucking father. Though hers was slightly different from mine.

"There are screams," she whispered. "Downstairs."

I wrenched my gun out of the nightstand and shot out of bed. "Hide under the bed," I ordered her. "And don't make a sound. No matter what."

Father would have dragged her into the middle of whatever the fuck was going on. But I refused. Emory's fears were bad enough already and she was only seven.

Once satisfied she was hidden, I crept downstairs. My pulse thundered in my ears as I inched toward the kitchen where the sounds were coming from. It was then that I saw it.

A woman tied to the chair. She was naked, her legs spread open with some tool I didn't recognize. Blood smeared all over her inner thighs, stark against her pale skin even in the dim light.

My father crouched behind the table that was turned over. Two other men on the opposite side of the kitchen. One hiding behind the large Subzero fridge and the other behind the island where we ate our breakfast. His back was to me and it would have been the easiest one to end.

Father's eyes flitted to me. There was blood on his shirt and his face. Instinctively my eyes darted to the woman still tied up, her chair in the middle of the crossfire. Was he trying to save her?

I had to save her, yet the need to kill my father was even stronger. I hated him. He hurt Emory and me, chipping away at our humanity one day at a time. But I couldn't let my hate outweigh the right thing to do. I couldn't sacrifice the woman who whimpered, bloodied and naked, in the middle of our kitchen.

So I raised my hand and shot one of the men. Then I aimed for the next one, just as he spotted me. I pulled the trigger and he attempted to dodge the bullet. But it hit him, lodging itself into his collarbone.

He fell to his knees, clutching his shoulder and neck, while my father jumped out of his hiding spot and rushed to him. I did the same, kicking the gun away, then rushed to the woman tied up.

She whimpered as I approached her.

"It's okay," I whispered as I reached for the knots on her wrists.

Father shot the surviving attacker in both knees. The scream pierced the air, both man's and woman's, causing me to cry in surprise. Why was she crying and looking at the attackers like that? Like she—

I swallowed hard. Like she cared about him.

Bile and acid stuck in my throat. Miscalculation. I killed the men who tried to protect the woman. My heart thundered against my chest and guilt was quick to lodge itself deep inside my heart and my soul.

My legs gave away, my sin too hard to bear and I fell down to my knees. I wanted to sink down through the tiled floor and let the ground swallow me. I was a monster, just like my father.

My eyes connected with the soft brown ones, full of anguish and pain. I caused it. I was directly responsible for it. I'd go to hell for it.

I had no idea who she was. I should know whose downfall I caused, shouldn't I? Yet, I didn't dare to ask her. Each soft whimper of hers laid blame. It screamed my betrayal at her innocence.

I had given my father open access to her.

Father stalked toward me and pulled me roughly to my feet.

"Pull yourself together," he hissed, then shoved me into an empty chair. "You did good, boy."

I had to fight the urge to spit in his face. I hated his guts so much that red mist marred my vision. This hatred choked me, threatening to swallow me whole and leave me in complete darkness. Yet, I knew I had to fight it. For Emory.

If I succumbed to the darkness, my little sister would have nobody left. She needed me.

Father moved to the only living attacker. He didn't try to crawl away; instead he crawled toward the woman. The woman he loved, I realized by the look in his eyes. I had seen it on TV when my old nanny watched her soaps.

Father lifted the man up with one hand and tied him up to the chair nearest to the woman. But far enough that he wouldn't be able to reach her.

Then with a cruel gleam in his eyes, Father's eyes zeroed in on the woman.

He unbuckled his pants, then whipped his belt out of the loops in one swift movement.

"Now, let's finish what we started," he purred as bile crawled up my throat. "Now, son, I want you to see how a woman is fucked. They're good for pleasure only. Nothing more, nothing less."

The screams filled the room, high-pitched and gutting.

First, he fucked her mouth so violently that she gagged. But the entire time, he kept a gun aimed at the attacker.

"If I feel one single scrape of your teeth, I shoot him again," Father grunted as he pushed himself deeper down her throat. It didn't end

there. Tears streamed down her face, with each passing minute I watched something slowly die in her eyes.

When he finished, Father squirted his cum all over her face. "That's how we treat whores. And you're all whores."

Letting his dick hang, like a disgusting, shriveled cucumber, he strode to the tied-up man.

"How does it feel, figlio di puttana, to know you'll never fuck her virgin pussy? Her virgin ass?"

Father reached for his knife and touched it to the man's bullet wound, then wedged the point into it. The screams rang, my blood buzzed and the scent of metallic blood filled my nose.

Miscalculation, my mind whispered. I missed my chance and chose to save my father, at the expense of an innocent.

Father glanced my way. "Did you learn something today, son?" Father muttered.

I nodded my head, but I remained numb. My answer wouldn't please him, might even earn **me** *a bullet.*

He untied the woman, then yanked her hair. Then bent her over the kitchen table, so she'd face me. Then in one forceful push, he buried himself deep into her ass. As he fucked her raw, her naked body sliding back and forth across the table, she kept her eyes on me.

Accusing. Broken. Hateful.

"Keep your eyes on him, whore," Father grunted. My hands shook, a roar formed in my throat, clawing to get out. "He's learning."

I learned that day that I'd never be able to coexist with my father.

That night, he threw the woman to traffickers. It was a retribution for her father's betrayal. Many years later, I searched for her. I wanted to save her, atone for my sins and explain myself to her.

"I didn't know" seemed inadequate. Yet, I had nothing else.

But before I got to her, Nico Morrelli saved her. She worked for him, even ran a shelter for abused women. Her eyes were still dark but her hair was white as snow. Like her innocence before my father destroyed it.

Pulling my thoughts from that dark day, I focused on now and the things I *could* fix.

"Violating the rules is a sure way to get us kicked out of the Syndicate," I finally said, leaving the past where it belonged. In the fucking past. "And that'll leave Emory vulnerable. Wynter too. The only way to protect them is to take over the seats of our fathers in the Syndicate."

A hot summer breeze swept through the large backyard, and memories of my time with Wynter at the beach a reluctant memory. I could almost smell her suntan lotion, hear her laughter, imagine her eyes shining with that mischievous gleam in her eyes.

I'd find her, if it was the last thing I did before I took my last breath.

It was the only hope I held now.

Chapter Thirty-Five

WYNTER

A week until Christmas.

Six months since the last time I saw him.

Uncle Liam, Davina, Juliette, Ivy, and I were in Portugal. I needed some time alone, so I'd told them all I'd meet them at their house. Uncle insisted we stay in the hotel. Probably because he wanted privacy with Davina.

I was happy for them. I really was. Except it was such a painful reminder of the short time I had something similar. Regardless if it was real or fake. God, it felt real. My heart believed it was real.

Rather than letting my mind wander back to the past, I flipped through the channels again. Figure skating coverage was just as intense here as it was in the States. And somehow I kept landing on Derek's and my number.

My failure, Mother called it. Her critique was right, and I blamed myself even more than my coach ever could.

Third place. They called it a disgrace for the ice princess. I fucking hated that title.

I watched as both Derek and I shot up into a quad Lutz. The

public put it on him, but it was all on me. I got distracted, lost in my mind and that goddamn song. I landed too close to my partner. The fall hurt like a motherfucker, but I kept going. Despite the song that had my heart bleeding and my whole right side that hurt like hell. It didn't match the pain in my chest.

The first song I danced to with Bas under the starry night and headlights of his car shining on us. That song should never be played again. "I Found" by Amber Run would forever be on my banned list. Because I couldn't listen to the words without feeling Bas's hands on me, his mouth on my skin, and his scent all over me.

Third place. It wasn't good enough. The whole right side of my hip was bruised and it ached. My ego might hurt even more and my heart was so used to the fucking pain by now that I barely noticed it.

The Winter Olympics would start in two months. The world speculated who would compete. I wanted out. Mother refused to even hear about it. I tried so hard over the last six months. If I was in singles, I could power through it. But not with Derek and the way I had to fight the flinch each time his hands rested on me.

"We still have a chance at gold," Mom protested when I tried to tell her I couldn't do it.

Except that I no longer felt the music, nor the passion.

"Is this the end of Star Flemming?" the announcer on the television screamed. *"She shone bright but every star eventually burns out."*

I threw the remote at the television. The worst part was that he wasn't wrong. I was burnt out. I had nothing more to give. All I felt was pain. I didn't even know how to come to terms with any of it.

Bas, his father, my mother, her ruined career, my father. I knew nothing anymore.

Sasha gave me facts, but there was so much more to the story that only my mother knew. Yet, I couldn't bring myself to ask her and cause her pain.

And this fucking pain in my chest was unbearable. I wanted it to ease so each breath I took wouldn't hurt so bad. I wanted to forget, so I'd be the old me. The old me that only cared about skating.

Someone knocked on my hotel door. I ignored it. Another knock.

"No room service needed," I shouted.

"Open the goddamn door," Juliette's voice came through and I covered my face with my hands. I couldn't deal with anyone. "I hear you replaying that stupid shit. Let me in before I break down this door and the hotel calls Dad."

I couldn't be left alone for just a moment, for Christ's sake. Was some alone time too much to ask?

As her pounding got more violent, I sighed and stilled myself for the mask I had gotten used to wearing. *"Everything's fine"* mask. I got off the bed and padded to the door, then unlocked it.

"I thought you left already," I muttered.

"Nope, you're not that lucky."

I rolled my eyes. Obviously. I sat back on my bed and Juliette threw herself on it.

"Get your mind off all the shit that happened at the championship," she said, exasperated. "You let things fester inside you too much. Nationals are done and behind you. You'll kick ass at the Olympics."

I stared at the screen, unwilling to comment.

"Her days as a single skater were amazing. Her talent is incomparable." Another announcer pondered, *"But maybe her ambition reached too far. She should have stayed in the singles."*

My lips thinned and I finally pressed the mute button. The announcer wasn't totally wrong. I skated better alone. Now more than ever, because more than ever, I hated having to trust someone to catch me as he swung me through the air. I trusted Bas and look how that fucking ended.

With a cracked heart, that's how. I didn't need a cracked skull too.

When I remained quiet, Juliette sat up and her arms came around

259

me. "I heard what your mom said," she whispered. "It wasn't just your failure. *You're* not a failure. You are amazing no matter what place you get."

Then why can't my own mother say that? I thought silently.

"You still have a chance at the Olympic gold," Juliette comforted. "If you want it. You have a right to say no."

My throat squeezed so hard that I couldn't utter a single word. So I just nodded. What was that saying... Every cloud has a silver lining. I tried so hard to find the silver lining, but it kept escaping me.

We stared at each other in thick silence and I returned my attention to the muted television where my failure played on repeat.

"I still remember that day when you stepped on the ice," Juliette said softly, breaking the tension that was so stifling I could hardly breathe. "I found a safe spot to sit down but you kept skating and falling. You were determined to stay on your feet." I turned my head to meet Juliette's blue eyes, wondering where she was going with it. "Yes, you had that crazy look on your face that said ice is your life." She rolled her eyes. "Let me tell you, it was the most annoying look. But it wasn't your love for ice that always fascinated me. It was your fucking determination."

I blinked at her unexpected comment. "Determination?"

"Fuck yeah, Wynter." She shoved her shoulder into me. "You're the most determined, annoying woman ever. I knew that when I was five and I know it today."

"Geez, thanks," I muttered. "I'm feeling loved."

She hugged me as if to compensate for her words. The truth was I didn't mind them. I never minded Juliette's honesty. Her crazy, unhinged ways... a bit. But never her honesty or directness. I loved her just the way she was though.

"I love you, Wyn." Her hands around me tightened. "But it's killing me seeing you this way. You shut down, refuse to talk about what happened." When I said nothing, she continued, "Don't think the yellow, faded bruises escaped me when you finally came back home." For all Juliette's reckless and wild ways, she noticed too much. "You don't want to share, I won't make you. Just know, no matter what, I'm here. I'll always be here."

Tears burned and my throat scratched. "I'm fine," I choked out, not able to say anything else.

"You say you're fine, but inside you, it's like you're still bleeding."

I wanted to spill it all out, tell her what happened. But I didn't trust her temper. She'd go on the warpath and pull in all the available resources to end every DiLustro on this planet. I told my best friends just enough. I'd rather leave it at the broken heart than attempted rape.

No matter what, I knew Juliette would go after him. The trouble was that I wouldn't be able to live with the knowledge that a certain man with coal hair and the darkest eyes no longer walked this earth.

Regardless if he played me or not.

Chapter Thirty-Six

WYNTER

I convinced Juliette to go on ahead of me. I promised I'd be right behind her. And I was, except as I approached the Nikolaev villa in the capital of Portugal, I took a detour. Just a few more minutes alone.

"Recalculating," Siri kept complaining. Taking the long way took a whole new meaning with me. I kept finding excuses to delay seeing them all again. I had avoided my uncle and all the Nikolaev family, with the exception of Sasha. Sasha showed up whenever he wanted to and checked on me. If I lived on the East Coast, I was certain I'd see him even more.

It was the only benefit of being in California at my mother's home. It was a different world.

Sasha even came along to Ireland three months ago when I went to visit Grandpa. The man made it his personal business to check up on me.

I roamed the old streets of Lisbon. It was a beautiful city. Ageless with a welcoming vibe. The weather was mild, though still cool. The breath of old colonial times was evident everywhere you looked. And so much history.

Not that I was into history. Especially when mine seemed so damn fucked up.

I watched the skyline of this old city. The spectacular hilltop vista from St. George's Castle stretched for miles. Davina's sister, Aurora, lived in a villa by the sea. Uncle Liam and Davina visited a few times. I'd been too busy training and avoiding everyone.

Even Juliette stopped spending so much time in California, busy with our new school plans.

Lowering myself on the thousand-year-old steps, I stared out into the horizon, my fingers tracing the bracelet on my wrist, my thumb finding the hidden kingpin pendant every so often and brushing against it. Even after all this time, I still couldn't find the courage to take it off.

"Are you hiding here?" A familiar deep voice came from behind me and I turned around to find Sasha Nikolaev standing there, leaning against the castle wall. He wore his signature three-piece suit that I hated ever since I met Basilio. Though truthfully, he didn't remind me of Basilio at all. Sasha was more MMA built. Bas was more... well, gorgeous.

"I'm not hiding."

Somehow, I wasn't surprised to find Sasha here. The man had some scary and seriously disturbing stalking skills. Much like his brother Alexei from what little I heard.

Sasha's eyes roamed over me, as they always did. He was like an annoying, overbearing brother, ensuring I wasn't hurt.

"Then why are you here, staring into space with that empty expression?" he challenged.

I shook my head tiredly. "What do you want, Sasha?"

Tense silence stretched, broken up only by the sound of the wind and distant noises of the city below us. I just wanted to sit down and keep those noises for my company. Just the thought of a social gathering and fake smiles was agonizing.

"Say the word, Wyn," he drawled. "And he's dead."

I blew an exasperated breath. "Don't you have enough people on your list to kill?"

He gave me his shark grin. "Some are business. Some are pleasure. I'm looking for some pleasure kills."

Narrowing my eyes on him, I regarded him with caution. "You're nuts. You know that, right?"

He shrugged.

"Yeah, but you like me."

I rolled my eyes. I wore my warm Lou & Grey black leggings and a large gray sweater. The temperature here was mild enough not to need a jacket.

"Yeah, but more from afar," I muttered. "Kind of like lions. Magnificent creatures but you don't want to be next to them."

He sat himself down next to me, uncaring of his expensive suit. "Don't tell me you're scared of me now."

I glanced at him sideways. "No, I'm not. But there is something deranged about you. And I have plenty of that with Jules." He gave me another one of his signature shark grins. "Honestly, I don't know why you and Juliette don't get along. You're both nuts."

"Is she into BDSM?" he asked curiously and I just about fell over. Good thing I was sitting down.

"You're joking, right?" I swallowed. I wouldn't tell him Juliette was a virgin. She was an all-talk, no-action type of girl when it came to sexual interaction.

"Yeah, I just wanted a reaction out of you." He shoved his shoulder into me playfully. "She's too young for me. You two are basically kids."

I scoffed. "Fuck you. I'm twenty-one."

"Ah, there is her spirit," he mused. "I wondered if nationals had crushed you."

And just like that, self-pity made an appearance. My eyes stung and I blinked to ensure no tears would dare make an appearance.

"Sasha, you're exhausting." My voice came out shaky and I twisted my fingers together.

"Want to talk about nationals?"

I stared out into the horizon, trying to find calm. Or my voice. Something. Anything. I was so sick and tired of this constricting pain in my chest. I kept thinking it would ease up—next day, I'd tell myself. Here I was six months later, and it hurt just as much as it did the first day. If not worse.

"I choked up," I whispered, unable to meet his eyes. "Derek swapped the music. It was—" I swallowed the lump in my throat. "The song meant something. It brought back memories and I just fucking choked. For a moment, I forgot I had a skating partner."

I peered at him from the side. He met my eyes and nodded, as if he understood. Somehow I thought he did.

"Your uncle's worried about you," he said.

"He worries too much," I mumbled.

"He hired Morrelli to dig up all the info on the friend that you were with when Davina was kidnapped."

I closed my eyes for a moment remembering that day. Ironic. That day I decided I'd stay with him. That very same day I left him.

"Will he tell him?" I rasped.

"I wiped the surveillance of the ice-skating rink. All the other city surveillance was already wiped out."

I put my hand on top of Sasha's big, tattooed hand. "Thank you," I whispered. I knew he didn't approve. I knew this was not how those men had each other's back. Yet Sasha still did it for me.

"Wyn, I think we both know you're not alright." He took my hand between his two big palms. My hand looked too small in his, but it wasn't that which fascinated me. It was that his touch felt safe. "I have yet to see you smile."

"I smile all the time," I protested weakly.

"Fake smiles are your specialty," he agreed. "I saw your old skating tapes and the new ones. You don't smile anymore."

"Maybe there's just nothing to smile about."

"Maybe," he answered pensively. "Or maybe it's time you tell your mother what it is *you* want. Or tell me it's okay to kill that bastard. Tell us all what will make you happy, help you heal and move on."

My nose and my throat were clogged from the tears that threatened to spill. I fought them desperately, trying to keep my composure. But it was for naught. I fell apart and buried my face into Sasha's jacket. After six months of trying to be strong, I lost my battle and broke down in public. I ugly cried, sobs shaking my body.

"I don't know how," I gasped out, my words full of despair. I knew what I wanted. *Bas.* Always Bas. "I feel so goddamn broken. One moment I had it all and the next moment—"

I couldn't finish the words and I buried my face deeper into Sasha's chest. It hurt so bad.

"I thought Mom loved my dad. She didn't," I cried, none of my words making sense. "Gio said she was his brother's, but he wanted her. I don't know anything anymore."

Sasha cupped my head and his pale blue eyes bore into mine. "Forget your mother, Wyn. She needs to handle her own ghosts, not put that on you. Forget everyone. Do what you want. Be happy for you."

I swallowed. Bas made me happy. With him, I felt content just being the average me. Not the skater. Not Uncle's niece. Not anyone, just me.

I sniffed. "You said Gio shot my mother. He ruined her career. And then there is this Russian mafia shit. But Bas, he never told me any of it. I—" My words faltered for a moment and then they rushed out. "I don't know if he used me. Or what Mother's deal was with Gio's brother. I want to ask her, but how do you bring up something like that? Whenever I ask about the past, pain crosses her expression and it guts me to cause it."

He held my gaze. "Are you sure you want to know?"

I nodded. Not knowing was what got me here. It made me blind and vulnerable to the DiLustros. Albeit something deep down told me that no amount of knowledge of DiLustro and my family's history would have kept me away. I would have still fallen for Bas.

"Your mom had an affair with Gio's brother. He was married and leaving his wife wasn't an option. For a while, almost a year, she lived in Chicago. A seventeen-year-old girl living with a married man in an apartment. They were happy from what I heard. Liam wasn't. Your mom eventually left DiLustro and got married. She had dreams of figure skating, and so did the man she married. Unfortunately, Gio had your mother in his sights too. He went after her, unwilling to accept rejection. I don't know all that happened there, but I know she was pregnant with you when she got hurt. Your father died, and officially, your mom and her newborn died too. Your uncle set her and you up with new identities."

"Gio DiLustro shot her," I whispered, dread filling my veins. "He told me himself. He gloated about it."

Silence lingered with my admission.

"I tell you this, Wyn. If they lay a finger on you, they're dead."

The conviction in his voice was firm and cold. These kinds of statements by Sasha made me realize he was a feared man in the underworld. Despite his casual attitude, he'd be the one to kill a person with a happy smile on his face. It was terrifying.

"You know, it makes no damn sense that Uncle and Mom let me skate and compete if we were supposed to be in hiding."

He shrugged. "It does. Your mom missed her chance to skate. So she probably wanted to live through you. Your uncle has Nico Morrelli's company erase information on your family on a daily basis. Maybe he thought that was enough. With everyone thinking you two had died and setting you up with new identities, maybe he thought you'd be safe."

"So many secrets," I murmured. For some reason, I kept one revelation that Gio told me to myself. "And this Pakhan?" I asked. "Why is the Pakhan so important?"

"It's power," Sasha said. "Pakhan rules a big portion of the Russian underworld and your connection to it would tilt the power in DiLustro's favor. It was the reason Gio wanted your mother."

"All of it is so fucked up," I murmured, closing my eyes and I rested my cheek against his wide chest while he held me tightly.

I found comfort in the most unlikely place.

The Nikolaev living room at Alexei and Aurora's home was huge.

All the guests were already here when Sasha and I rolled in. The Nikolaevs. The Ashfords. The Kings. Uncle and all three of my best friends.

The moment we stepped into the living room, everyone's attention shifted to us and the air grew quieter. It seemed to be the norm.

"Hey, you two," Vasili greeted us. He and Alexei seemed to be the only ones who didn't mind Sasha's and my friendship.

Cassio frowned and his wife patted his hand, calming him down while she held their daughter with her other arm and their son hung on to his leg. They had twins, Océane and Damon.

Uncle's eyes darkened and he growled. Actually growled. I told Uncle that Sasha just kept me safe but he got a different scenario in his head. Davina gently nudged him with her shoulder, then whispered, "Stop it."

"Hey, Brennan," Sasha greeted him with a wide grin. "Wyn and I had a nice, romantic stroll through Lisbon. It really is one of the most romantic cities in the world."

Sasha liked to taunt him.

I rolled my eyes. Aurora rolled her eyes. So did Vasili and his wife, Isabella. Alexei was too badass to roll his eyes. The Ashford brothers just looked amused.

"Stop it," I warned Sasha in a low voice.

Byron and Winston resembled each other, both leaned back casually against the mantel, sipping on their poison and watching everyone with those hazel eyes, while Royce and Kingston stood to the side, each with a beer. That family had some amazing genes.

"Good skating," Royce commended and I instantly stiffened. It wasn't good skating and everyone knew it. Kingston smacked him.

"Ignore him," he grumbled, his voice raspy. "I do. He's slow sometimes."

Alexei walked over to me, his wife holding his hand and baby on her hip. "Want a drink?" he offered.

I shook my head. "No, thanks," I muttered, smiling.

"No alcohol until she wins that gold, right?" Aurora chimed in, while Kostya kept reaching for me.

"Yeah," I agreed, my eyes on their son. It was so much easier dealing with the little ones.

I learned that Aurora was actually Basilio's cousin. Aurora's mother was Basilio's aunt. Small world, huh? Not that I could ask her anything about them. She had no connections to the kingpins or that side of the family.

"I don't know what it is with you and this baby," Sasha grumbled. "Whenever you're around, it's like nobody else exists."

Leaning forward, I smiled and took his little hand. "Hey there."

Kostya grinned his toothless smile and my heart just about melted. Then his little fingers grabbed a curly strand of my hair and pulled.

"Ouch," I protested. "When you get your hair, I'm gonna return the favor."

He smiled even wider.

"Hey, Wyn." Juliette joined us. She pecked me on the cheek. "I thought you were right behind me. Unless you and Sasha took a hanky-panky tour."

"Don't say hanky-panky in front of the little ones," I grumbled, then addressed Aurora. "Want me to hold him for a bit?"

My eyes shifted to Alexei, so did his wife's. He was obsessively protective, and I didn't want to go against him.

A nod and his wife shifted him over to me. "He's gotten big," I murmured softly, shifting him so he'd be comfortable on my hip.

"Babies grow," Juliette noted, rolling her eyes. "I hope he pukes on you. Because if you get on Davina's bandwagon and suddenly want a baby, I'm going to be the one to puke."

I chuckled softly. "Let's puke on Juliette, Kostya. What do you think?"

His hands and legs flopped excitedly and we all chuckled.

"Ugh, babies," she groaned. "We're too young for this crap. We should be looking for some fucker we can rob."

"Juliette," Uncle warned sharply.

My cousin, being who she was, just shrugged her shoulders. "What? We weren't going to rob anyone present." Uncle and Davina groaned. "Or people we know."

"Jesus Christ," he grumbled.

"Not to worry," Ivy joined the conversation, sipping on her eggnog. "We'll rob the cartel next. Then the Russians, present company excluded of course."

I shook my head. "They're joking," I assured Uncle Liam who glanced at his wife.

Davina nodded. "That's right. The last one went like shit and Juliette agreed no more heists. Everyone heard it."

"Yep," I agreed.

"If you need money for the school, just ask," Sasha offered. "These Russians still want to help."

Before I could answer, Juliette blurted, "I'd much rather rob you."

Juliette's expression turned pensive, as if she was seriously contemplating something and I really hoped it wasn't a robbery.

"I don't know why you two don't give it a go," Juliette told Sasha. "You get along great. And everyone says how true love comes from friendships."

Blinking my eyes, I stared at her speechless. She sounded serious. Not sarcastic or grossed out, but actually serious.

"I don't even know what to say to that," I muttered, shaking my head.

With Kostya in my arms, I headed to the couch and Cassio's son wobbled over to us. I lowered down to the floor and leaned my back to the couch so he could be at my eye level. It didn't take long for Vasili's kids to follow.

"You're really a magnet for the kids," Áine said softly.

"Probably because she looks like an angel," Juliette teased. "That hair of hers glows. Like damn glow sticks in the dark."

Kostya wiggled in my arms, twisting around so he could watch me. His clear, pale blue eyes met mine, and I swore when the kid looked at me, I felt lighter. His eyes were so much like his father's and his uncle's, it was kind of freaky. He didn't have a single physical trait of his mother's.

Conversation flowed, the atmosphere was light. Despite everything, it felt good being surrounded by people who cared about me and I about them. I only wished my mother could be part of it. Somehow it felt the older I got, the less I had her.

Some days I wished I could talk to her about everything. I wanted to ask her what happened, help her, and help myself. We were close, but only when it came to goals and training.

"How is the situation in New York?" I heard Vasili ask. I was half listening to their conversation, bouncing Kostya on my lap and playing peekaboo with Cassio's son.

"Fucking DiLustro is wreaking havoc." My spine stiffened and my eyes snapped to the group of men. None of them paid me any mind, except Sasha. I swallowed, looking away.

Sasha wanted to kill all the DiLustros and only his promise to me held him back. Sasha's promise to me reminded me of my own broken promise. Though if it was all a lie, it wasn't really a promise. Was it?

"Young Basilio is just as fucking crazy as his old man. He's attacking Russians in the city and all around. In turn they are attacking everyone else."

"Does Morrelli know anything?" asked Cassio.

"No, he doesn't have any useful information," Alexei answered.

"But why the Russians?" Uncle asked. "DiLustro never had an issue with them before."

"Who the fuck knows?" Cassio muttered. "Maybe he decided he hates them all of a sudden and wants to cause havoc. We know his papà is all about havoc."

They all lowered their voices, and I could no longer hear what they were saying.

I flicked a glance their way and caught Alexei's eyes on me.

Quickly averting my eyes, I felt my cheeks burn. My whole body. It was like my cells remembered that feeling while with Bas and it'd never give up on it. It was the type of addiction that stayed with you for the rest of your life.

I'd never forget him. Worst of all, I didn't want to.

Chapter Thirty-Seven

BASILIO

The obsession to find Wynter grew deeper and deeper. It wasn't healthy. It wasn't good for business. Yet, I couldn't give up. The need to find her burned hot. It was Christmas Eve and I wondered if the golden-haired principessa would be celebrating it in Russia or somewhere else in the world.

My phone rang and I glanced at the caller ID. Priest.

"Yeah," I answered.

"Are you coming?" Priest, Dante, Emory, and I would spend Christmas in Philly. I had avoided fucking Philly like the plague, but it was either sit it out in New York alone and risk seeing my fucking father, or spend it with family who actually had my back. Besides, Emory deserved to have us all there.

"Yes."

"Then stop dicking around and get your ass over here," he grumbled. "It's Christmas weekend. Give this hunt a rest." When I didn't answer, he continued, "Basilio, maybe she doesn't want to be found. Have you thought about that?"

Every goddamn day.

"Have you located Brennan?" There was no point in answering his question. He knew the answer.

"I did. He's in Portugal with his wife and her family."

I thought back to Davina's background that Angelo dug up. Just like Wynter's, there wasn't much there.

"I thought she only had a grandfather?" At this point, I started to think everything we knew was fucking shit. Maybe Angelo fed us crap on Father's orders.

"Fuck no, she's connected to the Nikolaevs through her sister's marriage."

Yeah, Angelo fed us crap. If this wasn't evidence enough, I didn't know what was.

"Her friends with her?" I asked.

"You didn't say anything about friends, so I only looked up Brennan, his wife, and Wynter. Though, everything with Wynter is a dead end. So either the girl is hiding or someone's hiding her trail."

"Have you hacked into my father's and Angelo's activity?" I wouldn't put it past them to do it and hide the trail.

"I have, and it's not them." He sounded sure. "You know that there is no way she didn't know, right?"

"Didn't know what?" I hissed.

"About the dispute between the DiLustros and Brennans. That she happens to be a descendant of one of the most powerful Pakhans in rússkaya máfiya. That she's a fucking Russian mafia princess."

I kept going back and forth, and as much as I hated to admit it, Priest was right. It was hard to believe she had not known about it. Even if I assumed she didn't know about her Russian heritage, she definitely knew about her Irish heritage and she withheld it.

It was still hard to believe that Wynter was the descendant of the Volkov family. She was part of the underworld all along. The resemblance to her ancestors was remarkable. It was as if she didn't inherit a single trait of the Brennan family.

Except her deception. She played me well. Not for a moment did I doubt her part in the underworld and there she had connections to the Russians and the Irish. No wonder my brutality didn't bother her.

And still I refused to let go of her.

"I'll see you soon," I finally said. "Keep my sister entertained and happy."

I ended the call and watched the deserted street.

Empty. Just like Priest's search on the Volkov descendants. He searched up everything on Winter Volkov. There wasn't much. She married the old Brennan and died young. We searched for information on Aisling Brennan, but that was a dead-end road. No pictures. Same when it came to her daughter. The only reasonable explanation was that Wynter was Aisling Brennan's daughter. The woman my father shot.

And although everything pointed to Brennan's sister being dead, there was no way she could be. Brennan must have changed Aisling's and her baby's identities.

Jesus Christ!

I let out a frustrated breath, the cold winter air filling my lungs.

At this point, I was certain my father's presence at my home that day wasn't a coincidence. Of course, I had no proof. I should kill him and be done with the fucker. If only it wouldn't bring down the Syndicate on us. I didn't care if it was just me, but it'd be held against Emory, Priest, and Dante too.

So instead, I focused on finding Wynter.

The hope of finding her grew dimmer and dimmer by the day, but I refused to let it extinguish. I wouldn't survive it. My humanity certainly wouldn't. I fucking needed her and I never needed anything. I never kissed a mouth that tasted like hers. I never experienced a touch that soothed and burned like hers.

I shook my head, frustration clawing at my chest. I was born to a monster and became one. Over the last six months, my darkness ruled

275

me. It ran in my veins like poison and Wynter's lightness was my only cure. I wouldn't stop searching until I found her. Until I made her fulfill her promise.

She said she would stay. I'd make her stay.

Time to focus.

I glanced around the street on the outskirts of Jersey City. There was only one restaurant on this entire street, probably the entire block. The Bratva didn't like competition in any area of life. The restaurant sat facing the murky, polluted waters of Newark Bay. The restaurant fancied itself on a water view. More like a sewer view. Leave it to a Russian to fancy up the view.

The street was empty. Most normal people preferred to stay home and celebrate Christmas Eve with their family. Russians weren't normal people in my book. Besides, they didn't celebrate Christmas Eve on the same day as everyone else. Worked for me.

I entered the restaurant and sat myself by the table that gave me the entire view of the restaurant and the shitty water.

There were only two men seated around. Probably a cook and a waitress back there somewhere. I locked eyes with a mustached man who looked like he was born in the last century by the way he dressed. Some kind of Romanov-style mustache. He couldn't be more than forty, but dressed like he was a hundred and forty. No fucking style with these Russians.

His eyes shifted around, nervous and panicked. Then he glanced to the door, whether debating to run or expecting reinforcements, I didn't know. It didn't matter. I'd kill the motherfucker whether he knew something or didn't. In my eyes, all Russians were guilty.

A waitress peeked her head out, checking to see if indeed there was a customer. My heart stopped. Golden-blonde hair. Our eyes met. Disappointment washed over me. They were the wrong color. She came out of the back room and more bitterness slithered through my veins.

Wrong hair too. Blonde but not quite the same shade. Straight.

You'd think after almost six months of hunting for Wynter, I'd get used to this feeling. Disappointment. Anguish. Regret.

She came up to my table. "What can I get for you?"

She looked beaten down. About Wynter's age, she looked battered mentally and physically.

"Whatever the evening's special is."

She nodded and went to the kitchen. While I unfolded the wrapped silverware never looking away from the mustache. Akim Kazimir, the Pakhan's most trusted man. The second man had to be his bodyguard, because while his boss ate and slurped like it was his last meal, the other guy just sat at the table.

I'll make it his last meal, I mused sardonically to myself. I just hoped the motherfucker didn't throw up all this shit he was stuffing himself with. It'd make cleanup a bitch, not that I'd be personally doing it. Or I might just have my men blow up this motherfucking water-view restaurant. It'd save us time.

It took no time for the meal to arrive, considering I was the only other customer. I didn't bother eating it. I sat back in my chair, watching the man who I searched for over the last few months.

It didn't take long for the waitress to come back, her steps tentative and her look hesitant.

"Would you like anything else to drink or eat?" she asked, her eyes flitting to the neighboring table. She knew damn well I didn't want anything else, since I hadn't touched a thing.

"You might want to stay in the kitchen for a while," I told her, my fingers wrapping around the steak knife in my hand. To her credit, she didn't flinch. She didn't look back to the neighboring table. I saw an understanding flash in her eyes and she slowly turned around, then headed to the back of the restaurant.

The fucker at the other table never stopped eating. He had to be sure of himself, considering I was alone.

The second the waitress disappeared, I threw the knife, the swish sound of it sliced through the air until it hit the bodyguard right in the throat. The clatter of the silverware and gurgling barely registered, and before the other fucker could do a thing, I was already at his table and stabbed my fork right through his left hand.

"Not so fast, comrade," I drawled, ignoring his yelp. "We're going to talk first."

"You fucking DiLustros are all crazy," he hissed.

"Ahhh, so you know who I am," I deadpanned. "Good, let's cut to the chase, then. Tell me where you have my woman."

He snickered. "What woman?"

"Ah, see, when you say it like that, I'm certain you have her."

He shook his head. "Who's your woman?" he whimpered.

"Wynter Star." Honestly, we couldn't confirm if that was her real name. I thought so since she always responded without delay. Besides, if she was hiding her identity, why pick her grandmother's name? Everyone knew the name of the Pakhan's daughter. Well, everyone except me until recently.

Lesson learned.

His eyes flashed with surprise and I realized my fucking mistake. I revealed my cards. He didn't know I was looking for Wynter.

No matter, he wouldn't get out of this alive.

He reached for the knife with his other hand and slashed it at me. My reflexes quick, I caught his wrist, then twisted it backwards, the sound of crunching bones filling the air. I grabbed his throat and squeezed hard.

"Now, let's play nice," I growled. "Shall we?"

He spat at me, at least he attempted to. He was lousy at that too, because the spit only drooled down his face. Fucking moron.

"You'll tell me what you know," I declared darkly. "And I'll make your death quick."

"Never!" he hissed.

"They all say that in the beginning," I said coldly, then smiled with all the cruelty swimming in my veins. There was no need to mask it anymore.

My father was a disgusting piece of shit with a sadistic streak, but in moments like this, it was welcomed. I let it taint my veins and take over.

His left hand still sported a fork stabbed in it and I reached for my gun, then shot him twice. One in the left hand and one in the right.

His eyes bulged and he yelped like a baby.

"There we go," I purred. "Both of your hands are disabled. Now talk." Blood pooled on the table, mixing with his disgusting dinner. "You can take your time," I told him, smirking. "I have nowhere else to be."

Well, except Philly but that was a different kind of torture. The self-inflicted kind.

"You're just as crazy as your father," he screamed, pain twisting his face. It made his mustache all wrong. Not that it was right to start with. "DiLustros are monsters. Filthy, sick monsters."

My mouth curved into a cruel smile. "Then you know what I'm capable of. You really want to keep all your secrets?" I pulled out my Ka-Bar knife and cut through his crappy Russian tailored suit. Then I repeated the move, except this time I cut through his flesh. A long line from his shoulder to his wrist. "I'm still practicing my fileting skills."

So I started slicing, separating his skin from his muscles and his high-pitched screams filled the room.

"I can do this for days," I said with a twisted grin.

"We're looking for her too," he screamed like a woman. I paused my movement and waited for him to continue. "Pakhan is looking for her too," he repeated, panting. "We want her and her mother back."

"You don't have her?" I asked to ensure there were no misunderstandings.

He shook his head, beads of sweat dripping down his forehead.

"We thought they were dead, until recently. We got a tip that she lived. Aisling Brennan and her daughter." Then he laughed, slightly crazy and psychotic, coughed out blood. "It was your father who gave us the tip in exchange for a bride. He wants to grow your power."

Fuck. Me.

Rage boiled inside me, consuming me. Just as the blood of this motherfucker soaked through my clothes, so did the hate I had for my father. I didn't think I could hate him more. I was so fucking wrong.

"He wanted an alliance, a marriage arrangement between DiLustro and Volkov," he continued, spitting blood all over himself.

"Which DiLustro?" I asked, my voice strangely calm.

"Don't know. He never said. Pakhan refused his despicable offer. Volkov wouldn't further dilute the bloodline with DiLustros," he choked out, then coughed again. "Brennans were bad enough."

I didn't fucking care about their bloodline. Wynter was mine. I was fucking desperate to rip into him and end his miserable life. But I couldn't do it too soon.

"What else?" I bit out, the fury simmering through my veins.

"Our men followed you two in Philly, but then they lost you." The black Land Rover. The men Priest and I tortured. "We were so close. And now she disappeared again. You and your father are to blame."

It was all I needed to know. The Russians didn't have her.

This time I gripped his throat and squeezed as hard as I could until the veins in his eyes began to pop and I felt bones in his throat crushing under the force of my grip. He kept fighting. Goddamn Russians had thick necks. So I brought up my knife with the other hand and sliced him ear to ear.

I watched the light extinguish in his eyes and his blood soak my hands.

Breathing harshly, I turned to find the waitress watching me with sheer terror in her eyes. I couldn't blame her.

"I won't hurt you," I rasped. "You can leave or I can help you disappear. Your choice."

She blinked. Once, twice. "My mother is the cook."

"Both of you, then," I offered, the adrenaline still pumping through my veins.

Where are you, Wynter?

Present

Chapter Thirty-Eight

WYNTER

Nine months without Basilio DiLustro.

Counting days without him became part of my routine. Regardless of what was going on in my life.

No matter how brutal the last two months had been.

They had been the most exhausting months of my life. Maybe it was the state of my mind. Even after all this time, Bas was a constant whisper in the back of my mind. Sometimes I even had a full-blown conversation with him.

Yes, it was disturbing, but it got me through.

"Man, even when you're sweaty you look fucking beautiful," Derek commented.

I smiled at his compliment. I liked Derek, but I worried about showing him that. We went out a few times, but I immediately realized my mistake. To me it was just a friendly way of hanging out and getting comfortable with my partner. To him, it was more.

So whenever we were required to make an appearance at an event or for a sponsor, I dragged my girls with me. Much to their dismay, but they always came through.

"Okay, one more time," my mother's voice came through the skating rink.

"Your mother is merciless," Derek grumbled, the corners of his mouth barely flexing.

He was right. She was merciless. It was almost midnight and our flight out was tomorrow. The Olympics didn't start for another five days, but we didn't want to risk the weather turning for the worse.

The two of us came to our positions, in the middle of the rink. I rolled my shoulders, Derek did the same. Sometimes we moved so similarly, it was freaky.

I turned my head to look at him. He wasn't a bad-looking man, with his brown hair and warm eyes. He was tall and strong, just a few years older than me. But I couldn't help but compare him to Bas. I compared everyone to him, and somehow, everyone faded in comparison to him.

Brad Pitt. *Nah, I'll pass.*

Theo James. *No, I'm good.*

Basilio DiLustro. *Yes, please and thank you.* Pathetic, considering he betrayed me. Clearly, my self-respect was lacking.

"Ready?" My mom's voice stopped my handsome-ranking comparison.

Both of us nodded.

The music came on. My favorite Dua Lipa song. I had to fight my mother and Derek on the choice of music. I won, though reluctantly. "Hotter than Hell" would be our freestyle, short program.

I shut my mind down, wishing Mom would let me skate with AirPods on. It was so much easier to tune out the world, but it wasn't allowed during competitions, so it made sense she forbid it during practice too.

The moment we started skating, I felt the weight lift off my chest. It was what I loved about this sport, though I preferred to skate alone.

The adrenaline from the last hour of skating still pumped through my veins.

"Perfect height," Mom commended. Derek and I flew through the air, doing side-by-side jumps together. Triple Lutz. Then the Axel jump. We had to be doing good because no corrections were shouted across the rink in her firm coach voice.

Probably another reason she wouldn't allow me headphones while skating.

Four minutes and thirty seconds.

And we were done. It was all that took for both Derek and I to breathe hard and choppy, our heartbeats racing. Our eyes met and we both knew it. We nailed it.

He cupped my face and I had to stifle a wince.

"That Olympic gold is ours." He beamed.

I nodded. The competition would be fierce, I knew it. But we worked hard and gave it our all. It was all we could do.

My eyes sought out my mom, our coach, sitting in the stands. A nod of approval. "We're ready."

We. This was for her, even before I knew the full story of what happened. I was happy about my achievements four years ago. After that, I skated to relax and get lost in it. I never imagined going back to it as a professional.

She stood up and I saw her wince, then she limped slowly down to the gate opening it to wait for us.

Derek and I headed toward her, where she already waited for us with skate guards. I took the offered plastic and slipped them over my blades. Derek did the same.

Then we stepped onto solid ground. Coach gave us her firm stare.

"Tomorrow we fly out," she started, then glanced at Derek. "You'll fly with us." Uncle Brennan secured a private plane for us. It made it easier to travel for sure. And safer. Then she returned her eyes to me. "You skated your best, Star. I'm proud of you." My mother was the only person on this entire planet who called me Star. It was my middle name, but according to her, it should have been my first. But she caved in to Grandpa. "You did well feeling the music and synchronizing your moves to Derek's."

I nodded, my breathing still slightly hitched.

"Do you ladies want me to drive you home?" Derek offered and I shook my head.

"No, thank you," I told him. "I drove Mom's car."

My Jeep was still in New York, but Mom had a car here despite that most of the time she couldn't drive. Her knee hurt her too much and she could never quite master driving with her left foot. She even had her knee replaced but it still bothered her.

Derek pecked me on the cheek, nodded at his coach, then turned around and was gone.

I sat on the closest bench and stretched my legs out ahead of me. Every single muscle in my body ached as I bent over and started undoing my laces. In my head, I was going over the list of things I had to pack and things I should talk to Mom about, but I kept avoiding.

Maybe I could just do it after the Olympics. I didn't want to upset her and ruin this moment for her.

"Your bodyguard came and checked on you." She broke the silence and my shoulders instantly tensed. She made it clear that she disliked Sasha. Since I came back to California, he'd been popping in and out, randomly. He appointed himself my guardian. I appreciated it, I really did. Except it made my mother agitated every time.

"Hmmm." I made a small noise. I hoped she'd drop it. I was certain she was just as tired as I was.

"I don't like him around you." Yep, no such luck. Even midnight hours couldn't tame her displeasure. I wished Juliette was here to distract her. She had become good at that.

"Sasha's a good guy," I mumbled, as I pulled on my Chucks a sharp pain pierced through my chest. *God, will it ever stop?* Every single time I put shoes on, the image of Bas kneeling down flashed in my mind. It started as a fairy tale and ended—

No, I couldn't think about it right now.

I set my skates into their protective case, then zipped my bag. I dug out the car keys from the pocket of the duffle bag, then picked it up off the ground and threw it over my shoulder.

"Are we ready?"

Both of us headed out of the complex and over the empty parking lot that was now lit up like a goddamn stadium. Courtesy of Sasha Nikolaev. To ensure there was nobody lurking in the dark when he wasn't around.

And my mother doesn't like him, I scoffed in my head. She was nuts. It should be exactly the kind of guy mothers should want for their girls.

I clicked the button on my fob and slid into the driver seat, then waited for my mother to settle in. It took her a moment since bending her knee caused her pain. I never complained about her taking her time. It was the least I could do.

Once she was inside, she clicked her seat belt and I did the same.

Just as I put the keys in the ignition and started the car, my mother spoke again, "Men like him, whether good or not, they destroy people's lives."

I shot her a sideways glance. I understood now why she'd say something like that. I didn't necessarily disagree either. But we were born into this world. The underworld. No matter how far we moved, that life was always a part of us. There was no escaping it.

"Mom, after the Olympics, I'm done with competing," I declared, changing the subject.

My mother's head snapped my way. "You're too young to retire."

I shrugged. "The girls and I want to start a school. I might open a rink and coach. I don't know. But I won't be competing."

Tick-tock. Tick-tock. Tick-tock.

"Why?"

I took a deep breath, then slowly exhaled.

"I'm doing this for you. You wanted this, not me. Single skating was my thing. Pairs was yours. Yours and—" My words faltered. I didn't want to cause her anguish, but just as Uncle kept me in the dark, so did Mom. Neither one of them bothered to enlighten Juliette nor me. Besides, the moment seemed opportune and there was just something easier about driving and talking. "Yours and my dad's, I'm guessing. But that was taken away from you when you were shot in the knee."

Mother's gasp sounded in the cabin of her little Honda car. My eyes flickered her way to see her pale and I fucking hated that I upset her. I could sort of see why Uncle kept protecting us, knowing that saying some things could bring pain. But eventually pain came regardless.

"What happened, Mom?" I whispered. For once, I wanted someone to tell me the entire story.

The silence stretched, and just when I was certain she wouldn't tell me, she started, "I don't know how much you know."

"Pretend I know nothing," I told her. "And tell me everything."

A dark and bitter laugh, unlike any I heard from her before, left her lips.

"Well, let's start with my father who kidnapped my mother from a powerful Pakhan." Her hands clutched around her thick gray sweater. She never bothered wearing a jacket. "But then he fell in love. Your grandpa can be quite romantic, you know." I nodded because I did know. The way he talked about Grandma could make you cry. "I fear you might have inherited that gene," she continued. I didn't say anything, because truthfully, I wasn't sure that I didn't. Juliette accused me once of being a realist with the most romantic of hearts.

"Anyhow, I was the product of that fiasco. Liam took care of me more than Father did. He grieved too much or maybe I reminded him too much of my mother. I don't know. I learned much later in life than you that I enjoyed ice-skating. I was good." I nodded. She had a good eye for everything ice-skating related. "Though I dare say, you're better." When I went to protest, she raised her hand and stopped me. "You are better, Star. And I am very proud of you. Both you and Juliette. I know I don't say it enough."

My throat squeezed and my fingers gripped the wheel so hard, my knuckles hurt. She rarely praised us. So the two of us made it a practice to praise each other. Even when we did dumb stuff. Like stealing money from the mafia.

Fuck, I wished Juliette was here to hear this. She needed this too.

Mom's left hand reached out and she placed it over my right one that clutched the steering wheel. "I love you, Star. Regardless of the history."

I swallowed hard. "What do you mean?"

"I moved to Chicago when I was barely sixteen. They had an ice-skating program and I *had* to be in it." The way she said *had* made me think she *insisted* on being in it. "Liam made it happen for me. My poor brother always tried to make things happen for me. Two months in a foreign city, I learned how to fool my guards. I'd pretend I went to sleep and then sneak out." I couldn't help but smile since it was exactly what Juliette and I did. "One night I ran into a man. I fell in love; I thought I'd die without him. I spent more time with him than skating. I wanted to be his whole world, just as he was mine. But I was way too young to understand the brutality of our world. It was too late when I learned who he was. A married man, with a child of his own already."

By this time, we were home and I parked the car. Neither one of us moved. We had never had conversations like this and I wasn't about to interrupt this one.

"I had a baby at seventeen and I lost that baby," she said, her expression full of pain, it broke my heart. I couldn't take it, so I leaned over and wrapped my arms around her. I hugged her tightly, wishing I could ease all her pain. Even after all these years, her pain was so vibrant. It didn't give me hope for healing and getting over Bas. "I came back to New York. Unfortunately, I caught the eye of Gio DiLustro." A disgusting shudder ran down my spine. I couldn't think of that despicable man without fear and disgust.

"Why did he shoot you?" I rasped.

"Because I refused him," she whispered. "Gio DiLustro wanted more power, and through my connection to the Volkov family, he thought he'd get it. Maybe he would have, or maybe not. I didn't care to find out. Liam kept him away from me while I put all my energy into skating with your father. He was a good man. It wasn't a passionate kind of love. More of the mutually caring kind. It was enough for me though. After the pain I experienced, I didn't want the kind of love that could consume you, only to leave you empty when without them."

Mom pulled away slightly and took my face between her hands. "You know what I'm talking about, don't you? Your distraction."

My heart stilled and went ice cold. If she learned about another DiLustro destroying our family and told Liam, it could cause more deaths. My family's. *Basilio's*, I worried reluctantly.

And like a coward I remained silent. I couldn't admit it. Not yet. Not now.

"Finish the story, Mom," I croaked, the words choking my throat and the vise around my heart squeezing.

"I got pregnant, skating took a pause, but I coached a bit. I couldn't stand to be away from the ice rink. I was about five months pregnant with you," she murmured, her gaze looking out the windshield and into the darkness. "Your father and I ran into Gio alone, right after he learned that it was his brother I gave my virginity to. So he decided he'd take it all away from me, to make me pay for my refusal. Your father, my skating, and you. He succeeded in the first two, but not you."

The past whipped around us, the cool winter air seeped through the windows, but it wasn't bitter cold like the truth.

"I love you, Mom," I whispered, hugging her tightly. "I'm so sorry."

I'm so sorry I didn't kill Gio DiLustro when I had the chance and ended his cruel life.

Chapter Thirty-Nine

BASILIO

It was mid-February. I didn't visit my sister, Emory, nearly as much as I should have. Dante and Priest were here too. We combined pleasure with business.

We took care of the business earlier. We secured a deal with a distributor and intercepted another gun shipment going my father's way. Customers grew agitated and displeased with him. Slowly but surely, they turned their backs on him and came running to us.

Eye for a fucking eye, Father.

The soft piano notes filled the air of my sister's living room in Las Vegas. She always had a fondness for luxury, opera, and everything chick flick. I fucking hated all that shit. There was only a short period in my life that I tolerated it. I didn't care to think about that period.

My jaw tightened as venom crawled through my veins, same as it did every time I thought of *her*. And I thought about her all the fucking time. It had been two hundred and eighty-nine days.

I looked for her everywhere. Yet, it was as if she never existed. Even Madame Sylvie disappeared.

"You should stop going on killing sprees, Basilio," Emory scolded.

Anyone else would shit their pants to say something like that to me. Not my sister and cousins. And lately, they'd been giving me advice more than I cared to hear it. "The men who work for Father will never betray him, you know that."

Yeah, so I expanded my hunting ground to men who worked for my father. Angelo got on that list too.

"Are you listening, Basilio?" she nagged.

"I'm trying really hard to ignore you," I grumbled. "But you're making it hard. Isn't there a man's heart you need to squash or something?"

She was just as damaged as me. No amount of my protection could have spared her our father's brutality. It left a mark. I still remembered her as she used to be. Soft and caring.

Our father wiped that shit out. Just as he did everything soft in our lives.

I still remembered her hiding underneath my bed, begging for a bedtime story so she wouldn't have to hear the screams.

"Isn't there a wife you need to find?" she retorted sarcastically. Nobody else would dare to suggest that. I'd gut them alive.

The notion of taking any other woman to bed was sickening. Love and affection had no room in our world. I had gotten a taste of it and it ruined me. For anyone else.

The rational part of me understood I couldn't remain single for the rest of my life. The sooner I secured an heir, the less chances of my father declaring another heir. He took another mistress after Thalia and the rumor was he was trying for another kid.

Because Emory and I were his greatest disappointments. Like I gave a fuck.

"No." Okay, as far as conversations went, this wasn't that great. I knew I had to marry, secure an heir. But fuck if I was in the mood for it.

There was only one woman who made me want to make that leap.

Out of the blue, Emory jumped to her feet and grinned.

"We're watching the Olympics tonight," she announced.

Dante and Priest snorted. I agreed with the sentiment, but I knew Emory always wanted more out of life than this life of the underworld. It was the least we could do. Grant her an evening watching the Olympics.

Fuck, it will be a long night.

The large fifty-inch screen came on and the broadcaster's enthusiastic voice filled the room.

Jesus H. Christ.

Dante, Priest, and I shared a glance. Dante rolled his eyes, smirking. He thought Emory was corny. He wasn't off base, but we loved her. Priest quickly wiped a hand across his mouth in a poor attempt to hide his amusement. He knew Emory would try to kick all our asses if she caught us laughing at her.

I should just come up with some poor-ass excuse and get the fuck out. If I said it was time to go hunting for Russians or anyone, they'd all believe me.

My mind made up, I stood up and adjusted my cufflinks. I opened my mouth to excuse myself for the night when the commentator started blabbing again.

"The next team is our ice-princess darling Star Flemming and her partner, Derek Konstantin."

"Oh my gosh," Emory gushed. "These two are everyone's absolute favorites. She's so fucking good at it, already won an Olympic gold medal in singles when she was barely seventeen."

I shot an agitated look at the television and nothing would have made me happier than to shoot the goddamn thing so it would go off. The audience cheered and screamed like new gods were born.

A pair stepped out onto the ice and Emory squealed, reminding me of the young girl she used to be a long time ago.

"Star had some rough times lately, but I know she'll come out on

293

top." Emory must have been her number one fan. Wonderful, from underworld to a fanatic.

I stood frozen, unable to look away. The two figures glided in perfect harmony, hand in hand. Dark hair and golden sunshine. Hair of the spun gold and light green eyes stared at the screen.

She was on television.

The familiar bright smile on a woman's face that I used to know so well. Her unruly blonde curls pulled up in a tight bun. She was slightly thinner, but it was unmistakably *her*. The only woman I had ever wanted.

The woman I had been desperately searching for.

"Yesterday the pair skated effortlessly. These two are amazing together! What chemistry!"

The commentator on the screen cooed in excitement as snippets of their yesterday's performance flashed across the screen. Twists. Spirals. Jumps.

Fucking Christ. No wonder her legs were so important to her. Images flashed like polaroids through my mind. The first night when she offered me five hundred bucks to catch her, claiming her legs were valuable. Her odd ballet lessons. The day we met at the ice-skating rink but she certainly didn't give the impression of being a champion.

Yet, now as I watched the screen, every move on ice reflected a professional figure skater. I didn't know jack crap about ice-skating, though you didn't need to know much to see that the performance yesterday was good.

"Let's see what kind of show they give us today. I have a feeling it will be spectacular. And if they deliver, we'll be seeing them tomorrow. I have no doubt these two are in the race for the gold."

Emory snickered. "If she doesn't win the gold medal, the Olympics are rigged."

I watched in a daze as a woman who looked like my Wynter skated to the middle of the rink, looking like an ice princess. Or a queen.

Dante shoved a glass into my hand. "Here, sit down."

For the first time in over a decade, I allowed someone to tell me what to do. My eyes glued to the screen, as if I was scared she'd disappear again. I watched them take their spot in the middle of the ice rink.

I watched her shake her shoulders out, take a deep breath in and then out, and then she was in the zone. Just as she was when I watched her take her ballet lessons. For fuck's sake, I thought she was training to be a professional ballerina. Not a professional ice-skater.

Star Flemming.

She gave me a different name. Wynter Star.

Her partner and she shared a glance. The audience was cheering them on. Chanting her name like they were celebrities.

Star! Star! Star!

Derek! Derek!

People were going nuts over them.

The two of them turned around at the same time to face the center of the ice. Her partner held out his hand to the side, and without even glancing his way, Star put her hand in his. The two were so synchronized, almost as if they shared the same breath and same thoughts.

I fucking hated it.

Her hand pressed against her chest, her neck gracefully extended as the notes of a song came up. The music started. "Unstoppable" by Sia. I couldn't tear my eyes off her.

She danced with him, but all I could see was her.

The music led her, her muscles relaxed as she danced expressing every single tune of the song with her movement. You felt her dance, felt her message. Fuck, she was unstoppable.

As she skated, her whole face glowed.

It made it impossible to look away from her. As if she felt every word and note of the song.

"Look at the height! Triple Lutz! And another. Look at those jumps! I have never seen such chemistry on or off the ice."

My grip tightened around the glass and ice rattled in it, protesting. Wynter's expression was of pure bliss. It was that expression which haunted me for the last nine months. It was the way she looked at me. Like I was her whole world.

"Wow, she's really good," Priest muttered.

"You think she's boning him?" Dante asked curiously, and I wanted nothing more than to punch him.

"Speculation has been that the two of them are a couple," Emory chimed in unhelpfully and unknowingly fed the rage boiling inside me. "She denied it, but her partner refused to confirm or deny, which feeds all the frenzy about them."

I'll hunt him down and kill him, I resolved.

"Impeccable triple Salchows, synchronized to perfection!" the speaker screamed, his words piercing through my brain. I had no fucking idea what that meant. Except that she flew through the air. She moved fast on the ice. So fast that if she fell, she'd break more than just one bone in her damn body.

"Look at that death spiral! Amazing! These two are truly unstoppable."

"Holy shit!" Emory exclaimed. "What a comeback!"

My sister was jumping up and down from the excitement while I felt my rage expanding in my chest, threatening to explode.

Wynter was arched backward on one foot, close to the ice as her partner spiraled her. One mistake and her skull would be split open. The next moment she flew through the air and landed on her feet. Emory's excited screams sounded distant, the rush in my ears drowning everything out.

"Triple Axel. Again, synchronized perfectly!"

They both landed at the exact same moment. As if they were one, body and soul. The way she looked on the ice took my breath away and I wasn't even sure it was in a good way.

"Look at that throw jump."

I fucking hated seeing her with him. His hands on her body. **"These two have the most amazing chemistry I have ever seen."**

Hate slithered through my veins. Venomous and powerful. I should stop watching it before I blow a gasket.

The performance ended, the final notes of the song ending at the same exact moment as their final pose. The audience went wild. The couple on the ice panted, both of them out of breath.

Then her partner lifted her by her slim waist, twirled her in the air and then pressed a kiss on her lips. I gripped my glass like my sanity depended on it, the cracking of glass mirroring the state of my heart and soul.

The sound of breaking glass filled the room and shattered around me. Hearing the broadcaster rave about the couple felt like a blow to the stomach. It stole my breath away, turned my blood to fire, then killed something inside me. I lost it.

I reached for my gun and pulled the trigger. The TV screen sparked. Then I destroyed every goddamn thing in Emory's living room.

Chapter Forty

BASILIO

P riest waved his iPad, the only undamaged piece of electronics that survived after I lost my shit.

I extended my hand but he narrowed his eyes. "I don't think so," he growled. "This is the only surviving piece in a five-mile radius."

After I had destroyed everything I got my hands on, Priest held on to his iPad like his life depended on it. Good thing too, because once the red haze over my brain retracted, I could think clearly again. And I put Priest to work. He'd dug up everything on Star Flemming. Clearly Angelo, my father's right-hand man, couldn't be counted on if he was unable to retrieve a single piece of information on the woman who the whole world knew. Fucking traitor.

"What do you have?" I asked him, staring into the dark of the night.

Emory and Dante sat in the room with us. My sister knew the athlete side of Wynter and was able to share everything she knew about Star Flemming. But I needed to know everything.

"All we had to do was look up Star Flemming and information

flowed," Priest dropped the bomb and all our attention snapped to him. "And guess fucking what?"

"What?" I grumbled.

"Brennan has a standing agreement with Nico Morrelli, wiping out all traces of his family on a daily, possibly hourly, basis. I find something on her and then it disappears. I was able to hack into Morrelli's web frame for all of fifteen seconds but it was enough to dig up her name."

I clenched my fists, the need to punch something so strong, my muscles actually ached.

"He hid her and her mother from the DiLustros after whatever had happened between Aisling Brennan and your father, Basilio. And he kept them off the Russians' radar."

The pent-up frustration stirred in my body. It recognized being close to my target and I wanted to pounce. But I had to be calculating and careful. Otherwise, I'd lose her, and next time, I might not find her again.

Priest's guy walked into the room and set a large desktop screen on the desk in Emory's office.

"Refrain from destroying this," Emory grumbled, glaring at me. "Do you need cables?" she asked Priest.

The latter shook his head. "I have it connected via Bluetooth."

Two swipes, the screen came on and Wynter's image filled my sight.

I froze.

She took my breath away. Every. Single. Fucking. Time.

She wore cropped black leggings, pink Chucks, and a loose pink off-the-shoulder shirt that came down to her mid-thighs. Her duffle bag thrown over her shoulder, her gaze was distant, as she smiled at someone. Paparazzi had to snap the photo as she was leaving one of her training sessions.

Fuck, she was so painfully beautiful. Her blonde curls gave a halo expression even in the picture. I knew firsthand how soft those curls were. Her hair trailed down her shoulders. Her face was flawless. But it was her eyes that got me. The way they shimmered, big and curious, even in the photo.

Now that I knew she was alive and well, living her life happy and free, all the while I was burning down this world, looking for her, red haze marred my vision. The anger that she'd left me was so strong, I had to choke it down. It burned in my throat, leaving ash and acid in its wake.

I wanted to make her hurt, so she had a taste of the pain I went through for the past nine months.

"Who's the guy next to her?" Dante asked. "It doesn't look like her skating partner."

"Sasha Nikolaev," Priest answered. "You'll see him a lot."

My gaze darkened and Dante snickered. "Fuck, I can see we'll have to kill him."

He wiped a hand across his mouth in a poor attempt to hide his amusement and thrill at the challenge. Fucking Dante was all about challenges. Crazy fucker.

"You can try," Priest retorted in a sarcastic tone, "but more than likely you'll fail. Sasha Nikolaev is rumored to be one of the best contracted killers for Cassio King, his gang, and the Nikolaev men. She has been under Sasha's protection."

"Getting sweet with a Russian, huh?" Dante egged on and I had to fight the urge to shoot him. "The irony of it all."

I couldn't think about Wynter and the blond prick on the screen; otherwise, I'd put a bullet in everyone's goddamn head.

"It's platonic between Nikolaev and the skating star," Priest added. It didn't ease the fury. I grabbed a cigarette and tapped it on the table, though I wouldn't light it.

"You have to admit, they make a striking couple," Dante mused.

Leaning back, I rolled a cigarette between my fingers and shot Dante a look that conveyed he was close to being my dead cousin.

"They're both too blond," Emory reasoned, trying to soothe my seething anger.

Priest flipped the screen, and unfortunately, it switched to an image of Sasha and Wynter together in Portugal. A reporter must have snapped a picture of them jogging together. I fucking hated how good they looked. They'd have pretty, blond babies.

Over. My. Dead. Body.

"Priest. Continue." My voice whipped through the air as a red mist blurred my vision. It turned out my mother was right to fear I'd become a mold of my father and the Syndicate. It was exactly what happened.

I still remembered the disdainful look in her eyes as she walked away, with little Emory in her arms.

"You'll turn into your father," she whispered as she walked away without a backward glance. She hated me before I even had a chance to prove to her I could be a better man.

For Wynter, I wanted to be a better man and she walked away without a backward glance too. After nine months of going mad, it turned out she was alive and well. Fucking skating.

Images of the woman who I've been hunting for the past nine months flashed through the screen. Gold medals. Competitions. Accomplishments. Travels. Friends.

"Freeze that," Dante barked, straightening up in his spot. "Who's that?"

An image of a woman with a face resembling Wynter's stared at us. Eyes that looked empty. Face that was drawn but spoke of beauty that faded in sorrow and resignation.

"That's her mother, Aisling Brennan," Priest answered. "Also Wynter's coach."

Dante shook his head. "It can't be," he muttered. "She looks like—"

"Like Wynter," I snapped, annoyed at his behavior. "I can see."

Dante shook his head. "No, she looks like my father's old mistress."

We all straightened up. "What?"

"I'd remember her anywhere. She looks like my father's old mistress. From way back, when we were kids. Her hair was black back then, but it could have been colored. Or a wig. She always hid her face behind sunglasses and her hair under her shawls."

The four of us shared a look. "Are you sure?"

"Yes, I'm goddamn sure," he snapped. "And the day I saw her bring the baby. Priest. You don't forget a woman who brought a baby to your door."

Priest had blond hair, his coloring different from the rest of us. Dante and Priest shared a father, but they had different mothers.

"Who's Wynter's father?" I kept my voice quiet, dread pooling in the pit of my stomach. I was too deep with this girl and incest wasn't in my fucking cards.

"Not to worry, her father was a figure skater," Priest assured me. "Her mother's skating partner."

"Are you sure?" I barked. I wouldn't allow any fucking obstacle between us, but that one it would be impossible to overcome. *Jesus Christ.* My uncle better not have fucked Wynter's mother and gotten her pregnant with Wynter.

"Yes," Priest confirmed. "Aisling Brennan underwent fetal blood transfusion to treat anemia in the fetus while she was pregnant with Wynter. The blood count of her fetus was too low and the condition was life threatening. They used her father's blood for transfusion while he was on his deathbed. Ivan Flemming. Fetus was Rh positive and the red blood cells were being destroyed by the Rh-sensitized mother's immune system."

"Okay, I'm assuming only parents' blood could have been used?" Emory inquired. "Because that sounded like a bunch of mumbo-jumbo shit to me."

"Wynter's mother is Rh negative and so are our fathers," Dante summarized it for her. "So are we. It means the probability of DiLustro being Wynter's father is null. Rh factors follow a common pattern of genetic inheritance. If both parents have a negative Rh factor, the baby will too. Well, Wynter is Rh positive."

"Thank fuck," I muttered.

Another image flashed on the screen. Wynter with her three friends. The quad team. The four sat together in Wynter's Jeep, somber and their eyes locked, probably contemplating the next heist.

Priest froze the screen and pointed to the woman. "Who is this?" He pointed to Wynter's red-haired friend with hazel eyes.

"One of Wynter's friends. The four of them burned down a guy's house. According to Wynter, they all went to Yale together." Of course, I couldn't be sure she told me the truth.

"She was in my club the night my armored truck got robbed," Priest declared, his eyes glued on the woman.

"If she was there, so were her friends," I told him.

"It means Wynter and her friends had something to do with the truck robbery," Dante growled. "Just like they pulled that stunt in my casino."

Why wasn't I surprised?

"The red-haired woman's mine," Priest growled. I cocked my eyebrow at the unexpected declaration.

"Well, if we are throwing around claims," Dante drawled, "the blue-eyed one is mine."

I smirked. "That one is psychotic," I deadpanned. "She burned down a fucking house."

Dante shrugged. Of course, it wouldn't bother any of us what they did. As long as they were ours.

Emory scoffed. "You three are idiots."

Ignoring my sister, I locked eyes with Priest. "I'm going to need to buy your Philly club, with the purchase date of last year."

"Why?" Emory asked, her brows knitted.

"Because I'm going to make Wynter settle that debt," I told her, smiling darkly. "Dante, is that illegitimate Ashford in Canada still asking for information on an Afghan supplier?"

She scoffed. "The fucker will never get it."

I grinned. "Never say never. I know Byron Ashford is trying to mend the relationship with his illegitimate brother. So we will use the Afghan supplier connection to blackmail our dear Ashford cousins to back us up."

"Why in the fuck do we even want them on our side?" Emory asked.

"We can't win against the Brennans, Nikolaevs, and Cassio's gang. But with the four Ashford brothers in our corner, the odds will be better. We have to plan for the worst-case scenario."

"Brennan's gonna want a war," Priest guessed.

"And he'll get it," I told him.

"Basilio, you're a scary motherfucker when you scheme," Emory remarked dryly. I'd be a scary motherfucker if I lost Wynter for good.

I turned my attention back to the golden-haired woman on the screen.

I'd marry that girl if it was the last thing I did on this fucking earth.

Chapter Forty-One

WYNTER

"You have done well, Star. Now finish it and bring home the gold."

I nodded, without turning to look at my mother.

At this moment, she was my coach. Truthfully, she had been more coach than mother my entire life. At least now after our conversation, I understood the reason behind it and I was fine with it. Maybe coaching was her coping mechanism, just as shoving all my feelings somewhere deep down in a dark abyss was my way of dealing with all the shit.

The familiar, dull ache swelled in my chest. I was used to it by now. I didn't think it'd ever go away. It might ease, but it'd be part of me until the day I died. Bas would forever drum through my veins with each heartbeat.

Derek stood behind me and his hands came to both my shoulders. I hated any man's touch but with Derek it was a necessity. I had learned to cope with it.

"Good?"

I kept my breathing steady. "Yeah."

I hadn't told him this would be my last competition. Mother knew and we both agreed there was no sense putting that burden on him. This was our home run. Once we won the gold, I had to put an end to all of this. Figure out who I was. Without ice-skating and without Bas.

Derek would have to find himself a new partner.

My eyes focused on the pair performing. We'd be the last ones on the ice. Go big or go home. I intended to go big, then go home. Wherever that was.

A tingle of awareness shot through me and I searched the crowd in the stands. It was packed. Fans with the banners for their favorite couples. I didn't see anyone who stood out, yet I couldn't shake off the feeling of being watched. And not by the crowd of fans.

It was the familiar kind of gaze that sent shivers down my spine. The kind that felt like a warm caress over my skin. Goose bumps rose along my flesh, and awareness touched my soul. God, sometimes I wished I'd felt nothing. Like Alexei Nikolaev.

Instead I felt so damn much, I felt like shattered glass on the inside, while on the outside, I tried to keep my shit together. Be the perfect skater. Be the perfect partner. Be the perfect daughter and friend.

I just wasn't perfect for anything anymore, but to be Bas's woman. A familiar need to scream scratched at my throat.

I blinked. Black suit. Broad shoulders. Pale blue eyes.

Alexei and Aurora stood with Davina, the latter two watching me with worry in their eyes. I smiled, while my throat squeezed. I was falling apart. I knew it. They knew it. The thread would snap. I just had to make it through one last performance.

"You don't have to do this," Davina mouthed. Her belly was so big, I was sure she was harboring twins in her womb. She assured me the doctors said there was only one baby.

"Just say the word," Sasha joined the three. "And we leave. Screw the Olympics."

Derek scoffed behind me. "Why would she want to leave? We are one last performance away from the gold."

This time I met Derek's eyes and shook my head. "Let's just stay focused," I rasped, my voice hoarse. "We do this and we're golden."

You're golden.

I felt Derek's hands on my shoulders again and couldn't help the flinching but I quickly hid it.

We've warmed up. We went through the routine one more time. There was nothing more to do. Just wait for our turn. I wanted it over with, but on the other hand, I worried about what that ending would mean for me.

"Your uncle is here," Derek whispered into my ear and it had me looking up. The last time my uncle came to my competition, it was at the last Olympics. Other than that, he didn't come around for my competitions. It just wasn't his thing.

I recognized him sitting next to Juliette and Ivy, Cassio and his wife on the other side of him. Even Nico, his wife, and kids were here. The whole damn underworld. I was surprised my mother didn't say anything about it.

The women waved their arms like crazy, grinning and more than likely screaming. They looked so fucking excited while I... I felt nothing. Dead on the inside.

Just so goddamn empty.

I shoved the feelings that threaten to rise up and choke me somewhere deep down in a dark hole. I couldn't feel it anymore. If the pain took hold of my throat, I'd lose before I even stepped on the ice. *We'd lose*, I reminded myself.

I swallowed the lump in my throat and lifted my hand, then waved it at my family.

My uncle and I came to an understanding, though tension still ran thick at times. We used Davina to soothe our tension.

The music ended and I returned my attention to the two figure skaters as they got off the ice.

Mom took my and Derek's hands into hers, zeroed her eyes on us and said, "You're both ready. Make me proud." She gave us both a smile, one of those rare ones. "It's your time. Go big." *Or go home.*

We both nodded. I slid my hand into Derek's and we made our way to the opening onto the ice. I took my skate guards off and handed them to my coach. My mother. Our eyes connected and I caught a flicker of worry in hers, but she quickly masked it. She was good at hiding her feelings. I was slowly catching up.

The second my toe pick hit the ice, the audience burst into a loud cheer. I zoned it all out. The wild crowd. The cheers. The chanting.

"They are going nuts over you," Derek murmured softly into my ear.

"And you," I answered automatically.

I used to live and breathe skating. It felt like home. Like love, so fucking right and invincible. And now I felt like a fraud, because the only way I could function on ice was by pretending that Bas was with me. It was always about him. He was my beginning and my end.

Hand in hand, Derek and I skated out toward the middle of the ice together. The crowd's screams got louder and wilder.

Star! Star! Star!

Derek! Derek! Derek!

We both got into our places. My hands and knees got into the position. Our eyes locked and the music started.

My first glide across the ice and everyone was forgotten. The song "Astronomical" by SVRCINA came on and Bas's face flashed in my mind. My body relaxed and the feeling of oblivion traveled through my veins.

Temporarily, I forgot it all. The pain. The past. The cruelty.

I floated between heaven and earth.

It felt like when Bas held me. Like the euphoria of a lover. I didn't think, I just let the routine and muscle memory guide me and all the while my heart was with the man I lost my heart to. The music mix changed to "Legends Are Made" and with the beat I went into a triple Axel, perfectly in sync with Derek's.

The adrenaline rush swam through my veins as we took a half loop and then we were leaping into the air into a quadruple jump in Salchow.

Another loop, the music and each move was part of me, buried in my bones. Ingrained in every fiber, just as Bas was.

I skated backwards, Derek forward as we shifted into a dance lift and the world spun in a circle. This was what I lived for, it was the best feeling in the world. The pain, the adrenaline, the exhilaration. It was my adrenaline shot, the only one that worked for me.

Until Basilio DiLustro.

Months of practice and pain from hitting the hard surface of the unforgiving ice. This was it. It was all for this. My breathing elevated, a sheer layer of sweat ran down my spine despite the icy temperature. Another crescendo reached its peak and *this was it.*

The death spiral.

Derek pivoted me around a curve holding my left hand, my body horizontal and low to the ice. I couldn't see anything, the only thing I felt were the motions, each move ingrained in me, anticipated. Then I was thrown, flying through the air, landing perfectly.

I heard screaming and cheers in the audience.

Coming to a perfect halt, our bodies lined up and both of our breathing heavy, I locked eyes with Derek. With our final pose, the music ended.

One breath. Two breaths.

"We did it," I breathed out, panting in and out. And we were fucking amazing if the cheers and screaming was anything to go by.

"Yes," Derek shouted, swinging his hand through the air.

I breathed hard, both my hands covering my face, and I bent over. My lungs were killing me.

"That's how the legends are made," the crowd screamed over and over again.

Despite it all, I smiled with disbelief and returned Derek's hug.

"We fucking did it," he whispered.

Chapter Forty-Two

BASILIO

"**Y**ou were on fire, Wynter." Brennan's voice was full of pride.

The entire group stood in the hallway, in front of the women's changing room. Wynter and her girl squad, Brennan and his supposed dead sister, the Nikolaev men, and their women. It looked like some damn family affair and I wanted to shoot them all and steal the golden princess. Though that might be a step too far.

None of them moved or bothered with the constant commotion of girls going in and out of the changing rooms.

I noted Nico Morrelli and Cassio King left with their families as soon as Wynter and her partner secured the gold.

"That was spectacular," he continued. "Grandpa watched the show from Ireland, cheering you on."

Liam hugged her and my fists clenched. It finally made sense why I ran into Wynter in Liam's home. She was his niece. All along, she had been right under my nose.

Though I'd agree with Brennan on one thing. Wynter on ice was a sight to behold. It was like she was born on it. Her elegance and speed as she skated were incomparable. She and her partner moved like lovers, living and breathing each other on that godforsaken frozen body of water.

Even Dante gaped with amazement at her jumps and her strength.

And me... It made me jealous of every frozen surface on this fucking planet. When she skated her eyes gleamed and her face glowed like candlelight in the dark of the night. Like she had just been thoroughly fucked. And I was fucking jealous. I wanted to melt every goddamn piece of ice on this earth so she'd only look at me that way.

And her partner. If he came anywhere near her again, he'd be a dead man. She'd only look at me like that going forward. Motherfucker!

"Thanks, Uncle."

Wynter took a step back, rolling back her shoulders. As if she couldn't release the tension plaguing her. I caught her glancing towards the area I sat in with Dante and Emory, as if she could sense me there. But there was no chance she could see us. Not with the crowd surrounding us.

Priest stayed behind, monitoring everything. Until we confirmed our suspicions, we couldn't risk him crossing paths with the Brennans. Besides, he was working on getting us a copy of hotel key cards and setting our escape plan in place. We'd need a hasty getaway once my plan was put in motion.

"You up for this?" I asked my sister under my breath. I had my pilot fly us out of Las Vegas in the middle of the night with no time to waste. My plan had been put in motion, and it had to happen today. Before she disappeared on me again.

It was the last day of the Winter Olympics. The winners have been announced. Wynter added another gold medal to her achievements.

Emory nodded. "Of course. We're going to have a celebrity in our family."

Two heartbeats.

"Oh my gosh," Emory squealed, going into her full fan mode.

Dante groaned next to me, muttering, "Too much."

Six pairs of eyes turned toward us but only one pair mattered. Recognition flickered in those light green eyes. Her mouth parted in shock and she stood frozen, as a wide range of emotions flashed in her gaze.

But the last emotion was disdain.

Not exactly the reaction I was going for. She still wore her costume with a blue windbreaker over the top of it.

"I am such a fan," Emory continued, rushing to Wynter. "I'm Emory. I've watched you skate since you were a kid."

Brennan frowned, his eyes narrowed on me. "DiLustro, what are you doing here?"

"DiLustro?" The ladies' soft gasps sounded, a flash of surprise crossing their faces. Wynter never told her best friends who I was. *Interesting.*

"Same thing as you, I presume," I retorted dryly, my eyes zeroed in on the woman who should have been my wife by now.

Brennan's eyes shifted to Emory, then returned to me. "Goodbye, DiLustro."

Not so fast, old man.

"Aren't you going to introduce me?" I drawled.

"No, I'm not," Brennan replied, his voice cold. My gaze darkened. Not that I expected a different kind of response from the head of the Brennan family.

I recognized his wife, Davina. She wobbled up to her husband, her hand on her large belly as she slipped her other hand into her husband's.

Tilting her head our way, she said to Liam, "Honey, I don't think Wynter is up for dinner. How about we just go back to the hotel?"

"Of course," Liam appeased his wife. The way she watched him, I was certain he offered her the sun and the moon. "Have Sasha take you to the hotel, Wynter."

A burn traveled through my cracked knuckles. They've gotten more than the usual amount of use over the last nine months. The need to punch Liam was like an itch I had to scratch. With Sasha, I wouldn't even bother with my knuckles. One bullet.

Wynter didn't move, her gaze settled on me. It was different from before. Curiosity in her eyes was replaced by something else. Disdain. Maybe even regret. Possibly both.

There was no trace of that smile I was used to seeing on her lips.

Emory took a step forward and extended her hand. "I'm Emory," she introduced herself. "I'm Basilio's sister."

Another flicker in Wynter's eyes. She slowly lowered her gaze, eyeing Emory's outstretched hand, then hesitantly took it into hers. Bringing Emory was a good move.

"I'm such a fan," Emory gushed. "And today's performance was amazing."

"Thank you." Wynter took her hand back and let it fall down her body.

"This is my brother, Basilio," Emory continued with a big smile on her face. She played her part too perfectly. I'd have to buy her a whole damn city for her persistence. "And my cousin Dante."

Wynter tipped her head, looking up at me. She never even glanced Dante's way, her light colliding with my darkness. My grip tightened, the need to touch her burning my skin.

I watched her swallow, the delicate bob of her neck. A polite, fake smile came to her lips. It was the kind she reserved for strangers.

"Nice to meet you," she acknowledged finally, her voice quiet.

I don't think so, principessa, I drawled.

"Actually, we already met," I drawled, pissed off she'd pretend she didn't even know me.

The three women shook their heads frantically. As if that would stop me. She was mine now and forever. "Remember, *Wynter Star*?"

"Ever heard snitches get stitches?" Juliette, the woman who Dante claimed, hissed. Then she glared at Dante while her cheeks flamed. It would seem Juliette remembered Dante all too well.

"But instead of ending up in ditches, you'll end up in my bed, sweetheart," Dante answered. Juliette flipped him the bird.

For all I cared, Juliette and her unhinged ass could go and get crazy with Dante. I adjusted my cuffs, my eyes focused on Wynter. Her eyes glanced at my hands, and for a fleeting moment her eyes flickered with the old fire. That same desire and lust.

Fine, I'd settle for lust. For now. I'd use it against her.

"Star, who's this?" The woman with a face that resembled her daughter approached us, her steps tentative. Her mother's eyes darted between Dante and me, like she was seeing a ghost.

Wynter's fingers wrapped around her right wrist, spinning her bracelet. Again and again. I zeroed in on it. It was the kingpin necklace that I had gifted her, turned into a makeshift bracelet. Her thumb kept brushing the charm, as if it soothed her.

"Nobody, Mom."

Nice! I was nobody to her and she was everything to me.

The crowd around us was too big; otherwise, I'd put my plan in motion right now. Then I'd show her exactly who I was.

Clearly, Aisling Brennan didn't believe her daughter, because she turned to her brother, her eyes fleeting back to Dante and me. "Liam?"

"I'll have it handled," he assured her, his eyes narrowing on us. "Wynter, let's go."

Sasha Nikolaev came up behind Wynter, his pale blue eyes narrowed on the three of us. The way he towered over her and with his fucking stocky MMA build, she looked like a kid in comparison.

"Ready to hit the sheets?" Sasha purred, a darkly entertained expression on his face. My jaw clenched and my fists tightened, fighting the urge to kill the motherfucker. He wanted us to attack. Craved it, in fact. He'd get his wish soon enough.

"Nice to meet you, Emory," Wynter said softly to my sister before turning to leave.

She walked away from me without a backward glance.

Would every fucking woman I cared for in my life walk away from me without a backward glance?

"You ready?" Dante asked, grinning with excitement.

Adrenaline sizzled under my skin but for a different reason. Dante hoped for a full-blown fight, while my goal was to kidnap the woman and have her out of this city before anyone even realized she was gone.

And if I was really lucky, I'd have my ring on her finger and knocked up before her family found us. Not exactly a dream wedding, but this called for extreme measures. Though I knew with certainty it wouldn't take her family months to find her. More like days.

I checked my gun and shoved it back into my holster.

"You plan on knocking her up?" Dante asked, reading my mind. "So you can hold the little babies over her head to keep her with you."

"Jesus, tell me that's not your plan, Basilio," Emory groaned.

"Let's focus on getting Wynter out of their clutches," I said as my mouth pulled into a dark smile.

"Brother, I love you"—Emory shook her head—"but you're a crazy fucker."

"Thanks."

Unbeknownst to the Brennans and the Nikolaevs, and any other fucking gang, we stayed at the same hotel as Wynter. In fact, on the same floor. It cost me a small fortune, but it'd be worth it. And if fucking Sasha Nikolaev was in her room, I'd shoot him. End him for good.

"Has Priest given you the key cards?" I asked tightly.

Two confirmation nods. "The pilot is ready too," Emory added.

I checked the surveillance of our floor; it was empty. At nearly midnight, most of the hotel was deep in sleep.

Chapter Forty-Three

WYNTER

I stared at the dark ceiling.

Bas was here. In the same city as me. I overheard Uncle talk to the Nikolaev men. Sasha wanted to move me tonight. Uncle wanted to wait until tomorrow and not alarm Mom.

Too late.

Just as I predicted, all it took was one glance at Basilio and Dante DiLustro for her to recognize them. She lost her shit and Uncle had to sedate her. *Fucking sedate her.* What in the fuck would happen if she knew I had fallen for one of them?

Sasha and I walked her out of the building and got her into the car. Then I helped her into her room and tucked her into bed.

"Is it him, Star?" she kept whispering. "He came back."

"No, Mom," I soothed her as her eyelids grew heavy. "You're safe. He's not here."

Now I lay in my bed, unable to find rest. I should be scared, but I wasn't. I should be surprised to see him again; I wasn't. For that moment, when I stood in front of him, his spicy scent wrapping around me, I felt whole again.

God, to feel so much for someone couldn't be healthy. Yet, I feared there was no cure. Deep down, I'd hoped he'd find me. Why? Maybe because I was a damn glutton for punishment. It wasn't as if I could get a happily-ever-after with him.

The look on my mother's face when she looked at Bas was heart wrenching. I could see the ghosts plaguing her, swirling all around her. When your boyfriend's father shoots your mother, it pretty much nulls your chances at a future. Right?

And then there was the issue of his deceit. I was an idiot to feel anything for him at all. So damn stupid.

Yet, I couldn't forget that moment our eyes connected. A simple glance from him could light me on fire and melt my soul. In the most consuming kind of way.

I shifted on the bed again, exhaustion heavy in my bones. Weeks and months of constant training were hard, but now it was all over. And again, I couldn't get my rest.

I had no clue what I'd do with myself. I needed to keep myself busy. Eventually, the school would keep me and the girls busy, but it'd be a while before that happened. Until then, I'd have to find a way to keep myself busy. I couldn't stand to have all this time to think.

Like now.

I felt tired, but my mind refused to calm. Thoughts whirled in my mind and they all revolved around *him*. Basilio DiLustro.

There had to be something wrong with me because a twisted part of me craved him. The son of the man who destroyed my mother.

The man I fell in love with. I knew he was a DiLustro when I asked him for help. I knew he was a killer. A criminal. None of it mattered to me, because I saw the man worth loving behind it all.

Until his father. Until the unknown past came knocking on the door. Until Bas's betrayal.

If I had known, I would have kept my distance. I would have

fought the attraction. I wouldn't have gotten close to Bas. I wouldn't have fallen for him

My mind mocked that unspoken statement.

"I wouldn't have," I protested in a whisper to the dark, empty room. The truth was that the attraction to him had been so damn different and curiously exciting. Such a new, unfamiliar feeling.

Yes, I had gotten good at lying to myself. Somewhere deep down, I knew the road would have always led me to Basilio DiLustro.

"Talking to yourself, principessa?" a familiar deep voice rasped. I shot out of bed to find two dark figures over my bed.

"What are you doing here?" I hissed. My heart beat hard and my lungs struggled to get air into them.

"You're going to fulfill your promise, principessa."

I opened my mouth to scream, but before a sound could break through, a hand covered my mouth, muffling it. With wide eyes, I watched him push a syringe into my neck. I attempted to struggle, my vision turning fuzzy.

My eyes locked on Bas's blurry face with disbelief.

"I told you I'd always follow," he whispered.

The last thing I remembered was a familiar spicy scent in my nose, filling my lungs and my eyes closed as darkness crept in.

Then there was nothing but an abyss.

Chapter Forty-Four

BASILIO

Wynter's body slumped in my arms.

Giving a terse nod to Dante, I lifted her small body and we left the room. I couldn't help glancing at her face. It was a bit thinner, dark circles under her eyes.

"There will be hell to pay," Dante muttered as we headed for the exit staircase. Running into someone at this hour was unlikely, but we couldn't risk it. It would leave a trail of dead bodies in its wake.

I kept checking on her pulse as we descended the staircase. Now that I had her, I was fucking scared to lose her again. I had no plans of letting that happen. Her hair hung loose, so fucking long and those bouncy curls that usually gave her a mischievous look now made her seem even thinner.

The moment we exited the hotel, Emory spotted us and started the engine.

"You sit in the front," I told Dante and he cocked his eyebrow, smirking knowingly.

He didn't know shit. I wouldn't let another man hold Wynter. She was mine now, and I'd be the only man touching her. Once in the car, my gaze lowered to watch her face. She looked like a fucking angel with that gold halo of curls around her head and pale skin. I trailed my eyes over the soft swell of her breast. Her breathing was shallow, and I pressed my finger to her pulse again.

"Don't fucking tell me you gave her too much sedative and killed her," Emory hissed, checking the rearview mirror.

"She's breathing," I said, never lifting my eyes from Wynter. "Focus on your goddamn driving and getting us out of here."

Wynter wore a slim tank top and boyshorts. Pink again. Some things never change, I guess. A light shiver rolled down her body and I cursed myself. I should have grabbed a blanket; it was the middle of the fucking winter with below-zero temperature in the mountains.

I was too fucking focused on the fact I finally had her. Why couldn't they have the Winter Olympics in the tropics?

Sliding my jacket off, I covered her body.

She stirred slightly and a soft moan sounded on her lips. And fuck if it didn't give me a goddamn hard-on. Yes, I was a sick bastard. But nine months without a woman would do that to you. Turn you into a cranky, ready-to-blow-a-gasket, horny kind of jackass.

It took us ten minutes to get to the helicopter, and another thirty to the jet waiting for us. Wynter never stirred again.

Like a thief in the night, I had stolen my bride.

Chapter Forty-Five
WYNTER

A constant hum of an engine came through the fog, demanding I wake up. I was still in the hotel room. What could that noise be?

I blinked slowly, feeling disoriented. I felt a warm body underneath me and a heavy arm around me. I went to shift but my movements felt slow and sluggish. My breathing picked up and icy terror clawed at my insides.

Clutching my fists, I pushed against the body, stumbling backwards. I struggled into a sitting position, the entire room spinning and my vision swam.

The man's face I loved so much came into focus and I blinked again.

"Bas?" I whispered, confusion swimming through me. "What—"

My mouth was dry and my body refused to listen as I scooted backwards, away from him. The vision of him was blurry and it kept moving.

"Go back to sleep, principessa." I heard his deep voice. I fought to keep my eyes open and lost.

The next time I woke up was in a car, curled into myself, and a jacket over me. The familiar scent was all around me.

I raised my eyes and found Bas in the back seat beside me. His dark eyes sent a shiver down my spine. The problem was that I couldn't distinguish whether it was fear or something else that wouldn't bode well for me.

I shifted up, struggling to sit up and Basilio's hands came to assist.

"Don't," I bit out, shaking his hands off my shoulder.

A driver who I recognized sat behind the wheel. Dante DiLustro and Bas's sister. She helped her brother kidnap me? The tension was palpable, my body ached and my eyes flitted around, touching the three of them.

There was no apology, no regret in any of their dark eyes.

"What have you done?" I hissed, my voice quavering. "Take me back. Right this second."

Bas grinned, wolf-like, his eyes filled with something dark and cruel. *A look very much like his father's,* I realized with terror.

"You'll fulfill your promise, principessa," Bas murmured, his voice dark and full of threat as his eyes raked over me.

And just like a fool, I drowned in them, letting him pull me into the abyss.

Hate him, Wynter. Hate him.

It was my only weapon against him. Yet, my heart couldn't find an ounce of hate for him. Stupid, traitorous heart.

The car came to a stop. I startled, my hands reached the door handle and I jumped outside. Though I instantly realized my mistake.

There was nowhere to run. I was in the middle of a desert.

Chapter Forty-Six

BASILIO

The sedative made Wynter weak as she stumbled out of the car.

I immediately lifted her small body into my arms and walked into Emory's house. We were back in Nevada. Far enough from everyone that we'd see someone coming from miles away.

"You don't know what you've done," she hissed weakly, her fists hitting against my chest. "They'll come for you."

I shrugged my shoulders. "Let them come. I'm counting on it, and if they try to take you away, I'll kill them all. I'll show them why they call me the Villainous Kingpin."

She stiffened and a bitter laugh escaped me. "What's the matter, principessa? Got more than you bargained for?"

She had fucking left me, moved on, without a second goddamn thought while I went out of my mind looking for her.

"I wasn't bargaining at all, jackass." Her eyes narrowed to slits. "I want nothing to do with you or your family."

Dante chuckled behind me and I fought the urge to punch him in his face.

Taking two marble steps at a time, I went into the bedroom we designated would be Wynter's while we were here. The highest one in the tower for my principessa with no way off the balcony.

I dropped her on the bed, her slim body bouncing against the soft mattress.

"Welcome home, principessa," I said, rougher than I intended.

"This isn't my home," she argued back. "You can't do this, Basilio. Take me back right now before anyone notices I'm gone," she demanded, though her voice was too breathless. Too throaty.

I traced my fingers down her slim throat. God, how she tempted me. "From now on, wherever I go *is* your home," I drawled.

Fuck, my cock was hard, straining against my pants, eager to finally taste her after all this time without her. I couldn't fucking stand another woman's touch from the moment I'd touched her and nine goddamn months was a long fucking time to remain abstinent. My fist only went so far.

"You're not home," she hissed. "You're the enemy."

My hand curled around her slim neck. She didn't push me away, though something dark flashed in her eyes. Fuck, it turned me on even more.

"You look pretty with my hand around your throat," I purred, wrapping my fingers tighter.

The glare she gave me would have frozen a man with a heart. Luckily for me, she ripped my heart out when she left me behind. Without a single thought.

Before I'd do something regretful and unforgivable, I let go of her tempting throat and headed for the door.

"Go to sleep, principessa," I said darkly. "Or I'll consider it an invitation to crawl into your bed and make you scream my name."

I shut the door behind me right as I heard her soft gasp.

Chapter Forty-Seven
WYNTER

The man had lost his goddamn mind.

Yet, something deep inside me quivered at his gravelly threat. Warmth and fear collided as my heartbeat drummed in my ears and pulsed through my veins. Bas always made me feel safe. He told me he'd never touch me without my permission.

I believed him. In the past.

Now, I wasn't so sure. His eyes reminded me too much of his father. He wasn't the same man anymore. And I wasn't that same woman any longer.

The dark sky outside matched the darkness in Basilio. Anxiety and ghosts ran through me, my heart hammered hard against my chest.

No, don't think about it.

I squeezed my eyes closed, hoping it'd shut my mind. It didn't.

The images and scent of his father, foul and frightening, were closing in. The way his cold, disgusting hands felt on me had terror crawling up my spine. His stale breath touched me and I fought the desperation to drag a deep breath into my lungs.

Fear wrapped around my throat.

We planned this. You are our ticket to the Pakhan and the Russians.

I couldn't be around his father again. I refused to let Basilio use me again.

And still there were so many days I wished there was just me and him, nothing else. No ghosts of our parents and our families. No deals to be made.

But power and money ruled the underworld. Money and power ruled Bas.

Even knowing all that, I craved the feel of his hands on my skin. It required steeling myself to accept Derek's hands on me while we skated. Yet, Bas wrapped his hand around my neck and my body shifted towards him, the same languid heat and desire flared in the pit of my belly.

Shifting to my side, I stared out the large French window as the stars glittered over the dark desert. I focused on my breathing and memories of Bas down on his knee like my own Prince Charming.

It was that image that kept me sane over the last nine months. The man who acted like a monster with everyone but me.

Not anymore. Now he'd become my monster too.

My eyes peeled open and the first thing I registered was Bas, sitting in the loveseat and his eyes shut. Asleep, his breathing strong and even. Lying on my side, I watched the lines on his face. Even in sleep, he seemed tense. His expression was harsh and his brows furrowed, as if he contemplated the next move in his sleep. He breathed darkness with every inhale; with every heartbeat of his. I felt it on my skin and in my soul.

Basilio DiLustro was my beginning. And I feared he'd be my end too. No matter how much I fought it. Oceans and continents apart would never be enough to forget him.

My eyes flickered to the window. It was still dark outside, not surprising. Winter nights were long. The full moon threw a glow over the desert. It made it appear beautiful, in a deadly kind of way.

Kind of like this man, I thought silently.

"Contemplating jumping out the window?" Bas's voice rang with something dark and taunting.

My eyes flashed to him. He shifted slightly and his face lingered in the shadows.

"It's creepy to watch people while they sleep," I breathed. My heart raced in my chest as I watched his familiar but somehow older, more exhausted face.

Did I do that to him, I wondered with a sharp piercing in my heart.

"You had a nightmare," he answered, running his hand across his face tiredly. "You were screaming."

I closed my eyes for a moment, cursing my stupid nightmares and cursing Gio even more.

When I opened my eyes, it was to Bas watching me, but this time there was no taunting or smugness on his face. God, it would be so much easier if he was a boy and I was a girl without all the fucked-up baggage behind us. Or without DiLustro's ambition to rule the world.

But Basilio was his father's son.

"Who hurt you?" His demand was uttered in a low voice, full of threat, though it wasn't aimed at me.

"Nobody."

Tense silence filled the space between us and a haunted expression flickered in his eyes before the cold mask took hold of his face.

"Do you often have nightmares?" he asked in a toneless voice.

Yes. "No," I lied.

I hated how weak and terrified his father made me feel. Vulnerable and breakable. One extra moment of hesitation, and his father would have raped me. And Bas left me to his father. To destroy me, like he had destroyed my mother.

Instead, I shot him. God, I wished I killed him. To avenge my mother. Was Bas here to avenge his father?

Bas stood up and I realized he still wore clothes, though his shirt was carelessly unbuttoned and his tie hung loose. It was as if he ran over here just as he was about to get undressed.

My eyes locked on his abs and that tattoo that I always admired in the past. The kingpin skull. I curled my fingers into my palms, fighting the urge to reach out and touch him. I still remembered how hard his muscles were under my palms and how warm his skin felt under my fingertips.

He moved closer to me, then sank down to his haunches, our faces only inches apart. This close, his gaze was more black than I'd ever seen it before.

"You left me."

Three words. Two hearts. One broken promise.

Chapter Forty-Eight

BASILIO

I waited for her to say something. Anything.

She said nothing, but the ghosts in her eyes were unmistakable. When I heard her screams in the middle of the night, the terror lacing her voice, it almost brought me to my knees. I couldn't wake her up, her skin glistening with sweat as she thrashed.

So I did the only thing I knew. The thing my mamma used to do the nights I was scared of my father. I started talking to her, keeping my voice low. She couldn't hear me, but it seemed to soothe her. I told her how I searched for her, night and day. How I'd never given her up because to give up meant living in the permanent darkness.

She was my light. My sun.

Without her, there was only darkness.

She was my calm in the storm.

When she walked away from me, she took the only light in my life, as well as my heart. Or maybe it just stopped working, I wasn't sure.

She was the reason I survived my wretched father and all the brutality in my world. All the roads led me to her, and God help me, I'd keep her.

At. All. Fucking. Costs.

I was nothing without her. Just a mirror image of my father and I fucking hated that.

Yet to her, I was nobody now. Nothing.

My teeth clenched, my gaze turned hard and I smiled darkly.

"You left me without a backward glance, principessa," I growled. "Why?"

Her lips thinned and her chin tilted up, stubbornly as defiance shone in her eyes. She wouldn't tell me. Not yet. But I'd hammer through those walls. Whether she liked it or not.

"You made a promise, and I intend for you to keep it," I told her.

Before this was over, I'd be her fucking everything.

"We should move her," Priest said tersely.

Dante, Priest, and I sat in Emory's office. It was barely eight in the morning,

I sat on the couch with my feet up on the coffee table. The office had girly touches to it. Pictures and flashes of pink and blue here and there. Despite the fact that Emory rarely ever wore color.

I sat back and cracked my knuckles. Over and over again. The restlessness ghosted under my skin, demanding I go check on Wynter. I wanted her within my sight all the damn time. I couldn't stop thinking about her.

She still smelled of honey and ice, just the way I remembered. When she finally calmed down from her night terrors, I couldn't tear my gaze from her. The way the moon glowed against her fair skin and made her curls glow.

The need to touch her seared through my veins but I refused to do it. Not without her permission. I couldn't fucking handle it if she looked at me the way my mamma did when she walked away from me. Or the way Mamma looked at my father.

"Are you fucking listening or daydreaming, Basilio?" Priest snapped and Dante gave him a tight look.

"Basilio just needs to get laid," Dante said, sitting opposite of me and smirking like a motherfucker. "Once he gets his ice princess to freeze his balls, he'll be back to normal."

"What the fuck is the matter with you?" Priest snapped, glaring at his older brother.

Priest definitely woke up with something up his butt, and I wasn't in the mood for it. He should go and recite someone's last goddamn rites. That usually got him in a good mood.

"I'm ready to shoot both of you motherfuckers," I growled, "if you don't tell me why in the fuck I should move her from here. Nobody knows about this place. Not even our own fathers."

"Everybody's gonna know about this place soon," Priest said. "You kidnapped a world-renowned Olympic skater."

What the fuck was wrong with my cousin? "You didn't complain when we came up with the plan?"

Dante must have sensed my bad mood because he chimed in, "Wynter had an interview scheduled for seven a.m. They noticed her gone right away. Priest was able to hack into the hotel surveillance. Brennan lost his shit. The big Russian wasn't far behind. The two got into it. Apparently, her bodyguard wanted to fly her out last night but Brennan refused."

"Well, that must have been entertaining," Emory butted in, strolling into the office like she was doing a fucking catwalk wearing combat boots and a holster. "Someone *had* to have the princess." She gave me a pointed look. "It will be so much fun when the Irish and Russians attack. It will be like a mafia world war. Maybe we can turn it into a bloody wedding reception."

"Shut up," I told all three of them. "Let me see the footage."

Priest pulled up his phone and opened the surveillance from the hotel. Sure enough, Brennan and Sasha Nikolaev were at each other's throats.

"They're already hacking all the surveillance and checking all the flight logs," Priest warned. "They're using Nico Morrelli. He's the best."

"I thought you were the best," I retorted dryly.

He flipped me the bird. "I am but Nico has a tech company that does only that for him. And with the Ashford brothers backing up Brennan, we're at a disadvantage."

"Excuses, fucking excuses," I grumbled. "The Ashfords won't back him up for long."

"Basilio, it won't take them long to find us," Priest warned.

I got up, buttoned my jacket, and turned to leave.

"Let them," I replied, before I left the three of them so I could go find Wynter.

"Get laid," Dante shouted behind me. "We can't stand much more of you like this."

I flipped him the bird over my shoulder and continued my path to the guest room on the highest floor, the one without any options of escape, where we stashed Wynter. After all, I met her climbing down her uncle's balcony, and I was certain it wasn't her first time sneaking out.

I barged into her room without knocking. My eyes wandered from the empty bed toward the wall, the balcony, then bathroom. She wasn't here.

I rushed out of there and roared, "Wynter!"

If she ran off, I'd lock her in next time. There'd be no freedom roaming the house. I was back in Emory's office, the three of them in the same spot where I left them with serious expression on their faces.

If they'd let her go behind my back, I'd crush their throats. Teach them a lesson, they'd never forget.

"Where is Wynter?" I bellowed, out of my goddamn mind. She wasn't in her bedroom. Not in the bathroom. Nowhere.

"She's in the basement gym," Emory answered, eyeing me suspiciously. "What the fuck is wrong with you?"

Ignoring her, I rushed out of the room and almost plowed into her guard.

With each step I took closer to the basement gym, the music grew louder. I opened the door and the bass speakers almost shook the walls how loud she had it turned up. She'd be able to wake up the dead with this kind of music. Some kind of angry version of Lady Gaga's "Paparazzi" song but screamed by a dude.

Wynter ran steadily on a treadmill, oblivious that anyone else was in the room. Blood rushed into my cock, watching her gorgeous body in a sports bra and skintight shorts that barely covered her ass. And fuck, she had a nice ass.

My cousins better stay the fuck away from here. I'd gouge their eyes out if they even look her way.

I caught her reaching for her ear, but her hand faltered and I realized she was used to having headphones in. I recalled she told me once that she liked to put headphones on and not hear anything, including her thoughts. It helped her concentrate.

I pulled up my phone and shot a message to Priest to get me Apple AirPods, every version and model and a new Apple burner phone. Then I leaned against the door and just watched her.

Probably made me some kind of psychotic stalker but the sight soothed me. As long as I knew where she was, I could breathe.

"She has some endurance." Emory's voice came from behind me and I stiffened. Fuck, I didn't even hear her approach me. I couldn't be oblivious to my surroundings, particularly with Wynter under my protection.

"She's an Olympic, two-time gold medalist, what do you expect?" Dante almost sounded impressed.

"Do you two have to be everywhere I am?" I grumbled. "And for fuck's sake, Dante, stop looking at her."

"I just can't help myself," Dante snickered. "She might prefer me to my cousin."

A growl climbed up my throat. "Dante," I warned before he said more stupid words.

"Yeah, you two will be lucky not to get shot by her uncle or one of those Russians she uses as bodyguards." The world had gone to hell in a handbasket if my sister was the only one who had some common sense left.

"What the fuck is wrong with Priest?" I asked them, instead of commenting on my sister's sound observation.

A fleeting glance the two shared didn't escape me. "What?" I demanded to know, my eyes glued to Wynter's form.

"He needs some time to come to terms," my sister said quietly.

"With?"

"He tested his DNA against hers." Dante didn't look pleased.

"And?"

"Priest and Wynter share the same mother."

Chapter Forty-Nine

WYNTER

I stepped off the treadmill, my breathing heavy. I had been at it for the past hour and a half. But it felt good. The stress reliever I needed, despite the little sleep I had.

Striding to the stereo, I turned off the music and turned around to find three pairs of eyes on me. I halted for a second, unsure why they were there. The look on their faces was grim and Dante glared at me accusingly.

Something deep inside me snapped and I glared at him back.

"What are you staring at?" I asked, my eyes narrowed on Dante. "You kidnapped me, remember? So you can't look unhappy about me being here."

Bas's sister chuckled and slapped him across the chest. "Man, she really doesn't like you."

I rolled my eyes.

Emory's sister was surprisingly... nice. For a kidnapper. Knowing I had a regimented training schedule, she came to find me in the room and offered me some gym clothes.

"Want to have breakfast with us?" she offered.

My eyes darted to Bas and I fucking hated it that it almost looked like I was asking for a permission.

"Yes, she'll have breakfast with us," Bas answered for me and my eyes narrowed on him in annoyance. Or maybe at myself, heck if I knew.

"I can answer for myself, thank you very much."

So I turned my attention back to his sister. "Yes, thank you."

"Jesus, they're not even married yet and they're bickering," Dante remarked, grinning like an idiot.

Then the meaning of his words sunk in and my eyes shot to Dante, then darted to Bas.

"Married?" I repeated, sounding like I didn't know what *married* meant.

"I'll take you to your room so you can get showered," Bas offered, then dismissed his sister and Dante. He grabbed my arm and led me up the stairs back toward my room. I didn't say anything, waiting for him to explain what Dante meant by his words.

The moment we were in my room, I whirled around and met his eyes. Dark, intense, burning with something I could feel deep down in my toes.

"What is Dante talking about?" I demanded to know, my breathing still choppy.

Bas watched me. Our gazes locked, his dark eyes dragging me deeper and deeper down into their abyss. Yes, there was harshness in them, ruthlessness and something unhinged. But also hints of vulnerability and pain that I caused when I walked away from him.

He towered over me, his eyes full of dark obsession. Then he bent his head, holding my gaze. Almost as if he expected me to step back. But I didn't. I held my head high and held his gaze. He closed the distance and his lips grazed my chin.

My heart beat wildly, like it was my first kiss. His mouth seared my skin, his scent seeped into my bloodstream. God, he was my poison. The sweetest kind that would end up killing me. I held my breath, while his lips moved down my cheek, until they met my mouth.

I held still, fighting the urge to lean into him. Like a moth moving toward the flame, waiting for him to ignite my wings.

Taking a sharp inhale, my breath caught in my throat when his hand came to my waist, his grip firm. My chest brushed against his and my pulse beat in my ears. His touch was just as searing as I remembered.

"Take a shower, principessa," he whispered in my ear, his voice laced with a rough edge. "Or I'll bathe you myself."

He turned around and stormed out, leaving me staring at the spot where he stood. Unable to tear my gaze away, I remained still.

My throat felt thick, the need choked my lungs and despair scratched at my chest.

I'd never survive him, not this time.

When I came out of the shower, I found clothes for me laid out on the bed. Just a simple pair of brand-new undergarments, black jeans, and a black crewneck shirt. It didn't take a genius to figure out it belonged to Emory.

She seemed to have a thing for black, but I was grateful to her. Once dressed, I left to head down the stairs. I found the kingpins of the DiLustro family whispering among themselves only to stop as soon as I walked in.

It was eleven in the morning and later than usual for breakfast, but with their criminal activities last night, namely kidnapping me, I imagined they all had a later morning start.

"Hello, Wynter," Priest greeted me, frowning deeply and watching me with a weird look in his eyes.

I stood for a moment, then tilted my head and strode to an empty chair. The furthest one from all four of them. They followed suit, taking their seats. Except for Bas. He came over and sat next to me. I shot him an annoyed look, but I didn't say anything.

"Do you have everything you need?" Bas asked as he placed a napkin on his lap.

"Do you Italians always wear a three-piece suit?" I blurted out, irritated.

A heartbeat of silence and the room filled with laughter. Even Bas. I hated how much I missed his laugh, how the sound of his laugh made me all jittery on the inside and sent a warm timbre rumbling down my back.

"Not always," Dante chuckled.

"When we fuck, we don't wear it," Bas commented, his voice laced with something dark and suggestive.

Duh, I knew that, but I didn't acknowledge his words.

"How long have you been skating?" Emory asked as she reached for the carbs on her side of the table. I guess it was her attempt to help me dodge a bullet.

"Long time," I muttered. Truthfully, I couldn't remember a time when I didn't skate.

As we all dug into our food, the four of them chatted while I just listened and ate. They stuck to generic subjects. After all, they were masterminds of the underworld. Unlike Juliette, Ivy, Davina, and me. The four of us were a catastrophe of the underworld.

I couldn't help but notice how comfortable Emory was with the gun strapped to her holster. She was like a badass femme fatale. Did her father teach her that or Bas?

A cold shiver ran down my back at the memory of her father. I hated his guts. There were so many nights I wished I pointed that gun to his head and pulled the trigger. He'd be dead and no longer part of my nightmares. He'd have paid for destroying my mother's life.

"Wynter?" Priest's voice pulled me back to the present company. Three sets of dark eyes and one set of blue eyes met me. Among his cousins, his hair and eyes seemed even starker.

"You okay?" Emory asked, frowning.

"Yes."

"What were you thinking about?" Bas asked.

How I want to kill your father. But I didn't say that, instead I answered, "Nothing."

"Umm, I asked why you switched from single to pair skating," Emory stated, her eyes sharp on me. She might not resemble her brother, but she was just as sharp as he was.

My eyes burned, and I blinked to ease the sting. The memories of their father's attack clawed at my chest with every shallow breath. But even worse, for my mother who had lost everything when she was my age.

"My mother's specialty was pair skating," I answered, my voice distant to my own ears. I turned to look at Bas. I ached for him, every minute of the day. It was a raw kind of ache, constantly present in my chest. It had become a constant companion from the moment I walked away from him. But my love for him was a direct betrayal to my mother. "She was shot in the knee. It ruined—" *Her.* "... her career. But then you knew that, didn't you?" I questioned, keeping my attention to Bas. The tension was so palpable, I feared it'd snap and leave death in its wake. "After all, you are your father's son."

Bas's eyes turned dark and hard, something harsh and brutal in them sent fear down my spine. For the first time in my life, I was terrified of Bas. I tried to hide it, I really did. But my hands shook badly as I tried to clench them together and my lip quivered.

If I started crying, I'd lose my shit. *Don't start crying! Don't start crying!*

Bas shot up from his chair and it landed back with a loud thump, making me jump in my seat. He stormed out of there with a dark expression on his face and his jaw clenched so hard, it had to hurt.

Dante and Priest were right behind him, leaving me alone with Emory and wondering if Bas knew what his father had done to me.

Chapter Fifty

BASILIO

My father shot her mother and Wynter knew it.

"Basilio, wait up," Dante called out and I turned to see both my cousins striding after me.

"Priest, hack into my father's records and see if you can locate his next shipment," I told him. "Dante, figure out the schedule for the Afghanistan supplier and keep it in your back pocket. In case we need it with the Ashfords."

I left them behind, striding through the large terrace door and into the hot desert sun that seared. It didn't compare to the fury consuming me on the inside. I had to cool off or risk losing my cool. If I did, I'd scare the living daylights out of her.

In all honesty, I shouldn't be surprised she knew. She probably knew all along. After all, it was her own mother who got shot by my father. Why did it fucking feel like I was the blind one all along?

Tension coiled beneath my skin, approaching the rapture, and I feared if I exploded, havoc would follow. I reached into my pocket and pulled out my pack of cigarettes. The same ones I had during my trip to Philly with her. The same pack she asked me not to smoke because she worried I'd get lung cancer.

I gave my head a small shake.

My reason went to shit when it came to the ice princess. I wanted every fucking inch of her body and soul, and all she saw in me was my father. Just like my mamma.

I let out a sardonic breath, while something tightened in my throat and my chest ached. Fucking ached!

So I lit a cigarette because that was sure to cure the ache in my chest. I inhaled deeply until my lungs burned, then exhaled softly. Nicotine spread through my veins, somewhat calming me. It was an unnatural kind of calmness, but I still relished in it. Or I'd lose my goddamn mind. All these months I refused to light a cigarette because of her words in Philly and here I was now, smoking one because of her.

Irony at its best.

My gaze settled on the desert landscape. I could see why my sister liked it here. Away from civilization and people. The scent of oil drifted from her outside garage where she spent most of her time, tinkering with junk. It was her escape.

What was Wynter's?

Calmness washed over me with certainty as I made my decision. It didn't fucking matter what Wynter knew or what my father had done. She was mine and I refused to let go. I'd warned her from the beginning I wasn't a good man, so it shouldn't come as a surprise to her.

My cell phone buzzed in my pocket, and I dug it out, flicking a glance at the caller ID.

Perfect timing for my cousins to call.

"Yeah?"

"Basilio." It was Byron Ashford, my ever-controlling cousin.

"Byron, to what do I owe this pleasure?" I drawled.

Silence rang for five heartbeats and I had no fucking intention to break it.

"You kidnapped Wynter who's under the protection of Sasha Nikolaev." My hand tightened around the phone, the plastic protesting my grip. If I never heard the fucking name, it would be too goddamn soon. "Why?" he demanded to know.

I ran my tongue across my teeth. "What's it to you?" I answered, a sardonic breath escaping me.

"She's a friend to the family. Basilio, if you—" Byron's voice held a warning, except it did absolutely nothing for me.

"You're not calling the shots here, Byron. Stick to your world, and I'll stick to mine."

"You're a prick, you know that, right?" A furious voice sounded in the background. "You fucking tell him he's a dead prick."

It sounded like Brennan's voice.

"Give my greetings to Brennan," I deadpanned.

"Winston, keep those two from killing each other," Byron ordered his younger brother, then I heard the door shut.

"What will it take to release her?" my cousin asked.

Nothing in this goddamn world would make me release her. She was fucking mine.

"She's staying with me. However, I hear you and your brothers are harassing Dante. We have something your brother in Canada wants. He'll get it, but only if you back me against Brennan and the Nikolaevs."

I wished I could see Byron's expression. It would tell me what he was thinking. Byron always tried to make up for his father's sins. The similarity didn't escape my notice, but fuck if I'd point it out. He'd want to do right by his half brother. This could possibly be Byron's only in with his half brother. The fucker in Canada was richer than Midas and he'd never need Byron's money and he definitely didn't want his father's last name. In fact, he despised the Ashford name.

345

"Are you going to hurt the girl?" he asked quietly.

"No."

"Then you got yourself a deal," he answered, although reluctantly.

Chapter Fifty-One
BASILIO

The next morning, I ordered one of Emory's guards to bring Wynter to the dining room. Dante, Emory, and Priest were already seated around the table, the tension in the air so thick, you could cut it with a knife.

A shared glance by Dante and Emory didn't escape me. "What?" I barked.

Dante cocked his eyebrow unperturbed. "I didn't say shit."

"But you thought it," Emory snickered.

"So did you," Dante told her.

"Would you two stop bickering like babies?" I snapped. "And tell me what's on your mind."

Emory shrugged. "I got a heads-up that Brennan is fifteen minutes away. He's coming for her."

"How did he find her so fast?" I knew it was only a matter of time, but I hoped it would take him longer.

"Nico Morrelli," Dante said.

"Goddamn it, we need to find a way to block that old man," I spat out annoyed. "Or work with him."

"It was stupid to kidnap her," Priest argued, his expression murderous. "It wasn't right, Basilio."

My narrowed gaze found his.

"Mind your own fucking business." I had never gone head-to-head with Dante nor Priest. But if they tried to take Wynter from me, I would. Nobody would fucking take her from me again. *Nobody.*

Priest shot up to his feet at the same time as I did. "She's my fucking sister. That changes everything."

I got into Priest's face while a burn radiated in my chest. "And she's my woman," I roared. "I swear to God, Priest. You touch her and I'll read you your own last goddamn rites."

Dante and Emory shared a glance, but they refused to interfere. Though we all knew if it came down to it, Emory would take my side and Dante would take Priest's.

"You're fucking blind when it comes to her." Priest refused to back down. Not that I expected him to. "You're so fucking obsessed you can't see the girl is scared of you. I won't let you hurt her."

My body slammed into Priest's and the dishes on the table rattled. "I'd rather slice my dick off than hurt her," I hissed. "You suggest anything like it again and I'll fucking end you."

In our entire life, I had never had disagreements with Priest or Dante. Ever! Until today. And it all boiled down to Wynter. Priest was right, I was obsessed with her. In fact, it was so much more than just an obsession. It was madness. It was love.

I loved her so fucking much. Life without her wasn't an option. She loved me once. I'd make her love me again.

Fuck, I was in so deep, I had no way of coming up for air.

"Basilio, she's related to Brennan and the Pakhan. She has some crazy Russian fucker for a bodyguard and she's a celebrity," Dante chimed in from his spot, though his tense shoulders didn't escape my notice.

"Did I ask for your opinion?" I snarled. "Wynter's staying with me. Anywhere I go, she comes along." I locked eyes with Priest. "Understood?"

He was silent. One second. Two seconds.

He nodded. "But if you hurt her, I'll fucking kill your ass. Cousin or no. Understood?" he threatened.

"Fair enough." I took a step back.

"You all are missing the point that Priest is related to the Pakhan too," Emory drawled. "And if the three of you morons hurt her, I'll kill you all."

"Let's all relax," Dante the peacemaker announced. "We have to work together, especially now that we have visitors coming."

"Basilio, does Wynter know she'll be your glue for the rest of your life?" Emory muttered, warning clear in her eyes. "You have to give her a choice."

My jaw clenched and my mood darkened. The fact was that Wynter would run if she was given the chance. I didn't need a mind reader for that. She left me once; she'd leave me again.

We were all seated now, seemingly calm but tension brimmed underneath us all.

"And what are you going to do, Basilio? Drag her down the aisle by her hair," she continued, egging me on.

"If I have to."

Someone cleared their throat from across the room, and the four of us looked over to find a guard standing by the door.

"Is this a good time?" he asked.

"Oh for fuck's sake," Wynter snickered behind him and sidestepped him. "I don't give a crap if it's a good time. I'm hungry."

Avoiding my eyes, Wynter strode to the seat furthest from the four of us and sat herself like a queen. Like someone who was used to getting her own way. Like someone who knew exactly how much she was worth.

It was what I loved about her when we first met. Her strong

349

personality. Her determination. And the way she watched me. Like I was her prince. The latter was no longer there.

One of the staff took her breakfast request and disappeared to go grab her food. Silence filled the room, Wynter's attention was on everything but the four of us. She was purposely ignoring us, and with every second that ticked, my anger rose.

That she would dare ignore me.

"Did you sleep well?" Emory asked her, trying to break the silence.

Wynter stiffened for a moment, then glared at all four of us.

"No, I didn't sleep well. You kidnapped me," she hissed. "I also had an unwelcome visitor in the middle of the night, gawking at me while I slept. For two nights in a row. It's freaky," she hissed, glaring at me. I couldn't help it, she had a nightmare. "I want to go home." Then she bestowed us all with a cold stare. "Now."

"You don't call the shots here, sweetheart," Dante mused, which earned him a small growl by our guest. "But since you're here, tell me how you won the poker game at my table last year. I've wondered about it for quite some time."

"And I wondered for quite some time how it felt when Juliette kicked you in your balls," Wynter snickered, then took a sip of her orange juice.

Emory stifled her laugh, earning herself a glare by our cousin.

"What?" Emory asked innocently. "You failed to mention that. I'd like to know how it felt too."

"It fucking hurt like a bitch," he grumbled.

"Why did she kick you in the balls?" Emory inquired curiously.

"Miss Flemming had a little heist operation going on," Dante drawled. "We came to intercept her card counting and her cousin fucking distracted me, then kicked me in the balls.

Wynter shrugged. "Honestly, I'm offended, *Dante*," she mocked him. "Calling our operation little."

Amusement crossed Dante's expression and he covered his mouth with his hand to hide it. It wasn't every day that someone pulled one over on us.

Wynter's breakfast was brought in at that moment, halting the conversation.

"Thank God," she murmured, reaching for her carbs. I had never met a woman who could eat as much as Wynter. I finally understood why with her vigorous ice-skating schedule.

"You don't have to eat it all in one sitting," Dante mocked her. Wynter just flipped him off and Emory's laugh filled the room. I hadn't heard my sister laugh so much in a very long time.

My eyes flickered to my sister, studying her. This would have been her if she had a normal life. She would have probably had friends like Wynter, getting into trouble and laughing. All the time. Instead, she was hardened. She hid it behind her petite frame, deceiving her enemies that she was weak. But she was no less ruthless than we were.

You had to be to survive our father.

The house shook and a booming voice traveled through the house.

"Where is she?" Brennan's demand rattled through the first floor, and the next moment, the dining room's door rattled open.

Well, that wasn't fifteen minutes.

Wynter shot off her seat, and so did I. Dante and Emory followed, both their guns drawn. Before Wynter could get close to Liam, I was by her side, my arm wrapped around her waist and lifting her.

"Let go of me, you brute," Wynter hissed as Brennan entered the room.

"DiLustro, get your hands off my niece right fucking now," Brennan growled.

Wynter kept trying to elbow me, twisting against me.

"You want to live," the blond prick I recognized as Sasha Nikolaev threatened, "you'll get your hands off her."

Brennan came with reinforcements.

Chapter Fifty-Two
WYNTER

Guns pointed in every direction.

Uncle held his aim at Bas. Sasha too. Luca held two guns pointed at Dante and Priest, while Killian held his against Emory who looked fucking amused. Like she was enjoying this.

Jesus! She was just as unhinged as her brother and cousins.

And Davina's brothers Byron and Winston Ashford came right behind my uncle and his allies. Though they didn't seem to be in the fighting mode, both leaning against the wall and their hands in their pockets. They watched the entire scene unfold like it was a live TV show.

What in the fucking hell was happening?

I jerked against Bas, attempting one more time to free myself.

"DiLustro, last warning," Uncle growled. "Before I put a bullet between your eyes."

"Fucker doesn't need warnings," Sasha spit, his worried gaze connecting with mine. "I say we kill them and be done with this shit."

My blood went cold with fear. For Bas. For Uncle. For everyone.

"Sasha, please—" I whispered, but I couldn't finish the sentence. He found me bloodied. He wanted to go back and kill every DiLustro. I had to beg him not to. He vowed he wouldn't, unless any DiLustro touched me again. "Please don't."

He shook his head, his pale blue eyes burned with fury. "Nobody gets away with this shit, Wyn. Not after what they did to you."

Uncle Liam's gaze ping-ponged between us. He had no knowledge of the deal Sasha and I made. Uncle didn't know Gio DiLustro almost raped me.

"What is he saying?" Bas gritted, his grip tightening.

"Yeah, what is Sasha saying?" Uncle echoed Basilio's words.

I shook my head, begging Sasha not to say anything. I didn't want anyone's death on my hands. Except for one DiLustro, but that one wasn't in this room.

"Fucking Russians with their big mouths," Dante gritted with disgust.

Luca King ran a hand across his jaw with sardonic amusement. "You think you're invincible, huh? Fucking kingpins."

My heart threatened to beat out of my chest as my eyes darted around the room. I'd give myself some serious motion sickness if I kept going.

"You didn't seem to mind us kingpins when you needed help with a certain lady," Emory mocked him. "Don't think I forgot yours and your brother's trip to Las Vegas."

I blinked confused. I had no fucking idea what they were talking about.

"God, you people are something," Winston announced while an amused spark flickered in his eyes. Both Ashford brothers didn't move, relaxed against the doorframe. They just needed a bowl of popcorn to make their entertainment full.

"Now, now, everyone," Byron deadpanned with that masked civility. He was just as brutal as the rest of the underworld. I'd stake my life on it. "We have to settle this like normal people. Let my cousins say what they want, and we can all come to terms. Without any bloodshed."

"Cousins," Emory sneered. "Just because your mother was sister to our father, doesn't make us family."

"I didn't call you family, did I?" Byron drawled, his eyes cold on her.

"Byron, your cousins are crazy," I rasped, my breath shaky.

Nobody acknowledged me. Byron and Winston had their eyes on the men ready to shoot each other. I felt like prey caught in the war, unsure which way to run.

Maybe stay with the current captor?

"I don't give a shit whose cousins they are," Killian spit. "They kidnapped a woman. *My cousin.* DiLustro's gone too far."

"Wynter is *mine*," Bas growled. "She is the payment for a debt owed." Confusion twisted in my stomach as my eyes frantically sought out my uncle and Killian, then Sasha. My sixth sense warned, but my brain wasn't coming up with the details fast enough. "Forty million dollars."

Realization slammed into me.

"Fuck," I cursed at the same time as Uncle. I attempted to elbow Bas but his arm around me wouldn't budge. Instead, my butt ground against him.

His lips pressed to my ear.

"Careful, principessa," he rasped low so nobody else could hear him. "You're giving me a boner, pushing up against me like that."

I instantly stilled, my eyes flashing to Uncle and Sasha. The latter looked like he was ready to start shooting and call it a day. My uncle was the strategic one.

"I'll have the money wired to you," Uncle assured him. "This morning."

A sardonic amusement flashed across Basilio's expression. "No can do, Brennan."

"What do you want, then, DiLustro?" Uncle gritted.

My heart hammered against my rib cage; it actually hurt to breathe. Something about Uncle's question had my survival instinct kicking in. And just like prey, I felt the need to run.

I turned my head around to find Bas's eyes shimmering with darkness. For a fraction of a second his eyes met mine, and something vulnerable flashed in those depths, it made my chest ache.

My breaths grew short as all the suppressed feelings slammed into me. The man I used to know offered me glimpses of his vulnerability, but just as I went to open my mouth, his expression changed back to a cold, dark mask.

"A wife," Bas replied and his gaze hardened as it returned to my uncle. A cold realization filled my lungs as I watched Uncle's eyes turn dark, like the deepest oceans during a violent storm. I had never seen this look on his face before, not when we got caught with our shenanigans and not when I lost my shit on him.

"Put an ad in the paper," Uncle bit out. "You won't have my niece. In fact, none of my family."

Slowly, like I was trapped in a slow-motion movie, I glanced at Dante, then Emory whose eyes flickered with regret.

"Why would I do that?" Bas drawled. "I already found my bride."

I shook my head, unable to breathe. Words escaped me and my heart squeezed in my chest. I couldn't marry him. I fell for him once and moving on almost destroyed me. I couldn't be around him; my heart would fall for him again. I wouldn't survive it.

The silence that fell upon the room was loathing and angry from Uncle and Sasha, annoyance from Luca King, thoughtfulness from the Ashford brothers and apathy from Bas.

"No, no, no," I breathed.

"She doesn't want you, fucker," Killian said, his voice cold while Bas's gaze burned through me.

I wouldn't survive my old lover.

Chapter Fifty-Three
BASILIO

She didn't want me.

I didn't give a fuck. She'd have me. Only me. For the rest of our lives.

The ice princess would be mine. Even if blood covered the altar as we said our vows. There was no getting away from it—for neither one of us.

"A member of your family stole from me," I drawled. "And this is my repayment. Or we'll have war."

"That club is not yours," Brennan growled.

"It's mine," I said, grinning darkly. "You should be getting a copy of the deed... right about now."

Everyone's phone dinged.

"Gentlemen, that would be the deed," Priest announced.

Brennan didn't bother retrieving the message, but his gaze shifted to Priest and his brows furrowed. Then he gave his head a small shake and came back to me with his niece in my grip.

Byron, my reluctant cousin, was the only one who checked it. His eyes shifted to me.

One breath. Two breaths.

"It's his," Byron acknowledged. "For over a year."

"I'll wire double the amount she took," Brennan offered.

I let out a sardonic breath. "Not good enough."

There was nothing and nobody that would do, except this woman in my arms. I'd start with tying her to me, then I'd make her love me. I'd have her loyalty, her trust, her love. I wanted it all.

And she'd give it. Just like she promised.

"Name anything," Brennan said dryly. "Anything, except for her."

I flicked a glance toward him and his reinforcements. Though unbeknownst to Brennan, the Ashford brothers were here to back us up, not him. If Alessio Russo, the illegitimate son of Senator Ashford, wanted our supplier's contact to enter Afghanistan, then the Ashfords would have to pay up.

Family or not. Nothing in this life was free.

My cousins and I were among the rare ones with the way to enter that country and Alessio desperately wanted in. At all costs.

"She's my term." I smirked. And denying me wasn't an option.

"You'll have your war, then," Brennan gritted. "You can't have Wynter."

Wynter's eyes frantically darted around the room. She stopped fighting me, her body tense in my arms.

"You guys can't be serious?" she whispered. "Tell me this is a joke."

"This is the way things are done," Luca deadpanned. "I thought you and your girl squad studied criminal activities."

"Shut up, Luca." Sasha's threatening glare would probably make a lesser man shit themselves. Unfortunately for all of us here, we were used to much worse.

"I was busy training," Wynter hissed at him. "I was a bit short on time to study your fucked-up, medieval ways."

Luca grinned. "I bet you Olympic gold this girl kills DiLustro herself at the end."

"I'm up for the bet," Byron chimed in. "I say she doesn't."

"Stop it," Brennan grumbled. "DiLustro, let my niece go. I'll wire a hundred million to you. And we all move on."

Dante whistled. "She's worth a lot to you, huh?"

"Everything," he admitted. "I made a promise to keep her safe. She's not safe around you. Just like her mother wasn't safe around your father."

My teeth clenched. I'd keep her safe until my dying breath.

"You can have a war, Brennan, but Wynter is mine either way."

Chapter Fifty-Four

WYNTER

U ncle's expression was murderous.

The detest and hate were so thick in the air it touched my skin as I stood frozen in Bas's arms, tasting fear.

For Bas's life. For Uncle's life. For everyone's life.

While nobody else seemed concerned, my heart turned to a block of ice.

Fear twisted so violently in my stomach, I felt the need to throw up. I couldn't let these men kill each other. I turned my head around, meeting Bas's dark gaze.

No words. No smile. Nothing.

Yet, there was this vulnerability deep down that I sensed more than saw. The ache in my chest swelled. If I didn't do something, it would mean violence and death. *A war.*

I knew what I had to do. What I should do. But self-preservation was a hard thing to overcome.

My gaze flicked to Uncle. We hadn't talked since I took my anger out on him months ago. I blamed him for too much. It was wrong and seeing firsthand he was willing to go to war to keep me protected highlighted it even more.

"I'll do it," I rasped. Basilio's arm around my waist tightened and I swore he pulled me closer to him. All the while a lump in my throat grew bigger and the tension hung over the room like a stormy cloud.

Uncle's eyes shifted to me. "Wynter, that's not what your mother wants for you."

"Neither is a war," I reasoned.

"Smart girl," Luca commended. It didn't feel smart.

"Wyn, no," Uncle protested. "No, you deserve so much better." Then he narrowed his eyes on Bas, and if looks could kill, the love of my life would be dead.

"I have to agree," Sasha chimed in. "I never agree with your uncle, but on this one. Just say the word, Wyn."

I shook my head. I'd never be able to say the word. Not when it came to killing the man I love. His father... yeah. But never Basilio.

"Wyn?" Uncle called out and I felt like such a cheat. He worried for me and I craved my villain with all my heart. I'd never be able to sever this love I had for him. My heart knew it. So did my soul and brain.

"I got this," I told him in Gaelic, holding his gaze. "Let me marry him and we keep the peace."

Maybe I'd at least get the chance to kill Gio.

I sat locked in my room.

Three of DiLustro's guards surrounded me and walked me to my room, then locked me in.

Uncle wanted to take me home. Bas refused. He didn't trust us. He believed I'd disappear at the first opportunity. I wasn't sure if I would.

I stared at the door.

I'd marry Basilio DiLustro. Before I learned our family history, it was a dream come true. Now, it was just... *complicated*. And there was the issue of Basilio's father.

I clenched my fists, letting my nails dig into my palms and relishing in pain. It was my resolve to kill him, make him pay for what he'd done. It was frighteningly easy to pull the trigger the last time. Especially when adrenaline and anger pumped through my veins. I could do it again.

All I had to think of was my mother and I'd find the courage to end him.

I headed back to the French window and stepped out on the balcony. The tiled floor on the balcony felt cool against my bare feet. I leaned back against the wall and slowly sank down. Pulling my legs up against my chest, I leaned my forehead against my knees.

I hadn't heard a gun go off and I took that as a good sign. Although I hated that they were having conversations about me, without me.

Glancing out at the horizon, the desert appeared endless, surrounding the mansion. The landscape became a reluctant familiarity.

I sat there, staring into the horizon but not really seeing it. I wondered if Mom was okay. I didn't even ask Uncle.

Jumping to my feet, I rushed to the door, and despite knowing I was locked in, I tugged on it. Then I banged like a madwoman.

"Basilio," I screamed as I banged my fist against the hard mahogany door. "Basilio."

I kept banging, my fists hurting from the impact.

Steps thundered toward the room and I paused.

"Basilio," I called out.

The door swung open and I came face-to-face with Dante.

"What the fuck, Wynter?" he grumbled.

"Is my uncle still here?" I asked frantically. He nodded. "I need to ask him about my mother," I breathed.

"Tell me what you want me to ask him," he growled with annoyance.

I shook my head. "No, I want to ask him."

For a moment he stood hesitantly. "For fuck's sake," he caved in. "Hurry, because they are getting ready to leave." I nodded and followed him. "And don't try anything stupid and make me regret this."

"You should regret kidnapping me," I hissed, my steps rushed.

We came into the foyer just as Uncle, Killian, and Sasha headed for the front door. Dante's hand wrapped around my forearm as I was about to rush to them.

"Uncle," I called out. Dante tugged me back and I shot him an annoyed look. "Dante, let me go."

Before he could say a word, Basilio was next to me.

"Release her *now*," Bas ordered, his voice cold, the warning sending icy shivers down my spine. His gaze was on Dante, dark and glaring.

Dante let go of my arm and Bas tilted his head in acknowledgement. I had no clue what the fuck that was about, but when I looked back to my uncle, he and Killian shared a fleeting glance.

"Uncle, how is Mom?" I asked, taking a step to go to him, but Bas held on to me now. I tugged on my arm. "Let go of me, Basilio," I snapped.

"You're not going anywhere without me," he warned and I let out a frustrated breath.

I took five steps and stopped, three feet from the three men who protected me.

"Mom?" I breathed out. "Is she okay?"

Bas remained next to me, the outline of his gun pressing at my back. A reminder if I did something stupid, it could end up in bloodshed. I wouldn't risk it, but I had to know she was okay.

"She's okay," Uncle assured me. "Juliette, Davina, and Ivy are with her."

"Don't... Don't leave her alone, okay?" I whispered.

"Never."

Ignoring Bas's hold on me, Uncle wrapped his hands around me and hugged me. It was kind of awkward with Bas at my back, allowing me to hug him with only one hand.

And then Sasha, God help him... or me... took a step forward and pulled me into a hug, tugging Bas right along.

"Hurt a single hair on her head, and you're dead," Sasha growled.

"Bring it on, blondie," Bas answered in a dark voice. Bas's lips curved into a snarl, his eyes hard and unrelenting. "And don't touch my woman again. Or I'll tear you apart."

"Fucking Italian devil," Sasha spat back at him.

"Russian prick," Bas sneered.

"Jesus, is this high school," I hissed. "I'll be fine," I told Sasha in Russian and smiling confidently. "You've taught me well." Something dangerous flickered in Bas's eyes and I quickly added, "Bye, Sasha."

Chapter Fifty-Five
BASILIO

The door shut behind the Russian prick and it was only then that I let go of Wynter's arm.

Brennan and I shook on the wedding, and only the wedding. It was a reluctant and barely civil accord. I didn't give a shit, as long as Wynter was with me. I told him, I'd take care of the wedding. He'd get the time and place.

"Eager to save him, huh?" I taunted her in a dark voice, but truthfully, I was so fucking jealous a red mist covered my vision.

Wynter glanced at me and shrugged.

"Sasha doesn't need saving," she spat back. "And if you'd kept a cool head, you'd have seen that."

A snicker sounded behind me and I followed it to where my cousins and sister stood, all three watching us.

"Cool head and Basilio when it comes to you don't go in the same sentence," my sister announced.

"Emory," I warned.

"It's true," she argued back. "And you know it is, so save us all the headache and listen to your soon-to-be wife."

Wynter stiffened for a moment, her breathing stilled and her eyes darted to me.

She swallowed before she asked, "When?"

"This Saturday," I told her. If I could even wait that long. "We'll get married in St. Patrick's Cathedral in New York."

"Hopefully it doesn't turn into a bloody wedding," Emory remarked.

"I have to echo the sentiment," Wynter repeated, looking at me pointedly. I ignored her insinuation. I couldn't make her any promises on that account. If someone attempts to take her away from me, there would be bloodshed. No way around it.

"Want to go for a walk?" I asked instead.

Her eyebrows shot up. "Why?" she asked suspiciously.

"It's been two days and you've been cooped up." She remained still, as if she didn't trust me to take her outside. "Let's go," I ordered her.

"Geez, I thought you were asking," she remarked sarcastically.

We headed down the back hallway and out the double-sided door. The moment the sun hit her face, her steps stopped and she exhaled, then tilted her face up to the sky.

I watched her silently. The look on her face took my breath away. Her long, dark blonde lashes fanned her face and her lips curved into a smile. First one I'd seen since I'd kidnapped her.

When she finally opened her eyes, she found me still looking at her. I didn't give a fuck. After nine months without her, I wanted to drink her in and get my fill.

"Principessa, why did you leave?" I had to know. She owed me that much. Hesitation flickered across her expression but she quickly masked it. "You promised to stay, and then left. Why?"

Her brows furrowed, as if she evaluated my words. Or my intentions. Then she started walking, averting her face from me. We walked in silence. If she thought I'd give up on finding the reason why she left, she was sadly mistaken.

I was relentless when I wanted something. And I wanted her. It's what kept me going for the past nine months.

"I have something to tell you," I started, breaking the silence that wasn't exactly uncomfortable.

Priest was her brother. She had a right to know and it wasn't right to keep that knowledge from her. Though I wondered how much she knew exactly.

"Don't tell me you're nervous?" she noted, her tone sarcastic.

"We're getting married," I started, ignoring her sarcasm. "We shouldn't have secrets between us." She scoffed but I ignored it. She'd come around. "Priest tested your DNA."

She stiffened but said nothing.

"You and Priest are half-siblings," I continued.

Her eyes widened and the shocked expression on her face revealed the truth. She didn't know.

"W-what?" she rasped, her eyes wide. "H-how?"

"You two share the same mother," I explained. She blinked, then blinked again, probably struggling to come to terms with it. "Twenty-five years ago, your mother and my uncle had a thing."

"A half brother," she repeated. "B-but she said she lost the baby."

My eyes snapped to her. "You knew?"

A heavy sigh slipped through her pink lips.

"She told me not too long ago." Her eyes darted to the horizon and gardens stretching around the several pools Emory had back here. "She said she lost the baby, not that the baby died," she whispered, as if she was talking to herself.

"You think she knows?" I asked her.

Wynter's eyes met mine. "I don't know," she murmured. "I don't know anything anymore."

Chapter Fifty-Six

WYNTER

Bas brought me back to my room after spending an hour
outside.

After the revelation about Priest, we no longer talked. I
didn't dare to tell him what I knew. I couldn't trust him. Though it
made me wonder why he trusted me with his information. He hadn't
even shared it with Uncle.

God, what a mess!

I couldn't call Mom to ask about it. Did she know? I must have
misunderstood Mom when she said she lost the baby. I took it that the
baby died.

With a heavy sigh, I came to a realization. I was on my own here,
until the wedding. Bas said my family would be there, along with their
guests. Whoever those were.

I walked back on the balcony and sat down. It became my go-to
place when I was bound to this bedroom. Closing my eyes, I rested my
head against the wall and listened to the wind rustling through the
desert. Unlike the city, it felt calming and soothing. Ironic considering
how I found myself here.

Bas asked why I left. Why? He'd know. He didn't really expect me to remain, not after that cruel performance by his father. Not after finding out that it was his father who shot my mother.

Last time, I put my faith in him. I trusted him blindly. I wouldn't repeat the same mistake again. I *couldn't* afford to repeat the same mistake again. It could destroy me. Mom. Uncle Liam. My friends.

I wasn't sure how long I sat like this when Basilio stepped out onto the balcony and my eyes flitted his way. I hadn't even heard him come in. While I changed into shorts and a tank top, he still wore his three-piece suit.

He crouched before me and reached for my chin, then nudged it up gently until our gazes met. His dark eyes watched me, searching my face.

I couldn't read his emotions, his gaze dark, yet warm. Something about him felt so *right*. So *warm*. So *mine*. But without trust, it was all for naught. With the history between our families, it was doomed from the start.

And still, I didn't push him away.

The air around us stilled, all noise drowned out by the beats of my heart. His rough palms cupped my face, and he brushed his mouth over the tip of my nose.

We'll destroy each other. The words remained locked behind my lips.

This man haunted my every thought for the past nine months. They say time heals all wounds, but mine just festered. The pain of his loss became permanent in my soul. The healing didn't start until I saw him again.

"I won't leave," I whispered a promise I knew he wouldn't believe.

He leaned in and kissed my throat, trailing a line down my throat. I sighed and tilted my head, giving him my submission.

"Liar," he rasped. I expected it, but my heart still ached.

The memories of promises I made him nine months ago would

forever work against me. Despite the electricity that burned between us, stealing all the oxygen in the room.

His hand lowered down to take my right wrist into his. He pulled back as his eyes took in the necklace he gifted me turned into a makeshift bracelet. I never took it off. Not even when I skated. I always wanted him with me, if even in such a small token.

He brushed his thumb over it. "Did you wear this with *him*?"

I knew he meant Sasha. Everybody always meant Sasha.

My lungs tightened and my heart gave a painful thud. Something about his assumption pierced sharply through my chest. I narrowed my eyes on him. Bitterness choked my lungs, taking my breath away.

"Go to fucking hell," I hissed. Fuck him for thinking I'd move on without a second thought. Fuck him for doing it so easily and assuming I did the same.

His gaze narrowed. "I've been there, principessa." A flicker of emotion in his eyes twisted my stomach. "I almost lost my goddamn mind when you disappeared. I searched everywhere for you."

He did?

"Ice princess," he muttered, regarding me with the darkness that pulled me deeper and deeper into the abyss.

"Don't call me that," I rasped, attempting half-heartedly to jerk my face out of his grip.

"How could you leave without a word?" He pressed his forehead against mine and my heart ached. It ached so fucking bad, I thought I'd die. "What happened? Why did you leave?"

A tear ran down my cheek and I wiped it away. I couldn't tell him. I didn't trust him. And yet, despair scratched at my chest, my instincts screamed to take him. Make him mine. Give him everything and demand everything.

"For weeks, I thought you were dead. Then I learned who you were." His bitter laugh was quiet. "Were you playing me the entire time? Collecting information for your uncle."

I stiffened, unsure whether he referred to my Irish heritage or the Russian one.

"Your father didn't tell you?" I breathed, a sliver of uncertainty snaking through my veins.

A dark chuckle vibrated between us. "Tell me what, principessa?" A few seconds passed and I held my breath. I didn't know why. I should seize this opportunity and lay it all out for him. But what if he took his father's side? What if he didn't believe me? "That my principessa was a liar and a thief?"

His accusation hit home. I didn't exactly lie to him, but I didn't tell him the truth either.

"I may be a liar, but so are you, Basilio."

He didn't tell me about my Russian heritage. He didn't tell me he wanted my connections to the Pakhan.

His pause was the only tell of his surprise, shortly replaced by a slow smile. "I do love your fire, principessa. And I'm always up for a challenge." I glared at him and his sardonic chuckle followed. "I should have known with the way you carried yourself," he murmured cryptically.

"You should have let me go home with my family," I muttered, tearing my gaze away from him, scared I'd drown in him. Every time I'd even begin to hate him, the image of the man I met, dancing with me under the stars with New York City lights in the distance flashed in my mind. Or the man on his haunches as he slipped my shoe on.

That felt raw, magical and so goddamn real.

"Never," he growled, low and almost feral. "I'm your family now. You're mine." When I didn't say anything, his hand wrapped around my neck and his fingers squeezed. Not hard, but just gently enough to warn. "If you leave me again, I'll hunt down every single member of your family and friends you have. I'll torture them until they tell me where you are. I own you now."

I am yours already. But I wasn't ready to admit it.

"You can't own a human being," I said in a quiet voice, tilting my chin up and meeting his gaze as I leaned my neck into his grip. "And if I leave, you'll never find me. None of you will." I let the words sink in before I continued. "But I said I'll stay. So I'll stay, unless you give me a compelling reason to leave."

My words slashed the air in the room, the battle of wills vibrating between us. Hot and heavy.

His grip tightened just a bit more and adrenaline rushed through my body. There were twisted, broken parts of me that enjoyed his dominance. He didn't scare me, not physically. The part I feared was him breaking my heart irrevocably and leaving me to live the rest of my life like a shell of a person.

Like my mother.

"I swear to God, Wynter. If you leave me again, you'll have death on your hands. I'll kill every single person you care about. I'll burn this entire world down."

His eyes hardened, the shadows inside them rising to the surface. "Give me your word you'll never leave," he demanded.

"Basilio, I already told you, I'll stay." I held his gaze. I wouldn't risk admitting to him that life without him scared me more than the darkness he harbored or any threats he dished out. But I'd give him this vow. "Despite the fact you're my family's enemy, I'll stay."

"If only I could believe your promises," he rasped.

"I'd also love to believe that you wouldn't hurt me," I retorted. "Or my family."

He gripped the back of my neck and slammed his lips against mine. Anger brimmed inside me and I tasted that same anger on his lips.

And still, his kiss felt so damn good.

I opened my mouth to protest and he took advantage and thrust his tongue inside. The pent-up need I had felt since the moment our eyes connected that winter day, a year ago, had erupted. I was lost to him, to his scent, to his heat.

"Fuck, you feel so good," he groaned against my mouth.

My hands wrapped around his neck, fisting his hair, pulling him closer. I needed his body against mine.

I moaned into his mouth and he groaned, then slid his hands down my neck, over my back and to the back of my thighs.

Without any effort, he lifted me. I wrapped my legs around him, relishing in how well our bodies fit together. Like perfect puzzle pieces. His fingers squeezed the flesh of my thighs, possessive, and his palm slid under my shorts to my ass as he walked us back into the room.

With a handful of my ass in his palms, he sat on the bed and I straddled his thighs. Our mouths drifted apart so he could pull the tank top over my head. The moment it was off, our mouths collided again. My shorts followed with a loud shredding sound.

It was raw lust and desire. Need for release. Yet for me, it was so much more. This hunger for him would be my undoing.

He gripped my hips, palms sliding up. Higher and higher. My sweet spot between my legs ached and I knew he was the only man who could ease that pain. His fingers brushed my inner thighs, as he bit my bottom lip with a gentle tug. Like he wanted to teach me a lesson.

He caressed the curves of my ass, while his lips traveled down my throat to the tops of my breasts. He nipped the soft skin and my head fell back.

"Bas," I breathed his name with a moan. I felt him everywhere, each nerve within me quivering with delight.

"Mine," he said roughly, while he caressed the bare curves of my ass. God help me, I was his. I had always been his and no amount of denial would ever change that.

His other rough hand slid beneath my bra and squeezed the flesh.

Pleasure was instant, rushing to my core, and I buried my face into his neck.

He pressed his lips against my ear. "Ask me."

"Please," I hummed against his neck, my hips grinding against him. I'd ponder and regret my choices later. Right now, I needed him like a wilting flower craved sun and water. "Please, Bas. I need this."

He groaned deeply, like my admission pleased him. He unclipped my bra and pulled it off. My breasts felt heavy as cool air brushed them. He pulled away, and his eyes skimmed over my breast with an almost reverent look. With something dark and possessive in his gaze that resembled madness. Maybe mine, possibly his.

He ran a thumb across my nipple, then leaned in and sucked a nipple into his mouth. A loud moan filled the room and my head fell back as I ran a hand into his hair, fisting it. He tugged on my sensitive nipple and I swore I felt the heat between my legs. He pressed the soft flesh of my breasts together, then bit, licked, and sucked from one to the other.

Flames curled low in my stomach and I grew wetter with each second.

"I can smell your arousal," he groaned against my flesh. "I missed your smell so fucking much."

"More," I begged, grinding against his erection with a panting noise.

"You want it here?" he asked, his hand covering my pussy through the thin fabric of my panties.

A desperate moan and a nod of my head. "Please."

His thumb slipped under the strap of my panties, tugging it down. Then he pressed his lips to my ear.

"Take them off for me," he commanded. It didn't even occur to me to object. With eager hands, I pushed my panties down my thighs, adjusting on his lap. A few times I accidentally ground, or not, against his hard erection and he released a ragged breath.

He stared at my pussy with a gaze as dark as midnight. My hands trembled as I put them on his shoulders, gripping the material of his suit.

"You are my fucking vice," he groaned, his tone harsh. Like he hated that he found me desirable. "This little body belongs to me and nobody else."

His hand ran up my thigh and around to my ass, pulling me harder against him. Then his fist tightened in my hair, tilting my face to his and his gaze hard.

"Say it." His demand was ruthless,

His face came up to mine. Our lips were inches apart and our gazes drowned in each other.

I should fight him. Deny him. But there was no sense in lying to him, at least in this regard. "My body belongs to you and nobody else," I breathed. "I'm yours."

Always and forever.

He ran a thumb across my lips and I parted them, my tongue brushing against the tip of it. I held his gaze as we sat chest to chest. Heartbeat to heartbeat. He leaned in and brushed his lips down the length of my throat.

I tilted my head to give him more access, the move submissive. I didn't care. I trusted him with my body. He might be the ruthless kingpin, my villain, but he knew my body better than even I did.

"You feel so good," he groaned against my throat. The heat of his lips sent a sizzle between my legs. As if he knew it, his palm snaked between our bodies and pressed against my clit, applying the smallest amount of friction. His hand was rough, and I was already so damn close. I didn't need much. I bit my lip to hold in a groan.

Bas watched his hand between my legs through his heavy lids. His palm moved at a tortuous grind against my clit, and frustration bubbled within. He knew exactly how to get me off, but he was withholding the pleasure on purpose.

"Stop fucking teasing me," I snapped, glaring at him with my cheeks flushed. I wanted to get off and all he was doing was building my frustration.

His hand stilled, as if he was surprised by my fire, and after a second that stretched like hours, a low chuckle escaped him.

He nipped on my jawline in punishment, then lifted his dark eyes to mine. The hint of darkness tainted his next words. "What happened to my sweet principessa?"

"She died," I breathed. It felt like a part of me had truly died that day.

"You want to come?" he rasped darkly. I nodded and he slipped two fingers through my wetness and pushed them inside of me.

I arched my back, dug my nails into his shoulders, and groaned in pleasure. This was rougher than anything before, yet the pleasure was enhanced by the pain. He slid his thick fingers in and out, both of us breathing raggedly.

"When I take you again, I'm going to be rough," he said harshly.

His words only seemed to spark a fuse inside me and adrenaline unfurled in my veins like a shot of a powerful drug, as he thrust his fingers back into me. He hit the spot deep inside me. My body shuddered and my eyes rolled back as my insides clenched greedily around his fingers.

Hot pressure expanded and I squeezed my eyes tightly shut, reaching for those heights. Bas smacked my ass with his other hand. My eyes shot open to find his darkened gaze on me, passionate and deep.

"Eyes on me, principessa," he rumbled, the tension in his shoulders visible. Then he smacked my ass again and the unexpected sting sent a vibration to my core. I moaned against his lips, breathing his air.

Judging by the rumble that vibrated in his chest, he liked my reaction. The next spank was harder. Firmer.

"Ouch," I complained.

"Because you left me," he gritted, then spanked me again.

It brought fire that was enhanced as he continued to slowly fuck me with his fingers. I watched him through my half-lidded gaze before lowering my gaze to watch his fingers slick with my juices, pumping in and out of me as my hips ground shamelessly against him.

My whole body trembled with the impending release, like a volcano threatening to erupt. I was so wet, it was dripping down his hand and my leg. A shiver rolled down my spine, every muscle in my body quivered, and he took my mouth for a rough kiss. And all the while I ground against his hand and panted as I climbed the peak. My nails dug into his biceps, the impending release curling down my spine.

"Who are you thinking about?" he asked through clenched teeth. His fingers thrust hard, circling deep inside me and making me see stars. "Who?" he demanded coarsely.

"You," I whimpered.

As if he wanted to reward me for my admission, his thumb pressed on my clit, and another finger eased inside. My insides clenched and my body shuddered at the extra pressure. Pressure built and built.

Another thrust of his fingers and he sent me over the cliff as I gripped a fistful of his hair.

Heat exploded through every fiber of my body, my vision dimmed, and my heart pounded to keep up with the scorching blood pumping through me, stealing my breath. My skin burned as I gasped for air and all the while his fingers moved slowly, in and out of me.

The ringing in my ears faded, the fog in my vision cleared and his fingers remained inside me. My face buried in his neck, I inhaled deeply his scent, making a soft noise of appreciation. He smelled so good, like whiskey, sin, and spice. So masculine. So mine.

Warmth spread through my body as he wrung the last pulse from me, and in the moment, I didn't care about our fucked-up families' history, about the past, or the way he kidnapped me. I just cared about *him*. With me.

I kissed up his neck, humming a soft noise of appreciation. Inhaling his heady scent was my own brand of alcohol. Post-orgasmic bliss made me feel raw and vulnerable. I was completely naked and he was completely dressed.

I brushed my fingers over his erection, feeling his thick, hard length and the wanton in me wanted him. *Now*. Inside of me. He was so hard and big, and my body still remembered how he felt inside me. My pussy clenched, ready for him to claim me.

My eyes met his, and I held my breath. I knew he could see my desire in them, but he must have seen in them something else too. Because he let out a frustrated breath, kissed me on the lips and then tucked me under the blankets.

"Go to sleep, principessa," he rasped. "Soon."

I lay on the bed, staring blankly after him as he stood up and walked out the door.

A raw ache pulsed through my chest. A single tear ran down my cheek and a choked sob escaped me.

He warned me he was a villain when we met. He never warned me he'd steal my heart.

Chapter Fifty-Seven

BASILIO

The image of Wynter naked against the wall, her skin flushed by her arousal, burned in my brain. I was hard as a rock and ready to take her. After nine months of dreaming and fantasizing about her, she was finally in my grasp, and I was determined to make her mine. Brand her. Fuck her senseless.

Yet, it was all wrong.

Her eyes, the color of cool lakes, watched me with so much distrust it fucking tore at my chest. There was no trace of that look she used to have for me. Blind trust was gone.

Fucking bullshit.

She left me without a backward glance. I felt fucking crazy over the last nine months imagining her hurt, tortured, or dead. I waited for an explanation. It never came. My father was a sadistic, lying snake, so asking him was out of the question. I tried Angelo and that led nowhere. I suspected he withheld information, but short of torturing it out of him, he wouldn't disclose it.

Still, my cock wanted inside her tight, wet pussy. It didn't care about the reason. Just her. She was mine, from the very moment she landed in my arms. And I'd burn this whole motherfucking world down to keep her. Nobody would take her away from me again.

In my own bedroom, I lay down in my bed, silently cursing myself for taking it so far. Now I was rock hard and risking getting blue balls. Except the need to touch her was an itch that demanded to be scratched. I had to feel her soft skin, or risk losing my goddamn mind.

So I succumbed to the temptation. And now, restlessness ghosted under my skin, demanding I go back and take her.

Fuck me. Dante was right all along. I was way too hung up on Wynter. I was so deep into her I didn't know the way up.

This woman fucked with my brain and my heart. But she was mine now and there was no chance I'd ever let her go. She had a body I wanted to bury myself in, but most of all, she had a soul that I wanted to consume.

She gave me lust. She gave me her body. But it wasn't enough.

I would take all that she promised me.

Getting sleep tonight would be a moot point.

So I lay in my bed, wearing just my boxers, my head against the stack of pillows and my eyes locked on the skylight. The dark sky was full of stars but all they fucking did was remind me of her. The girl who slept in the room within my reach; the girl I wanted to consume.

The tension itched my skin, demanding I get a release. My cock wanted to be inside her tight, wet entrance. My own personal haven.

I took my cock in my hand, imagining Wynter's soft hands wrapped around my dick. She'd pump up and down, too gently at first, but I'd show her how to do it harder. I squeezed my dick hard, pumping it up and down, stroking it and all the while images of Wynter writhing underneath me in pleasure flashed through my mind.

A board creaked, tension shot through me before I reached for my gun and opened my eyes.

I found Wynter staring at me with wide eyes, her lips parted.

I stilled, wondering how long she stood there. I didn't even hear the goddamn door open.

"How did you get in here?" I grumbled.

She padded towards me, her bare feet silent on the hardwood. God, those long, lithe legs would be the death of me.

"I—I don't want to sleep alone," she whispered, licking her lips and her breathing slightly ragged.

My desire flooded my veins and my cock throbbed painfully. Fuck, this was the wrong time for her to seek me out. My control hung by a thread.

"Principessa," I murmured, unable to turn her away.

Chapter Fifty-Eight

WYNTER

God, watching Bas jerking off was so erotic that I forgot about the beginnings of my nightmare. His guttural noise as his fingers pumped up and down made my pussy ache. My heart thundered in my chest and fire burned in my veins.

I took one step. Then another. No protest left his lips, so I closed the distance to his bed and climbed onto it.

I couldn't tear my eyes away from his hand wrapped around his big, thick cock. The faint sounds of the song I recognized came from somewhere else in the house. The song "Ashes" by Madi Diaz whispered words that I could feel in my soul.

He started pumping his cock again, up and down, his soft grunts mixing with the tunes of the song, making it forever deliciously filthy.

The haze in the air thickened; it burned with each inhale. I lifted my gaze up to his face to find his hooded gaze burning with desire and on me. My tongue swept over my lip and a whimper bubbled in my throat.

My skin burned, my heart raced and my breathing was choppy like I just skated a ten-minute program at high speed.

The tip of his cock glistened with cum, tempting me with its taste. I remembered how good he tasted.

My hand reached out to his hard cock, wrapping my fingers around his strong ones.

"Fuck, principessa." His voice was tortured, the tension streaming off his body.

"Let me," I rasped.

He removed his hand too eagerly. The moment my hand touched the skin of his shaft, a loud groan echoed through his bedroom and straight to my core. It didn't matter that he just gave me an orgasm mere hours earlier. I wanted him again.

I started pumping his smooth, hard length, up and down, while he watched me through half-closed lids. He looked so strong and vulnerable at the same time, his muscled body a sight to behold.

"Bas," I whispered, swallowing hard. I craved him so much, it was an ache I felt everywhere. "Can I taste you?"

Both his hands grabbed my waist and he lifted me on top of him. My knees spread, straddling his strong thighs. My pussy was so close to his cock I could feel his heat and a throbbing ache pulsed between my legs.

But this was for him. He gave me pleasure and now I wanted to give him his.

I lowered down his body and licked his shaft from base to tip, my eyes on him. He sucked in a strained breath and his eyes grew hazy. A shiver ghosted down my spine, and I moaned with his cock in my mouth.

His hand grabbed a fistful of my hair, his eyes watching me with a half-lidded gaze. I ran my tongue around his head and sucked him in and out of my mouth.

"Take all of it," he said harshly, tension vibrating through every cell of his body. Even more disturbing was the way my body responded to his bossy tone. Wetness pooled between my legs and my pussy throbbed.

This was only the second blowjob I'd ever given, but this one felt different from the first one. It was more desperate, his thrusting into my mouth jerky, like he was teetering on the edge.

I took all of him in my mouth, my breasts rubbing against his thighs and causing friction over my thin top.

He moved my head up and down, controlling the rhythm. He thrust deep, his cock hitting the back of my throat, and my eyes fluttered shut, moaning with need.

He tasted salty and so fucking addictive.

"Look at me," he ordered roughly and a shudder passed through my body as my gaze flicked to him.

"Mine," he muttered.

I hummed my approval, squeezing my thighs together to ease the ache. While still gripping my curls with one hand, his other caressed my cheek like I was his everything. Just like he did all those months ago.

Raw emotions flickered in my chest, and I feared he could see my love for him shining in my eyes. He continued fucking my mouth and I let him. Because he was my everything.

His groans rumbled through his chest, our gazes locked as he kept thrusting in and out. Deeper and harder, and his groan turned into a hoarse sound as he spilled into my mouth. I swallowed and licked my lips, never breaking our eye contact.

I sat back on my heels, still straddling him. Bas's chest rose up and down, his harsh breathing filling the silence between us and darkness pooled like whiskey in his gaze.

Then without a word, he pulled up his boxers. Then he tugged me flat on his bare torso and his hands wrapped around my waist. I pressed my cheek against his chest and listened to his heartbeat.

It was the first time in over nine months I slept without night-mares plaguing my dreams.

Chapter Fifty-Nine

BASILIO

I woke up with Wynter's curls in my face, her scent all over me and her face pressed against my chest.

She looked so peaceful, her breathing even and her palm resting over my chest. I didn't want to move and wake her up.

I started to suspect the black shadows under her eyes were the result of her nightmares. If only she'd trust me enough to tell me what they were about. It had to be bad if she willingly came to my bed.

From the moment I met Wynter, I'd wanted to protect her. The last nine months hadn't diminished that urge. If anything, the need grew fiercer. Yet something happened and I'd bet all the money in the world my father had something to do with it.

I kissed the top of her head, my chest hurting with all these fucking emotions. She was the only one who held the power to my destruction and didn't even know it.

And fuck, when she took me in her mouth, her pink lips closing around my shaft, I almost lost it. I could have exploded right then. That was how much she impacted me. Her soft expression locked on me and her noises as I fucked her mouth were what erotic dreams were made of.

I ran my fingers through her silky hair, her breaths fanning my heated skin. My one hand was still wrapped around her arm and I couldn't stop running my thumb over her soft skin.

Another three days and she'd be my wife. I almost wanted to drag her to the justice of the peace and be done with it, but I promised Brennan it'd be done properly.

We'd fly back to New York today, but I didn't want to go back to my old place. Until I learned exactly what my father had done, I wouldn't risk having her anywhere close to that bastard. So I'd take her to the new penthouse I bought and not a single soul knew about. Nobody had access to it but me.

She stirred in my arms and her eyes fluttered open. Our gazes connected and her lips curved into a smile.

"Hey," she murmured sleepily.

For a fraction of a moment, she reminded me of that girl from nine months ago. Her eyes fluttered shut again and a contented sigh left her lips.

"Morning, principessa."

Her eyes opened again and she jerked up into a sitting position. The air stilled, her gaze darting around the room. She blinked slowly, then wiped a hand over her eyes.

"I slept all night," she murmured absentmindedly and confirmed my suspicion about her nightmares.

"You did," I confirmed.

"Did I—" She hesitated before she continued, "Did I keep you awake?"

I shook my head. "I just woke up."

Relief flashed across her face, but then she looked away. My throat tightened and my mouth filled with a bitter taste. It was like she couldn't bear to look at me. Then she shifted away from me, combing her fingers through her hair and looking anywhere but at me.

Like she couldn't stand the sight of me.

"We fly back to New York today," I bit out harsher than I intended. She instantly paled. "I have a penthouse I just bought. Nobody else knows about it, so we'll stay there until the wedding."

"Nobody?" she asked quietly, nibbling on her lower lip nervously. "Not even your father?"

"Nobody," I confirmed. "Not my father. Not even my sister and cousins."

"What about the wedding?" she rasped. She pushed an unruly piece of hair out of her face, a small tremor in her hand. "Will your father be there?"

"No."

What the fuck happened that day?

Half a day later, we were in New York, taking the elevator to the top floor of my new penthouse.

The elevator beeped and came to a stop to open to the space that was already decorated but fairly empty. On the way here, I ordered a delivery of groceries, clothes for Wynter and myself as well as an early dinner.

I motioned for Wynter to enter and she took hesitant steps into the large foyer.

"I've never stayed here, so there will be things missing," I told her. "Let me know whatever you need and I'll have it ordered."

She peered at me from under her lashes. "If you get me a phone, I can order it myself."

Truthfully, I had already ordered her a phone, AirPods, and an

Apple Pro. Why didn't I give it to her? Because I was worried she'd take off.

Fucking sue me. I never claimed to be a good guy.

She refused to open up, which left me suspicious of her real intentions.

Her eyes roamed the room and she stepped up to the large French windows. Emory had gotten her a pink sweater dress that came down to her knees and white Ugg boots. It made her look like a true winter princess.

And unfortunately, the girl made me rock hard. All the goddamn time.

She took two steps to the left and opened the door, then headed out on the large rooftop terrace. I followed and watched as she leaned over to check the steep way down.

"No climbing down from here," I said as I leaned beside her.

She actually smiled. "Not unless I get a helicopter," she retorted back. Before I could say anything else, she added softly, "Bas, I said I'll stay."

Except, she said that the last time and then she left.

Everywhere I turned, she was there. Her scent. Her eyes. Her body, just waiting for me to claim it. I took my jacket and vest off, then the holster and followed by placing my gun in the nightstand.

I was surprised she hadn't asked to sleep in the guest room. The answer would have been no, but I still expected her to ask it.

Maybe she wanted me after all. At least in the fucking bed.

Goddamn it, it should be enough. Any other man would be elated to be wanted by a woman like her.

Except, I wanted everything. Her body, heart, and soul. Fuck, I wanted to be part of her every heartbeat. Her every thought. I wanted to be her whole world. Just like she was my whole world.

The bathroom door opened and she came out wearing the tiniest pink boyshorts and a black top. Jesus, she was trying to kill me.

"Which side of the bed do you want?" she asked, motioning at the bed.

"Closest to the door," I said, my control hovering on the edge.

She sauntered to the other side of the bed and bent over, giving me a full view of her glorious ass.

Temptation had a name. It was Wynter Star. She was mine. She'd always be mine.

I had no idea what in the fuck she was looking for, but I wished she'd stop bending her ass and giving me all kinds of ideas that would take us all night to execute.

"Are you going to keep staring at my ass?" she asked, straightening up, then turning around to meet my eyes.

Her green eyes turned a darker shade and her parted lips begged to be kissed. Or fucked. I couldn't quite decide. Then I scented her arousal and it was game over for me.

One second, I was on the opposite side of the bed; the other I had her pressed against the wall. My body slammed into her, pushing her back against the wall. I shoved my hips into her and a soft gasp slipped through her lips.

Without warning, I hooked my fingers into her waistband and pulled them down her legs, lowering myself down on my knees at the same time.

Snaking my hand between her thighs, I found her soaked and a satisfied growl vibrated through my chest. I wanted to pound my chest. My woman was soaking wet.

For me.

My hand cupped her pussy and I hummed with satisfaction when her back arched, pushing further into my hand.

"You crave this," I groaned. "Just like me."

"Don't be so satisfied," she murmured, her voice husky and her eyes half-lidded. "It's just a normal r-reaction."

Without warning I slapped her pussy, lightly.

A moan vibrated between us, and as if she realized too late what happened, her eyes snapped open. Though she didn't push me away. Either she was too stunned. Or too excited.

Before she'd have time to ponder on it, I brushed my fingers against her core. I watched her pink pussy like a man dying of thirst. I inched my face closer to it and inhaled her scent deep into my lungs.

Her back arched off the wall and her eyes fluttered shut. I watched bliss cross her expression. I had been dreaming about having her for so goddamn long. I wanted her begging for my cock, but the damn woman had a strong will.

She had changed. The young woman with open smiles and reactions hid from me now. But it was right there and then that I decided, I'd hunt every man down who had the pleasure of seeing her unravel since she walked away from me. And I'd kill them.

I'd be the only man on this earth who has seen her fall apart when she reached her peak.

I slid my fingers inside her wet folds, and this time, a soft moan escaped her. Her insides greedily clenched around them and I thought I'd fucking come just from that.

"Tell me you want this," I rasped against her pussy, my eyes glued to her face. I watched her lower lip caught between her teeth. I regretted not hearing her moans.

"C-can we just stop talking?"

I rose to my full length, ready to pull my fingers out of her folds when her hand flew to my wrist.

"P-please, Bas." Since I slammed back into her life, I fucking thrived each time she called me by the nickname she gave me. The wanton need in her eyes eased my anger, but it wasn't enough. I wanted all that she promised me before she left me.

Her light green eyes watched me through lust-filled half-closed lids and I knew, no matter what, I'd do anything for her when she looked at me that way.

Pushing my fingers back inside her clenching pussy, her mouth parted and I slammed my mouth against hers. She bit into my lip, the sting shot through me, but when her tongue licked over it, my fucking chest exploded.

This woman was rougher, more demanding than the woman who walked away from me nine months ago. And I fucking loved it.

Our mouths clashing, our tongues dancing together, my fingers slid in and out of her. In and out. My cock throbbed painfully against my pants, but right now, I wanted to see her unravel. For me.

"Bas," she moaned into my mouth, her hips bucking. She was close. With this woman, my blood burned hotter and the word *mine* seared into my chest.

Wynter Star DiLustro. *Soon!*

She ground against my hand, her moans filling the room. I knew when she approached her orgasm. Her hands frantically held on to my shoulders, her fingers digging into my skin.

"That's right, principessa." I nipped her earlobe. "Give me everything."

Her head fell backwards, exposing her neck to me. I bit into it, gently nipping and marking her. I wanted the entire world to know she was mine.

Thrusting my fingers in and out. In and out, her grip on me tightened. I stilled my hand movement and her eyes shot up.

"No," she said frantically, her hips grinding against my hand. "Don't stop."

I chuckled darkly. "I'll finish you off," I promised coarsely. "But you'll get on your knees and suck me off."

I needed her mouth around my dick to get me off so I'd make it to our wedding night. Then I'd fuck her all goddamn night. Slow. Hard. Fast. I had nine months of fucking to make up for.

Watching Wynter's face, I could tell she wanted to tell me off. But she wanted to come even more.

"I can get myself off," she murmured, but at the same time her hips ground against my palm, hungry for friction.

"But it's not the same," I drawled. I'd know. I had been getting myself off for the last nine months. I couldn't stand to fuck any other woman. The scent was off. The hair color was off. Everything about them was off. "Is it, principessa?"

I skimmed my mouth over her neck. Licking. Nipping. "I'll make you come so hard. Then I'm going to eat your greedy pussy." A whimper vibrated through her chest and straight to my groin. "And after I lick off all your juices, I'll bury myself so fucking deep inside you and fuck you so hard that you'll be screaming until your throat turns raw."

"Yes," she panted, her eyes closed. I wondered if she pictured her other lovers. The thought burned like acid through me.

"Open your eyes," I ordered harshly.

She obeyed without question, and something in her eyes calmed me. Without prompting she leaned forward, her lips barely an inch from my mouth.

"Get me off," she whispered, her tongue licking my mouth. "And I'll suck you off."

No sooner her last word was uttered, I slammed my mouth against her at the same time my fingers thrust into her. Hard. We kissed like two desperate people. I finger-fucked her like her orgasm was the last thing I'd see on this earth.

Her hands ripped my shirt off, eager to take it off me. Her small palms felt cool against my heated skin. And God, I could feel her touch all over. On my back, on my shoulders, on my chest. As if she was as hungry for me as I was for her.

"Ahhh... Ah.... Ahhh, Bas," she gasped.

"Open your eyes," I ordered, jealousy a dark thought in the back of my mind. She obeyed without delay, probably scared I'd deny her pleasure. Our eyes locked, her shimmering green depths as she fell apart. I kept thrusting my fingers deep into her, uncaring how rough I was. I needed this as much as she did.

"Oh my God," she moaned, watching me through heavy eyelids.

I chuckled darkly. "No, not God," I drawled, my cock hard as a goddamn rock. "Your soon-to-be husband."

"More," she begged, her hips bucking.

I curled my finger inside her and hit her spot. And she spiraled out of control.

"Yes, yes. Bas, p-please." Our mouths clashing together, I drank her moans and pants. Her pussy clenched as she fell apart for me. For me! Nobody else. It was enough to sustain me and sate this rage I had felt since she left me.

Her juices dripped down my knuckles, over my hand. I was tempted to get down on my knees myself and lick her, tongue-fuck her, eat her up so she'd fall apart for me again. But I'd spill in my fucking pants. I was close.

"Your turn," I said, a tad bit too harshly.

Her eyes sparkled like the stars, her breathing heavy. She had that sated look on her face, the mixture of bliss and wonder. Just like before. My insides hardened thinking about before.

She fucking left me.

Her hands roamed my chest, her touch light and gentle. I pulled my fingers slick with her juices and brought it up to her lips and smeared it over her bottom lip, then brought them to my lips. As I sucked my fingers clean, her eyes never wavered from me. Her tongue swept over her lower lip, the sight maddeningly erotic. And she wasn't even trying.

I fucking hated how much I fucking needed her to keep my sanity.

"A promise is a promise," she whispered.

She pushed my shirt off my shoulders and it landed soundlessly onto the floor.

"You're not good at keeping promises," I told her darkly, my mood souring remembering her last promise.

She promised to stay with me, to never leave me. And then she left me without a backward glance, without a single note. She left me to go mad looking for her.

Something flickered across her expression but she said nothing. Instead she lowered herself down onto her knees and fumbled with my belt. I couldn't wait, so I took over, got rid of my belt and unbuckled my pants.

Then my hand wrapped around the back of her neck and I gripped it tightly. The anger in my chest burned, like acid and wildfire. A bad combination.

She pulled my briefs down my legs and her tongue swept across her lower lip. Maybe she wanted me as much as I wanted her too. For now, I'd tell myself that. Otherwise, I'd lose my fucking shit.

Her little hand wrapped around my cock and she leaned in, her tongue lapping at the crown of it.

"Fuck," I groaned, my hips thrusting into her mouth. She couldn't get away, my hand keeping her locked in place. I widened my stance and pushed further down her throat. "Look at me while I fuck your mouth," I instructed, my control shaking hard.

Her gaze flicked to me, soft and full of lust.

"Fuck," I muttered. I almost shot off my cum as I sank my cock deeper into her mouth.

God, she looked perfect on her knees, her mouth full of my cock.

My breaths came out heavy as I watched her with a half-lidded gaze. She was perfection. Her cheeks flushed, her eyes shining as she gazed up at me as she sucked me deeper into her mouth.

Our rhythm in sync, I began to move faster. Harder. Deeper. Her throaty moans vibrated through my dick, sending shocks all the way up my spine.

Her hands grabbed at my hips, her fingers digging into my flesh. She was getting off on this as much as I was. Her head bobbed up and down with enthusiasm and my abs shook with the need to come down her throat. But I wasn't ready. I wanted to prolong this heaven.

"You're mine," I growled, thrusting deeper into her throat. "Every inch of you."

I thrust deeper and faster into her wet, hot mouth. The only sounds filling our room were my ragged breaths and her muffled moans. I didn't take it easy on her, as if each rough thrust was a punishment for what she put me through. Her gurgles came from her throat but she didn't stop me, didn't push me away. In fact, she pulled me closer.

"You're going to swallow every last drop," I said, my voice hoarse. She blinked her eyes in agreement. "Because you're mine." I started thrusting into her, faster and deeper into her throat. "And I'm yours."

Her grip on me tightened, while a moan vibrated deep in her throat. Fuck, she liked my claim. At least at this very moment she did.

I came harder than ever, my cum filling her mouth and dripping down her chin. My orgasm burned through me, wild and hot, though it didn't compare to the feelings I had for her. They would be my downfall, I knew it. But I couldn't stop them. She consumed me and breathed life into me. Without her, I was bitter and angry, a shell of a man. With her, I felt everything. Each breath, every smile, every look.

A pale pink flush stained her cheeks, her gaze on me and her mouth parted. She looked like a goddess on her knees. And the look in her eyes... I could convince myself that she felt *something* for me.

Something, I scoffed in my head. Hate was a feeling too. Though she didn't look at me at this very moment like she hated me.

So I fucked her and made her scream my name all night.

Chapter Sixty

WYNTER

I woke up with a heavy hand wrapped around me and the scent I'd come to know so well. My body ached with the sweetest exhaustion. Some things we'd done last night would make a much more experienced woman blush.

And when he muttered something in Italian, I fucking melted. *Melted!* I wanted to ask him what he said, but then his tongue slid inside me and I forgot every damn language but moaning. He fucked me slowly, in every possible way, murmuring soft words in my ear.

Our bodies fit perfectly together. His hands branded me; his mouth gave me hope; his heart owned me.

For a few moments, I just lay there, staring out the large window that covered one entire wall of the bedroom with the city spread across the horizon and a startling realization hit me.

No nightmare.

Two consecutive nights without nightmares and both while I slept with Bas. I felt better. Rested. As if he felt my revelation in his sleep, Bas's hold on me tightened. *Comfort.* He was my comfort.

Shortly after we arrived at Basilio's fancy, new penthouse, our clothes and groceries arrived. Bas and I put it all away. It felt natural, almost as if we picked up where we left off before everything blew up. Before his father.

The air was tense, like he waited for something.

I glanced over my shoulder and he looked so damn tense, even in his sleep. Like he expected me to betray him. Except, I didn't. It was he who betrayed me by never revealing his true intentions.

The attraction was there regardless. But maybe if he'd told me all he knew and kept his fucking father away, I'd have kept my promise and not walked away like his mother. Even so, it hurt me to know that my actions made him colder.

Maybe instead of running, I should have sought Bas out. I started to get an inkling that maybe, just maybe, his father's visit didn't go exactly as Bas planned it. I'd have to confront him about what happened.

Returning my attention back to the window, I looked at the city skyline. Maybe I should have trusted my heart. Goddamn it, I didn't know. But now that I knew the pain, I was hesitant to trust him fully.

I couldn't help but laugh at the irony of Mom keeping Juliette and me out of the underworld, only to sink ourselves into it elbows deep.

And our past came back to haunt us with a vengeance.

Mom! And Priest!

Did she know? He wasn't at the Olympics, so she wouldn't have seen him. A half brother. So technically that makes him Irish, Russian, and Italian too. Right? So why in the hell would they even need me to make a connection with the Pakhan?

It was pointless. I'd never figure it out, not unless I flat-out asked and demanded all the answers from Bas.

Careful not to wake him up, I slid out of his grip and got out of bed. I glanced down at myself, wearing black boyshorts and a pink tank top. He bought me tons of pink stuff, and when I asked him why so much pink, he grumbled something about it being my color.

I padded barefoot to the kitchen, unsure what to do with myself. There was no gym here, no equipment. Nothing. He said his Hampton home had a gym and he'd get me whatever I needed.

Yet only one thing kept coming to mind when I thought about what I needed. *Him*.

But he hadn't mentioned words of love, and I stubbornly refused to admit it. God, I wished I had a phone so I could call... Mom? Someone who could tell me what was normal in this situation.

I glanced around the kitchen. Even this room had a large bay window overlooking the Hudson River. From all the way up here, the city appeared tranquil and the only thing that betrayed it was the movement of cars.

Two more days.

I'd be his wife. Though after everything last night, I felt like his wife in every single way except in name. My cheeks burned with the memory of everything that happened last night. It was almost as if Bas was trying to make up for all the lost time and cram it all into one night of fucking.

There was no mistaking it—that was fucking. There was nothing gentle or loving about it. God help me, I loved it.

If only I could marry him—just the two of us and nobody else. No, no... the two of us, my mom, Uncle, the girls, and Sasha. He could have his cousins and sister there also. I'd forgive them for the kidnapping. After all, Priest was my brother, Emory is his sister, and Dante is... Well, I wasn't sure what he was.

A sigh shuddered out of me and trepidation fluttered deep inside me. It wasn't because of the forced marriage. After all, I wanted to marry Bas nine months ago. I was scared of seeing his father.

What if he tried something again?

My hands shook as I opened the fridge door. I stared at the contents, focusing on ingredients. Lots of fruit, pre-made pasta meals, almond milk, spinach, and Greek yogurt.

"Banana, blackberries, almond milk, spinach," I muttered, forcing my mind away from the dark thoughts. "Banana, blackberries, almond milk, spinach."

My stomach rumbled. I glanced over the door, in the direction of our bedroom and my lips curved into a smile. The idea hit me like a lightning bolt.

"Wakey, wakey," I whispered gleefully. I stood at the island and pulled my hair into a messy bun, then started my search for a blender. "Aha," I exclaimed quietly, careful not to wake up Bas... well, at least not that way.

I peeled the bananas and tossed them into the blender. Then I washed blackberries, spinach, and added them into the blender. Almond milk followed, and with a wicked grin on my face, I pushed the on button.

The roaring blender filled the morning silence and I grinned as I listened to it grind. I could already picture Bas moaning and groaning, cursing the day he dragged me here.

Easily rectified, I mused to myself, keeping my finger on the ice crush button. But the tightness in my chest immediately followed. I loved him so much it freaking hurt. It was the kind of maddening love that ached, but you refused to let it go because it was part of your every breath. Every heartbeat.

A sharp sting on my butt cheek caused me to jump and I let go of the button to spin around. Of course, I knew it was him. Nobody else was here, but still my heart thundered in my chest.

Bas stood in the kitchen, two feet away from me, wearing only a pair of black boxer briefs and his black hair tousled. His piercing gaze was glued to me and mine to his abs, covered with the kingpin skull tattoo along his right side. The tattoo I licked last night.

My cheeks heated and longing burned with an ache in the pit of my stomach. I burned for him with such a raw need that it scared me.

Well, this backfired rather quickly.

"What are you doing?" he grumbled, his eyes on me but something dark and all-consuming flared behind his eyes.

"Breakfast smoothie," I breathed. "Want some?"

He should really put some clothes on and hide that body. His prancing around was cruel to weak women like me, tempting me. My palms remembered the feel of his abs, they itched to touch him again. I wanted to trail the line of hair below his navel with my fingers, feel his muscles tense and his control snap again. *For me.*

God, help me. He was turning me into a sex-crazed woman.

"Are you going to stare at me all day?" His voice was deep, sending shivers down my spine with a rough caress.

I swallowed, the heat rushing to my cheeks. Suddenly, my bright idea didn't seem so bright, because seeing Bas in his boxers gave me different kinds of ideas.

The kind that would take us back to the bedroom.

Basilio drove his car with confidence and control. Just the way he fucked.

My pulse fluttered and a throbbing ache traveled between my thighs. This man would be the death of me, because all I could think and feel was him. So many unspoken words lingered in the air and I couldn't find the beginning to start unraveling the past so we'd find ourselves back at the day when I fell into his arms.

The sun shone brightly and the air felt humid but we left the windows rolled down. He drove in silence and I couldn't help flicking a gaze his way. Darkness glinted all around him, even under the bright rays of sun, but I couldn't help but stare into it.

"Where are we going?" I asked.

He just told me to put on a bathing suit and grab a beach towel, then left it at that. His head tilted to the side, meeting my gaze before returning it back to the road.

"Beach."

I rolled my eyes. "I figured that when you told me to put my bathing suit on. But where?"

I looked at his profile and saw a small smile appear on his lips.

"Curiosity killed the cat," he drawled.

He flicked a gaze to me and dark amusement shone in his eyes.

I raised a brow, surprised at his teasing. The warm air brushed my cheeks and whipped my curls around me. This moment almost reminded me of how it felt before... before his father.

"This cat might kill Basilio DiLustro," I remarked casually but my smile kind of ruined the threat.

He grinned. "If I had to choose how to die, it would be by your hand, principessa."

Raw pain slashed through my chest at the thought of Bas dead. Just the thought of it shattered my heartbeats one by one and I knew that nothing would ever be the same if he no longer walked this earth. I wouldn't be the same.

The car came to a stop and I immediately recognized the area. My uncle's Hampton home was nearby. I straightened into my seat.

"The Hamptons?" I asked, my eyes darting back and forth. "Are the girls here?"

He shook his head. "No, they are with Davina and the baby in California."

My shoulders slumped. "That's right, I forgot. Davina had the baby."

Last week, right after the attack at Emory's home. I missed it

403

because of Bas. Uncle begrudgingly called Bas since I had no electronics with me. Then he handed the phone to Juliette who promptly cursed Basilio out and told him she'd cut him into tiny little pieces when she got her hands on him.

Family reunions will be so much fun, I thought dryly.

"This is my place," he interrupted my thoughts. "I want you to see where we'll be having the reception." I tilted my head and watched him in silence. "I want you to see the setup and get your input." I blinked, slightly confused. Was this his olive branch? "Whatever you don't like, in the house or for the wedding reception, we can change."

"Okay," I finally said while emotions tugged at my heart, urging me to lean over and kiss him. He was my center of gravity and life without him was pointless. But then so was the pride that held me back.

The engine of his black Chevy Corvette extinguished. The two of us exited the car, and he came around to take my hand into his, then handed me his cell phone.

"Call her," he offered, his voice warm against my ear.

I took his phone, though something deep down in me rebelled. "I want my own phone back, Basilio," I demanded softly. "When—" *When will you trust me?* But I had to be scared of his answer because I couldn't get the words out. "I won't leave," I promised.

He reached in the back seat of his Corvette and grabbed the beach bag. You'd think he'd look ridiculous carrying a large pink bag, but no. He looked fucking hot, with his aviator glasses, black dress pants, and a white short-sleeve shirt. I could spot a glimpse of his ink on the side of his abs through it and warmth rushed to the pit of my stomach, despite my agitation at his distrust.

"Whatever," I muttered and slid open his phone and froze at the picture staring back at me.

Bas's screen saver was our selfie from nine months ago when I drove Priest's Jeep to the beach. When we got to the beach, I insisted we take a selfie and he appeased me. He snapped the photo just as I turned to tell him to push the button so the two of us stared at each other when the selfie was taken.

I looked completely and utterly infatuated with him.

Chapter Sixty-One

BASILIO

"**Y**ou locked my sister in your penthouse?" Priest growled.

I met with Dante, Emory, and Priest at The Eastside Club. Tomorrow was our wedding day and I needed everything to go smoothly. I needed my ring on her finger before I lost my shit.

The four of us sat around the office that used to belong to Liam. An authentic Picasso painting was the only thing to witness our discussion.

"To keep her safe," I told him. Yeah, it wasn't the best plan, but fuck, it was the only one I had. Until now, nobody knew about that place. But I trusted my cousins and sister. Although Priest was acting like an overbearing nutjob of a brother. "Emory, I need you to go and stay with her tonight. Dante will escort you two to the church with our men tomorrow."

Emory rolled her eyes. "I can't believe you're even bothering with the tradition of not seeing your bride the night before your wedding. Considering you broke all the other traditions."

I flipped her the bird.

"He's superstitious," Dante mocked.

"He's an obsessive idiot," Priest spat out. "You can't keep her locked up and shackled for the rest of your lives."

I shrugged.

"Watch me." Until she learned to love me and pledged all her love to me, I wouldn't take any chances. Yes, it was morally questionable, but it got me through and it held my darkness at bay. If I lost her, I'd—

Yeah, it wouldn't be good for the world.

Priest lost his shit and shot up. I did the same, and before his big body could slam into me, I dodged him by shifting to the right. The sound of wood cracking, splinters protesting and the desk crumbled down.

Before he could do anything else, I grabbed his wrists and held my knee to his back.

Both Emory and Dante shot to their feet.

"Priest, she's my wife. You'll stay out of it," I warned, my voice calm and cold.

"Not yet, she's not," he roared. He jerked his arm, uncaring if he dislocated his shoulder. It was one thing my cousins and I had in common. We'd cut our arm off, as long as we got to our goal. "Did you ask yourself if she'd be your wife if you gave her a choice?" Every goddamn minute of the day. "Pick another woman, not my sister."

"She was mine before she was yours," I hissed. "I love you, Priest, but I won't let anyone stand in the way of me and my wife. Understood?"

Not heaven. Not God. Not the devil. Nobody would keep me away from her ever again.

"You men are fucking idiots," Emory chimed in, annoyed and agitated. "We need to discuss tomorrow. And the fact that Father summoned you."

"Agreed." I glanced down to Priest. "Are you calm enough?

Keeping Wynter and Emory safe tomorrow and my father away is our priority."

Priest grumbled something under his breath but nodded. I let go, my body still not relaxed in case Priest lost his shit again.

He rose to his full height, brushing off the little specs off his suit. He was still pissed, it was evident in the tension of his shoulders, his tightened jaw, and his darkened eyes.

"I'm calm," he finally gritted through his teeth. "I'll always have your back, Bas. But I'll have her back first."

I nodded. "Fair enough."

"This is too much tension for me," Dante announced, grinning like an idiot. "It's like a soap opera."

"I didn't know you watched those," Emory remarked dryly.

"I don't, but the little glimpses of it I caught when you're watching it was enough to relate."

Emory flipped him the bird. "Maybe my brother and I will kick Priest's and your asses. For old time's sake."

"You can try, cuz," he drawled, smiling with a clear challenge in his eyes. I shook my head. We used to do those when we were kids. It always ended with someone's broken bone.

"Okay, that's fucking enough." I slid my hands into my pockets and walked over to the wall with the Picasso painting. "I have to go see Father after this. If something happens, you two watch over Emory and Wynter."

"I don't need to be fucking watched over," Emory hissed, her eyes flashing with lightning. I ignored her, focusing on Priest and Dante.

"I'm sure he got word of the wedding and wants to know where his invitation is," Dante guessed the same thing that I thought.

"Don't kill him yet," Emory warned. "I know you want to, but it'll bring a whole set of new troubles to us. To all of us and that won't help Wynter. Just be patient, our time will come."

Not fucking soon enough.

"Either way, he's not coming tomorrow." Over my dead body would he come anywhere near my woman. Or Emory. Or Wynter's mother for that matter. My father fucking shot her and ruined her career. "Emory, you'll stay with Wynter in the penthouse."

"I feel honored," she mused. "I get to stay in your secret penthouse."

I ignored her comment. "If Wynter has a nightmare, just talk to her. About anything, keep your voice low and just talk."

Three sets of eyes watched me with scrutiny I didn't like. "Jesus, you're whipped," Dante broke the silence. "I mean, I knew it but I just didn't know how whipped you truly were until this very moment."

I flipped him the bird. "I'm not whipped enough to kick your ass unless you shut the fuck up."

"Okay, so maybe Wyn will be happy," Priest muttered pensively.

"Wyn?" Emory and I asked at the same time.

Priest shrugged. "It's what those close to her call her."

Did Sasha call her Wyn? She never asked me to call her Wyn. For fuck's sake, I had to get a grip. I'd call her mine, wife... nobody else would ever get to call her that.

"Dante, you won't spend the night at the penthouse, but be there first thing. And, Priest, monitor the place. If anything unusual happens, just get Wynter out."

He'd keep her safe, even at his own expense. I trusted him on that matter. I just didn't trust him enough to bring Wynter to the church so I could finally put a ring on her finger. I suspected if she begged him to take her away, he'd cave.

Because she was his sister.

My father sat in his office.

It reeked of alcohol, antiseptic, and fucking dead flesh.

My eyes flitted to his knee. It was fucked up. Looked like shit. It stank even worse. Not that I gave a damn. He should have been shot through his black heart.

Ever since he got shot, he rarely sat behind his desk. He couldn't stretch his knee far enough. Instead, he had to sit next to the table and prop his leg on a stool.

"Finally! What took you so long?" he spat out.

"Traffic." It was after rush hour traffic. It was a bullshit excuse. We both knew it.

His eyes regarded me closely, that face that my mother detested staring back at me and I knew it was the same face I'd have in my old age. But I'd have Wynter. She'd keep the light in my life and keep me from becoming my father.

"So you're getting married." It wasn't a question. A statement. An accusation. A judgment.

"Yes."

"To Brennan's girl."

"Yes." Fuck him. He couldn't stop me from it. Let him bring the entire fucking Syndicate down on me, I refused to give *her* up. I'd set up enough cash and residences around the world to hide us.

He stood up, reaching for his cane. It was just barely out of his reach but I didn't bother moving to help him. He never helped a single person in his life.

Finally grabbing it, he stood up, that fucking cane wobbling. God, what I wouldn't give to smash his skull with it! End him for good.

"I'm guessing Brennan doesn't want me at the wedding." *I don't want you at the wedding.* But I remained silent. Let him come to his own conclusions. "Alliance with them will be good. You better get some more property out of them for taking an Irish cunt for a wife."

A growl sounded in my throat. It was impossible to hold it back.

His eyes flashed in victory and his lips curved with a dark laugh. I still said nothing.

"You should move into our family home once married." *Never gonna happen.* "After all, you were raised here. You'll want your children raised here."

The fuck I would. I planned on burning this motherfucking place down to the ground the moment he was dead.

A vein throbbed in my temple, my rage wanted out. To make him suffer. To end him, once and for all.

"I have my own place," I bit out. "We'll live in our own house and make our own memories." Happy ones without your fucking ass in it.

"Angelo will wire your place," he said. That fucker would never step foot in my home again. "Brennans are not part of the Syndicate. We need to protect the interest of our organization."

"Send Angelo to my home and he's a dead man."

I turned on my heel and stalked out. Or risked murdering the man on the spot.

Chapter Sixty-Two
WYNTER

B as really thought of everything.

From the massage, bath with scented oils, facial, manicure, and pedicure, as well as makeup and hair team. The only thing I didn't have was my friends. He didn't trust them nor me.

Dante picked both Emory and me up from the penthouse and drove with me to the cathedral in the back of a luxury Rolls-Royce. They were my security, or more accurately my guards. Bas didn't trust anyone but his family. Once we pulled up to the front of St. Patrick's Cathedral, a swarm of men wearing black suits filled the entrance.

I spotted Davina, Juliette, and Ivy and my hand gripped the handle. "Stop here," I told the driver. "They made it."

Davina assured me nothing would stop them from coming, but I still worried. After all, she just had a baby.

Dante shook his head. "We'll pull up at the side and you can wait inside until the ceremony starts."

I flashed an annoyed glance his way. He resembled Bas a lot, with his dark hair and dark eyes. He was built similar to Bas, but there was something different about Dante. While Bas and Priest had something unhinged and crazy about them, I couldn't quite get a read on Dante.

My eyes shifted to Emory. She looked pretty in a soft pink dress. She was to be my bridesmaid along with Ivy, Juliette, and Davina. Honestly, the whole thing felt like a circus. A fancy circus.

Once the car came to a stop, Dante and Emory helped me out.

The train on my dress was too fucking long and Emory quickly picked it up so it wouldn't drag on the ground. Such a tentative criminal, I thought to myself and a hysterical laugh bubbled up my throat, but I quickly swallowed it down.

Dante eyed the surroundings, his hand under his jacket on the gun, ready to shoot anyone who dared approach us.

Like I said, a fucking circus.

"This is bullshit," I murmured, as several paparazzi spotted us and rushed our way, already snapping pictures. "It's too long to walk in with these heels."

Dante chuckled, offering me his arm to help me walk in my high heels. Put me on ice and I'd stay steady. Put me in heels, and I was bound to fall.

Once inside, my heels clacked against the marble floor. Once we took a few turns, Dante stopped and opened the door to the rectory for me. The faint organ sounds played in the distance and Dante extended his hand, telling me to step inside.

My gaze flicked to Emory, then to Dante.

Emory shot me a comforting smile. "It will be over soon," she murmured.

"Can't wait," I grumbled as I walked in, then realized I was being kind of bitchy towards her. "Umm, thanks for—" My words failed me. She helped Bas kidnap me, but she also went out of her way to make me comfortable. "I guess for everything," I muttered.

"No problem," she replied, smiling widely. "I know you and Bas will be happy together." A heartbeat of silence. "He's tough on the outside, but he's a big softy on the inside."

A soft inhale of air. I would have described him exactly the same before the incident with his father.

When I remained silent, she continued, "For as long as I remember, he has been protecting me from our father at his own expense. It's about time he found his happiness. Even if he stole it."

Every cell in my body filled with hope. That dangerous hope that could lift you high.

"Thanks, Emory."

She tilted her head, then shut the door. I almost expected to hear the click of the lock but there was nothing.

I was left in an unlocked room. Maybe it was a test? I stood in the middle of the room, unsure what to do until the ceremony started. It was then that I caught the reflection of myself in the mirror.

My blonde curls were pinned up in a bun with pearls weaved through it. The dress was stunning. The pearls and the silver embroidered in the dress shimmered, catching light each time I moved. It hugged my body and came down the long train. It made me feel like a princess and I had nobody to share it with.

I had no idea who would be part of this wedding since I had no part in planning it. Truthfully, I had no idea who did, and with such a short period for preparation, I expected it to be a small affair.

I heard a soft sound and turned my head in its direction. The wall rug that hung over the east wall shifted and out of it came Juliette and Ivy.

"Jules!" I gasped, scrambling to my feet. "Ivy! What are you doing here?" And then I threw myself into their arms, wrinkling up their beautiful pink bridesmaid dresses. "I am so glad to see you," I squealed, blinking my eyes hard and scared I'd ruin my makeup.

"Duh, isn't it obvious?" Juliette retorted. "Saving you."

I glanced around after she uttered those words, almost expecting someone to barge into the room and for hell to break loose.

"No saving me," I whispered. Somehow I wasn't surprised Juliette would come up with a plan to save me. "I don't want you in trouble."

If Bas found them here or overheard Juliette's words, I feared what he'd do. The man I was marrying today was a different man than the one I walked away from. Besides, I promised him I'd stay.

"The DiLustros are nuts," Juliette announced. "You can't marry that loony bin that kidnapped you, no matter what Dad says."

"And what did Uncle say?" I asked, unsure what to do with the two of them.

Ivy waved her hand. "That you have to pay the debt for the four of us stealing that armored truck."

Well, that kind of summed it up. But it was a lot more than that.

"Wyn, you cannot do this," Juliette hissed. "I won't let you sacrifice yourself."

"It's not—" She didn't let me finish.

"And do you know what Dante DiLustro did?" she continued, her voice high-pitched. "He asked Dad for my hand."

"For your hand?" I asked, confused.

"He asked Dad to fucking marry me," she spat out. "I should have cut off his balls rather than kicked him in them."

I blinked, watching her cheeks flush. My cousin never blushed. Fucking ever. But something about Dante DiLustro got Juliette riled up. Every time.

"What did Uncle tell him?" I asked curiously.

"Fuck no," she said. "That's what. Thank fuck. Otherwise, I'd use today to kill him rather than saving your ass. Now let's go before that freak DiLustro shows up. We have only minutes to clear out of this block."

The door was wrenched open with a loud thud against the wall, the wood frame rattling. Basilio stood there, his expression dark and stormy.

"You're going nowhere," Bas growled. "And you're certainly not taking my bride. Get out!"

All three of us shrank back at his murderous expression.

He knew that Juliette was all talk. Right?

"Bas, they're my bridesmaids and best friends," I choked out, flicking a glance at my friends.

Juliette got herself together, masking her initial reaction, and glared at him. Her hands came to her hips and she took a step, like she'd come at him.

"Listen, DiLustro," she spat out. "It's fucking wrong to kidnap people. And now dragging her down the aisle. Have you no shame?" Then she snickered as if she remembered something. "Oh, that's right. None of you DiLustros have any shame. Like your fucking cousin. Bunch of Italians." Her eyes came to me, satisfied she gave Bas a piece of her mind.

Ivy's eyes darted between all of us, wide with a flicker of uncertainty.

Bas took a step towards Juliette and towered over her, though he didn't touch her.

"And you, Juliette, do you have no shame?" he deadpanned, narrowing his eyes on her. "After all, it is you that started this shit when you set that house on fire."

Juliette flinched, and for a moment, I thought she'd start crying.

"Stop it, Bas," I croaked, not wanting to see my cousin cry.

"Your cousin has to learn there are consequences to all actions," he gritted out. "And she practically pushed you into my arms when she went nuts. So maybe she should look in the mirror if she wants to blame someone."

Oh, fuck. Why did he have to be so brutally honest?

I tugged on his sleeve and begged him. "Bas, that's not fair."

Bas stilled. "Get lost. Both of you," he growled at her and Ivy.

"Go," I mouthed.

Ivy took Juliette's hand and pulled her along, scurrying out the door, instead of the secret passage. The wedding hadn't even started and it was already turning into a catastrophe.

Alone with Bas, his coal-black gaze narrowed on me. It was only now I noticed his fitted black tuxedo. It made him look darker and ominous, but also so damn handsome.

I held his gaze, drowning in his dark possessiveness that sent shivers over my body. His chest heaved up and down as a silence full of tension swirled through the air.

"You were going to run, principessa," he said softly, his gaze darkened. I shook my head, but before I could say anything, he continued, "Don't lie to me. I heard her plan to clear the block. You didn't disagree."

Anger slowly rose within me. "It's because you barged in like some devil ready to kill," I snapped back.

"You tell that witch of a cousin to mind her own business and leave the two of us to ours."

"Why don't you just start pounding your chest and roar '*mine*'?" I hissed, annoyed. "Jules just wants to protect me. All she knows is that you kidnapped me, so what in the hell did you expect from her?"

He took a step, bringing us chest to chest. "Tell her if she ever dares to suggest a stupid fucking idea that will put you in danger again, I'll make her regret ever speaking to you."

A tremor ran through me at his words. I must have lost my mind because his darkness tugged at something deep inside me.

He leaned forward until his forehead rested against mine.

"Today, you're mine. My wife. Nothing and nobody will keep me from you," he whispered thickly.

My insides caught on fire as I held his gaze.

"This is all wrong," I said, thick emotions squeezing my throat and making it hard to breathe. "It shouldn't be like this."

Basilio grabbed my wrist in an iron grip and pulled me towards the door. My eyes snapped to him, alarmed.

"What are you doing?" I hissed in a small voice. I tried to pull my wrist out of his grip. Unsuccessfully.

He held on tight as if he worried I'd escape. Didn't he believe my promise?

"I'll never hurt you," he hissed, dragging me down a long hallway. I scoffed at that declaration. What did he think he was doing now? "But I won't tolerate your refusal. You're mine, and the sooner you realize that, the better. You run; I'll follow. You touch another man; I'll kill him. Remember that for the rest of our days."

My step faltered and my eyes widened. Where was the man I fell in love with? The warm brown eyes were replaced with a dark, cold gaze that could freeze this earth, never mind my heart.

I shook my head, whether it was at my thoughts or his actions, I wasn't sure.

"We're getting married," he growled, then tugged me forward.

"B-but we can't walk down the aisle together," I protested weakly. Bas had lost his goddamn mind.

Pulling me along, we reached an arched doorway. The entrance to the main chapel. Jesus Christ! He was serious. He'd drag me all the way down to the altar where the priest waited because he didn't trust me to walk down it alone. In front of all our guests.

"Bas, please be reasonable," I pleaded. He ignored me, continuing to pull me forward.

My throat was tight, my heart thundered, stealing my breath away.

His father had done this to him. His mother had done this to him when she left him as a boy. I left him. And now that he found me, he believed I'd leave him again.

The moment the guests saw us, a soft murmur spread through the church. There were no sounds of awes and soft gasps. Instead, I was met with shocked gazes and loud murmurs.

The walk down the aisle of the massive church was over too quick. The music played announcing my walk. The white and red rose petals covered my path and I found it ironic that it matched our story. Blood and innocence. Except there were no innocents here.

Unconcerned with anyone else, Bas's steps were rushed, and he didn't stop until we stood in front of the altar, a shocked priest staring at us. So did a hundred or so guests. I recognized some; others I didn't.

Out of the corner of my eye, I saw Uncle Liam and Killian step forward, furious looks on their faces. My eyes sought out my mother, but she just sat there with a slightly empty look on her face.

Basilio's groomsmen, dressed in vests and dark dress pants, wore no jackets but holsters were clearly visible. Three groomsmen. Dante DiLustro, Priest, and Killian.

Three bridesmaids. Juliette, Ivy, and Bas's sister, Emory. My eyes flicked back to Mom, wondering if she saw Priest?

It would seem Killian and Emory were thrown to the wolves, to stand on the wrong side of the fighting ring.

My eyes connected with my best friends' gazes. Comfort. Support. Love. And of course, their shock.

"What the fuck are you doing, DiLustro?" Uncle snapped angrily. "Get your hands off of her. We agreed on marriage, not to you abusing my niece."

Bas's grip on my hand tightened and a small whimper escaped me.

"Get your hands off her, DiLustro," Sasha warned, showing up out of nowhere and gun already pointed at Bas. "Or I'll kill you. Right now!"

Sasha's brothers came to stand behind him, Quinn stood right behind Uncle and Killian, while Dante and Priest came behind Bas. The only ones that seemed unconcerned with this volcano about to erupt were the Ashford brothers. Though they did come to stand behind Bas.

"You go too far, DiLustro," Sasha growled, his eyes furious on Bas. "For this, you'll die."

Oh my God!

There'd be bloodshed in the church. On my wedding day. In front of all the guests. The Ashfords. Nikolaevs. The Morrellis. The fucking world.

I shook my head, unable to utter a single word.

"Try to take her away from me and I'll kill you," Bas roared as he shuffled me to his left and pulled out a gun from under his tuxedo. His eyes narrowed on Uncle and Sasha. "You and your entire fucking family."

The buzzing in my ears drowned out the guests' murmurs. Blood rushed through my veins.

"He doesn't mean it," I breathed, shaking my head. I shoved at Bas and came to stand in the middle. "It was just a misunderstanding," I told them all, my eyes darting around. "It's all good. Please, for fuck's sake, put your guns away."

Whoever planned this wedding should be fired!

Chapter Sixty-Three

WYNTER

The priest performed the ceremony, shaking like a leaf against the breeze.

The ceremony and words uttered during it were a haze. I focused on my breathing and people who would kill Bas if I lost my shit.

Do. Not. Lose. Your. Shit.

I loved my villain. It was stupidity. Suicide. Except that I couldn't forget his smiles. How he caught me from the balcony. The way he slipped the shoes onto my bare feet.

That was so damn pathetic even without saying it out loud. He kidnapped me, drugged me, and I loved him. He was psychotic. Maybe I was too.

Bas whispered his vows into my ear, his words a dark promise. "Nobody will separate me from you. Not gods. Not heaven. Not hell. You'll forever be mine. I'll have you, and you'll have me. Until death do us part."

I couldn't decide whether it was a romantic vow or just a mad obsessive one.

Basilio's strong hand took mine and without hesitation slipped the ring onto my finger. My heart drummed vigorously under my rib cage but my fingers didn't tremble. My face was a perfect mask.

In front of a hundred witnesses, our fate was sealed. The unfamiliar faces of New York, Chicago, Philadelphia, New Orleans, and even Washington witnessed the union. The shackles were permanently placed on me.

But none of them knew I accepted those shackles nine months ago because I fell in love with the monster.

My eyes darted to Davina. She had married my uncle. It wasn't under perfect circumstances and they made it work. They were happy. But they didn't have the history that the two of our families had.

"You may kiss the bride." The priest's words penetrated my thoughts.

I raised my head and met Basilio's dark, liquid gaze. Those eyes that swept me off my feet from the moment he caught me that night. It seemed ages ago, like it happened to two different people. He wasn't the same; neither was I.

He bent his towering frame to bridge the distance between us and he took my mouth without hesitation. Our first kiss as husband and wife. Soft. Possessive. Heartbreaking.

My lips parted, the warmth of his lips a welcomed sensation. His tongue brushed over my lower lip and a moan filled the air between us.

I took his lower lip between my teeth and bit hard into it. His body stiffened but he didn't jerk back. Nothing. He ended the kiss, his tongue sweeping over the sting, as if he relished in the pain.

Our eyes remained locked as he pulled back, something dark and possessive in the depths of his stare. A shudder passed through me, though I wasn't certain whether it was in anticipation or fear.

He took my hand and a tight smile masked his expression as we walked down the aisle past the guests and towards the exit of the church. Outside, the limo already waited for us and we headed straight for it.

"Wait, I want to ride with—"

"You're riding with me," he growled, a warning clear in his voice.

"Shouldn't we thank the guests?" I rasped. "I barely got to see my family. My mom."

I still couldn't believe she was back in New York. It would have been okay if she couldn't have made it, especially considering how she reacted after seeing Bas and Dante. Uncle hasn't said much and I hoped they didn't sedate her to convince her to come.

"We'll do that at the reception."

The whole drive to the reception, Basilio's Hampton beach estate, the air between us was so tense, you could slice it with a knife.

Chapter Sixty-Four

WYNTER

Basilio and I stood by the archway, his hand holding mine. Like the perfect wedding couple.

His Hampton home was very elaborate. Too elaborate for someone so young; it seemed a bit extravagant. The white marble building could easily house thirty people. There was a line of expensive cars that circled the driveway. They all belonged to Bas.

Dozens of waiters waited outside holding glasses of champagne at the ready, along with small trays of appetizers.

As we stood, waiting for the first guests to arrive, we'd almost appear like happy newlyweds. *Almost.*

He bent down, his lips brushing my ear and whispered, "Smile, principessa."

His hot breath sent a delightful shudder down my spine and a memory flashed in my mind.

"I found you." His breath was hot in my ear as our bodies moved together, the slow tunes of his car speakers filling the air. The stars flickered above us and the city lights shone in the distance, but all I felt and

saw was him. "I want your lips and your body because you want to give it. Not because you want to repay the debt."

Those times with him, I was the happiest. I never thought it would bring us here. The memories tasted slightly bitter after everything that had happened but I still wouldn't trade them for anything. Those were fuel for my heartbeat, regardless of whether it was in pain.

I opened my mouth to assure him, again, that I really wasn't going to run, when the first guests arrived in front of us. Uncle and Davina, along with their newborn. A handsome baby boy, Aiden.

"You good?" Uncle grumbled, his eyes on me like he expected to find evidence of abuse. I didn't put it past him to kill Bas and call this whole charade over.

I forced my brightest smile. "Yes, wonderful." From the corner of my eye, I could see Bas eyeing me suspiciously. Uncle studied me too, and somehow, I doubted either one of them was fooled. "Is Mom okay?"

Uncle nodded. "She insisted on being here."

Surprise washed over me. "Really?"

He couldn't blame me for doubting him. After twenty-one years of refusal to even visit the East Coast, all it took was a wedding for her to come.

"Yes. She refuses to miss any more moments. Her words; not mine."

Oh.

"Congratulations, Wyn." Davina hugged me, little Aiden in her arms sleeping peacefully. "You look beautiful."

She held her newborn with so much love, it brought tears to my eyes.

"He's so small," I whispered, scared to wake up my nephew in her arms. I brushed my fingers lightly over his cheek and little Aiden never stirred. "He's my nephew, right?"

Uncle pulled me into a hug. "Yes, your nephew." Then he whispered into my ear, "You want to be a widow?"

I pulled away and shook my head, hoping he was joking. Though you never could be sure with a crazy family in the underworld.

The Ashfords were next in line. "Wonderful wedding," Byron congratulated, then turned to Bas. "You got your woman. I'll expect that contact."

My eyes curiously ping-ponged between the two. "What contact?" I asked hesitantly.

Bas shrugged. "My cousin here has a half brother he wants to make peace with."

"I'd never seen such a ceremony," Royce Ashford announced. "And I've been to quite a few. That priest probably put in for his retirement right after marrying you two. Though that kiss at the end... yeah, smoochy, smoochy."

I blinked at his odd comment. Bas flipped him the bird while the former grinned, mouthing *psychopathic fucker* right back at Basilio. Royce and Bas were the closest in age, so maybe they understood each other better.

"Ignore him," Kingston grumbled, the look in his eyes frightening. Of the four brothers, he made me feel the most uncomfortable. He gave off Alexei vibes and you knew he'd kill you without losing any sleep. "Congratulations."

I nodded my thanks but remained quiet. It wasn't like they'd believe me if I beamed like a gushing, over-the-moon bride.

The next guests were Aurora and Alexei with their little one. Honestly, I was surprised that families with little ones didn't disperse. Especially after that fiasco in the church.

My eyes searched behind them but Sasha was nowhere to be found. For a moment, I met Alexei's eyes but his unmoving gaze portrayed nothing.

"You look lovely," Aurora said, then leaned over to kiss me on the cheek. "Sasha had to go cool off for a bit."

"Ah, okay," I muttered. It might be for the best, though I regretted not seeing him.

Kostya's hand reached out. "Mine," he wailed.

"Jesus, he's already possessive," Aurora mused. "Must be the genes."

Surprising all of us, Bas chuckled. "Ah no, little buddy. She's mine. You find your own princess."

Aurora's eyes flashed to him in surprise. "I didn't know you joked, cousin," she muttered.

Taking a step closer to her, I took Kostya's little hands. "When I'm done with this charade," I murmured into his hair, then kissed his forehead. "I'll come and get you."

The never-ending line of guests took a lot longer than I thought.

———

I had no idea how we ended up with so many guests with such short notice. My cheeks ached from the fake smile I held for so long.

Every so often, I risked a glance up at Bas. He'd meet my eyes every time. Darkness and flames burned deep in his gaze. He was my love, lust, and happiness... despite it all. I couldn't fight it. He was my flame and without him I wouldn't live. I'd just exist.

"Bas?" I whispered so nobody else could hear us.

His gaze found mine and the memories of all our firsts flashed through my mind. There was so much I could see in the intensity of his gaze that I feared whether he felt it too. Or was it just my imagination?

"I wasn't going to run," I murmured softly. "In the church."

A rumble of satisfaction, or maybe disbelief, traveled up his throat and he bent his head to press a kiss to my mouth. But he said nothing, leaving me to wonder whether he even believed me.

We were in this for better or worse. We'd have to learn to trust each other.

"Bas?"

"Hmmm."

"Can we talk tonight?" The day of Gio's attack would have to be addressed. He had asked me why I left. Repeatedly. If we didn't clear the air and come to some agreement, it wouldn't be a good start to our marriage.

"I was hoping we'd do more than talk on our wedding night," he answered, his dark eyes full of sinful promises.

"But maybe we can talk about the day—" I paused for a moment. It was hard to think about that day, never mind talk about it. "Talk about the day I left," I finished.

Surprise flickered in his eyes.

"Tonight," he agreed.

He slipped his hand into mine, and we headed to our seats where the soft music filled the large backyard with views of the Atlantic Ocean stretched for miles around.

Once seated, Davina took my hand that clutched my dress and squeezed it gently. "It's almost over."

Our table seated Mom, Uncle, Dante, Emory, Priest, Ivy, Juliette, Killian, and Basilio's uncle. My eyes darted to my mother who sat stiffly next to Uncle Liam. I couldn't help but remember what she had told me about falling in love with Gio's brother. It had to be Bas's uncle.

I wanted to apologize to her. Hug her and tell her Bas wasn't his father. Tell her Priest was the son she lost. She hadn't even glanced to their side of the table. Although I caught more than plenty of gazes flickered her way—by Priest, Dante, and their father.

I didn't know what to think of it.

Dante rose from his chair and clinked his glass to get everyone's attention. I tried hard to focus on his toast but my ears buzzed so loud, I heard nothing but the thunder of my own heart.

Uncle was next. From the corner of my eye, I caught the tattooed, bulky body moving gracefully through the tables to sit down at the Nikolaev table. I shot up and everyone's eyes came to me.

I froze and Sasha's eyes met mine. A terse nod and a resemblance of a smile. I breathed a sigh of relief. It was his reassurance that he wouldn't hurt Bas.

Davina took my hand and tugged me down. Slowly, I lowered myself back into the seat. Bas's lips tightened and his dark eyes held mine. He leaned over, his breath hot against my earlobe. "If I catch you with him, he's a dead man."

A strangled laugh escaped me. I worried about protecting Bas from Sasha, while my reckless husband threatened to kill him. How perfectly ironic! A fucking circus.

My uncle started his toast. "From the moment Wynter was born and I held her in my arms, I gave her and my sister a promise. I swore I'd keep her safe." His eyes narrowed on my new husband. "She's my family, and no matter her last name, if she hurts, I'll come for her."

"Nothing beats that speech," I muttered under my breath except everyone at our table heard it.

"I bet I could outdo him," Juliette snickered.

I shook my head. "Please don't."

She grinned. "Only because I love you."

"And she wants your Jeep," Ivy added, which earned her a glare from Juliette.

"Juliette is not getting a car," Uncle snapped. "Not until she can prove she is safe to others and herself while driving."

"That would be never," Davina scoffed.

"Hey," she protested. "I've gotten so much better."

"In your fucking dreams," Davina muttered.

"Don't say cuss words in front of my nephew," I warned her. "It's fucking rude."

"I'll buy you a new car," Dante chimed in, his eyes on Juliette. "All you have to say is yes."

And if looks could kill, Dante would be dead.

A round of snickers followed and another clink had me turning my head curiously to almost falling off my chair. My mom stood up, her eyes on me.

"I'd like to make a toast," she started in her soft voice. "Would that be okay?"

My throat squeezed. She hated attention on her, and yet, she wanted to make a toast. I nodded.

"Of course," I choked out.

A waiter rolled over a cart with a big-screen TV and nodded at my mom. She tilted her head in thanks and then turned to meet my eyes.

"I know I haven't said enough how much I love you," she started softly.

"It's okay, Mom," I rasped, emotions squeezing my throat.

"I am thankful every single day that the day I lost so much, I didn't lose you." The lump in my throat choked, knowing she meant the day Gio shot Dad and her. "You have exceeded my wildest dreams and made me so proud." She twisted her hands. "On and off the ice, my little Star." I let out a shuddering breath and I felt a big hand squeeze mine under the table. "From the moment you were born, you were my light. You and Juliette kept me going."

Her eyes darted to Juliette, then returned to me.

"I made a little video of pictures and recordings for you," she announced softly. "I have one for Jules too for when she gets married."

"You might as well hand that over now," Juliette muttered. "I'm never getting married."

Then she glared at Dante and I had to bite the inside of my cheek or laugh. A round of laughter followed Juliette's proclamation and Mom pushed the start button.

I stared at the screen. A picture of Mom at the hospital with me in her arms appeared. A sad, soft smile. Pictures I had never seen rolled. First roll. First steps. First ice-skate. Me sprawled on the ice, my hair a wild mess. It was my first jump and my first fall.

"I still remember that one," Juliette muttered. "After you fell, you turned over and kissed the ice. Disgusting."

My throat burned and the lump in it made it hard to swallow. I remembered it too. I was so happy on ice. I really was. Some people search their entire life for something to be passionate about. I found mine before I learned to write.

Then a clip of a video played. My first competition. First day of school.

"I didn't know you kept recording all that," I murmured softly, glancing at my mom.

"How could I not?" she rasped. "I knew the time would fly and leave me without you."

I shot up from my seat and took three steps to her, wrapping my arms around her.

"I'll always be here," I vowed. "I love you, Mom."

Inhaling deeply, I tried to stop the tears from falling in front of everyone.

"I love you too, Star. Always." She rarely gave us emotions. Sometimes Juliette and I grumbled about it. We *knew* she loved us, but she rarely said it or showed us affection. So when she did thoughtful things like this, it shook me to the core.

She pulled away and our gazes locked. "Your distraction found you." A sharp inhale of my breath echoed between us. How did she know? Guilt swam in my chest and in my eyes, and I opened my mouth to start explaining myself, when she continued, "Be happy, Star. And your distraction"—she flicked a gaze to Bas—"better worship the ground you walk on. Or I'll take a page out of my brother's book and have him killed."

A choked laugh escaped me. My mother had never even raised her voice at anyone. I couldn't imagine her threatening to kill anyone. Until now.

She looked back at my husband. "Make her happy, Basilio." Or else hung in the air.

Bas nodded, his gaze meeting mine consuming me. "I will," he vowed. "I swear on my mamma's life."

Fuck. I might end up bawling my eyes out today. "Go back to him," Mom whispered into my ear. Each step I took towards him felt so much more. Fuck, it almost felt like finding my way back to him.

This romantic side of me would be the end of me, I thought wryly.

Servers began bringing the food around. It looked like strictly Italian cuisine. Everyone ate, the slight tension around our table was evident but somehow I didn't think it had anything to do with Bas and me, and it had everything to do with Mom and Franco DiLustro.

A band started playing and Bas stood, holding out his hand. "Time for our first dance, principessa." Something about the way he looked at me had my heart flutter, and unwillingly, our first dance came to mind.

Different times, different circumstances. And the same song, I realized with a startling realization.

With my heart in my throat and probably stars in my eyes, we headed to the floor. We didn't say anything, the guests were silent or maybe they faded into the background as he pulled me against his chest.

The holster under his vest pressed against me and our eyes connected.

"I found you," he murmured, almost softly as the tunes of the first song we danced to under the starry sky over nine months ago filled the backyard of his Hampton home.

The tables were set up in circles around the large dance floor so everyone could get a front-row view of the bride and groom. But to me, nobody was there. Just the two of us, like nine months ago.

Our bodies moved together, like we've done this a million times.

"Why this song?" I murmured softly.

He bent his head, his lips against my forehead. "Because no matter where you go, Wynter, I'll follow."

I wasn't sure whether it was a threat or a promise. But my heart melted just the same.

I danced with so many people and smiled so many fake smiles that when Sasha finally came up, I breathed a sigh of relief. I didn't have to pretend.

"Hey," I greeted him, smiling softly. "Where have you been hiding?"

"Staying out of your husband's reach," he grumbled. "Either I'll kill him or he'll kill me."

I shook my head. "He won't."

As long as I kept my distance from Sasha. Apparently over the last nine months, Bas had become obsessively crazy too.

"Has he hurt you?" His jaw was clenched, his muscles tense.

"No." It was the truth. Physically he'd never hurt me. "Thank you for—"

My words faltered because I knew it wasn't what he wanted to hear.

"For not killing him," he finished for me.

My fingers curled around his bicep. "I love him," I admitted softly. "Just the thought of living without him shreds me to pieces."

He sighed. "It has to be something in the water," he muttered. I frowned and he shook his head, dismissing his weird comment. "I take it as a good sign that his father is not here."

Memories slammed into me. The foul breath in my face; Gio's grip as he pushed against me. I shuddered and lowered my eyes, and kept my focus on Sasha's tie.

Gio DiLustro left a mark.

"Wyn, I swear—" he started to talk and I shoved the past into a corner.

"I'm fine," I said. "You trained me well. And if I come face-to-face with Gio, I'll kill him."

Another growl vibrated between us. What was it with these men and growling?

Sasha, just like his brothers, could be scary. That blond hair and pale blue eyes with the danger vibes that screamed from every pore. Basilio had the dark allure that was hidden below his gentlemanly exterior. With Sasha, no amount of suits and polish would hide his ruthlessness. Whether it was ink that covered most of his body or that stocky MMA body frame, I didn't know.

But unlike his brothers, I didn't fear him. Maybe because he held me while I bawled like a baby. Or maybe because he took care of me after what happened with Bas's father.

Aurora and Alexei swayed next to us, their little Kostya protesting and reaching for me.

"I can take him," I offered. My eyes stayed on Alexei just for a second before they shifted to Aurora. She was the safe alternative.

"I don't know why he always squirms for you," she murmured.

I shrugged. "I'm a baby whisperer."

"You get knocked up and I swear to God," Juliette showed up on the other side of them, dancing with Ivy, "this friendship is over. With you and with Davina."

"Good thing we're family, then," I retorted. "No escaping us."

I shifted little Kostya on my hip who cooed happily. "Mine," he claimed, pulling on my curl.

"Okay, buddy," I mused. "You're a bossy little thing, you know."

Just like it seems to be the trend in the Nikolaev family, he had pale blue eyes and bleach-blond hair. He'd be a gorgeous boy one day. Sasha and I kept dancing, Aurora and Alexei barely two feet from us. Alexei had some seriously obsessive, psychotic ways, but his wife didn't seem to mind it.

"Your husband won't be happy about a one-year-old stealing his wife," Aurora teased.

"It would serve him right," Sasha grumbled and little Kostya's eyes snapped to him.

"Shhh," I soothed him before he'd start crying. "Your uncle is a grumpy one."

"I don't give a shit what I promised you, Wyn," Sasha growled. "I see one single hair on your head hurt, and I'm coming for all of them."

Nothing beats an appointed psychotic big brother and psychotic new husband.

Chapter Sixty-Five

BASILIO

"**D**on't tell me your wife is ignoring you?" Dante mocked, and I wanted nothing more than to punch him.

I leaned against the wall, watching her dance with Sasha Nikolaev and my blood fucking simmered. I wasn't fond of the little Nikolaev baby either. He watched her with stars in his eyes, like she was his own personal toy.

"They would have made a striking couple," Priest remarked, showing up out of nowhere. He'd been eyeing Ivy, Wynter's friend, like it was his full-time job. And that was on top of staring at Wynter's mom. My uncle refused to say anything about Priest's mother but secured himself an invitation to the wedding. My father didn't. "Can you imagine how blond their little babies would have been?" Priest taunted.

I'd return the favor to the fucker, and by the looks he'd been shooting Ivy's way, and her flushed cheeks, it would be sooner versus later.

"Too blond," Emory observed, punching Priest in his gut. "Their babies would have blinded everyone on this planet. I mean, proof is right there with that kid she's holding."

Both Sasha and Wynter had golden, fair hair. While she looked more like an angel consumed by a devil next to me, next to him, she appeared angelic in the embrace of an angel. A fucking corrupt, fallen angel but still a goddamn angel.

I watched her hand the baby back to his father and mother. Thank fuck; otherwise, the picture-perfect family already seared into my mind. This fucking jealousy burned hotter than the sun.

"Have you heard that Wynter's mother hadn't been on the East Coast in over two decades?" Dante asked under his breath.

I met my cousin's eyes. I nodded, but didn't elaborate. It was the only condition Brennan put on the wedding. No Gio. It wasn't as if it was a hardship. I hardly spoke to the man since Wynter's disappearance nine months ago.

My father was a cruel motherfucker, but I'd never let him hurt her. In fact, I'd keep him as far away from her as possible. It would be best for everyone if I ended my father, but if it came out, it'd come to haunt not only me, but my wife and all my family.

The beat picked up and I turned my attention to the dance floor to find Wynter whirling, still dancing with Sasha.

"I don't think that's the first time those two have danced to that song," Dante said as he shifted back on his heel, his hands in his pockets.

Wynter and Sasha started lip-synching to Jaymes Young "Don't You Know" both smiling, like this was their own goddamn wedding. I left my cousins and sister standing there and headed for Sasha and my wife.

Sasha's eyes darted to me and they darkened a bit. The cold, calculating bastard that he was, he drawled, "You know I love you, Wyn."

"Love you too, Sasha."

Burning fury burned through me and it took all my willpower not to pull out my gun and shoot the motherfucker. It simmered under my skin, making me want to lash out at all of the Nikolaev men.

"Sasha, let Wynter dance with her husband," Vasili, his brother, said, his tone cold and annoying, heavy with their Russian accent. Brennan insisted they be invited and now I regretted it. I'd much rather kill them.

"Only if she wants to," Sasha retorted, eyeing me like he was ready for a fight.

I shifted forward but Wynter dropped his hand immediately, while Vasili grabbed his younger brother and tugged him along to his table, hissing something in their heathen language.

I quickly took Wynter's hand and made her dance the rest of the song with me.

"You really have to calm down," she remarked with a heavy sigh.

"Then stop dancing with other men," I warned.

She rolled her eyes. Fucking rolled her eyes at me!

"You used to be more fun," she muttered and then as if she realized she slipped, her eyes snapped to mine.

A lazy smile curved on my lips. "The last time we danced I had to beat up another man for touching what was mine. Maybe I need to up my game," I drawled.

"Don't hurt Sasha," she warned, and it fucking annoyed me she would care whether he was hurt or not.

"Time to throw the garter!" Dante shouted and both of us turned our heads to find Juliette glaring at Dante. My cousin grinned at her, like he was ready to devour her. He'd had a fascination with her ever since she kneed him in the balls. You'd think it would have the opposite effect, considering how much that shit hurt. But no, my unhinged cousin took it as his own personal challenge.

The crowd circled us and someone brought over a chair. I sat her down, then hunched down and cocked my eyebrow at my wife. She

438

sat there, her eyes frozen above my head, and her hands clutching her dress so hard, her knuckles turned white.

I followed her gaze and found it on my father. Where in the fuck had he come from? My eyes found Priest and Dante, the two nodded and surrounded him. To my surprise so did Sasha who looked ready to pounce on him.

And all the while, my father was grinning and his eyes were locked on my wife.

"When will we see bloodied sheets?" my father exclaimed and Wynter flinched, then narrowed her eyes on him. Sasha growled and Brennan reached for his gun. Wynter's mother paled and my uncle, of all people, found himself next to her and shielding her body with his.

"You haven't heard," Wynter said, tilting her chin up and giving him a proud smile. My father couldn't see Wynter's hands curled into a fist on her white dress because I hindered his view. "He popped that cherry a while back." Someone started choking behind us, but I didn't turn to see who, keeping my gaze locked on my father. "The only blood you'll see tonight might belong to a DiLustro."

Atta woman, I thought proudly.

A deadly quiet filled the chilled air and guests stilled, every man shielding their own family with their hands on their guns. The tension was louder than an explosion, and the anger burned my chest. My fingers twitched with the need to pull out my gun and shoot the motherfucker, consequences be damned.

The only thing that stopped me was Wynter. I felt her tremble under my touch and I didn't want to cause her more distress.

My uncle nodded at Brennan, then moved towards his older brother. I followed the two of them, my uncle ushering my father into the house, and I didn't turn my back to them until my father disappeared from view.

Wynter watched them too and the look in her eyes was haunting. It tore at my black heart.

"Principessa," I murmured softly and her eyes lowered to me. Slowly the tension in her shoulders eased, but the anguish still lingered in those green depths. That talk she promised me had to happen. *Pronto.* "Just watch *me*," I told her and she nodded.

I cupped her calves, her skin soft and warm under my rough palms. She went to lift her gown but I stopped her. "I'll find it," I rasped.

Gently, I slipped off her heel and our first date flickered to the forefront. When our eyes met, I knew she thought of it too. That day in Emilia's shop. The first kill I did for her; it wasn't the last.

I slid my palms up slowly until I reached her thighs. I could feel goose bumps on her skin, a little tremor rolling down her body. But she held my gaze, as if she found strength in it. I reached higher and higher, until my fingers brushed her garter on her right leg. I lifted her dress, just enough to put my head underneath it, my face against her soft skin.

Kissing the skin right above her knee, I closed my teeth around the garter and dragged it down her leg until it fell on the floor. She lifted her foot and I grabbed the ruffled piece of fabric. Then I slid her heel back on.

"Just like Prince Charming," I heard her murmur softly. "Villain Charming."

"But always yours."

I stood up with the garter and helped her up onto her feet, then wrapped my arm protectively around her.

"Who wants to get married next?" I shouted.

Men gathered around and Wynter's laugh pulled my attention away. Her eyes shone and I followed her gaze to find them on Sasha who was taking a step back.

"You know you want it, Sasha," she teased mischievously.

The latter rolled his eyes and took another step back, just for good measure.

Wrapping my arm around my wife, I raised my free arm and threw the garter at the crowd of single men. It didn't surprise me to see Dante diving for it, then putting it between his teeth to turn and stare at Juliette.

She flipped him off, then turned her back to him.

The crowd disbursed and Wynter got distracted by her friends and Emory.

I strode towards my two cousins, and once we were out of everyone's earshot, I asked, "How in the fuck did he get in?"

Priest's face was grim. Dante's wasn't any better. "Father is getting him under control."

I kept my face neutral, aware of gazes thrown our way, even if my blood boiled with fury. It was the only thing Brennan insisted on. I didn't give a shit that my father was the head of the New York Syndicate for as long as he was alive. I wouldn't bring the sick bastard around my wife, nor my sister.

"What happened?" I growled in a quiet voice.

"Our dad is taking care of him," Dante hissed. "Leave it to Gio to show up uninvited. He'll get him out and stay with him."

"Thank fuck," I muttered.

Priest's eyes kept darting to Wynter and her mother. His mother. I had no fucking idea if Wynter's mom knew she had a son. She kept her gaze away from my uncle and most of us DiLustros.

Not that I could blame her, considering the DiLustros destroyed her life.

Suddenly, the music was turned up so loud the speakers shook. Everyone's gazes turned to Wynter and her girlfriends in the corner, their faces bright with animation as they all laughed. Whatever it was, all four of them and Emory laughed so hard, they held their stomachs.

The song "Problem" by Natalia Kills lyrics kept screaming and the girls kept shaking their heads while Juliette kept saying something in her crazy animated way. Wynter reached out and turned down the song.

"It doesn't say anything about bending ass," Emory snorted, her cheeks actually flushing.

Ivy shrugged. "Well, we've been singing it with bending ass, so we're sticking to it."

Wynter's silvery laugh traveled through the air. "You and Juliette have been singing it the perverted way."

Juliette flipped off her friends, turned the music back up, then hopped on the table and started to shake her ass to the song still blasting through the speakers. Emory laughed hard and I was happy to see her getting along with the girls. It was something she never had before.

"I heard you were stupid enough to ask Brennan to marry Juliette?" Priest asked in a bored tone.

Dante slipped his hands in his pockets, his gaze never wavering from the dark-haired woman who had trouble and unhinged written all over her.

"I gave it a try," he drawled. "One way or another, I'm gonna have that girl."

Dante smirked and I could already sense trouble on the horizon. I narrowed my eyes on him. "Just don't fuck it up, Dante."

Dante rubbed a hand over his jaw. "Not to worry," he assured me, though somehow it set me on edge. "I will be the perfect gentleman."

"Even when she kicks you in the nuts again?" Priest asked on a snicker.

"I hope the red-haired one cuts your balls off," Dante drawls, dragging his eyes away from Juliette.

The music was lowered and the Nikolaev men laughed at whatever Wynter said. My wife found a way to have little Kostya in her arms again and was kissing his little hands.

"Jesus, she's really good with little ones," Dante muttered, watching her help little Kostya push on Sasha. The big brute pretended to fall over and Kostya giggled loud, flapping his hands and legs. Then Wynter did it again and Sasha pretended to stumble backwards.

I loved and hated how at ease she was with the Nikolaev family. It was my jealousy, I knew it. Before she'd tell me she loved me. Those words no longer slipped past her lips.

Forcing my face to stay calm as I watched them all, my wife's eyes darted around, as if searching for someone.

Chapter Sixty-Six
WYNTER

I didn't see my mother anywhere.

My eyes skimmed over the crowd of guests and nothing. My uncle was there but there was no sign of her. She hadn't left him all day.

Giving Kostya to Aurora, I excused myself and went searching for her.

Maybe she went to the bathroom, I thought.

I went into the house and turned down one hallway. Servers were busy going in and out.

"Excuse me." I stopped a woman with long blonde hair. "Did you see one of our guests coming down this way?" When she stared at me blankly, I continued, "My mother."

She shook her head. "The other hallway," she muttered. "The one on the right."

"Thank you." I rushed back from the way I came and took the right turn down the long hallway. I practically ran, opening each door on my way. I'd made it almost to the end when I heard a whimper.

I barged through the storage room door to find Gio's hand wrapped around my mother's neck, the look of sheer horror in her eyes. A body was slumped on the ground and I recognized Basilio's uncle. I had no fucking idea what happened here, but I wasn't having it.

"Get the fuck away from her." I flew at him and hit him on his head. He didn't even flinch and his grip must have tightened on my mother's throat because her eyes bulged and she clawed at his hand, desperate for air.

"Get your filthy hands off her," I screamed, beating furiously at his back. "I'm going to kill you."

My mother's petrified face stared at me and I refused to let this man win. I jumped on his back and bit into his shoulder. His yelp was music to my ears.

He pushed my mother off and she stumbled down onto her knees. "Useless whore," he spat, though I was unsure who he was talking to. Mom or me.

"Get it through your thick head," I hissed. "She doesn't want you. And neither do I."

His eyes glared at me, dark and ruthless, promising a painful retribution. Let him fucking try.

"How is your knee?" I sneered. "It should have been your skull I shot."

Mom's gasp filled the room but I didn't look away. "I bet no woman will want you with that fucked-up leg of yours."

He raised his hand and slapped me hard across the face. My ears buzzed and a metallic taste filled my mouth.

"Run, Mom," I croaked while all Gio's attention seemed to be on me. He went to turn his eyes on her, but I quickly said, "This time, I'm going to kill you, Gio DiLustro," I said with conviction. "For what you've done to my mother. And for what you've done to me."

This time, his hand curled into a fist and flew across the air. I dodged it from hitting my face, but not quick enough to avoid it hitting my shoulder.

"I'll show you how we present the bloodied sheets even with your cherry popped, you whore."

Chapter Sixty-Seven
BASILIO

I stalked closer to the door and a red mist filled my vision.

"This time, I'm going to kill you, Gio DiLustro." Wynter's voice was strong, but underlined by trembling. "For what you've done to my mother. And for what you've done to me."

My mouth pulled into a snarl and I lost my shit. He dared touch my woman. I'd slice him up, piece by fucking piece.

His fist connected with her shoulder and pain flashed across my wife's face but she held it in.

"I'll show you how we present the bloodied sheets even with your cherry popped, you whore."

Pulling the knife out of my holster, I charged against him. My hand wrapped around his throat in a crushing grip and I pressed my knife against his lower abdomen.

"You touched her," I roared. "You fucking touched her."

He never saw me coming; he was so intent on the two women. Wynter's mother was on the floor, next to my uncle.

Father grasped my hand, choking the life out of him and his eyes bulged.

"Y-you can't kill me," he choked, his breathing ragged. "The Syndicate will obliterate you. Kill all the DiLustros, including your wife."

I twisted the knife in his abdomen, fucking hating that he was right.

"You'll die one way or another," I said, a twisted grin curling my lips. "Like my wife said, your blood will be spilled today. Not hers. Never hers."

"The Syndicate will—"

He didn't get to finish his words because I pulled out the knife and stabbed him again. His scream vibrated against the walls and it was the best fucking soundtrack.

I'd torture him, but then I'd have to run. I'd have to take Wynter and hide her so this sick motherfucker would never find her.

He opened his mouth to say something and I pushed my knife deeper into him. Pained gurgles filled the air.

"Basilio." I recognized Dante's voice behind me.

"Wyn, you okay?" Sasha lowered down on his knee, checking on my wife. I should be checking on her, except I lost my shit.

My eyes shifted to my wife, never releasing my father from my grip. Sasha was talking to her, but her eyes were on me.

"Principessa," I murmured, regret lacing my voice. How badly did my father hurt her? I'd seen through my life what he was capable of. A feeling of dread settled in my stomach. Would she see my father each time she saw me? Would she hate me?

I finally understood why she ran. She had every right to keep away. I knew my father was to blame. He had hurt her mother and he hurt Wynter. And I wasn't there to protect her. That fucking bastard.

He'd made enough hell on this earth.

My uncle Franco stirred and Wynter's mother leaned over him.

"Are you okay?" She watched him with trepidation.

"Dad." Priest came down to help his father, his eyes looking to his mom. The two locked eyes and Wynter's mother looked away as shame flashed across her expression. *She knows.*

I'd bet my life she knew Priest was her son.

Uncle Franco sat up with assistance from his son and his woman. Because the way he looked at Wynter's mother, there was no mistaking that she was his woman.

"Who knows we're here?" Uncle asked.

"Nobody," I rasped, squeezing my father's throat slightly harder. Unfortunately, it wasn't hard enough to kill him. "Just the seven of us. Eight including this filthy father of mine."

Wynter stood up, Sasha lingering behind her like a dark shadow.

"Basilio, you know none of us can kill him," Uncle Franco rasped, rubbing the back of his head. A large bump told me Father must have hit him from the back. Backstabbing bastard.

"I can kill him," Wynter said firmly, but we all shook our heads.

"You are Basilio's wife now. You kill him, it's on your husband," Uncle explained.

Wynter's mother swallowed. "I could try."

But all of us immediately shook our heads. That woman was not a killer.

"I will," Sasha chimed in. "I have no connections to the fucker and I've been denied that pleasure for nine months now. The longest I had to hold off on a kill. It's worse than blue balls."

Wynter shot him a sideways glance and shook her head.

"Nobody wants to hear about your blue balls, Sasha," she snickered and it was right there and then, I knew. My wife never slept with Sasha Nikolaev. Then her eyes came back to me, soft and shimmering.

"I'll owe you big-time," I told Sasha, my eyes never wavering from her. I hoped she'd forgive me. One day.

Because no matter what, I couldn't let her go. It'd take a better man than me.

I shut the library door behind me, then locked it. There would be no need for witnesses and I definitely didn't want interruptions for this.

The library was on the opposite side of the manor, but the voices of the guests could still be heard.

"We have to talk," I rasped, cupping her face. Her one cheek was red from where my father hit her. The anger boiled so hot inside me, I had to choke it down.

"Yeah, I think so," she agreed.

"Tell me why you left." I *needed* her to tell me the whole goddamn story.

A slow shuddering breath left her, a hint of panic in that green gaze that fascinated me.

"I—I waited for you," she admitted. "Then your father showed up and—"

Her voice faltered and the pain in her expression hit me right in the chest.

The sound of music played in the distance, vibrating softly against the windows and reflecting the anguish in my wife's face and my chest. It was like a stab and twist to the chest.

"Whatever it is, it's okay," I whispered, knowing exactly what my father did to women. I've witnessed it plenty of times. "We'll get through it together," I promised. "And I'll make him pay."

My chest burned, the need to make my father pay *now* like flames that readied to set into a full-blown wildfire.

"He showed up," she whispered softly. "He said you two planned for it. That you left me there knowing he was coming. You only wanted the connection to the Russians." I stilled, holding my rage back. It burned through my chest like acid and I had to take a moment to swallow it down. "He tried to—" She swallowed hard, the gulp loud between us. "He tried to rape me, but he didn't succeed. I escaped and Sasha found me."

Her teeth tugged at her bottom lip and she averted her gaze, looking somewhere behind me. I was glad she avoided looking at me, because she'd have seen the crazy monster that her words unleashed. That demanded retribution. The monster inside me rattled the bars of its cage, demanding to set him free so I could avenge my woman.

My wife.

"He will pay." My voice sounded distorted by the rage buzzing in my ears. "For what he did to you and your mother. And many others."

We were in the Nikolaev specially designed basement for torture. Let's just say Sasha Nikolaev was a crazy motherfucker, but I was seriously considering redecorating my own torture room.

I smashed my fist into his face. "You touched my wife," I growled.

His bones crunched under my knuckles and nothing ever sounded so fucking good.

Gio's beady eyes found me, and for the first time in my life, that cruelty in his gaze was replaced by fear. Angelo's dead body lay limp next to him. The only reason he got a fast death was because he let Wynter go when she came out of the house bruised and bloody. Rather than force her back in for Gio to finish her off.

"She wasn't your wife at that time," he tried to reason in a hoarse voice. It only pissed me off more.

Dante, Sasha, Priest, and Uncle watched from their spot against the wall, letting me have this moment. For nine months, I went crazy, hunting every Russian bastard in a hundred-mile radius.

It was all his fault.

I dragged him off the floor and shoved him into a chair, then tied him up. He attempted to struggle. Unsuccessfully.

"It's time for you to get a taste of your own medicine, Father." The last word tasted bitter on my tongue.

Images of him attempting to rape my wife played in my mind on repeat. How scared she probably was. She didn't have a single cruel bone in her body and that bastard tried to force himself on her. He lied to her, letting her believe that I knew about it, knew about who she really was.

No fucking wonder she ran.

With my knife, I leaned closer to him and smiled cruelly as I pressed the blade against his skin and sliced it across his chest. His blood trailed down his bare skin as he begged for mercy.

"Did you show my wife mercy?" I snarled. She waited for me, in my place, where she should have been safe and my father fucking attacked her. "Did you show my mother mercy?" I smashed my fist into his side. "Or Emory?"

"I gave you everything," he spurted out, blood trickling down his mouth

Another fist into his nose. "Or any other woman?" I punched him again.

I sliced his forearm. Then his ear. His thighs. His finger. The memory of the voice in my head while I searched for Wynter was too fresh. Too raw. He almost cost me my woman.

Another few hours of torturing him and my breathing heaved. I felt blood splatters on my face, my hands were soaked with my father's blood. I wasn't back to one hundred percent but this was too good to miss. Too good to shorten.

My cell phone rang and I glanced at it.

Wynter's grinning face greeted me. My wife was calling.

"Principessa," I answered. "Is everything okay?"

"Yes. I was just wondering if you'll be coming home soon?" Such a simple question. Yet it gave me the best feeling in the world. Coming home to her was the highlight of every scenario.

"I'll be home soon," I told her. "Is Emory with you?"

My body screamed for rest. We'd been at this for the past twenty-four hours. Our wedding turned bloody after all, just as Emory predicted. Except in the best way possible.

She chuckled. "Yes, she and the girls. And my mom."

Good, I didn't want her to be alone.

"Your uncle's men watching the house?" I asked her.

My men guarded her too, but for the first time, I didn't mind reinforcements.

"Yes, it's like a military base."

"Good, I'll see you soon."

I ended the call and looked at the bloodied state of my father. He wasn't worth any more of my time.

Turning around, I held out the knife to Sasha. I was grateful he took care of Wynter after her attack, but there was a part of me that still envied it. It should have been me helping her heal, easing her wounds.

Sasha pushed away from the wall and walked up to me. Taking the knife from me, he nodded then stared down at my father.

The look of pure hate shone in his eyes as he watched him. It matched my own hate.

"This is for Wyn and her mother." He got down on his knees and got closer to him. "For every woman you hurt." He raised the knife above my father's chest, then leaned even closer.

He jabbed the blade down into my father's black fucking heart and left it there.

"And this is from a mutual friend." Then he pulled out his own knife and sliced his throat. "Gia, remember her?"

My father was too weak to confirm. Though it didn't matter. He'd remember her and think of his sins in hell.

"I'll see you in hell," I growled.

Four hours later, I was finally home.

I called Brennan ahead of time to tell him the deed was done. The debt to the Brennan family that started over twenty years ago was paid. Then I showered and changed before going home. Nobody could see me covered in blood, especially not on the night he'd turn up dead.

My father was dead. After decades of wishing him dead, he was finally gone. Forever.

Uncle Franco, Dante, and Priest had already come by the house. Apparently, Uncle and Wynter's mother went to his own penthouse. No fucking clue where Dante and Priest went. Nor Emory. Brennan took the women back to his place, leaving Wynter and I to start our honeymoon.

Finally!

My body throbbed with dark hunger for her. I had yet to take my time and savor her body since I kidnapped her. The crazy part of me wanted to save it for our wedding night.

When I walked into my Hampton home, the house was quiet and dark.

"Where is my wife?" I asked my man watching the front entrance to our home.

"Upstairs," he answered. "She asked me to give you this."

He extended his hand with a small sealed envelope. Opening it, I read the message.

If I'm asleep when you get home, wake me up.

It was almost ten at night and I knew she'd probably be asleep. She was like a toddler with a sleep schedule. I nodded at him, crossed the foyer, then climbed the stairs two at a time.

When I entered the bedroom, I found her curled to the side and asleep. Her short pink nightgown hiked up to her waist, exposing her ass in a matching pink thong. I should let her sleep, yet even as I thought about that, I dropped to my haunches and placed my hand on her smooth thigh that was outside the covers.

The curve of her bare ass was tempting me, begging me to bite it. Yet, I couldn't do it. As if she sensed my presence, her eyes fluttered open and our gazes connected.

"You're home," she murmured softly.

"Always," I vowed softly. "I'll always come home to you."

Chapter Sixty-Eight

WYNTER

Bas had already lowered to his haunches in front of our bed, our faces close together.

For some reason the day he proposed to me came to mind. The day I broke my promise to him. After seeing his reaction to his father, I regretted not trusting him more. He deserved all my trust.

"He's dead," he said, a hint of vehemence showed through his every word. "He'll never hurt you again."

Relief slammed into me as I released a shuddering breath. "I should say I'm sorry," I whispered. The truth was I wasn't. Not in the least.

His face inched closer to me. "Why?"

"Because he was your father."

His shoulders tensed and a growl vibrated in his chest. "He was a sadistic asshole. Never a father. He tortured both Emory and me with his cruelty. It should have never touched you."

I reached out my palm. "It should have never touched you either," I murmured softly. "Nor your sister. I should have never put his sins on you. Or at least given you a chance to explain. He scared me, and when I barely got out of it alive, I—"

Inhaling a shaky breath, I pondered the right words to tell him. I didn't want to hurt him more. I told him the abbreviated version in the library.

As if he read my thoughts, he said, "Everything. Tell me all of it."

I swallowed, hating those memories.

"When your father showed up unexpectedly, he offered me money. I refused. He convinced me you two were in it together. That you left on purpose to let him—" God, why was it so damn hard to say those words. His forehead came to mine and there was so much pain in his gaze that it shattered my heart into a million pieces. "Anyhow, he attacked, I fought back. It was a close call, but then I remembered your gun. I saw it when you gave me the necklace."

My hand wrapped around my wrist, the bracelet always having that calming effect on me.

"He didn't rape me, I swear," I told him and a flicker of relief and something raw bled through every pore of him. "But his words about my mom hurt just as bad," I choked out. "He didn't think I'd shoot him. Then he started talking about my mom. How he shot her in the knee and took her career away. My dad. How he killed him."

"My brave woman," he rasped while his gaze bore into mine. "You shot him in the knee."

"Eye for an eye," I breathed. "Though I wished so many times since then that I had just killed him."

A quiet noise of anger crawled up his throat.

"Next time, though I'll make sure there isn't a next time, you come to me. Not Sasha. Not your uncle. *Me.*" Somehow with this man nearby, I didn't think anyone would dare to come after me. "I'll always protect what's mine. And you, Wynter Star DiLustro, have been mine since you landed in my arms jumping off that balcony."

I averted my gaze, embarrassed that I was so stupid to believe a single word from Gio DiLustro.

"After all he told me, after what he tried to do..." I closed my eyes remembering that last day and a single tear trickled down my face. "It just seemed impossible to find my way back to you."

Silence was deafening and a heavy tension filled the space between us. A choked sob slipped through my lips. "I'm a shell of a woman without you, Bas."

His palms cupped my cheeks. "Look at me, principessa," he demanded softly. I opened my eyes and found his dark eyes intense on me. "I want *you*," he rasped, his thumb gently brushing over my bottom lip. "Only you. All your firsts and your lasts. I want to be your beginning and your end. Because you are mine. I'm a shell of a man without you. Fuck your connections. Fuck your family. Just you and me."

His lips brushed against mine. Sweet. Soft. All-consuming. It was the kind of kiss that could break your heart and mend it within the same breath.

"I have something for you," he murmured against my lips.

Pulling slightly away from him, I regarded him curiously. "I saw all the shoes you kept," I breathed.

He shook his head with amusement.

"I couldn't bear to get rid of them, but it's not the shoes." His nose brushed against mine. He pulled something out of his pocket. He held a little velvet box in his hand. "This is what I went to get that day." He opened the box and the most gorgeous engagement ring sat in it. Princess-cut diamond with tear-shaped emeralds surrounding it. "It matches the wedding band."

"You held on to it all this time?" I croaked as my heart raced in my chest, longing for him.

"I will always follow." His palm brushed across my cheek and I leaned into his touch, soaking up his warmth. "A day without you is hell on this earth. Promise me you'll never leave."

I pressed my lips to his, softly and possessively.

"I'll never leave, Bas," I rasped. I watched as he slid the ring on my finger. "Wherever you go, I'll follow."

These vows were ours. For our future. For our happiness.

He grabbed the hem of my nightgown and pulled it over my head, leaving me in only my thong. My skin burned with the need to feel him on me, inside me. His mouth crushed mine, devouring me. Deep and consuming. When I parted my lips, his tongue slid into my mouth and I moaned.

I burned like a match, needing him with desperation. He pushed his hand into my hair, fisting it as his lips left mine and trailed down my neck. He stood up and his weight settled on top of me. It felt so good, so right.

His one hand lifted my thigh and I wrapped my legs around his torso, his erection pressing between my legs. The ache between my legs throbbed and I arched up into him, grinding myself against him.

Desire burned, sparks flew, and hearts glowed.

I tugged on his shirt and he paused to pull it over his head. Then his mouth was back on my skin, nipping at my breasts and all the while his hard cock grinding against my hot pussy.

I was delirious with need. Nine months without him was far too long. Now, I needed to overdose on him. I ground myself on his hard-on, desperate to get myself off. The friction between us was delicious, my greedy pussy clutching his shaft, needing him inside me.

The sound of shredding cut through the air. I didn't care what he ripped or destroyed, as long as he kept fucking me.

Angling his cock into me, he felt hot and hard at my entrance. My muscles clenched, hungry for him, needing him with desperation.

"Bas," I begged in a breathless voice.

"Beg for my cock, principessa," he rasped, his mouth nipping at my earlobe.

I turned my head and his eyes seared through me. I grabbed his face, and pulled him closer.

"Please give me your cock," I breathed. As he placed a scorching-hot kiss on my lips, he slid all the way in with one hard thrust. My body welcomed the intrusion, turning my blood hot. He thrust inside me in long, deep strokes. Hard and relentless.

"Fuck, I missed this," he grunted, pounding his hard, thick shaft into me.

I clenched around his hard cock, my breath caught in my throat. The rush of feelings swarmed my body, taking every powerful thrust of his.

"So fucking good," he praised, his voice guttural. Those three little words had me panting with crazed lust, on the verge of an orgasm.

My pussy and my insides had been molded to the shape of his cock, welcoming his intrusion. He was my missing puzzle piece. Whimpers and moans left my lips, his eyes bore into me with a crazed possessiveness.

"Ahhh, please," I pleaded. Every inch of me was on fire. He had to extinguish it. Each thrust of his widened and stretched me, bringing me closer to the pinnacle. I'd never felt so deliciously full in my life as I did when Bas fucked me, relentlessly and hard. My back arched off the bed, every thrust began to kindle a spark and spread from my clit outward.

My head thrashed against the pillow, my neck exposed to him. I was so close, reaching for the stars. His big hand curled around my neck, and with a slight squeeze, my body shattered. This was what I needed; his domination, this intensity.

A moan tore from my mouth, his name on my lips as my body exploded. An orgasm shuddered through me, overwhelming me. Heat pulsed through every fiber of me, tremors shaking my body.

When I came down, it was to Basilio's dark gaze on me.

"Who fucks you?" he growled, resting his forehead against mine.

I shivered. "You."

He'd get any admission from me after such an intense orgasm. "Who else?"

"Nobody else," I breathed.

"Until my dying breath, just you and me," he grunted.

"Yes," I panted, a languid sensation rushing through my bloodstream. "Just you and me."

Satisfaction rumbled in his chest. His thrusts shallowed, his muscles tensed, and with a grunt, he spilled inside me, his own body shuddering.

"You feel amazing, principessa," he purred, his breath hot against my skin. His thick cum trickled down my inner thigh and my chest swelled at the praise. "You are mine."

I sighed with contentment.

Because Basilio DiLustro was mine.

Chapter Sixty-Nine

WYNTER

Happiness started with the letter B and ended with the letter O.

We spent two days in his bedroom. We fucked, kissed, fucked again until I was so sore, it hurt to walk. Best damn honeymoon ever.

I didn't need Paris. Nor Venice.

As long as I had this man with me, I floated. He was my entire world.

And when he gave me my wedding present, I choked up and started crying. He bought me an ice rink. My own ice rink.

"I didn't get you anything," I grumbled softly.

"You are my gift," he drawled, then pressed his face between my legs and I just about burned like a star.

I had made so many promises over the last two days. Never leave him. Always trust him. Never let another man touch me. Always wear his ring.

There was one thing we never talked about. Other women he

might have had over the last nine months and other men he believed I had. It was as if both of us were scared of what it would do to us.

The past no longer mattered. Only the future.

He was all mine, and I was all his.

I was so happy, I feared something else was bound to happen.

I blow-dried my hair, wearing only another set of pink undergarments. I sauntered into our shared walked-in closet, digging for something to wear. We were meeting Mom, Priest, and his father.

My mother's boyfriend. Or something like that.

I'd just think of him as Bas's uncle. Mom having a boyfriend was a foreign concept I couldn't quite grasp.

Then this afternoon, we'd attend the funeral of Gio DiLustro. I'd rather not, but the etiquette required it. Especially since Bas would officially be taking his place in the Syndicate as the head of New York.

A sharp sting on my ass had me spinning around to come face-to-face with my husband.

"Bas!" I exclaimed undignified, but failed because a big smile played on my lips.

"You can't walk around half naked and expect me not to get a boner," he growled as he picked me up and tossed me on the bed.

I laughed, pulling him down with me. The moment his weight settled on me, I released a sigh. I spread my thighs and pressed against his erection.

"Tell me what you want," he growled, his breath hot in my ear.

"You," I breathed out. "Inside me."

"You two are a whole hour late," Priest grumbled as we approached the table.

I noted my shoe was unbuckled. My step faltered. These were the shoes he bought me nine months ago and I didn't want them ruined. Just as I was going to lower down, Bas beat me to it.

"Let me," he murmured, his fingers skimming over the back of my ankle and sending goose bumps over my skin.

A round of gasps and wows echoed but all I could do was stare at him. I breathed this man. I felt safe with this man. He killed his father to keep me safe. Well, technically Sasha gave him the last blow but Bas made him suffer first.

Bliss hummed through every inch of my body as I watched him buckle the strap and then stand up to his full height. Without him, life was a painfully slow death.

"Why can't you do this for me?" An unfamiliar voice had me turning my head just in time to see a woman smack her date on his chest and then turn to watch my husband with hearts in her eyes.

I slipped my hand into Basilio's. It might have been a silly move, but I wanted the whole world to see he was mine.

"Come on, you two," Basilio's uncle called out to us.

Squeezing my hand in comfort, Bas ignored everyone and bent his head to press a kiss on my lips.

"Don't be jealous," he murmured against my lips. "You're the only one for me."

My lips curved into a soft smile and my heart swelled, I feared it'd explode from these feelings that boomed inside me.

We strode towards the table where Mom, Priest, and his father sat at Eleven Madison Park restaurant on Madison Avenue in the heart of New York City. They secured a window seat that overlooked Madison Square Park. The street outside was busy with pedestrians, despite it being a chilly day. The beautiful weather drew the people out, eagerly anticipating spring.

"What the hell were you two doing?" Priest added.

I blushed crimson, avoiding looking his way. I feared if he saw my eyes, he'd know exactly what we were doing.

Bas just shrugged his shoulders. "Been busy."

"They're newlyweds," Bas's uncle defended us. "Let Bas enjoy his honeymoon."

"Hi, Mom." I went around the table and hugged her. "Are you okay?"

She pulled away to look at me. She looked beautiful, wearing a light green sweater and white jeans combined with a pair of white flats. Her hair was up in a bun, and for the first time in my life, she didn't seem to have ghosts lurking in her eyes.

Taking both my cheeks between her palms, she held my head firmly. "Next time, you run. Don't try and save me." I shook my head at her words. "I was scared he'd take you too. That, I wouldn't have survived."

"You're my mom," I whispered. "I love you. Of course, I'll always save you."

She shook her head, sadness crossing her expression.

"You might not think so after today," she answered enigmatically.

Priest offered a terse nod and Bas's uncle extended his hand. "We never officially met. I'm Franco DiLustro."

He wore a three-piece suit and so did Priest, both ready to attend Gio's funeral. I wore a simple black dress that reached to my knees with black shoes.

"Wynter," I murmured, accepting his hand hesitantly. "How is your head?"

A dark expression passed his face. "It's good, thank you."

Unsure what else I could say to him, I offered a tight smile and took the seat Bas pulled out for me. Once we all sat down, the waiter showed up and took Bas's and my order.

With the waiter gone, it was Franco who broke the uncomfortable silence.

"I hear you play poker," he drawled.

I shifted uncomfortably, my eyes looked to Priest. "Yes," I muttered, wondering how much Franco knew.

"You got yourself a good game at Royally Lucky," he continued. Well, it seemed he knew a lot.

"Star beats my father at poker and chess," Mom chimed in. "She's really good."

"Sometimes," I murmured.

The waiter came back and placed my caramel mocha in front of me. I wrapped my fingers around my cup, my shoulders slightly tense.

"Going for calories already, huh?" Mom teased.

I chuckled uncomfortably. "Figured I could enjoy all the stuff I've been craving."

Bas's hand came to my leg under the table and squeezed in reassurance. "She earned it," he told Mom.

"Fuck yeah," Priest agreed, shooting a slightly disapproving look my mother's way. "Two-time Olympic gold medalist, she can eat and drink whatever she wants."

"Watch it, son," his father countered. "Show respect."

"How are you feeling, Star?" Mom asked. "I got inquiries for interviews from a few of your sponsors."

I shook my head. "I told you, Mom. No more competing for me." I glanced at Bas and he nodded. "Basilio bought me a wedding present. An ice rink. I want to clean it up, rename it, and maybe coach." I clenched my fingers and Bas's fingers interlocked with mine, his thumb brushing softly against my palm. I found the move to be soothing. "If you want, we could coach together. Not sure if you're staying in New York or—"

Mom and Franco shared a glance and the smile that man gave her told me he loved her. I didn't know their full story but I was happy for my mom. She finally got her happiness. It was only fair.

"Well, I'm thinking about moving to Chicago." She beamed.

I grinned. "Chicago is good," I agreed. "Closer than California."

And she won't be alone.

"You'll come to visit?" she asked.

Bas and I shared a glance, and he nodded. "We'll visit often. You have to visit us too."

Priest huffed a frustrated breath. "Why don't we tell Wyn and Bas the information you told me?"

Priest was agitated. It was evident in his tense shoulders and the way he shook his head in disgust. I still haven't come to terms with Priest being my brother. I had no idea how to behave, especially since Mom hadn't said a word about it. Neither did Priest.

Mom's heavy sigh shifted the air between the five of us and I couldn't help tensing again.

"Remember what I told you about a baby I lost?" I nodded, swallowing hard. "Well, Priest... Christian, he's your half brother."

"Huh?"

"He's—"

I waved my hand. "Yes, I knew that. Basilio told me after Priest ran a DNA test." Confusion marred Mom's face and I turned to Priest. "Your real name is Christian?"

He just shrugged. "Don't tell anyone."

"I won't," I promised. This felt slightly awkward. I felt like this wasn't the bomb about to be dropped.

I turned to my mom who was watching Priest with a longing in her eyes. I didn't understand her history.

"Mom," I whispered, and her eyes came back to me. "Why did you tell me you lost the baby?"

Mom blinked, then blinked again. "I didn't tell you everything, Star." I stilled, waiting for her to tell me whatever else she had to get off her chest. "My grandmother, your great-grandmother went mad when she lost her daughter. Her husband, the Pakhan, declared war on the Brennans and swore to kidnap every descendant of the Volkov family from them."

"What?" I breathed confused. "Why?"

"My mother, your grandmother, was an only child," she explained. "They were robbed of their heirs. So when I had Christian, I risked his life. Not to mention that Grandpa and my brother would have gone crazy. Franco was married and I—" Yeah, it wasn't the ideal scenario but why leave her baby behind.

"Franco and I decided it was best to hide Christian. It was the safest option. Then I returned to New York and eventually married your father. When Gio..." Her eyes flitted towards my husband, and this time, I squeezed his hand in comfort. "When Gio attacked and killed your father, a perfect opportunity presented itself. Liam had me proclaimed dead, changed my identity, and the Pakhan stopped hunting. But nine months ago, Gio alerted them to you, Wynter. They don't know about Christian, but they're coming for you."

Bas growled next to me. "Let them fucking try."

Chapter Seventy

WYNTER

Gio's funeral was lavish.

There were a lot of attendees but not many grieving faces. And I had a feeling the ones that were grieving were fake.

The weather was beautiful and somehow it fit the occasion. Was it wrong? Fuck no. Gio DiLustro was a sadistic bastard and this world was a better place for it. I stood next to Bas, his sister on the other side of him. Dante, Priest, and Franco were here too. My mother wasn't. Even in his death, she feared him.

Basilio's face was an unmoving mask. Many men approached us, giving their condolences. He held my hand with his left, needing to keep his right hand free.

"Just in case," he said.

Emory was slightly pale, but as the guests cleared out and Dante, Priest, and their father left, it was her turn to throw a rose on her father's grave, she whispered a hiss.

"Rot in hell." She threw a scrunched, rotten red rose and left without a glance.

A shudder rolled down my spine, not wanting to know what she endured to hate her father so much.

The funeral wasn't long and I was glad for it. A few men of the Syndicate rounded off to the side, discussing business and that seemed to take longer. All the while, Emory remained with me.

"How come you don't get to be there with them?" I asked her, tilting my chin toward the group of men.

"I don't have a small brain," she muttered under her breath and I had to stifle my laugh.

Her eyes, as dark as Basilio's, came to me and she grinned. "I'm happy to see you and Basilio come to terms."

My eyes gravitated back to my husband to see him already watching me. He winked, I smiled and then his attention was back to the group of men. Yet, I knew the entire time he kept me in his sights.

"You know, he caught me falling off my uncle's balcony," I told her with a soft smile. Her raised eyebrow told me she didn't. "He's my fairy tale."

"I didn't take you for a romantic," she scoffed.

My eyes found my husband again. "Only when it comes to Bas."

It was after six in the evening when we headed home.

Bas sped down the road, covered with flurries. The last visit from Mother Nature I guess. It wasn't the ideal road condition for his Bugatti.

I glanced toward him, his body tense and expression dark.

"Basilio—" I started but never got to finish the sentence. Something collided with our trunk and my body jerked forward.

My head snapped behind us to find the headlights of a black SUV. A Land Rover. Bas suddenly floored the gas, but so did the driver of the SUV. Another ram into the back of Bas's car.

"What's happening?" I whimpered.

"Fucking Russians," he hissed.

"How do you know they're Russians?" I asked him, my eyes glancing behind us.

"They always drive damn Land Rovers."

"D-do you think it's my—" I couldn't quite force the word great-grandparents past my lips. "Do you think it's the Pakhan?"

"I don't know." Except his body language told me he thought it was exactly them.

I shifted around, my hands shaking. Bas must have noticed it, because he tried to comfort me, "I won't let anything happen to you."

"Both of us," I rasped. He cocked his eyebrow and I clarified, "Don't let anything happen to both of us."

"Both of us, then," he agreed. He took a sudden twist of the steering wheel, making a sharp right corner. "Head down," he barked, his voice tight and cold.

Without delay, I obeyed and leaned forward. No sooner than I did, bullets started flying. The passenger window exploded and so did the rear window. Both my hands covered my head while Bas kept driving.

My face was pressed against my legs, my body jerking with each sharp turn Bas took. The bullets kept flying and I turned my head to my husband's. Fear choked me. I finally got my fairy tale and now this bullshit.

I kept my gaze on Bas, wishing I could do something to help him. He was in a clear line of fire and it terrified me. He kept his cool but I didn't. I felt tears prick at the back of my eyes and I prayed we got out of this alive.

Somehow Basilio managed to pull his own gun and started shooting at the SUV. More shots came our way. He kept shooting but he was at a disadvantage, trying to drive and shoot at the same time.

And I felt useless.

He turned another corner and my body slammed against the door, my head hitting the handle.

"You good?" Bas asked, worry laced his voice. He was being shot at and he worried if I was good.

"Yes. Tell me how to help," I asked.

"Get my phone," he barked. "Right pocket."

I reached over and pushed my left hand into his pocket. It was the only thing in his pocket, so I pulled it out.

"Dial Dante or Priest."

I nodded and swiped the phone open, then started scrolling down his phone book. "D. D, D there is not a single name with D here," I told him frantically.

"Under Cousin," he clarified, his eyes above me. "Fuck," he snarled and I followed his line of sight.

More shots rang out, the deafening sound of bullets against the metal of the car. I couldn't stop flinching, my eyes darting around with fear. The terror gripped my throat and the fear of losing Bas to death was the biggest part of it.

A loud hiss to my left had me whirling my head. Bas never slowed down the car and kept shooting at the men after us, but he was hit.

"Bas, you're hit," I cried out.

He didn't slow down. He kept firing another round of shots. His sleeve was soaked with blood and I straightened up to help stop the bleeding. I couldn't bear the thought of him in pain. My hands shook, our eyes connected. There was still so much I wanted to say to him. So much I wanted to do with him.

"Bas, I—" His hand landed on my head and pushed it down just in time to hear a bullet fly by my ear. In agonizingly slow motion, I watched the bullet graze his head and blood spurt on my face and all over him.

The car spun out of control, and with the last sense of reason, I pressed the call button to his cousin. The faint ringtone mixed with the firearm and screeching tires. The car shot toward a guard rail and I was certain this was it for us.

I turned my head to see him one last time.

"I love you, Bas." Our eyes locked, my mouth moved but I couldn't hear my voice. Something flickered in his eyes and I had to believe he knew what I said. I couldn't die without saying those words one more time.

An ear-shattering noise sounded as we crashed against the rail. The car tumbled and my body jerked back and forth, flying through the air. The safety belt cut into my neck, digging into my collarbone. My head hit something hard, and then a loud explosion split my ears.

My vision turned black, my ears rang, my whole body hurt. But I could hear voices. Russian voices in the distance. My body lay limp and my eyelids refused to open. The sudden silence was deafening. Eerily scary.

For several heartbeats, I remained still. Listening.

A car engine roared, but it didn't move. Whoever attacked us was still here. Ignoring my throbbing headache and pain, I forced my eyes open. My vision was blurry and dots swam in the air everywhere I looked. I blinked once. Twice.

My sight cleared and I noted the smoke surrounding us.

I turned to the driver's side and my breath was cut short. Bas was slumped over the steering wheel. Blood soaked his whole sleeve, dripping down his fingers. There was also blood on his temple and fear unlike ever before took hold of my throat.

Was he dead?

I felt panic rise in my throat but I choked it down. Instead I listened for any sound from him. Anything. I held my breath, praying silently to anyone who was listening.

Don't let him die. Don't let him die. My throat was raw, so many emotions choking me.

473

That was when I saw it. His fingers twitched. Like he wanted to keep on fighting.

He's alive, my mind and heart sighed in relief.

The harsh Russian words neared and I looked frantically around Bas for his gun. I couldn't let them finish us. The smell of gasoline traveled with the smoke and drifted into my lungs. I kept still while my eyes darted around, panic spread through every single cell of me.

Smoke and heat filled the car, and I feared we'd burn alive if we remained here.

Gun! I spotted Bas's handgun by his foot. I couldn't waste any time. Ignoring my aching body, I unbuckled my seat belt and shifted forward to the left. Then I grabbed the gun and shifted around to the right.

Two men stood ten feet away from the car, and without thinking about it, I put my finger on the trigger and pulled it.

Bang.

I missed. Fuck! I forced myself to calm down and aimed. Just the way Sasha taught me.

Bang. Bang. Bang.

I hit them. They stumbled. One fell down to his knees. The other followed. The latter raised his gun but I pulled the trigger again. *Bang. Bang.*

He fell over, blood quickly pooling around him.

I killed a human. The realization hit hard but I didn't regret it.

Sparks popped under the hood. With no time to waste, I grabbed the door handle and started pushing. It wouldn't budge. I picked up my legs and placed the bottom of my Chucks against it, then applied all my strength into pushing it open.

Thank God I changed out of my clothes before heading home after the funeral. It was an odd thought while you tried to get out of a wrecked car.

"Come on," I grunted. I kicked the door. Again and again. The hood of the car was burning and panic rose inside me. I started kicking frantically, then alternated to using my shoulder.

The door swung open. My hands and legs shook and tears streamed down my face. My muscles burned, but I couldn't stop. I rushed out of the car and around toward Bas's door.

The fire was spreading quickly, reaching the windshield now. I gripped the car door and tugged hard, grunting while my muscles screamed in protest. The door flew open unexpectedly and I fell back on my ass.

The smoke filled the car while fire licked at the windshield. Fear gripped my lungs, burning them raw. Smoke and gas drifted into my nose and down into my lungs, making it even harder to breathe.

I stumbled to my feet and reached for Bas. He hadn't worn a seat belt, so I just wrapped both of my hands around his bicep and I started pulling on him. He was much stronger and bigger than me, but giving up wasn't an option. He would never leave me behind.

The fire was spreading way too quickly and Bas was too heavy for me to move quickly out of the range in case the car blew up. Frustrated tears pooled in my eyes and my sight turned blurry but I refused to stop.

"Please, Bas," I whimpered. "Just don't die on me," I pleaded out of breath. Blood quickly soaked his dark hair and dread pooled in the pit of my stomach. Each step I took felt lead-heavy. But I kept going until we were a safe distance away.

I dropped down to my knees. My eyes searched over his body, alarmed by the amount of blood pooling around his head. I leaned over his face and felt the gentle breath sweep against my cheek. With shaky fingers, I brushed my fingers over the pulse on his throat.

"It's there," I breathed with a relieved sigh. The pulse was there.

I closed my eyes, overwhelming relief washed over me. And I prayed, promising God anything and everything. As long as Bas stayed with me.

My eyes stung and my chest felt tight, making each breath I inhaled hurt. I couldn't live without this man on this earth. I might survive knowing he was somewhere on the planet, walking and breathing. Healthy and alive. But I wouldn't survive his death.

"I love you, Bas," I whispered, holding his head on my lap. "I have never stopped loving you. I promised I'd never leave you. I walked away but my heart stayed behind." I bent my head and pressed a soft kiss on his forehead. "Please stay with me."

He barely stirred and I froze, almost scared I imagined it. "Bas?" I rasped.

I held my breath, waiting for him to move again. Say something. Anything. When he didn't, my heart sunk. Maybe I should keep talking? I didn't know.

"Bas, please don't die," I pleaded softly, whispering against his clammy forehead. "I love you so damn much it hurts. There has been nobody since I walked away that day, and if you leave me, it'll break me. Please just hold on. For me."

A loud screech of tires had me raising my head. A black Land Rover. Another one. My eyes frantically searched around for the gun. It lay discarded close to the burning car. For a second, I remained immobile, hesitant about what I should do. I didn't want to leave Bas, vulnerable in his unconscious state.

Except, without a weapon, we'd both be vulnerable. I laid his head down on the cold dirt ground and I scrambled over to the burning car. I reached for it and it burned my palm. A small whimper sounded in my throat, but I ignored it.

I heard the door of a car shut behind me and I whirled around to find a woman stepping out of the black Land Rover. She had a fur coat on that came down to her knees and a matching fur hat.

She wore sunglasses, and if the scenario was different, I'd swear she was an old Hollywood star. The way she moved, with elegance and confidence. I almost expected her to have one of those long skinny cigarettes in her fingers and bring it to her lips. Three men who looked scary as fuck surrounded her, their eyes and guns on me.

I shuffled back to Bas's immobile body, the handgun gripped between my fingers.

Putting my hand on his chest to ensure myself he was breathing, I raised my hand and pointed it at them.

"Stay where you are," I demanded with the courage I didn't exactly feel.

To my surprise, the woman stopped, then whispered something to her men.

"Wynter Star Volkov."

The woman's voice was low and soft. And most of all creepy.

She took her sunglasses off and her eyes met mine. They were dark brown, but something in her eyes scared me even worse than in Gio's. She took a step, then another.

I shot a warning shot, just about grazing her stupid animal-killing fur hat. "Stop right there," I growled.

"You look like your grandmother," she said in her soft voice that was fucking creepy. "Winter was my whole world. The only good thing in my world."

I stiffened. Was she—

No, she couldn't be. This woman with an olive skin tone couldn't be Russian. Maybe she worked for the Pakhan.

"Who are you?" I bit out.

"I'm your great-grandmother." Her eyes darted to my husband. "Sofia Catalano Volkov. And you, my child... You'll be coming with me."

"The fuck I will," I spat back. "You shot at us. My husband! And I'm not your fucking child."

"Do you know who I am?" she asked, ignoring my outburst.

"Duh, you just told me."

She chuckled, her laugh creepy. "I was the first payment in my family to the Belles and Mobsters' fucked-up arrangement, sold to the notorious Ivan Petrov. His Pakhan saw me and took me for himself. I went through hell, but I came out on top." I held my breath, unsure where this was going. I never heard of the arrangement she was talking about. "I made the Pakhan fall in love with me. And then I had my daughter. She was my whole world."

I swallowed. "That has nothing to do with me. Or my husband."

Another creepy laugh. "But it does. Because it is men like your husband and like your uncle who play with lives. It is men like them who have taken everything from me. I will take everything from them. But I need someone of my blood to take my place. Rule this world and make these men regret ever taking my baby from me."

"W-where is your Pakhan?" I asked, something in my subconscious tickled, nudging at me. Except my headache was becoming worse.

Her cackle hurt my ears. The woman had to be crazy. A certified nutcase.

"Pakhan?" Her shrill voice was making my head hurt. "I'm the fucking Pakhan. I rule it all."

My mouth might have dropped to the ground. Or maybe I hit my head harder than I thought.

"Aim guns on him and shoot," she ordered softly in Russian. "You hit her and I'm going to have you and your entire family gutted."

Jesus, she was a nutjob!

They raised their guns. I didn't think, just acted as I threw myself over Bas's body and covered him with mine.

If they couldn't shoot me, it was the best defense.

I heard the click before the bullets started flying. But they never came. I kept my husband's body covered, glancing over my shoulders. It was only then I registered the roar of an engine and screech of tires.

"Just hang on," I whispered in my husband's ear. "Reinforcements are here."

At least I hoped to God they were. Whoever it was had the Russians running. They killed one, wounded another but the crazy woman made it all the way to her car.

That was when I saw it and I could have cried from the relief that slammed into me.

Dante and Priest were here. Thank God, they tracked the phone.

"You'll get your last rites now, bitch," I hissed.

Chapter Seventy-One

WYNTER

Mom kept throwing glances my way.

Ever since we arrived at the hospital, it had been a never-ending parade of poking and probing. And questions. So many damn questions. My temples throbbed, the smell of smoke and blood lingered in my nose and my lungs.

But the dominating emotion was fear. For Bas.

I wouldn't survive it.

My gaze locked on his pale face. He should have woken up by now. It had been hours since all hell broke loose. The crazy bitch, my great-grandmother, got away. Sasha, Priest, and Dante showed up in the nick of time. Killed all her men. Apparently, the woman had reinforcements coming right behind her too.

"Star, are you alright?" Mom's voice had me turning my gaze to meet her eyes. Even with her brows drawn together and a worried expression on her face, she looked happier than I've ever seen her before.

Priest's father stood a few feet away from us, giving us privacy but his eyes were on Mom the entire time. As if he worried she'd disappear. Priest stood by his father, but it was harder to read him.

He was still coming to terms about all these revelations.

"Yes. I just need Bas to be okay." I held Mom's gaze, wondering how she was doing. "How are you?"

Her eyes darted to her son, pain crossing her face. "I'm better than I've been in a long time. I just wish—" Her voice failed her and I took her hand in mine, squeezing gently. She let out a heavy sigh. "I just wish I could make him see that I meant well. Yes, I left him with his father but it was to protect him."

"He'll come around, Mom." I truly believed that. It might take him time, but deep down, under his crazy last rites and unhinged look in those blue eyes that now I knew were the Brennans' blue eyes, he was a good man. "Just give him time. It's a lot to find out in such a short time. And we don't know what he's been through."

You don't just wake up one day and decide to read men their last rites before you kill them. At least, I hoped not. There had to be something traumatic that got him to that point.

"There hasn't been a day that went by where I didn't think about him," she whispered her admission. "I never wanted to leave him, but it was the only way to keep him hidden."

Our gazes locked, all the secrets that our families kept, dancing around this hospital hallway. They were big secrets. The kind that should have never been kept from us, but I realized at this moment, I didn't fucking care about any of them. They brought me here, to this very moment. To Bas.

The only thing I needed was for Bas to be okay.

My eyes sought out the man who I had fallen for from the moment I landed in his arms. Okay, maybe not that very moment but the second he slipped that shoe onto my foot, his eyes like black diamonds, I was lost to him. As long as he was by my side, I'd live through anything.

"You kept a lot of secrets," I told her, keeping my gaze on my husband. "You, Uncle, and Priest's father. Yes, it was wrong. But it brought me Bas."

"Your distraction," she murmured softly.

My lips curved into a smile. "Yes, my distraction. It wasn't right to keep all that from us. To keep Priest from his mother. But help him see that despite it all, you did it for a good reason and it brought him something good. Find what that good is and don't give up on him."

It was the only advice I had. The best I could come up with.

"I don't deserve you, my little star." Her voice trembled slightly and I turned to see a lone tear rolling down her cheek.

Wrapping my arms around her, I squeezed her tightly. "Oh, Mom. You deserve it all. Now just go and get it. You were good to Jules and me. We were lucky to have you. But now, Priest needs you. Don't worry about us. If we need you, we know how to reach you."

Franco DiLustro strode to us and I took a step back, letting him comfort my mother.

"How about we go home?" he suggested. "You need rest."

She shook her head. "No, let's wait just a bit longer."

The two of them walked away, leaving me standing with Priest by my side. Silence stretched, although I couldn't say it was an uncomfortable one.

The beeping sound of the machine, signaling Bas breathed, soothed my worry and I just focused on that. Bas was still asleep, and even in his state, he looked like a force to be reckoned with.

"Are you two admiring Basilio sleeping? Reminds me of reversed Sleeping Beauty shit." Sasha's voice came from behind me and I whirled around to find him standing behind me with Alexei and his wife, along with Nico Morrelli and his wife. "I mean, I know he's handsome and all that, but I dare say, I'm even more handsome."

I scoffed and rolled my eyes. "Your hair is too blond."

"Have you checked yourself in the mirror lately?"

My eyes darted between all of them. "Thank you for showing up when you did," I said seriously. "If you hadn't—"

I couldn't even think about that.

My eyes shifted to my brother. Jesus, it still shocked me to think of him as my brother. "If I forget to thank Dante, please let him know. Okay, Priest?"

He nodded, the expression on his face grim. As if on cue, Jules's screech echoed through the hospital hallway and she stormed off.

"Those two are playing cat and mouse," Bianca, Nico's wife, mused. "Guess who's the mouse?"

And Jules was making the chase all the more thrilling.

"We should announce my connection to you," Priest said, changing the subject. "It will take the heat of the crazy bitch away from you."

Bianca winced and opened her mouth to say something, but Franco and Mom were back.

"Absolutely not," Mom hissed. "I didn't sacrifice all those years to put you in harm's way now."

"I've been in harm's way all along," he snapped and my mother paled.

"Priest, you can't say shit like that to our mother," I scolded him.

"Your mother," he growled low. "Your mother, Wynter."

Mom's expression broke and her sobs shattered the air.

"We'll talk about this later," Franco warned his son. "In private."

"Good luck finding me," Priest snapped. "I'm done with asking permission. You do your thing, I'm doing mine."

Franco and Mom shuffled away. I knew we could resolve all this tension and past ghosts that seemed to have left a mark on all of us. The question was how long would it take.

"So I know this might be a bad time to bring this up," Bianca started tentatively. "The woman. Your great-grandmother."

"The crazy bitch," I added helpfully. "I kind of prefer that."

Bianca shared a fleeting glance with her husband. "Yeah, about that. Well, she's my great-aunt. Sasha said she gave you a name. Sofia Catalano."

My brows shot up.

"Are you for fucking real?" Priest asked exactly what I was thinking.

Nico shoved his one hand into his pocket, looking all casual and lethal. "Dead serious."

Priest and I shared a look.

"No offense, but the bitch is dead the moment I get my hands on her," Priest announced. "For what she did to my cousin and for putting Wyn in danger with her psycho attack." I nodded my agreement. "And don't expect family reunions if that woman is there."

I love my brother.

It took about five minutes for Priest to chase everyone away. Well, everyone but Sasha. I couldn't help but smile as I watched them both. I truly felt rich. Now, if only my husband would wake up, I'd be complete. The doctor assured me he'd be fine, but until I could drown in those dark eyes, worry clawed at my chest.

"You know, Sasha, I got Wynter," Priest broke the silence. "I'm her brother. I'll take care of her."

Sasha shrugged his massive shoulder that I've used to cry on. Quite a few times.

"I knew her first," Sasha drawled. He was technically wrong though, and by Priest's shark grin, he knew it.

"Ah, wrong, Russian," Priest drawled. "I knew her first. In Philly."

"That's right," Sasha said, looking bored as fuck. "When she robbed your ass."

"It's just money. And she's my sister. But that wasn't her first trip to Philly."

"Okay, little dude," Sasha deadpanned. "But you make the kid cry, and I'm gonna beat your ass."

"Hey, hey, I'm not a kid. I'm a married woman," I protested.

Neither one of them paid any attention to me.

"Okay, old man. You can try but you won't succeed," Priest growled. His arm came around me, pulling me into a hug. "She's my sister."

"Umm—"

With my eyes wide, I watched Sasha but his expression revealed nothing. They wouldn't get into a fight here. Would they?

Then he grinned. "You keep her safe," Sasha said. "And if you need help, you call me."

With a wink, Sasha strode away, leaving me with Priest.

"So, Christian," I started, reverting back to his real name since it was just the two of us. "Possessive much?"

"Nah." He kept his arms around me and I raised my head to meet his eyes. "Only of my family."

"Does that extend to our mother?" I asked softly. His face darkened. He didn't confirm it, but he didn't deny it either. "Give her a chance," I murmured softly. I remembered the day she told me about her baby she lost. Of course, back then I understood it differently. "She's an amazing woman with a big heart that got broken."

He remained silent and I wrapped my arms around him. I felt him stiffen for a moment but then he slowly relaxed.

"If you won't do it for her, then do it for me." It was a bold request, considering we weren't close. At least not yet.

"She abandoned me," he gritted. "Once she was pronounced dead, she could have come back for me and raised me with you."

Jesus, how bad did Priest have it?

Chapter Seventy-Two

BASILIO

eep. Beep. Beep.

My head felt heavy, painful throbbing in my temples. My mouth was dry, like someone stuffed cotton in it. I swore every single inch of my body hurt. Like I'd been beaten senseless.

Kind of like when I was a kid and too weak to fight back against my father. I groaned, then tried to move but it seemed impossible.

Beep. Beep. Beep.

What the fuck was that annoying noise?

Beep. Beep. Beep.

I'd shoot the fucking thing. I twitched my fingers to grab it, but all I felt was soft skin.

God, what the fuck happened?

Then the events slowly came back to me. The drive back after the funeral, the attack. Hearing Wynter's voice through the fog in my brain.

I love you so damn much it hurts. There has been nobody since I walked away that day, and if you leave me, it'll break me. Please just hold on. For me.

Fuck! I had never held on so desperately as I did when I heard those words. For her.

The statement shouted loud in my brain. There had been nobody for her.

It had been the avoided topic between us because I knew if she confirmed there were others, I'd dig up those names and bodies would be piling up. I didn't want anyone else who walked this earth to have tasted what I had. The selfish prick in me wanted it only for myself.

I slowly peeled my eyes open, blinking hard against the light, only to find my wife curled up beside me, her hand wrapped around my torso.

Her wild curls hid her face, and I couldn't resist reaching out gently and brushing a few of her golden curls out of her face. Fuck. My chest tightened seeing her like this. Her lips were slightly parted as she breathed and her thick lashes rested against her skin. She furrowed her brows as if she was thinking even in her sleep.

She was born for me. The conviction was hard and firm. Every single breath I'd taken from the moment I was born, it had been for the moment when she'd stumble into my life. I couldn't live without this girl because I had been hopelessly and irrevocably in love with her from the first moment.

"There hasn't been anyone for me either, principessa," I rasped, my throat raw. There'd never be anyone else for me.

Her eyes fluttered open and our eyes met. She blinked, then blinked again as if she couldn't believe what she was seeing.

Then she sat up and her eyes roamed over me. "You're awake?" she whispered. Before I could answer, she threw herself at me, showering my face with kisses. I didn't even care about the pain, as long as she kept kissing me. "I was so worried, Bas. How are you feeling?"

She went to pull away, but I tugged her back to me. "Better now that I've been thoroughly kissed." Then she buried her face in my neck and her lips skimmed over my skin, placing small kisses. "Did you get hurt?"

"No, I'm good," she murmured, inhaling deeply. "Just a little head bump."

"She has a concussion," Priest's voice came out of nowhere. He leaned against the door, both hands in his pockets. "She refused to leave your side and the only reason the doctors let her harass your ass was because she's a famous Olympic skater."

I chuckled, the small movement causing pain but I didn't give a fuck.

"What happened?" I grumbled.

"My crazy sister threw herself on you when the crazy old Russian bitch ordered her men to shoot you," Priest grumbled casually.

I tensed and searched my wife's eyes to see the truth in them.

"Principessa," I growled.

She shook her head, narrowing her eyes on me. "Don't you *principessa* me! First, you would have done it for me. So don't you dare preach to me," she said, slightly annoyed. "Mom, Uncle, and Priest have done it enough. And second, the old crazy woman told those men she'd gut them if they hurt me. So it made complete sense to be your shield."

It was smart thinking but it still sent a fucking shudder through me. If something would have happened to her, life without her would be impossible. Nothing ever fucking got to me like this woman.

"Who was she?" I grumbled. Her eyes flitted to Priest, then came back to me. "What?"

"It's the Pakhan," Wynter explained softly. "My great-grand-mother is the Pakhan and she wants to destroy all of the underworld. Make them pay for losing her daughter to my grandfather."

"She won't stop coming after Wynter," Priest said, the tone of his voice cold. My cousin was protective of family. He'd be overprotective of his sister. "We need to make her aware I exist. That way she'll back off."

Wynter shook her head. "Absolutely not. Mom will never forgive us. Forgive me, if we let that happen."

A slightly bitter laugh escaped him. "She didn't seem concerned with me for the past twenty-five years. She shouldn't start now."

Sorrow flashed across Wynter's face. "Christian—" she whispered softly. "She thought she was protecting you."

"I feel like I missed a whole fucking conversation here," I groaned, shifting slightly. "What the hell is going on?"

Priest shrugged. "I'll let your wife fill you in." Then he turned around to leave.

"Shut the fucking door," I demanded.

Priest flipped me the bird. "No sex in the hospital."

He didn't shut the goddamn door.

Chapter Seventy-Three

WYNTER

O nce Priest was gone, Bas pulled me back into his arms. I pressed my face against his chest and inhaled deeply that familiar scent. Last month had been a whirlwind, but it wasn't until I saw Bas bleeding that it hit me. Life was too damn short and I refused to waste a single moment holding back.

He was mine and I was his. Nobody would ever take him away. I'd lie, steal, and kill for him.

"Now tell me what I missed," he ordered, the kingpin in full form, back in control.

I didn't mind it though. It was who he was. He'd warned me from the beginning and I went into it eyes wide open. His father caused an obstacle but Bas tortured him for me. Sasha killed him to protect us.

"Well, I should start by saying that my great-grandmother is batshit crazy," I sighed, remembering that unhinged look in her eyes. "Priest, Dante, Sasha, and his brother showed up at the perfect time. Otherwise, the Pakhan's bodyguards would have peeled me off your body and shot you, then probably dragged me to somewhere in fucking Siberia."

"The fuck they would," he growled, his voice dark. "I'd come for you."

My lips curved into a smile. "Even in death, huh?"

"Nothing will ever keep me away from you. Not death and not the fucking Pakhan." If there was anyone who could make that happen, it was certainly Basilio DiLustro.

I brushed my mouth over his. "Thankfully, that's not necessary. Your cousins and the Nikolaev men killed her men but she got away." A shudder rolled down my spine remembering that freaky look in her eyes. "However, the world is a small place because apparently, the woman is Bianca Morrelli's great-aunt or something. Sister of her grandfather's. Sophia Catalano. Alexei recognized her."

"Fuck, the world is too small," he muttered.

"Well, my brother wants to sacrifice himself and make it known he's a descendant of the Volkov family too. Mom and your uncle object. Mom in particular. She sacrificed raising him, and if he went ahead and did it, she feels it was for nothing."

With a pensive look, his hand around me tightened. "Priest is stubborn, and in my experience, if he decides something, nobody and nothing will stop him. Does Dante know?"

I swallowed. That didn't bode well for anyone. "Yeah. He's pretty much pissed at everyone. Mom, your uncle, and me..." He stiffened, but didn't interrupt. "And Juliette is not helping. Something happened between the two of them, and as she was leaving the hospital, she keyed his car and smashed his windows."

"Jesus Christ."

"My thoughts exactly," I murmured. "And now Cassio and his gang are all up in arms about this Pakhan too. And then there were the Ashfords. Byron showed up too. He checked on you, then harassed Dante about a debt owed. It was like a soap opera here."

He shook his head, a small smile pulling on his lips. "Maybe it's good I slept for a bit. Byron probably wanted to confirm himself that I wasn't dead. If something happens to me, the seat in the Syndicate goes to him as the closest kin who's not a member."

"It's a cluster," I mumbled. "And I thought training for the Olympics was hard."

He chuckled, then brushed his lips against mine. "You'll be my Kingpin Queen." His grip around me tightened and I felt his hand roam down my hip. "I want to fuck you again."

A spike of heat ran through my veins but I fought it. "Absolutely not. The nurse will kick me out."

He let out a frustrated breath and my gaze flicked to his that burned dark and hot. "If I have a hard-on, I'm out of the danger zone."

"You're crazy, Bas," I rasped, glancing at the door. A doctor walked by and I quickly shoved his hand away. "Stop it. I'm serious."

The doctor paused at the door, shot an annoyed look at both of us, then left. I turned to look at my husband and realized why the doctor scurried away. My husband's eyes threatened retribution if he entered.

"You're the worst patient," I murmured, lying back down against him. His one hand ran a path down my back, then back up, almost absentmindedly. When he didn't say anything for a while, I searched his face. "What are you thinking about?"

"You're related to Nico Morrelli," he remarked pensively.

I lifted my head and rolled my eyes. "I guess through marriage."

"Nico is part of Cassio's gang. It might make for weird family reunions if the Syndicate and Cassio are not on the same page."

I cleared my throat uncomfortably. "It will be weird anyhow because when Sasha found me after your father—" My words faltered and I felt Bas's body tense underneath me. "Anyhow, he took me to Cassio's place and his doctor. Cassio was adamant about calling Uncle and I sort of threatened him."

His chest rumbled with a laugh he was trying to suppress. "What did you say to Cassio?" he said, approval ringing in his voice.

"That I'd blame him if he sent me back to Uncle," I admitted, slightly ashamed. "I didn't want Uncle Liam to go after you. I didn't care about your dad getting hurt in the process, but never you."

"My queen," he murmured softly.

I scoffed but his words made me smile. "The whole thing is kind of weird. Stealing from Nico, threatening Cassio. It won't make for a good reputation."

He chuckled and winced the next second. "What is it with you girls stealing money? You know we're rich, right?"

I grinned. "Really?"

He nodded. "What's mine is yours," he said, his dark eyes shining with amusement.

"That's good to know," I said. "What's yours is mine and what's mine is mine."

His hand tugged on my hair. "Ours, principessa. Everything is ours. Now tell me why do you need the money?"

"The girls and I want to start a school," I told him. "When we burned down Garrett's house, we realized how inept we were at handling crime. We were born in the underworld and didn't even know how to go about erasing the surveillance after that prick Garrett threatened us."

"You came to me. That was the right thing to do."

I shook my head. "No, we want to be able to do it ourselves too. Anyhow, after you erased the surveillance, we kept the money we stole from Uncle and decided we'd start a school. To help sheltered daughters of men like... well, you." He stared at me like I was crazy. "The school will be for both boys and girls though. We don't discriminate."

He stared at me and I started to wonder if he thought he could stop me.

"I fucking love it," he finally said. "I'll give you the money for it."

I raised an eyebrow surprised. "You love it?"

"Yes. It was exactly what Emory needed. Priest, Dante, and I taught her what we knew but it was hard for us to fight the urge to protect her from some things. A school like that... it would have been perfect."

At this point, I was smiling so wide my cheeks ached. I didn't care. "And it will be just a few hours from the city. So win-win. I can be your wife, coach, handle school stuff, and we can have kids that will be a big part of it."

"You want kids?"

"One day," I whispered. "You?"

Bas's gaze was full of possessiveness and he pulled my head so my forehead rested against his. Inhaling a breath, he kissed me so softly, it made my heart ache. It was the kiss that could break my heart or make it soar to unimaginable heights.

"Only with you. I want it all but only with you."

My heartbeats slowed and happiness vibrated beneath my skin. It was the kind of love that was raw, passionate, and all-consuming. The kind of love that made it all worth it.

"Bas?" I started in a hesitant voice. His eyes were closed, his jawline covered in stubble. I pressed my lips to his jawline, the skin slightly rough against my mouth. "Is it true what you said?"

"Yes," he murmured, opening his eyes. God, I loved his eyes. I loved his taste and smell. I fucking loved everything about him. Even his psychotic ways. "But which part are we talking about exactly?"

I kissed a line down his throat. "There hasn't been anyone for you?" I whispered my question, running my tongue up his throat.

He cupped my face and brought it close to his. I closed the distance and kissed the corner of his mouth. It was easier to kiss him than drown in his gaze and let him see how scared I was that he'd see how much I loved him. It was the insane kind of love that consumed you and could destroy you. Still, there was no stopping it for me.

He swallowed my sigh in his mouth, kissing me wet and rough until he nipped my bottom lip.

"There has been nobody else for me, Wynter. You are my star, moon, and sun. I love you and I'll never give you up. It'd take a better man than me. It's a good thing we've established from the beginning that I'm not a good man. I'm a villain."

My heart glowed in my chest and fire spread through my veins. "But you're my villain. I love you," I breathed, my throat choking with all these emotions. "After I left, I felt dead inside. My mom said love shatters you but it's not true. Giving you up shattered me."

"Fuck, principessa," he rasped, kissing me with a new kind of possession and demand. "We're in it for life. I'll make you happy, I promise."

I smiled, tasting salt on my lips. "I'll make you happy too, Bas. I promise."

He was my fairy tale. My villainous prince.

Epilogue

BASILIO

Seven Years Later

St. Jean d'Arc School Opening.

Unofficially, the school of badass females. Though there are plenty of boys in it.

"Daddy, when I get big, can I go to school here?" my four-year-old asked. My little Miss Independent was the spitting image of Wynter. Her big green eyes shimmered as she met my gaze. She knew how to play me, like a goddamn fiddle.

And I let her. Every damn time because I couldn't bear to see her unhappy. Fallon, true to her name's meaning, knew how to rule a room and the people in it. Much to Wynter's dismay.

My wife called it payback for the shit we'd done. I called it a fucking blessing.

"Only if I come," my eldest chimed in. Even at six years old, Grayson acted like an overbearing big brother. "Nobody touches my sisters." He was a fucking terror and occasionally took protection of his two younger sisters to a whole new level.

Our youngest, twenty-month-old Noelle, flapped her legs and arms, excited to hear her big brother's voice.

"You're not coming," Fallon screeched her protest in indignation. "Badass females. You're not a female."

She raised her hand like she was going to smack the shit out of her big brother when I snagged her hand.

"No hitting, Fallon," I scolded her and her green eyes filled with fire. "And no bad words. Mommy won't be fucking happy if she hears it. And I promised your mamma, I'd always make her happy."

With her blonde, curly pigtails, and her big eyes, she looked like an angel. Until she got pissed off. Then she was a fucking monster in disguise.

Did I mention Fallon had a fucking Irish temper?

Just like her damn aunt Jules.

Our family was a fucking nightmare. But I wouldn't change it for the world.

"Hitting is bad," I explained, my voice stern.

The baby squirmed in my arms like a wild animal, squealing, "Down. Down."

"Whatever," Fallon muttered, rolling her eyes. *Are four-year-olds even supposed to roll their eyes?* Fuck if I knew. All I knew was that Fallon would drive a fucking saint to drink.

"Hello, Mr. DiLustro." Two sets of blue eyes met mine. Nico Morrelli's eldest daughters. Their father and mom slowly approached us with their own little hellions.

"Hannah. Arianna." I could never figure out which one was which, so I just let it go. "Looking forward to going to school here?"

"Hell yeah," one of them answered. "Can't wait to taste freedom."

Yep, those two would be trouble.

"Hey, Basilio." Bianca was first to greet me, leaning in to press a kiss to my cheek. Yes, these women were setting some new, supposedly normal, standards around here. Nico growled and his wife rolled her eyes. Their twenty kids ran around wild. Okay, maybe not twenty but lots of kids. Twins. How in the fuck they kept them straight, I had no fucking idea.

"Down, down," my youngest demanded again. The little monster was a wiggle worm. "Me want," she babbled.

Noelle knew how to make her wants heard.

"I see the kids are doing good," Nico announced. "You must be proud."

My eyes darted back to where my wife stood. Proud didn't even begin to describe it. "More than proud."

Bianca chuckled. "And to think you had to drag her down the aisle."

Of course, it was a topic of discussion almost every holiday. Fuckers.

Bianca reached out for Noelle's little hand that kept reaching for her aunt. Or was it cousin, fuck if I knew. The family connection was complicated, connecting my wife to Bianca through the crazy Pakhan.

"From what I hear, Nico forced you down the aisle too," I mused while lowering down to set my toddler down.

She chuckled. "Right you are. Best fucking day ever."

I grinned. I couldn't quite figure out if we had corrupted our women or vice versa.

All three of my kids took off in the direction of their mother who stood surrounded by the new students. Some fascinated by her ice-skating career, and others asking questions about the school.

"I'm gonna say hi to Wynter," Bianca announced and I nodded. Minutes passed in silence.

"It never goes away, huh?" Nico's remark had me raising my eyebrows. "The worry constantly lingers that something could change it all. Take it all away from us."

My eyes sought out my wife again. He was right. The worry never truly ended. No matter what, it probably never would. I'd worry about my wife and our children until my dying breath.

"It never goes away," I confirmed.

Nico dispersed to go help his daughters get situated into whatever dorm they'd stay in. I'd talk to Wynter about putting extra insurance on that building, because those two were sure to wreak havoc.

My wife's eyes flickered my way and instantly my chest grew full. Yes, I ruled the Syndicate alongside my cousins. Yes, we still dealt with illegal shit. And fuck yes, I killed anyone who tried to threaten my family.

But at the end of the day, I'd always come home to them. To a house full of children, toys scattered around, and my wife as she attempted cooking. She was better at ice-skating and running the school, but my wife was not a quitter. My cook made sure of it.

Noelle found her way to her mother, grinning and reaching up her chubby arms. I could hear her faint demand. "Up."

Before my wife had a chance to pick up our baby, Grandma snatched her up.

"Where is my baby girl?" Aisling cooed at her. "Guess what I have?"

Wynter's mom found a cure to aging. Though it only worked on her. My wife swore she had never seen her mother like this. She glowed from happiness. And my uncle spoiled her rotten. The woman deserved it though.

"Ummy beaws!" Noelle squealed excited and instantly opened her mouth.

It was her favorite junk food. Out of nowhere, Fallon and Grayson found themselves next to their grandmother. Little rascals.

The salty ocean air drifted from the shoreline. Despite the girl squad sucking at their criminal activity, I had to admit they did well with this project. They had found the perfect location, the large acreage of woods hiding them from the nearest road of nosey passersby and the ocean views on the opposite side.

My wife's hands wrapped around my waist from behind, her touch sending a small shudder through my spine. Every. Fucking. Time.

At this rate, we'd end up filling the school with our own kids.

"Hey, husband. How is your stay-at-home-dad job going? Or is being the kingpin more to your liking?"

I brought her around to my front, so I could get lost in her eyes. She was my own personal heaven. "Well, I have another ten hours to go. We only managed to spill one juice box and a handful of animal crackers inside the car. This kingpin will forever be happy to spend a day with our kids. And you, principessa."

Her soft chuckle vibrated against my chest. "You did good," she murmured. "You're as good at your daddy job as you are at your kingpin job."

There were days I was so goddamn happy, I feared it was all a dream. I'd wake up and realize I was still searching for the love of my life, hunting down the Russians and all other villains on this earth.

"I love you," she murmured and satisfaction ran hot through my blood every time she said those words to me. Nothing mattered more to me than her and our family. My cousins and hers came to visit. The dream family we both always wanted came true.

Her bottom lip came between her teeth and an alert instantly shot through me. "What's the matter?"

"Why do you think something's the matter?" she questioned.

"Because I know you."

"You do," she confirmed. "How do you feel about another baby?"

I stilled, searching her face for any sign that she was joking. There were none.

I cupped her face and ran a thumb across her cheek. "Are you happy?" She nodded, her lips parting and a blush rising to her cheeks.

"Then I'm happy. We can have as many babies as you want." A corner of my lips lifted. "Nothing makes me happier than making them."

She rose to her tiptoes and breathed against my mouth. "I'm so fucking happy that it scares me sometimes."

I leaned in to nip her bottom lip. "The only one allowed to scare you is me, principessa. Anyone else, I'll kill them."

THE END

Acknowledgments

I want to thank my friends and family for their continued support. To my alpha and beta readers—you are all amazing. Thank you to **Susan C.H.** and **Beth H.** who always have my back. You are amazing and I don't know how I'd get through some of these without you!

To **Christine S., Denise R., and Jill H.**—you ladies rock! And to a countless number of others—THANK YOU!

My books wouldn't be what they are without each one of you.

To my editor, Rachel at **MW Editing**. Your questions made my stories so much better.

To my rockstar cover designer, **Eve Graphics Designs, LLC**. Where would I be without you?

To the bloggers and reviewers who helped spread the word about this book. I appreciate you so much, and hearing you love my work, makes it that much more enjoyable!

And last but not least, **to all my readers**! This wouldn't be possible without you.

THANK YOU! Thank you all! I couldn't have done any of this without you!

Eva Winners

Connect With Me

Want to be the first to know the latest news?
Visit www.evawinners.com and subscribe to my newsletter.
FOLLOW me on social media.
FB group: https://bit.ly/3gHEe0e

FB page: https://bit.ly/30DzP8Q

Insta: http://Instagram.com/evawinners

BookBub: https://www.bookbub.com/authors/eva-winners

Amazon: http://amazon.com/author/evawinners

Goodreads: http://goodreads.com/evawinners

Twitter: http://Twitter.com/@Evawinners

TikTok: https://vm.tiktok.com/ZMeETK7pq/

Made in United States
Cleveland, OH
23 December 2024

12577039R00298